Anouschka Zagorski

SUPERSONIC

life in the legal fast lane

a novel

SUPERSONIC: Life in the Legal Fast Lane

Published in 2018 by
AG Books
www.agbooks.co.uk

AG Books is an imprint of
Andrews UK Limited
www.andrewsuk.com

For my daughters Anastasia and Isabella

And for my soul sister Karmen

"At his best, man is the noblest of all animals;
separated from law and justice he is the worst."

Aristotle

"No one saves us but ourselves.
No one can and no one may.
We ourselves must walk the path."

Buddha

Contents

1

New Kid in Town

My name is Chloé. Chloé Krakowski.

I have never really liked my name. When I tell people my first name I have to spell it out, several times, very slowly. It's hard to pronounce it correctly. English or Americans usually say clou-ay, similar to clown but without the 'n' at the end. Germans either pronounce the "Ch" as in the French word *charmant*, which it sounds far from. Or they ignore the accent on the 'e' at the end and say *Klö* or—worse—*Klo*, a German term for toilet. You will thus understand my weakness for French people. Of course they pronounce it correctly: *Clo-ayhh*. It sounds like a declaration of love, like a light April breeze touching the branch of a cherry tree on the Champs Elysée. Until they get to the last name. It's a stumbling block. At least it's hard to forget, once you have been able to remember it.

It's Friday, 28 April 2006. Today, on my first day as senior associate lawyer in the Frankfurt office of Pratt & Wonkey, one of the world's finest law firms, I had already heard various versions of my name from the people I had encountered so far. The nameplate on my office door had also been spelt wrong—it read *Chloe Karbowski*. When I had pointed this out to the receptionist, who had shown me to my new office, she placed a short phone call to the office manager who had sent a grumpy handyman to exchange the plate. Once he had gone I sighed deeply. This was a promising start. Or not.

I sat at my new wooden desk and looked around my office. It was just large enough to hold a desk and two chairs. It had a locked window to the outside with a view of the surrounding towers of the Frankfurt financial district. Black book shelves covered both sidewalls up to the ceiling. Opposite the window, half of the inside glass wall consisted of a sliding door.

I felt somewhat exposed, like sitting in a glass cage. Still, it was better than on the other side of the glass wall: Across the narrow passageway, secretaries were sitting at group desks in an open plan area without any chance for privacy. And they were all talking with each other at normal volume. I had left the sliding door open in order not to appear abrasive. However, their chatter was starting to get very animated.

"And then he said he needs the entire document re-formatted by tonight."

"Nooo! You're kidding!"

"Can you imagine? As if I haven't got better things to do!"

"Well, if he hadn't spent three hours at lunch yesterday he could have done it himself!"

"Three hours? Again?"

"I'm telling you, and I could smell his breath afterwards!"

"Oh good morning, sir!" The chorus went when a partner or other senior lawyer passed by.

"Sorry, I don't have time for this now. I have to bind thirty copies of this pitch document." This was directed at a junior lawyer. The ladies made sure to appear to be very busy.

I, for one, intended to have better things to do than to listen to the gossiping coming from outside my office. I got up from my chair, gently closed the door so as not to draw their attention, returned to my desk and perused the piece of paper lying on top of a pile of documents. Maybe I simply didn't have anything better to do after all.

The said piece of paper was an email from a client at AB Bank containing short instructions to draft a letter to a corporate borrower waiving its default in its loan repayments. It was a simple little document that, often, the bank may even get its own in-house lawyer to do—unless it was a very large loan going into seven or eight figures. In that case the bank would instruct its outside counsel and the assignment would finally land on the desk of some legal trainee or junior lawyer. After over ten years in legal practice,

I had not expected to have to draft such a document myself ever again. Earlier on, my new boss, Tracey Taylor, had handed it to me.

"I thought that you could handle this for me—could I have a look at it in about twenty minutes? The client needs it this morning. Thanks." And off she went again before I had the chance to ask any questions.

Stop—my new boss?

Oh. My. God. What the hell was I doing here? How on earth did I get here? And why had she given such a basic piece of work to me? I was confused. I had accepted this position, as Senior Associate in the Banking and Finance legal department of Pratt & Wonkey, to become her successor, that is her replacement Partner, as it was planned, after twelve months, for her to relocate to head office in London. To me at least that meant that I should follow her around and start taking over her work. One year earlier I had left my previous firm Solomons where I had been partner and local head of department. After taking some time out, I had been looking for a firm where I would be appreciated and work at the appropriate level of seniority. And now she asked me to draft a simple waiver letter, *and* she wanted to check my work. I hardly had any choice at this stage—I would have to make a few things clear later on.

I had less than fifteen minutes left. I checked the pile of documents—the loan agreement to which the letter related had one hundred and eighty-six pages. Great. I had not switched on the PC yet, let alone attended the induction course on how to use the firm's IT system. The course was to take place on the coming Monday, which would be my official first day. There would be no time for that now. I found the switches for the desktop and the monitor and turned them both on.

Please type your user name and your password.

I tried my full name without any accent or space. When that did not work, I tried ChloeKarbowski. You never know.

Damn. How was I going to find that out quickly? I was just starting to wrack my brain when somebody slid the door open, startling me. I expected seeing an impatient Tracey. Instead it was the smiling face of Jerome Panzer. He had been introduced to me as Tracey's assistant, and who was also now to work for me—a male secretary if you like. Not very tall, he was a little podgy and had kind teddy bear eyes.

"Hi Ms. Krakowski. This is from IT—I put it on your desk yesterday but I noticed earlier that it had disappeared." He handed me a piece of paper containing three lines of writing:

Name: Chloé Krakowski
User Name: KRAPW
Password: 12345

"Brilliant timing! I was just trying to log on!"

He grinned. "No problem. Just let me know if you need anything. The top button on the phone is my direct dial."

"Thank you so much!"

Jerome retreated and was just about to slide the door shut.

"Oh and Mr. Panzer?"

"Yes?"

"Please call me Chloé."

"Then you will have to call me Jerome."

"With pleasure."

I watched him closing the door and sighed with relief. Tracey had already told me that he was the best assistant Pratt & Wonkey was able to offer. Judging by his initiative I tended to agree with her. For now I had to share him with her but that would only be a matter of time. Time! I had less than ten minutes left. I logged on, found the word programme and quickly created a new document on the C drive while I checked the provisions of the loan agreement referred to in the client's email.

To: [The Borrower]
From: [The Facility Agent]
Date: []
Re: €238,964,900 Credit Agreement dated 23 June 2005 (the Agreement)

> Dear Sirs,
>
> We refer to the Agreement. Capitalised terms used herein and not defined otherwise shall have the meaning as set out in the Agreement.

Talking about reinventing the wheel. For sure Pratt & Wonkey's know-how database had plenty of precedents for this kind of document and plenty of legal trainees to draft it. But I had not met any legal trainee yet and Tracey had assigned the task expressly to me. I typed as quickly as my special method (two hands five fingers) allowed. Done. I had no time left to find out how to use the printer. I opened outlook, created a new email message, typed Taylor into the addressee section, selected Taylor, Tracey: BK (FR) from the drop down menu and inserted the letter as a file from my desktop. It worked.

> Dear Tracey,
>
> as requested, please find attached the first draft of the waiver letter. Perhaps we can discuss when convenient for you. Kind regards, Chloé.

I pressed 'send'. It had taken me 23 minutes. I relaxed my shoulders, leaned back and breathed out. Not even a minute later the telephone rang. I checked the display. It read *Taylor*. I picked up.

"Hello, Tracey?"

"Hi. Could you come and see me please. Thanks." She had hung up before I was able to reply.

I got up and smoothed my black Chloé dress. Yes, Chloé, like my name.

It was rather a coincidence but I did love the Chloé collection since Phoebe Philo had become the chief designer. Each season I treated myself to one or two special pieces, or rather outfits once you include the shoes, handbags etc. I felt I deserved it, I certainly worked hard enough and earnt enough money. Perhaps it was more than one or two pieces—but these handbags were just to die for. It all started with the Paddington handbag—the softest leather, gorgeous colours and the absolute ingenious detailing, such as the huge padlock. I had placed my beige Eastwest Paddington handbag behind my chair in the empty bookshelf (never, never on the floor!). It should be safe there, next to the framed photos of Marie and Noëlle. I ensured my girls were always with me, even if only in a photo. I looked down at my clover green Jimmy Choo pumps, which they had chosen for me that morning: "Mummy, wear these, they look like lucky charm shoes!" That would provoke the secretaries' chatter again outside—I was not really dressed like a normal female lawyer. Maybe they would get used to it.

I walked down the corridor with a straight back, passing by the secretaries and ignoring their suddenly animated whispering, which I had expected. I had turned two corners before I noticed that I'd walked in the wrong direction. I remembered from my brief tour the same morning that Tracey's office was at the exact opposite side of the building. I quickly turned around and walked back. When I passed the secretaries again I thought I heard them suppressing a giggle. As I finally arrived at my destination I put on my nicest professional smile and knocked on the sliding glass door. Her office was thrice the size of mine, containing a small meeting table in addition to her desk from which she now looked up. She raised her upper lip and bared her large front teeth.

"Hi. Please, have a seat. Thanks for your email. I have some comments on your draft. You might want to incorporate those and then send it to the client before lunchtime." She handed me a printout of my draft waiver letter. It was full of red ink manuscript comments, deletions and arrows. I stared at it.

"Yes, of course. Uhm, sure."

"Good. Another thing. The credit agreement needs to be amended. I have forwarded you the email from the client summarising the required changes. The client needs it by Monday morning, so if you send it to me by Saturday evening, I can review it beforehand."

I hesitated. My official starting date at P&W was May 1st which was the following Monday. I had only come into the office, at her suggestion, to get the initial administrative things done. The weekend was reserved for fun things with Noëlle and Marie.

"Right. Of course I am happy to do the draft, Tracey. The thing is—I need to look after my daughters during the day, so I can only really work when they sleep. Would it be ok if I send you the draft on Sunday morning?"

Tracey's smile faded. Small red spots became visible on her neck.

"I see. I find in these situations that one can organise childcare. At least that is what I do, and I would expect that you prioritise your work accordingly."

"Sure. And I usually do. Unfortunately I do not have childcare for this weekend, especially at such short notice. I will do my best and send you the draft Sunday morning at the latest." I got up, my heart pounding fast. She stared at me silently and raised her eyebrows. Her ears started to redden. The spots on her neck had become darker.

"I see."

"Thanks, Tracey." I quickly left her office.

~

"You did the right thing," Isabella said five minutes later on the telephone. "You have got to make your position clear right at the start. She is crazy! You haven't even started yet and you're supposed to work all weekend? Doesn't she have kids of her own?"

My best friend, Isabella, was a local concept storeowner in her mid-forties and married, without children, to a wealthy Saudi businessman. I had not been her customer long before we realised how our souls were connected and we became friends. Having lost my mother in my early twenties, I was also drawn to Isabella's maternal ways. The fact that she had rung at the precise moment I had returned to my office was a typical instance of how connected we were. The blood in my head had still been pumping so loudly that I nearly did not pick up the receiver at first.

"Yes, she does!" I replied. "And they are younger than Marie and Noëlle. That's why I am so shocked—I would expect her to understand. I think she hates me already."

"Rubbish—she will get used to you not sucking up to her. And you are not supposed to be her minion, are you?"

"Strictly speaking, yes. I am an associate and she is my supervising partner—in other words, my boss."

"But you were also a partner in your old firm."

"That does not change my status here at Pratt & Wonkey. Even if they pay me nearly as much as a junior partner, it does not make me one."

"You lawyers and your hierarchies. I don't understand any of that. I just know you are a great lawyer and very good in your area of expertise and a super lady with great style. Obviously your new boss can't appreciate that—she is probably jealous."

This made me laugh. "Aw. You speak like a true friend! But you're right. I mustn't let her get me down. I am just feeling a little insecure, I didn't expect this kind of behaviour from her. She seemed nice when I met her for that lunch after my interview. In any event I do have to prove myself here and impress everyone. Talking of which—I am impressed you tracked me down."

"Well, when you did not answer your mobile I did some research. I may not hold any academic qualifications but I'm clever," she giggled. "Anyway, don't worry dear, you will show them how brilliant you are!"

"I hope you're right."

After we hung up, I looked out of the window and got thinking. I really didn't have any possibility of organising childcare for the weekend. My neighbour, Jana, already took care of the girls after school during the week and occasionally babysat them at night. I didn't want to ask her to look after them all weekend as well. Hugo had gone to a weekend seminar, so he wasn't an option either.

Thinking of Hugo made me dreamy. The gorgeous, sexy Otorhinolaryngologist Dr. Hugo Walter—blue innocent eyes, boyish charm, much less boyish and not so innocent body…

My thoughts were interrupted by a knock on the glass door. I reluctantly swivelled my chair around. A pretty young woman with long dark hair, wearing a navy trouser suit and a crisp white blouse, beamed at me.

"Hi! You must be Chloé? I'm Jessica. I'm also in Tracey's team." She said this very quickly with a distinct North American accent. I got up and we shook hands.

"Hi, Jessica. Nice to meet you!"

"I thought you weren't starting until Monday?"

"That's right, but Tracey suggested to come in a day earlier to set things up."

"Right! That makes sense. Listen, I was wondering whether you'd like to come for lunch with me and a couple of other colleagues?"

"Oh, sure—I'd love to!"

"Great! We'll meet at the elevator in about fifteen minutes—see you then!"

When she was gone I took the telephone receiver and pressed the speed dial for Jerome. He answered immediately. "Hello Ms. Krakowski, what can I do for you?"

"For starters, you can call me Chloé. I thought we agreed on that."

He laughed. "I am sorry. Old habits die hard."

I chuckled. "Well, you should acquire a new habit."

"Agreed—many thanks for the reminder. Can I do anything else for you, Chloé?"

"Yes. It's about the waiver letter I gave you."

"I just sent it to you."

I checked my inbox. Jerome's email had arrived a minute ago. I quickly read through the draft. "Great, thanks! That looks good—we can send it like this to the client at AB Bank with a short cover note."

"I'll do that on your behalf. Are you going out for lunch?"

"Yes. Jessica asked me to join her. I'll be back in about an hour."

"Fine. See you later."

I hung up and checked my watch. 12.45. The girls would still be at school. I would not be able to reach them until late afternoon. I swivelled around on my chair and looked at the silver picture frames I had placed on the shelves behind me. Two little girls with laughing faces looked back at me. I started welling up. I missed them so much every minute I was away from them. How could I even consider handing them off for the weekend? I would manage to get the draft contract to Tracey in time. I sniffed and placed the frames on my desk so that the photos were now visible from the outside through the glass door. If Tracey passed by she would be able to see them. Just to ensure the message was clear.

Jessica was waiting by the lifts together with two young men wearing grey suits. She introduced me.

"Chloé, this is David Byrd, my fiancé—I believe you already met briefly on your department tour this morning—and this is Mike Jones. He works with Frank Smith who was just made partner. He is involved in most of Tracey's real estate finance deals, so we work together quite a bit."

We exchanged niceties and got into the lift. I looked them over inconspicuously. Their appearance was nearly identical—both had very short hair and wore round horn-rimmed glasses. The one Jessica had introduced as Mike was taller than her fiancé David. Like Jessica they were in their late twenties or thirty at most, which made them ten years my junior. That feeling of being in the wrong place arose in me again. Should I not be at lunch with Tracey or with my friend Patricia's husband, Michael Stone who was also a partner in the banking group and whose office was a few doors down from mine? But nobody had asked me. Something was wrong.

Mike led us into the nearest steak restaurant. I would have preferred sushi or a spicy Asian noodle soup but if you are the new kid in town you should first follow the others. Follow and observe. On our way Jessica had told me her life story. She was from Connecticut and had a German father. After finishing her law degree at Yale she came to Frankfurt to study German finance law. That was where she met and—as she embellished—fell in love with visiting professor David Byrd. He worked in the banking department of Pratt & Wonkey and organised a summer internship for her. At the end of the four weeks P&W offered her a full-time job—"naturally" at a lower salary than the European junior lawyers as she was "only" a U.S. qualified lawyer. When she hesitated, because she also had an offer from the well-known New York firm Rosenblatt, Weinstein & Stiller, David made her an offer she could not refuse: He proposed to her. She said yes and went back to the U.S. to sort out her working visa. Once in New York, she headed directly to Tiffany & Co. and purchased, with her parents' credit card, a one-carat diamond engagement ring. A ring, which she had already decided upon at the tender age of thirteen.

"Of course David reimbursed me afterwards—it wasn't very romantic but it was so much cheaper than buying it here!" She proudly stretched out her left hand, displaying a shiny Lucida diamond ring and blew a kiss to David who had turned around upon hearing his name.

"Oh wow! It's blinding—I need my sunglasses!" I joked.

We took the nearest unoccupied table. The others, even Jessica, ordered steaks with potatoes. I glanced at her in wonder. She was very slim. She noticed my look.

"Actually I have to eat heartily otherwise I get too skinny."

"Lucky you!" I looked around and spotted the salad bar. "Oh good—I think I'm going to go for the salad."

"So, Chloé, where did you work before P&W?" Mike asked while we were waiting to order.

"I was at Solomons for five years. I helped to build the banking practice, especially in the area of asset finance—you know, financing aircraft, ships, trains and so forth."

"She was a banking partner and is supposed to succeed Tracey next year! Then she will be my boss!" Jessica added with enthusiasm.

"And how come you are only an associate now?" David asked.

"Well, initially, I was actually discussing Partnership with P&W, then a position as counsel—for some internal political reasons neither were possible at this time," I replied. "That then turned into the package senior associate with concrete partnership prospects. Tracey is supposed to show me the ropes for a year until she moves back to London so that I can take over afterwards."

David frowned. "Aren't they planning to move house this summer?"

"Her husband and children are moving next month," Jessica confirmed. "I guess she'll commute."

"I didn't know that. Interesting. Wow. I couldn't be separated from my children—I'd go crazy! But then I guess she'll follow her family soon."

"You've got kids? How many?" Mike interrupted me.

"Two girls—Marie just turned five and Noëlle turns eight soon."

"Really? How do you do manage that with *this* job?"

I raised my hands. "I don't manage it alone—I have childcare. But I do admit, it's like juggling: As long as all the balls stay in the air it somehow works."

"And your husband?"

"My hopefully soon ex-husband has moved back to France and only sees the children during their school holidays. We split up two years ago. I have a boyfriend but he has a demanding job himself—he is an Otorhinolaryngologist."

"A what?" Mike looked puzzled.

"Oto-rhino-laryn-gologist: an ear, nose and throat doctor. He's busy running his own surgery, so he can't take any time off to allow me to work. It is up to me to figure out how to manage being a working mum. But I am used to it—I didn't stay at home for very long after they were born and I've always worked full time." I took a fork full of lettuce.

David added, chewing: "Except that full time in our job means day and night! You don't get to be a Partner without working your butt off."

I started to shift uncomfortably on my chair. This started to sound like an interrogation.

"Yes, that's true, of course. To be honest, I don't know either how I manage or have ever managed. It's hard and I am constantly sleep deprived but, somehow, it works. Maybe I am just a bad mother." My attempt at humour worked as they all laughed. But it wasn't a joke. Trying to cope with all my duties, both at work and at home, never seemed possible and it seemed that something always slipped.

"However, I just spent several months on sabbatical where I had a lot of time with my children, that was fantastic. Although, I must admit, I did start to miss work after a while!" That prompted some more laughter. "The girls are at school until mid afternoon so there isn't that much quality time during the week anyway. Our weekends are sacred though."

"Oh dear," Jessica sighed. "I don't think I have had a weekend off since I joined Tracey's team."

"I am not surprised." I gave her an account of Tracey's instructions regarding the amendment of the AB Bank loan agreement. Mike and David took the opportunity to discuss the latest news on the impending football world cup, which, maybe unsurprisingly, they were more interested in than the moaning of a single mother.

Jessica was horrified. "What? I thought I was going to have to do that! I was with her in the conference call, with the client, and before he could say anything she offered to have the draft ready on Monday. The client said mid-week would be fine but she insisted. But that's so silly! It's a job for a junior lawyer plus you haven't even started properly yet!"

"I know. But she asked me, so I'll do it. I did the waiver letter, too."

"No—that's ludicrous!"

"I'm telling you, and I got it back with every word moved to a different place."

"That's normal—Tracey always does that to my work. But in your case I would have thought she wouldn't check at all!"

"What can I say? I guess we need some time to get to know each other."

Jessica frowned. "Still, it's weird. Look, just send me an email if you need any help at all. I check my blackberry regularly over the weekend—firstly, because Tracey expects that and secondly, we have several clients who work on Sundays."

"That's really kind of you. I should be able to manage, but it's good to know."

I felt grateful for her solidarity. But something felt wrong. It started to dawn on me that this job was quite different to what I had expected and, to a large extent, had been promised. I could either leave or make the best of it.

I was annoyed with myself. How could I have let this happen?

2

Indecent Proposal

"Thank you for coming, Ms. Krakowski." Dr. Richard Keel, Managing Partner of Pratt & Wonkey (Germany), greeted me at the door to the conference room. He led me inside and waved his hand in the direction of four people sitting on the far side of a large conference table. "I guess you know Michael Stone and Gunther White, and these are Tracey Taylor and Francis Mayer. Tracey heads the English banking law team and Mr. Mayer is head of real estate finance."

I made my rounds, shaking each person's hand with a polite smile and took the chair on the opposite side of the conference table. Indeed, I already know the first two gentlemen.

I had met Michael Stone ten years before as an associate in the Frankfurt office of Howard Hewitt, the largest law firm in the UK at the time, and now, in the world. Somewhat stiff and grumpy at first, he turned out to be reliable and collegiate, with an intelligent sarcasm and a dry sense of humour. I had been all the more surprised when he unerringly and confidently started to court Patricia, a lively, somewhat naïve and party-loving Irish secretary. He got her pregnant within a few months and, finally, the week before the birth of their first son, married her at a short registry office ceremony in her home town of Limerick in the southwest of Ireland—at which he spent all night drinking whisky with his jovial father-in-law. Patricia O'Reilly—pronounced Pet-ri-sha, not Puh-tree-see-ah—had become a good friend and favourite drinking mate of mine shortly after my arrival in Frankfurt. Both single and new in town, we went on a discovery tour of the bars and their male patrons. Like me Patricia was fond of having one or two cocktails too many but as she could not hold her drink, I regularly had to take her home. The next morning she would show little remorse, quiz me to ensure that she'd done nothing that she would be too ashamed of (which was usually the case) and be ready to make plans for the next night out. Therefore, it was, not least to herself, a surprising reversal of fortune that less than one year later she, of all women, was the wife of the conservative lawyer Dr. Michael Stone, who wasn't at all her usual surfer and ski instructor type. Ultimately she was grateful to have someone who, as she said, kept her on the straight and narrow and who made her feel secure. She could have easily ended up unhappy with some random tennis coach.

"Would you like some water?" Michael Stone pulled me back from my thoughts.

"Yes, please. Thank you." I gave Michael a conspiratorial smile. He ignored it. It had primarily been his doing that I had been invited to this interview.

While Michael got up to get another water bottle from the sideboard, and the others passed around the coffee pot, I looked at Gunther White. He was in charge of Asset Finance—my area of expertise. I had encountered him in the past as opposing counsel on transactions or at industry-sponsored conferences. He seemed to be an unassuming man who neither exuded the air of, nor tried to look like, a partner in a big law firm. On the other hand, all three men present had one thing in common: they wore ill-fitting suits and unimaginative ties. They also looked a bit crumpled—as if they had been working all night and had not been home to take a shower and change clothes. The dark circles under their eyes confirmed my impression.

In contrast, Tracey looked neat in her starched white blouse. She was not wearing any visible make-up. Her skin had the sort of pink shade of pale that would probably never tan. She wore her strawberry blonde hair in a plait. Large grey pearl earrings dangled from her slightly protruding ears, which emphasised her Buddha-like earlobes. She scrutinized me with her pale blue eyes, their blonde lashes hardly visible through her narrow steel-rimmed glasses. I had noticed her looking me up and down initially and sitting down very quickly after greeting me. She was shorter and rounder than me and even though I was only wearing plain black

Chloé palazzo pants, a short black Chanel-style jacket (a brilliant item from Zara) with a white Petit Bateau T-Shirt and black Jimmy Choo slingbacks, I could sense her discomfort. Maybe I should have chosen differently to the limited edition Louis Vuitton Vienna handbag, but it was the only black bag I possessed. Also, it gave me that extra bit of confidence that women have when they own such a desired object. In order to achieve that purpose, men spend even more money—on the golden Montblanc fountain pen, the newest Rolex watch, the Porsche.

Tracey cleared her throat.

"Thanks for coming, Chloé. I understand you have just taken a year out after having been partner at Solomons for nearly five years. I think we would like to understand the background to this?"

"Yes, of course. There are actually two questions. One is why I left Solomons and the other is why I took time out. As for Solomons I was quite happy there, at first, and built up my practice from scratch within a relatively short period of time but then the management changed and I got very frustrated with the internal politics. As for the time out, that decision was a personal one. My husband and I separated and that was very hard for my children. I wanted and needed to look after them. Whilst it was, I admit, perhaps not the cleverest decision, from a career perspective, it certainly was a good one as far as my children are concerned."

"I can sympathise with that," Keel interjected. "And it is very admirable. The good thing is you still have your reputation in the legal market and that is exactly what we appreciate here."

I rewarded him with a smile. "I agree—my time out did not make much difference. Firstly, I stayed in touch with my most important business contacts and secondly, last year was a quiet one for the asset finance market so I have not missed any big transactions."

"That is correct," White nodded. "Our team has been busier on real estate financings than on aircraft financings. Furthermore, the number of film financing transactions, which is also part of Ms. Krakowski's expertise, has dwindled since the introduction of the new media funds laws. These investment fund structures were lucrative for the investors as they enabled substantial savings on their tax bill. Sooner or later the tax authorities were bound to put a stop to those."

"Yes, unfortunately!" I added. "That was an incredible deal flow!"

"Then I do not quite understand what type of work you intend to do here," Francis Mayer commented. I looked at him properly for the first time. Despite his comment, he did not seem hostile. He had asked the question with honest astonishment.

Michael beat me to it.

"Ms. Krakowski is to replace Tracey when she returns to London," he explained impatiently. "This saves us having to get expensive secondee partners from London every few years. She is a German national and an English qualified lawyer with over ten years' experience in the German market and all kinds of banking transactions. This is perfect for us."

"Well, that's nice. I am the head of the banking department here in Frankfurt and I am only now being informed of this," Mayer replied.

"If you read your emails, Mr. Mayer, you would have known about this for quite a while," Michael quipped.

"Do not worry, Mr. Mayer," Keel reassured, shooting a glance at Michael. "Of course all decisions require your consent—there is no question about that. I must admit though, to my shame, that I have not read your CV, Ms. Krakowski. Could you please summarise your professional career for us?"

The tension created by the verbal exchange between Mayer and Michael subsided noticeably. Apparently Keel was used to mediating between them. Michael leaned back in his chair, folding his arms and biting his lips. Mayer raised his eyebrows and looked out of the window. Tracey was busy typing an email on her blackberry with her thumbs. Only Keel and White smiled at me encouragingly.

"I will try to be concise," I replied, and meant it. It was a long and unusual story. It is a well-known interview technique to let the candidate talk. On the other hand, all lawyers love the sound of their own voice. I wanted both to sell myself as well as possible and to give those present plenty of opportunity to talk. I took a sip of water from the glass in front of me and began: "I studied two years' German law when I finished school before moving to London University for the undergraduate law degree course. After that, I did a postgraduate degree in Oxford, followed by Bar School. When I was called to the Bar, I got a pupillage and then tenancy in commercial chambers in the Middle Temple in London. Two years later, I moved to Frankfurt to work at Howard Hewitt in the Asset Finance and Banking department. That is where I met Dr. Stone." I turned to Michael who nodded slowly. Then I looked at the other four each in turn to see if I still had their attention.

"Five years later, I was offered non-equity partnership at Howard Hewitt," I continued. "At the same time I received the partnership offer from Solomons to build their banking law practice in Frankfurt. I decided to accept that offer as I regarded it as a greater challenge and a unique opportunity to do things in my own way. After two years, I became an equity partner at Solomons. Three years after that, I left Solomons, took some time out and, now, here I am."

Tracey looked up from her blackberry. "What kind of position did you have in mind if you were to join us?"

I hesitated. "I have been a partner for five years, I know how to build a practice and lead a team—these qualities can be put to best use if I play a leading role and take an active part in the management side." I was not going to under-sell myself, time out or not.

"I have already informed Ms. Krakowski that partnership will be difficult since we can only have one English banking partner based here at a time. That will only be possible upon your leaving, Tracey, i.e. next year at the earliest," Michael added.

Tracey returned to typing into her blackberry and said nothing.

"In the meantime we do have the counsel status," Keel suggested.

Mayer interjected. "That is not really an official status yet. Nobody really knows what it means and it is not necessarily on the 'Partner track.'"

"Whether as associate or as counsel, you would have to go through the whole partnership selection and assessment process again. You wouldn't really want that again at this stage in your career, would you?" Tracey asked with a slight smile, looking up only at the last two words.

"Actually I have already been through it three times—once at Howard Hewitt and twice at Solomons. If necessary, of course I would do it a fourth time. At least I have had plenty of practice," I intoned.

Tracey's smile froze. "You would also need to commit to a fifty to sixty hour week. We are very busy."

"Indeed, you did over eighty hours last week, didn't you, Tracey—almost as many as Mr. Mayer and me, ha, ha!" Keel exclaimed with a booming voice.

"Indeed," Tracey confirmed coolly.

"Ms. Krakowski is not a rookie, after all. Would a non-partner position be at all acceptable to you?" White turned to me. "How would that be construed in the market?"

"That would depend on the overall package and my prospects. P&W is a first class firm—this could be a very good platform for me from which both sides could benefit. We could market this well."

"Exactly! I can see the headlines of the legal press: *Asset Finance Star Krakowski Moves to Market Leader P&W*," Keel raved. I beamed at him. This man had the right vision. The others would come around.

"I suggest we discuss this amongst ourselves later and now give Ms. Krakowski a tour of the 25th floor. I am happy to do that," Keel said, concluding the discussion, and rose from his chair, impressing with his, almost, seven feet stature.

"With pleasure." I rose as well and extended my right hand towards Mayer first and then the other three to say goodbye. "Thank you all very much for your time. It was very nice to meet you. Tracey, I hope to see you again soon."

Keel held the door open for me. "See you all later. Michael, I'll give you a buzz," he shouted into the room before closing the door behind us.

That same evening Michael called me at home.

I had just put the children to bed, slipped on a soft shirt and some cosy Juicy Couture lounge trousers and finished my first glass of Chablis. Marie had needed a long cuddle. She knew how to demand what she required emotionally. Her sister was more reserved. At only just eight years old, Noëlle was already so independent and proud. She also knew exactly what she wanted and made her own decisions. She never made emotional demands but, if I did not gently impose my love and tenderness on her, she would retreat. I knew this feeling too well.

I went to the sound system and chose an Ella Fitzgerald compilation. I sang along quietly. When Noëlle was still a baby, I would sing '*Everytime We Say Goodbye*' to her as a lullaby. One night—she was too little yet to talk but big enough to sit up in her cot—she had looked at me with her big serious eyes, placed her tiny digit on my lips and said "psshht". I had laughed, though had felt slightly indignant since I considered my singing to be passable. I then tried another classic lullaby but she did the same. "Pshht". That was the end of the lullabies. That memory always made me smile.

"I just quickly wanted to get back to you—can you talk?" Michael began. His voice was as crisp as my white wine. My heart beat faster. My mouth was dry. I grabbed my wine glass. Empty!

"Yes, of course—no problem." Now I had to walk to the fridge, take out the bottle and—this was the difficult part—pull out the cork, all without making any noise.

"We think you would fit in very well at P&W and would like to make you an offer."

My heart missed a beat. "Okay?"

"As we already said, partnership is not on the table." I knew that when Michael had to convey unpleasant news he became very curt and undiplomatic.

"What about the counsel status?"

"Nah. Too complicated. We would have to get all offices and the other practice groups on board, and the corporate partners are not cooperative because we are trying to get rid of some of them. So listen. You join us as an associate. We'll pay you the same salary that Ingrid offered you. And when 'that' Tracey finally leaves next year we'll make you partner."

I cleared my throat in order to suppress my giggle. It was too funny how he spoke about Tracey. I pulled myself together. Ingrid was a former colleague who had been recruited by a large U.S. law firm with which I had also been interviewing. "I have to think about it, Michael. Black & Chase have offered me salaried partnership."

"Well, only you will know whether you would get along with Ingrid. She will grab, for herself, whatever work she can get and will drop you the moment you fail to fulfil your financial targets. P&W is clearly the better firm and we have a huge amount of work. Also, you don't have to do any build up work like at B&C—you would be in charge of the entire English law team in the banking department."

I pondered this for a moment. "Thank you, Michael. I will let you know by the end of the week. Will that be OK?"

"Yes, of course. I don't want to talk you into it but I do recommend you consider it seriously."

"I will," I promised and hung up. Damn.

The magic word: Partner. In the legal world, there are essentially two categories: the first category comprises those partners who do not have any share in the firm's equity. They are usually called non-equity partners, salaried partners or (sometimes) local partners. The second category consists of those who do—they are the equity partners. To become Equity Partner is the equivalent to the Holy Grail for practically every lawyer in private practice and, in larger firms, it can correspond to having a licence to print money. Even amongst the partners, there is a hierarchy: equity before non-equity or salaried. All decisions are made by the equity partners but the real power lies with those in top management positions and—perhaps even more importantly—the so-called 'rainmakers', the ones with the highest billing figures. But above all, a Partner is a Partner. Why was that so important to me when one firm had offered the same money as another?

To a lawyer, in a big firm, status means more than money. Money is a pleasant side effect of the status but one has little time to enjoy it when one spends day and night in the office—*unless your name is Chloé Krakowski and you shop online during a long, multi-party, boring conference call, purchasing a dress from the new Miu Miu A/W collection at net-a-porter.com (and shoes of course, without which no outfit is complete). It was a treat for all the hard work and deprivation—but certainly not to make fashion statements in the office. To wear that dress for the benefit of my fashionably challenged colleagues would indeed be, as my hopefully-soon-to-be-ex-husband would say, comme la confiture pour les cochons—like feeding pigs with jam. A waste of a good thing.*

No, money is not the primary objective in this Olympus-like world. At most, only the other partners within the same firm and your financial adviser know how much you make. Also, earnings may fluctuate, depending on revenue. Status is everything because it means power. Once you are finally made partner, you will want to remain a partner. When a partner is asked to leave the firm due to their underperformance—meaning billable hours or receivables continuously below budget—his next destination and earnings are almost secondary, as long as he can keep his title as Partner. A Partner is perceived to be 'somebody' and is invited to participate in exclusive business shaping meetings, which take place behind closed doors, where associates' security cards do not work. As a partner, you can behave as if you own the place (because theoretically you do). You can delegate as much work as possible to your hungry associates who are chasing the partnership carrot that is being dangled in front of their noses. When you mention (with feigned indifference) to someone in the legal world that you are a partner, you secretly expect the kind of awe and admiration usually reserved for Greek gods or their modern counterparts, Hollywood stars. Once you have been to Olympus or the VIP-area, you do not want to be excluded from it again. And Black & Chase offered me the golden ticket.

However, Ingrid Nordström was, as Michael Stone had stated, indeed an unpredictable entity. I met her for the first time at the annual Howard Hewitt summer party some eight years earlier. I was eight months pregnant with Noëlle and about to embark on my statutory leave. She had been sent by the London office to fill in for me during that time.

All tanned and in a white shift dress, she made a beeline for me as soon as she spotted me at the party. Blonde and attractive, I thought with suspicion. They better not try to replace me permanently, just because I am taking, a short, maternity leave. She must have sensed something because she immediately made it very clear that she was only there for the three months and had no intention of staying one minute longer than necessary. As I began to relax, she told me about her little daughter, which, of course, warmed my heart, and then relayed the latest gossip from the London office. We had a great time. She fulfilled the stereotype of a cheerful Swedish woman who could hold her drink. Behind her casual exterior, however, she was made of steel. On my return from maternity leave, her secondment contract was extended and we became rivals for the position of banking partner. Even though she was my senior, it was I who won the race, which she acknowledged graciously. When I then declined the offer of partnership at Howard Hewitt in favour of Solomons, and the firm did not pass the offer of partnership, that had been made to me, on to her, she triumphantly showed her hand. It turned out that whilst on the HH partnership track she had been in negotiations with Black & Chase, a distinguished and very profitable U.S. law firm with a reputation for being tough with and demanding of its partners. They had opened an office in Frankfurt and offered her immediate equity partnership. It was a far more prestigious position than that which Solomons had offered me and I didn't begrudge her it. Thus there were no longer any impediments to us being friends. And now, five years later, as head of banking at B&C, she was able to offer me a job as a local partner—'baby partner', as she called it. So her world was finally in order.

I thought hard. Was it really so much better to be an associate at P&W with concrete prospects of becoming head of the department in one or two years' time? Tracey did come across as a bit difficult but I was sure I would be able to get on with her. We both had children and could be allies in a man's world. Her return to London was also set in stone. What prospects did I have with B&C if I did not achieve at least two million Euros in billables in my first year? The noise of a key in the front door interrupted my thoughts.

"Hello, my angel!"

It was Hugo. He was still wearing his work clothes—white Ralph Lauren polo shirt and white Levi jeans, both unfortunately a little on the short side since they had not been available, for someone of his height, at the street-market he had visited last winter in Bangkok. Never mind, his mother had let the jeans down with the help of some white cotton material and it did not matter to him that when he stretched his arms, one would see the white ribbed vest underneath his shirt—as long as he did not have to spend any money on clothes. I sighed inside. It was a pity that such a beautiful man dressed so badly.

"Hello. Didn't you have time to get changed?"

He usually took a shower and changed in his office after work. His outfit would then be thrown into a basket, which he would take once a week to his mother's to be washed and ironed. I wisely refrained from interfering. I had enough washing to do, anyway, with all his other clothes.

"Nah. I am going to go for a run in the woods. So, how did it go today? Where have you been again? With Patricia's husband, wasn't it?"

He came into the kitchen and planted a cheerful kiss on my lips. He pronounced her name 'Pad-risha'.

I could not stop myself. "*Patricia's* husband," I corrected him.

"That's what I said. How did it go?"

He nonchalantly took the bottle of wine out of the fridge and poured the remaining liquid into a glass. I crossed my arms. "Michael just called. They want to make me an offer. Two fifty plus bonus—same as Ingrid has offered, but no partnership."

"250,000 Euros a year? Angel, that's great! Although I don't really appreciate my girlfriend earning more than double of what I earn." He protruded his lower lip.

"It is to your advantage as well. Otherwise, we would hardly be able to afford to live in this house."

"I'm just kidding!" he replied hurriedly. "And what are you going to decide?"

"It's really hard as B&C offers immediate partnership, but, puts on immediate billing pressure, and I don't know whether I will be able to fulfil that straightaway—I did take a year out, after all. Partnership at P&W is only possible in one or two years' time but I won't have to build up a business because I will be filling an existing position."

"Who do you trust more? Whom can you rely on—Michael or Ingrid?"

"Michael, I think. He has proven to be reliable in the past and Patricia is one of my closest friends."

"Then I would choose P&W. Trust your gut feeling."

"You're probably right. I'll sleep on it."

"Good idea." Grinning mischievously, he came closer. He grabbed my hips and buried his head in my neck. "Mmm, you smell so good. Success makes you even sexier." His face slid down towards my chest. I giggled, pretending to fight him off.

"I knew you wouldn't really mind if I got a well-paid job."

He looked up with feigned outrage. "I never said that I mind and I do so love to see you in a suit and heels." He started fiddling with the buttons of my shirt. "But I love even more to see you without any clothes at all."

"Hey! I thought you were going to go for a run and then take a shower."

Meanwhile he had unbuttoned my shirt and pulled me towards him. "Later," he murmured and kissed me passionately.

That night, I did not make any further decisions concerning my career.

--- original message ---
From: Chloe Krakowski [mailto:C.Krakowski@gmail.com]
To: Michael.Stone@prattwonkey.com
Cc: Richard.Keel@prattwonkey.com
Re: Employment contract

Dear Michael,
Thank you for sending me the employment contract. It seems to be missing the usual provisions regarding the health insurance and pension contributions. I understand 50% of which is usually paid by the employer. Can you confirm this?

Best regards
Chloé Krakowski

--- original message ---
From: Stone, Michael: BK (FR) [mailto: Michael.Stone@prattwonkey.com]
To: C.Krakowski@gmail.com
Cc: Keel, Richard: BK (FR)
Re: Re: Employment contract

We do not put this in our employment contract because it is mandatory law. The employer pays half of the health insurance and pension payments.

Best regards
Michael

--- original message ---
From: Chloe Krakowski [mailto:C.Krakowski@gmail.com]
To: Michael.Stone@prattwonkey.com
Cc: Richard.Keel@prattwonkey.com
Re: Re: Re: Employment contract

I thought so.
Many thanks and have a nice day!

--- original message ---
From: Richard.Keel@prattwonkey.com
To: Stone, Michael: BK (FR)
Cc: C.Krakowski@gmail.com
Re: Re: Employment contract

Michael, Ms. Krakowski just gave me a new idea to further increase the profitability of the banking department: we could generate exceptional income by not contributing to our employees' health care and pension plans.

Just kidding!
Best regards
RK

--- original message ---
From: Ingrid.nordstroem@blackchase.com
To: C.Krakowski@gmail.com
Re: Business Plan

Hi!!
All clear from NY! We can take you on as a salaried partner. The partners in London and Frankfurt are supportive - no need to go to New York for an interview. I will arrange all. Should be done by month end.

The Frankfurt partners want a chance to meet you - will arrange for a meeting the week after next. You can then also meet some of the associates in the team. BTW, the salary as discussed is no probs.

The business plan you sent over is good. So now just one more meeting!

Will be great to have you on board.

Ingrid.

--- original message ---
From: Chloe Krakowski [mailto:C.Krakowski@gmail.com]
To: Ingrid.nordstroem@blackchase.com
Re: Re: Business Plan

Dear Ingrid,

Thank you for everything and for being prepared to give me a chance. I have thought it through and I have concluded that I am not ready for the pressure to meet your billing and business development expectations. After having been subjected to the internal politics at Solomons and having been out for the market for so long, I have lost some confidence. I think the route that is mapped out for me at P&W will enable to me to get back into the market with less pressure. I am sorry if you are disappointed now but I would hate for you to be even more disappointed later. Don't be mad at me please.

Chloé.

3

She Works Hard for the Money

On Monday, 1 May 2016, my first official day at Pratt & Wonkey, I arrived in the office just before 8.30 a.m. After depositing my bag and switching on the computer I found my way to the tea & coffee room and examined the coffee machine. It had various buttons—espresso, cappuccino, coffee short, long, with or without milk, with or without sugar. That looked promising. I pressed the buttons for cappuccino, extra strong, no sugar. The machine ground the beans and spat the liquid into my Starbucks New York mug. I had brought it from home when a glance into the room's cupboards on the previous Friday had shown me a vast selection of only chipped and faded mugs.

"Mornin'." Michael strutted into the room, holding a mug in his hand. "You're early," he declared.

"Good morning, Michael. Well, the girls have to be in school by eight. The office is on my way back," I explained what he already knew.

He grunted, took some coffee from the thermos (which I had already tried and immediately had poured down the drain) and marched out again. "See ya."

It did not sound unfriendly. Before I could reply he had turned the corner. My mobile rang. I checked the display and answered: "I knew it could only be you at this early hour!"

"Well, good morning to you, too, Ms. Krakowski!" Patricia's voice shouted into the loud speaker of her car phone. "How's the fun factory? Is my husband treating you well?"

"Actually, I'm in the tea & coffee room and he was just here to get a coffee. He seems to have been in for a while."

"Sure—I do the school run, so he can be in the office early. Doesn't mean he will be home before nine or ten."

"Yeah, I know. Well, I have to be home at eight at the latest to take over from Jana and there is no way I can leave any earlier than seven thirty. I think people here are expected to stay until at least eight, if only to demonstrate presence and eagerness." I whispered the last bit.

Patricia let out a short laugh. "Do you remember how the guys at Howard Hewitt would leave their desk lamp and PC switched on, files open on the desk and a jacket hanging over the back of the chair?"

"I do! I think it's the same here. Apart from the fact that this is rather silly and a complete waste of electricity, I am hardly going to leave any item of my lovely and expensive wardrobe in the office. As you may remember, I need to leave my desk in order or, even better, cleared so that it can be cleaned properly and I can start the next day fresh and newly inspired. I know I'm a bit neurotic."

"A bit? I don't know about a bit!" Patricia laughed. "I am so glad I don't have to do this anymore. Anyway, I just called to ask you and Hugo to dinner this Saturday. I want to have a nice proper dinner before all those football parties start next month. Are you free?"

"Oh—great idea! I'll check with him, but I think that works. Can we bring anything?"

"No, don't worry. Just be there at about seven thirty. You can bring the girls and they can watch *Madagascar* with the boys. I'm going to buy the DVD."

"They'd love that, thanks! Now I better get to work." I spotted two secretaries walking by.

"Okey-dokey! Have fun!"

I checked my watch. It was nearly 9 a.m. If I reduced my lunch break to a maximum of thirty minutes it would leave me about ten and a half hours, which I could fill with chargeable work. Nobody was going to be able to accuse me of working less just because I was a mother of two. In addition, there were still a few hours left after the children went to bed. On the other hand, it was very important to spend that hour between 8 and 9 p.m. with the girls as well as trying to keep quality time at the weekend for the girls, of course. The previous of which Tracey had nearly spoiled. I had worked all night Friday until the early hours of the morning and again on Saturday night after I had put the girls to sleep in the evening. Tracey had received her document at exactly two minutes before midnight. I was dead tired but at least I had been able to spend the day with Noëlle and Marie.

As I walked back from the tea and coffee room, I passed by the office adjacent to mine and briefly stopped for a peek. It looked like utter chaos inside. There were piles of papers and documents on the floor. The desk looked as if a hurricane had swept over it: opened books, files, sheets of paper unstapled and highlighted in yellow or edited in blue, note pads, tea mugs, pencils were lying around. I shuddered. I wouldn't be able to stand that mess for five minutes. The chair was still empty. I glanced at the plaque outside the door. Jacob Wronski. The name rang a distant bell.

I went into my office, sat down and looked at the monitor while carefully taking a sip of the hot cappuccino—extra strong, no sugar. I shuddered again. It tasted like a mix of dust and water plus a bit of stale coffee squeezed through an old sock. I put the mug aside and clicked on the internal mails.

--- original message ---
From: Taylor, Tracey: BK (FR)
To: Krakowski, Chloe: BK (FR)
Re: Amendment Agreement

Hi Chloe,
Thanks for this. I will review and we can have a chat on Monday. Have a good weekend.

Tracey

The email had been sent on Sunday morning at 0.02 a.m. Goodness. Either she slept with her blackberry under her pillow and had turned on the audio alert for incoming mails or she really had sat by her laptop all night. I sent her a brief reply along the lines of "anytime, whenever it is convenient for you" and started to look through the files, which Jerome had placed on my desk.

Sometimes I asked myself what I was doing in this job. Staring at the monitor all day and either reading a document, typing or speaking on the telephone, or everything at once—this had little to do with the picture I had had in my mind since childhood. My mind wandered back to when I was about nine years old. One evening, by my bedside, my mother told me about her father whom she had never met—shortly after her birth, he fell in the war in Russia. He had been a lawyer with a promising career as a judge. She showed me some faded black and white photos of a young, attractive man with short black curls and a self-confident smile. His face showed intelligence and determination.

"Mummy, when I grow up, I'll be a lawyer!" I declared. "I want to go to court and fight for justice!"

She hugged me tenderly. "Yes, that's exactly what you will do, my little doll. I know it."

And somehow I knew it, too. A few years later I watched a black and white movie on TV—*Witness for the Prosecution*, a courtroom drama set in the Old Bailey directed by Billy Wilder based on a play by Agatha Christie. Tyrone Power plays the part of a man charged with the murder of a rich old widow. Marlene Dietrich plays his German wife who is to exonerate him and Charles Laughton plays his defence barrister—the old, sick, rotund, grumpy and brilliant Sir Wilfried Robarts. I was fascinated, not by the beautiful charismatic murderer or his mysterious wife, but by the clever, rhetorically brilliant and shrewd Sir Wilfried. Wearing the black barrister's gown and white horsehair wig he sits rather casually in court and sips on a cup of tea from a thermos flask which his nurse has prepared for him and which he has secretly spiked with brandy. But as soon as the prosecuting counsel makes a mistake during his examination of a witness, he jumps up and coolly states his objection. Then he rises for the cross-examination of the housekeeper and with a few sentences reduces the witness to utter incredibility. That is what I wanted to be, exactly that! Wearing a white horsehair wig, the gown streaming behind me, and being a brilliant orator! Not old, fat and sick, but beautiful, like Marlene Dietrich. I wanted it all.

Right now I was further away from that dream than at the beginning of my career, when I was indeed working as a barrister in London. Instead of working in old venerable chambers I sat in a skyscraper and made use of my talent for verbal reasoning by drafting two hundred-page credit agreements based on standard precedents. Most of the time, all that it took was to reflect the commercial terms correctly—such as the interest rate, duration and security for the loan etc.—and to adapt the provisions to the context of the transaction. Sometimes, however, an unexpected commercial or legal issue required the careful and creative drafting of a new provision covering all eventualities. That was fun. I would then not be able to let go until I had it absolutely right. When negotiating the point with my counterparties, I would apply a mixture of logical reasoning and charm, which, on the whole, worked very well. At least, it had until now. I felt that Tracey was yet to be convinced of me and that I would have to work hard to gain her trust.

~

"Hi Chloé, how are you? Did you have to work all weekend?" Jessica was standing in the door later that morning, as I was ploughing my way through the documents.

"Hi Jessica—well, almost. It was a bit of a late night effort but I sent Tracey the draft just before midnight on Saturday. That might have been too late for her. I haven't spoken to her yet."

Jessica frowned. "Well, technically it was still Saturday night when you sent it to her. And anyways, it's a question of principle, right? She shouldn't ask you at such short notice to work all of Saturday."

"As long as she's happy with it. How about you—did you have to work yesterday?"

"Yeah. We had a conference call with those clients I told you about. But at least I could do that from home. David had to come into the office."

"Poor you. You may have told me already—which partner does he work for?"

"Francis Mayer. He is very demanding of his associates and works all the time himself. But if all goes according to plan, David should be made partner the year after next."

"Wow. He is quite young, isn't he?" So Byrd was Mayer's special prodigy. Interesting.

"Thirty-three. But it's what he wants. So we definitely won't be getting married before then." She curled her lips. Byrd's working hours and the effect on their relationship seemed to a sensitive topic.

"Hey, don't expect any marriage advice from me—I'm in the middle of a divorce!" I joked.

A tall dark-haired man appeared behind Jessica. "Hello, Ms. Krakowski. Hi, Jessica."

I looked at him with a question mark. "Hello?"

"I'm Jacob Wronski—I have the office next door." He offered to shake hands. "We kind of have met already."

"Right." I struggled to remember him.

"The Australian Gas transaction? December 2001? You were at Solomons then. We spoke on the phone a few times. I work with Gunther White." He seemed disappointed and probably thought I was a stupid arrogant cow.

I did remember the transaction very well and also that P&W was on the other side but thought that I had only dealt with White. Wronski must have been very junior at the time. I quickly glanced him over. He was tall, had large blue eyes and his suit was well cut. He was not as gorgeous as Hugo but there was something about him. I smiled at him.

"Of course—Australian Gas! Such a messy deal, and just before Christmas! What a coincidence that we are now office neighbours. By the way, I thought associates were on first name terms."

He grinned. "Yes that's correct. So, a warm welcome from the other side of the wall; if you need anything just let me know."

"Very kind of you, thanks!" I followed him with my eyes as he left the room.

Jessica raised her eyebrows.

"You really do know a lot of people in the legal world!"

"Yeah, I guess. The asset finance market is small and the number of specialised lawyers a mere handful," I explained. "Gunther White is one of them. But I never met *him* personally," I whispered and pointed my right thumb behind me towards the wall which I shared with Wronski's office. I did not want him to be able to hear us.

"Oh you will get to know him—he is quite a character."

"Is he? I am intrigued."

"No, not like a womaniser. He does tend to make a lot of sexist jokes, but I don't think he means them. You kind of know that, underneath it all, he is a decent guy."

"Hm. I remember now in that transaction we had a call at least once and he did seem nice. Anyway—his room is a mess."

"That's not that unusual—have you seen some of the others? Actually, mine is not that tidy either—although I try! Yours looks spic-and-span though."

"I need to have my room tidy—it makes me feel more balanced and calm."

"And your outfit is, again, impeccable! I love that suit—is it Armani?"

"No, it's actually vintage Alberta Ferretti. In my case, that means it's about three years old," I laughed. "I'm afraid I'm a bit of a fashion addict. Shoes, bags, you name it. I can get quite gaga over a handbag." I rolled my eyes.

"I think you look amazing! I would be thrilled if you gave me some fashion advice—I am so useless sometimes!" She looked down at her suit.

"Not that you need it but, of course, with pleasure. I must warn you though. When friends ask me to help them clothes shopping, it usually leads to an excessive use of their credit card!"

"Oh I'm fine with that! Maybe we can do a little bit of shopping at lunchtime some day." Jessica glanced at her watch and startled. "Shoot, I nearly forgot—Tracey asked me to ask you to join the conference call we have with Frank Smith at one!"

"Sure, no problem. What's it about?"

"It's a really complex real estate finance transaction we have been working on for a couple of years. To start with we represented the banks and now, at the refinancing stage, we represent the investor, a private equity group based in the U.S. who are investing in German real estate. The loan is over two billion Euros, made in various tranches to a large group of special purpose German companies and partnerships set up by the investor. These entities together purchase a portfolio of over a thousand buildings and apartments, which were sold by local authorities in German cities like Frankfurt and Hannover. I think Frank is the only one who has a complete overview."

"Is there anything I should read beforehand?"

"Tracey didn't say. And honestly, I wouldn't know where to tell you to start. Which reminds me again—I better go and prepare for this call. No chance of getting any lunch in before the call." She screwed up her face. "I'll pick you up just before one," she said and disappeared through the sliding door.

Three hours later Tracey, Jessica and I were still sitting in Frank Smith's office for the conference call. So far, it had been about very specific real estate and corporate law questions. Smith had spoken most of the time. Tracey and her team were to discuss any issues that might have an impact on the English law credit agreement. Whilst Jessica had been scribbling away on her notepad I had tried to follow the call despite lacking any knowledge of the background. After a while my mind had started wandering and I had to make a big effort not to fall asleep, to still look interested and nod knowingly from time to time when any financing-related aspects were addressed.

I was startled when I heard my name mentioned. "Ms. Krakowski, you should know, being a trained barrister."

Smith looked at me expectantly. Oh shit. I had not been listening. I smiled nonchalantly. "Which aspect in particular do you have in mind?"

"The interpretation of the term *gross negligence*," replied Smith. "Is there a precise difference to *negligence*?"

I opened my mouth to respond when Tracey cut me short. "Actually Chloé doesn't practise at the Bar anymore. We will ask the litigation department in London and get back to you after the call." She turned her attention back to her blackberry.

"Indeed, you are right," I continued, turning to Smith. What the heck? This was not an issue of procedural laws. "English civil law does not distinguish between *gross* and *simple negligence*. Either you breach the standard of the *reasonable man* or not."

Jessica nodded in agreement. Tracey continued to type a message into her blackberry. Smith seemed satisfied and turned to the speakerphone. "So, Ms. Krakowski also says that there is no difference."

"It would do no harm in this case, though, to add the word *gross*, if you feel more comfortable with it," I added. Jessica had quickly shown me the relevant provision of the credit agreement.

"Ok thanks, that's really helpful." The client's voice sounded metallic.

Tracey suddenly leaned forwards towards the speaker. "That's fine, Jack—please let us know if you need any further details."

I stared at her. Maybe I had been a bit too forward. Ultimately, she was the boss. It seemed that in order to make any progress in this job, I would have to play the role of the *good* associate—no, *senior* associate, if you please.

The call was over.

"We should send Jack a memo about the issues we discussed, especially the point about the hereditary building rights," Tracey said.

"Fine, good idea." Smith was absently leafing through a statute book.

"Why don't you prepare that, Chloé?" Tracey asked me innocently.

"Uhm, uh—sure. I'll have a go."

"That would be very helpful. Do send it to me first. I'll have a look at it." Smith seemed grateful.

"I'll give you some more background," Jessica offered.

Super. What the hell was a hereditary building right??

“That wasn’t really fair.” Jessica said when we had returned to my office.

“To be honest, I found it a little difficult to follow everything, especially the hereditary building right stuff. It’s really not an area I have dealt with before.”

“Actually, we do need to know quite a bit about German real estate law issues because, ultimately, we also have to deal with them in the credit agreement.”

“I realise that. I guess I will have to get some sort of idiot’s guide or resort to the method all lawyers use: learning by doing. That’s how I became an asset finance specialist!” I laughed without humour.

That is the way it is—in big law firms, hardly anybody takes their time to explain something to you; you have to find out for yourself. It doesn’t seem to bother anyone that, even if you don’t make any mistakes, you could easily overlook something important that you just didn’t know about. However, the more experience you have as a lawyer, the more you heighten your awareness of new issues.

“So what kind of deals have you done in the past?” Jessica asked.

“Mainly everything to do with the financing of assets, often combined with a leasing structure—we’re talking aircraft, trains, container ships, high tech equipment. The deal Jacob mentioned this morning was about thousands of gas meters—not very glamorous!”

“Jerome told me you had also done some movie financings.”

“That’s right. The way that worked was the producer obtained financing to buy the movie rights and then leased them back to the distributor who made the money with the film once it was finished and paid fixed monthly licence fees to the producer.”

“Wow! That sounds so glamorous! So what kind of movies?”

“Big budget Hollywood productions. They became very popular amongst investors because the tax breaks were so huge—the entire production cost could be deducted in the same year. Sadly the tax authorities put a virtual stop to these structures. Some film investment funds got a very bad press because the financing structures were thought not to be genuine and the directors had to pay enormous fines or even go to jail. None of my deals though!”

“That’s so cool! So did you meet anybody famous?”

"I wish! I travelled to L.A. several times for negotiations with the studios' lawyers and even offered reducing my fees if somebody introduced me to George Clooney, but that didn't work!"

"Too bad!" Jessica giggled. "Maybe you should have asked for Brad Pitt!"

~

It was 7.30 p.m. and I was starting to get nervous. I had only managed to write the first introductory paragraphs of the memo. I would have to leave the office soon to pick up the girls from Jana's house. The memo would need to wait until later that evening. My phone rang. The display read *Taylor*, making me feel instantly queasy. I picked it up and forced myself to smile.

"Hello Tracey?"

"Hi. I was wondering when we might expect your memo."

"I'm still working on it. I'm trying to get to grips with the deal structure as well. It seems quite complex." That was a huge understatement.

"I was going to go out now and grab a bite to eat. I'll be back in a couple of hours, so it would be good to have it by then. In the meantime I will send you my comments on the draft you prepared at the weekend. You can then revise that after you have finished the memo."

I gulped. "Sure, Tracey. Will do."

"Thanks." She hung up.

I felt upset—not because I had to finish the memo that evening, but because Tracey had managed yet again to impose her will on me. I shied away from personal confrontation—I had only just started this job and wanted to make a huge effort. It would not be wise to take on my boss, the one person who had total power over my professional development. We had already gotten off to a bad start last Friday. Maybe then I shouldn't have made it an issue at all but should have just said, 'Yes, of course, Tracey,' like I had done just now.

I wearily took the telephone and dialled Jana's number.

"Jana Jurec?"

"Jana, hi. It's Chloé."

"Chloé, sweetheart, what's up, are you ok?"

"So-so. I'm being kept in the office. I'm so sorry. Can you take the girls home and to bed? Hugo should be back by nine. They should be asleep then so he won't need to do anything."

"Sure, don't worry. I've still got your keys and Dean will be late tonight as well."

Dean was a hard-working electrician and Jana's husband. They lived in the house right opposite ours. As Jana only worked in the mornings she was able to look after my girls in the afternoon. Jana did not have any children but was longing to get pregnant and gave all her maternal love and attention to my girls in the meantime.

"You are an angel! May I speak with them please?"

"Of course. They are with me in the kitchen. I'll pass you first to Noëlle."

"Hello Mummy," Noëlle's little voice squeaked through the phone.

"Hello my sweetie, are you ok?"

"Yeees. Jana made pancakes!"

"Wow, that's so nice of her! With icing sugar or with Nutella?" I knew the answer. Noëlle loved Nutella.

"With Nutella! But Marie had hers with icing sugar."

"Sounds yummy! Very good! Listen, my little darling, mummy has to stay in the office and will come home a bit later—Jana will take you to bed and wait until Hugo comes home, ok?"

"But why? When will you come home?"

"I've still got a lot of work to do. You'll be asleep already when I get home. But I'll come to your room and give you a kiss, ok?"

"Mhmm. Okay."

My big little girl. I swallowed hard. "Then sleep well, my darling, and good night! Let me speak to Marie. Kiss kiss!"

"Kiss kiss, byeee. Good night."

"Hello Mummy." Marie sounded tired.

"Hello my sweetie, how are you my darling?"

"Fine."

"I already heard you had yummy pancakes!"

"Yes."

"Listen, sweetheart, I wanted to say good night because mummy is going to be late and will come home when you are already asleep."

"Okay."

"Fine, so Jana will look after you and I will come and give you a kiss later, alright my love?"

"Okay."

I smiled. Marie was nearly five years old. Her monosyllabic answers on the telephone were in stark contrast to Noëlle's liveliness. But Noëlle was already eight and felt in charge when I was not around.

"Good night, my angel, sleep well. Mwah mwah." I blew kisses into the air.

"Good night, mummy, you too." I heard her rustling then she hung up. My sweet child—she didn't know it was far from bedtime for me.

That evening, and each other evening that week, I stayed in the office until after ten o'clock.

Saturday came and we took the girls to Patricia and Michael Stone's house for dinner.

It was more of a mansion than a house, surrounded by a landscaped garden and protected by a high brick wall. Having parked the car on the side of the road in front of the house, we passed through the wrought iron gates and walked up the gravel path, Marie holding my hand. Noëlle ran ahead to ring the doorbell. The door opened and my eyes fell down on Lucas, the youngest member of the Stone family. A cuddly toy lion dangled from his hand. He looked at us without any emotion. I bent down towards him.

"Hello Lucas, are mommy and daddy there?"

At that moment Michael appeared, carrying an open box with wine bottles. "Hi! Sorry about that—Patricia is in the kitchen and I was getting more wine from the cellar. Please, come in." We stepped inside the entrance hall. He turned to his son. "Now, Lucas, why don't you take Marie and Noëlle to the TV room. We'll be there in a minute to check on you guys."

"Ok daddy," Lucas replied and looked at the girls expectantly.

I nodded to the girls. "Go ahead."

"Come on Marie." Noëlle took Marie by the hand and led her away.

"There you go." Hugo handed Michael the wine bottle we had brought.

"Thanks, excellent. Ah, there she is."

Patricia appeared, wearing a pink apron over her black dress and looking flustered. "Hi guys! Sorry—I am trying this new recipe and just had a tricky moment. Lovely to see you." She greeted us with a kiss. "Gorgeous outfit, madam!" she remarked upon my white linen Chloé dress and tan wedge sandals.

"Thanks, darling, and thank you for the invitation—the girls have already disappeared in the TV room with your boys," I said as she hugged me.

"They'll be fine there—the boys are just watching *Nemo* for the umpteenth time but we'll put on *Madagascar* afterwards. I have to excuse myself again though, I must go back to my kitchen—Michael, can you please offer Chloé and Hugo a drink?"

"Do you need any help?" Hugo asked her.

"Actually, you could help me get some dishes from the top cupboard—even Michael is too short to reach it."

Michael rolled his eyes. "Come on Chloé. Let's get you something to drink."

I followed Michael into the reception room. He placed the bottles from the box as well as the bottle we brought on the side table. "Red wine ok? I decanted a bottle already." He pointed to a carafe filled with dark ruby red liquid.

"Yes, please."

He poured two glasses and handed me one. "So how was your first week? I see you have been working late."

"Yes, it's been very busy. I haven't really seen the girls all week. But you know what that's like."

"That's the job. It is what it is. When you are the main breadwinner it's what you have to do."

I took a sip of the wine and contemplated that statement. Before I could reply Hugo and Patricia walked in. Hugo carried a tray with what looked like four mini quiches.

"Right!" She exclaimed. "We've been to see the children, they are all set and we are ready to start with the first course. Hugo, could you give each of us a plate please? Chloé, why don't you sit on that side, and Hugo here at the end of the table. Michael, sit. All—please start. The quiches are not going to get any hotter."

We all sat down at our designated places. Michael poured more wine.

"This looks amazing, Patricia! Four perfect little single quiches—it must have taken you all afternoon to do this."

"Well it's not like I had any help from my husband."

"Patricia is annoyed with me because I had to work this afternoon," Michael explained.

"And why should I not be? You already work all day and night on weekdays and most Sunday afternoons and I always have to do everything," she complained coldly.

"Actually, my girl here has been notably absent from home too. Patricia—you and I can open a lawyers' neglected family club," Hugo joked.

Michael drew his breath. "I feel so sorry for you guys. It's useless explaining. You will never understand what it is like to be a partner in a law firm, the sort of pressure we are under."

"Chloé did not work like this when she was a partner at Solomons," Hugo objected.

"If she wants to be a partner at P&W, she will have to. Look at Frank Smith, our newly elected partner, and David Byrd, the candidate for next year. They live and breathe for the firm. I bet you if I called them now and asked them to draft a hundred page agreement by tomorrow morning, they would drop everything and go to the office straightaway."

"And I bet you they would not keep their wives and children for very long," Hugo retorted, throwing a glance at Patricia who pursed her lips as if to say *I told you so*.

"Anyway!" I said cheerfully. "Let's enjoy this lovely meal, shall we? So, Patricia, have you and Michael decided on the secondary school for the boys?" And with that I managed to steer the conversation away from any mines and into safe waters.

After dinner Patricia got up to change the music. When the beat began she started dancing and held a hand out to Hugo. "Come on Hugo—remember? Rihanna—*SOS*—this is *the* summer song! Same rhythm like *Tainted Love* which I'm sure Chloé and Michael will remember from *their* youth in the Eighties!"

"Yeah, sure!" Hugo got up from his chair and started shimmying towards her.

"Come on, we are not that much older than you guys—five years!" I protested.

"What do you mean by Hugo remembering?" Michael asked.

"I bumped into Hugo at the Bristol party on Wednesday," Patricia panted as Hugo twirled her around. Patricia and Hugo giggled. I exchanged glances with Michael.

"Ah, I see. My dear wife is partying while I am working late."

"Oh don't be so stuck up, *Michèlle*," Patricia retorted. "You need to have some more fun!"

"And you need to slow down with the wine."

She ignored him and continued twirling, singing along to the refrain: "S.O.S., please, someone, help me!"

"S.O.S., help me!" Hugo bellowed cheerfully, still dancing.

"I'm definitely not letting you drive!" I shouted at him. I turned to Michael. "We should go soon, anyway. It's also getting late, for the girls."

"Sure. I'll let the children know and perhaps you can get these two to calm down again before the neighbours call the police because they think someone is really crying for help." He got up from his chair and left the room. I watched Patricia and Hugo dancing happily in oblivion and wondered where all of this would lead.

~

The month of May passed by. I saw the girls only in the morning and at the weekends, and Hugo only when he was asleep or as one of us was just leaving the house. I felt like I was a bad mother. Yet Noëlle, Marie and Jana had the patience of saints. Hugo did not understand why I worked late every evening. As if it were fun not putting my children to bed and being sleep deprived. Nor did anybody take over my household duties. I would hang up the washing and clean the kitchen late at night.

But each morning I would still get up at 6 a.m., prepare breakfast, help the girls to get ready and take them to school. Then I would drive to the office, hair and make-up done and perfectly styled. I would joke around with Jerome, chat to the secretaries who had their desks in front of my office—yes, I had managed to break the ice—and work like a dog. I ran up chargeable hours as if there was no tomorrow, determined to show Tracey and Michael just how tough I was.

4

A Big Fat Greek Wedding

The month of June arrived and brought with it two main events: the football world cup in Germany and the wedding of Alex and Alexia.

I had met Alexia, an advertising agency executive and Greek by birth, when I started dating Hugo. Her future husband Alex Baker, ten years' her junior, was also a doctor and Hugo's friend. Alexia and I quickly established a friendship independently of that of our men. She possessed a rare mixture of affection, intelligence and a dry sense of humour. On top of that she was beautiful and a loving mother to her sweet little son, whom she had so far raised by herself, as well as to Alex's son from his previous relationship. When Alex finally proposed to her just after her forty-seventh birthday, she decided with her incredible energy and willpower to fulfil her dream of a white wedding on the Greek island of Santorini. It'll be like My Big Fat Greek Wedding meets Sex and the City, I thought as I was packing my bag on a Wednesday morning. I expected no less from Alexia.

Hugo and I were due to leave the next morning on a flight to Athens with a connecting flight to the island. The girls were staying with Hugo's parents for the weekend. I decided to pack the day before because that evening I was due to attend the office afterparty for the JPMorgan Chase Corporate Challenge. I wanted at least to show my face at the party even if I did not participate in the race (Running for over five km? Do I look like I do that sort of thing? You must be joking.).

I packed my new green Diane von Furstenberg sleeveless silk wrap dress which had a white leaf pattern, and—in case I was going to panic when looking at an item of clothing which blatantly breached my rule "I don't wear patterns or bright colours"—an LBD by Valentino, adding dark grey Chloé Paddington sandals and my beige Chloé Paddington handbag. For the black tie evening I had a black asymmetric gown by Narcisso Rodriguez with golden Jimmy Choo sandals and a vintage clutch.

"Uh, angel, do you think I can take this with me? It's not washed but I only wore it once."

Hugo held a dress shirt right in front of my face. I inspected it carefully and frowned.

"Goodness, no. There is a stain on the right sleeve and the collar is quite grey."

"Oh. Do you think you could?" He looked at me like a puppy.

"Yeah, alright. Leave it here. I'll wash and iron it for you by tomorrow morning." I didn't know when I was going to find the time though.

"Thank you my angel, you are so great!" He grinned and patted my bottom.

"I know," I sighed and brushed his hand away. After all, I was not his maid. I bet he'd love it though if I wore a short black skirt with a white lace apron and bonnet.

"Mummy, where's my blue dress?" Noëlle shouted from her room downstairs. "And Marie has to brush her hair!"

"Yes! I'm coming!" Pure morning stress! I just about managed to keep my voice from sounding hysterical.

Now my blackberry was blinking. It was probably an email from Tracey. Even though it was only 7 a.m. she would expect an immediate answer. I tensely clicked on the button and typed in my password. Thank god—it wasn't from her. Hmm. It was from Lars Helman, one of my former partners at Solomons. One year after my departure he had also left Solomons and joined Howard Hewitt.

--- original message ---
From: Helman, Lars [mailto: Lars.Helman@howardhewitt.com]
To: Krakowski, Chloe
Re: Ciao

Heard you're active in the market again. Nice to have you back. Lunch? Drinks? Dinner?

L

My heart skipped a little beat. Lars and I had been quite close at Solomons, for the entire five years I had been there. He was shrewd with a dirty sense of humour and managed to sell his arrogance as charm, his Prince Albert of Monaco looks being helpful with the ladies. His professional success was based on his deal making rather than technical legal skills, which is why I had not taken him that seriously as a lawyer, being a bit of an intellectual snob myself. He would delegate all the grinding work to junior lawyers who revered him and wanted to be like him. For all those reasons I did not trust him but somehow despite, or maybe because, of everything I felt, sporadically, attracted to him. I had never found myself in any situation in which I would have had to consider this seriously. During our time at Solomons we were both married with children as well as partners in the same firm and the same office. Those were two absolute taboos. At least as far as I had been concerned.

--- original message ---
From: Chloe Krakowski [mailto:Chloe.Krakowski@prattwonkey.com]
To: Lars.Helman@howardhewitt.com
Re: RE: Ciao

Lars! How nice to hear from you.
With pleasure. When, where?

Chloé

--- original message ---
From: Helman, Lars [mailto: Lars.Helman@howardhewitt.com]
To: Krakowski, Chloe
Re: RE: RE: Ciao

Let's be spontaneous.
Tonight?

Oh dear. I was tempted to see Lars but how was I supposed to squeeze that into my already packed day? Maybe we could meet during the race so that I could still make it to the after party. I didn't have time to ponder on this—Noëlle called me again. And we had to leave for school.

--- original message ---
From: Chloe Krakowski [mailto:Chloe.Krakowski@prattwonkey.com]
To: Lars.Helman@howardhewitt.com
Re: RE: RE: RE: Ciao

8 pm Villa Kennedy Bar.

--- original message ---
From: Helman, Lars [mailto: Lars.Helman@howardhewitt.com]
To: Krakowski, Chloe
Re: RE: RE: RE: RE: Ciao

Can't wait.

OK, maybe that was a bit flirtatious but we always did that. Lars was not to get any ideas though, after all, I was with Hugo—even if that relationship had become quite strained in the last months—and as far as I knew Lars was still with a Polish Solomons partner who was based in Warsaw, for whom he had left his wife of twenty years and their four children. So I put on the least spectacular outfit I could think of—black cropped tapered Chloé pants and a black Michael Stars T-shirt, which I made ready for the office with a chunky silver T&Co. necklace, elegant Prada patent sling-backs and a cream Louis Vuitton monogram vernis handbag—and ran downstairs to help the girls. I found the blue dress for Noëlle and brushed Marie's thick curls. Once I got them both safely seated in the SUV we drove off to school.

The day passed in no time. Since most of my colleagues either participated in the race—it was an acceptable excuse not to work for a few hours—or went to watch it, and others because of the expected traffic chaos had gone home early to continue work from there, the 25th floor was nearly empty after 6 p.m. The last lawyers who had squeezed their pale legs into running shorts and slipped on the lemon yellow T-shirts had marched off like heroes going to war. I breathed a sigh of relief. Finally, I was able to concentrate on drafting the credit agreement, which I had been discussing on the telephone with Laura, a client from Holland Bank, for several hours. My new trainee lawyer from London, Jason, had been busy taking notes and was now preparing the conditions precedent—or CP—list. Since the glass pane, which constituted part of the dividing wall between our offices, had been removed we could talk with each other without having to move from our desks.

"Chloé? Sorry, can I just check," Jason said with a raised voice. "Did Laura say that they want the land charge registration prior to paying out the loan as well?"

"What she said was we should try to have it as a condition of the drawdown of the loan. But it's unlikely that the land charge will be registered that quickly. If that's the case, the bank can think about waiving it as a CP and make it a 'condition subsequent.'"

"Uhm, right. But then that means if the borrower does not manage to get the land charge registered in time, the loan has to be repaid?"

"Normally, that would be the consequence, although the bank would be likely to grant another time extension. So let's add it to the list of CPs for now. That increases the pressure on the borrower to register the mortgage as security for the loan as soon as possible."

"I understand. Thanks." Jason was learning quickly but he had only recently arrived in the banking department and didn't yet know very much about security for real estate loans. Actually, neither did I but my learning curve in the last four weeks had been very steep.

I made the amendments in 'track changes' mode directly into the document and sent it to Laura, with a copy to Tracey. I checked my watch. 7.45 p.m. Perfect. A quick check in the mirror—fine, nothing special. Lars would notice immediately if I had made more effort with my outfit, and would construe that as an invitation. I definitely wanted to avoid making any such impression. Absolutely definitely.

~

Gentle piano music reached my ears as I was crossing the lobby of the hotel. There were only three people sitting at a table in the bar, which was otherwise empty. I chose a bar stool and ordered a champagne cocktail, which arrived shortly thereafter. I took a large sip. It felt good. My blackberry was blinking its peaceful green light. I relaxed.

"Hello darling."

Lars suddenly appeared at my side and gave me a kiss on the cheek. Typical. Overly intimate and very direct.

"What are you drinking?"

"Champagne cocktail."

"Looks good. I'll have a Whiskey Sour." The last sentence was directed at the barkeeper.

"Lars, how lovely to see you. I am quite surprised that you are not participating in the race for your new firm."

"I'm not completely bonkers," he replied dryly. He looked me up and down. "By the way you look tasty. How's the ear doctor?"

I laughed. I somehow enjoyed not having to beat around the bush. "Actually he has been getting on my nerves lately. I've got to work a lot and he is only complaining. I heard enough of that when I was married to Jean."

"Baby, I always told you we should get together. We would be the dream team."

"Yeah, sure! And how is dear Magda?" I retorted.

"We are separated again for now. It became all so exhausting. The constant commute between Warsaw and Frankfurt. Besides she insisted on having another baby with me. Really! I already have four, I think I've made enough of a contribution to the world's population."

"I understand both sides here. I'm sure you'll work it out."

He made a discarding gesture. "Whatever. For now I'm actually glad about it." He grinned and came closer. "You really do look tasty."

I leaned back a little, almost falling from the stool. My heart was beating fast. "Anyway…why don't you tell me, how did Howard Hewitt recruit you and how is it going there," I asked casually.

He stopped in his movement and frowned. "First I'll order more drinks."

He waved at the barkeeper and pointed at our glasses. "Same again. And when those are empty as well, same again." He turned back to me. "Where were we? Oh yes, right here." He pulled me towards him and gave me a full kiss on my lips.

"Lars! What are you doing!" I stuttered, still slightly numb, when he let go of me.

"I should have done this ages ago. I've been thinking about it for the last six years." He handed me my glass. "Cheers, darling. And now I will tell you everything you want to know."

I was stunned. It was like a scene from a James Bond movie. And I was the Bond girl. Cool. Sexy. OK, more like a Bond Lady. I listened to his stories and did not notice that my glass once empty kept being replaced with a full one. I forgot all the negative things from the last weeks—Tracey's bullying, the hard work, the feeling of being completely left alone with everything. I felt desired, understood, appreciated. By this successful and confident man.

Several hours and drinks later we were in his apartment—with a bottle of champagne, even though I already had had really quite enough to drink—making out on his sofa. When I suddenly realised I was down to my underwear, I sobered up on the spot.

"This is as far as it goes, Lars. I am not going to sleep with you. Not tonight, anyway."

"Darling, please. I have to have you, please, quickly," he urged and fumbled with my bra. "You are so gorgeous!"

I jumped up. It was absurd. "No. Stop. I'm sorry, but not like this and not now. I do like you but I am not interested in a one-night-stand. Apart from which I really have to go home."

I collected my clothes and started to get dressed. He leaned back and grinned. "OK. Shame. But do take your time getting dressed. I love to watch."

There was a loud drumming noise in my head. Who, where, what was I?

"Angel, get up. We have to go to the airport."

I knew that voice—it belonged to Hugo. Hugo? Airport? My memory returned in a flash. Fragmented images of the cocktail bar and Lars and his sofa were shooting through my brain. I opened my eyes in horror—only to close them again. I moaned. There was far too much light and my head was killing me.

"Oh dear, you don't look too well—I guess you had a hard night?" Hugo asked joyfully.

"You can say that again," I mumbled into my pillow. Just please leave me alone, I thought. I don't want to get up. I want to sleep and forget.

I pulled myself together and nearly crawled to the bathroom and into the shower. I let the hot water run down my back for several minutes and slowly started coming back to life. As I emerged I heard somconc knocking.

"Just a moment!" I wrapped myself in my bathrobe. When I opened the door, Hugo's mother Gertrude was outside offering me a steaming cup of coffee.

"Ohhh." I accepted it gratefully.

"You look dreadful, dear!" she exclaimed.

"I feel absolutely dreadful," I whispered slowly. "I feel nauseous and dizzy."

She scrutinised me. "That must have been some office party."

"Hm, so-so." I avoided her eyes.

"You have seemed generally rather exhausted since you started that job. But try and have a relaying weekend, darling. You need a bit of time off, what with your work and the children and the household—I don't know how you manage it all. Hugo could help a bit more. Shall I talk to him?"

"No, thanks. It's OK. I'm fine. You are already a huge help. I can't thank you enough for taking the girls this weekend."

"Are you kidding? Here's me waiting for grandchildren so you are doing me a favour! Now you just get ready so you get to the airport in time." She smiled and turned back to descend the stairs.

I got ready as quickly as was possible under the circumstances, threw my make-up bag in the suitcase and zipped it up.

"Are you ready now? The cab's here." Hugo came in to take my luggage.

"Yeah. I just want to say goodbye to the girls."

I went downstairs. They were playing My Little Pony with Gertrude in Noëlle's room.

"Bye-bye my little darlings." I went to hug and kiss them.

"Bye, mummy, have fun!"

Bless them. They never complained about any of my absences. The pang of guilt felt just great with my hangover. I pulled myself away and went outside where the taxi was already waiting. Hugo was sitting inside, impatiently drumming his fingers on his knee.

"Where do we have to go?" he asked.

"Terminal 1, Olympic Airways," I instructed the taxi driver feebly. I was trying to concentrate not to lose control over my stomach.

Twenty minutes later we arrived at the airport. Any more time in the shaking car and I would have lost that control. We found the check-in desk for Olympic and joined the queue. I decided that if I moved slowly it would be better for my head. Eventually it was our turn. A large-busted lady with a huge curly hairdo and an even more hugely made-up face sat behind the counter. I stared with fascination at the amount of big gold jewellery one single person could wear.

I handed her our passports. "To Athens please."

"Tickets please." She expectantly held her right hand open.

I asked myself how long she would be able to keep her arm suspended like that, with all the bangles, bracelets and rings she was wearing. I rummaged in my bag. My insides seemed to get even more twisted. "Oh no."

Hugo looked at me with expectation. "What is it? You did book this, didn't you?"

"Yes but—I left the tickets at home." My carefully maintained façade was about to burst and bring me to tears along with it.

"Then I am afraid we can't take you on this flight," the lady said and looked behind us. "Next!"

"No, please! You have to take us! We have a connecting flight in Athens, to Santorini! We are going to a wedding!" I pleaded with her.

The lady shrugged her shoulders and began to speak rapid Greek with the couple who had approached behind us. Hugo's face turned to stone. "Let's get out of the queue."

I started to cry. "I'm so sorry, it's all my fault. I'm so stupid!"

"Where are the tickets?"

"In the drawer of my desk at home! They've been there since December when I booked—I completely forgot about it!"

"Then call my mother—maybe she can bring them over!" Hugo suggested.

I took my blackberry out of my bag and dialled home. "Nobody is answering! They have probably gone to the playground!"

"Then we can forget about it. That's just great!"

"Wait—I'll try Jana! She's got a key!"

The phone on the other end rang three times, four, five—then the answering machine came on. Oh no. I was just about to hang up when I heard Jana's hurried voice.

"Yes, hello?"

"Jana! Thank god!"

"Chloé? Did you not just leave for the airport?"

"Yes—but I forgot the tickets! They are in the desk drawer. The plane leaves in less than an hour! Could you maybe help?"

"Gotcha—I'm already on my way! Terminal 1? I'll call you when I'm there!" She hung up.

I turned to Hugo. "Jana is bringing the tickets. I so hope we will be able to make it! Please don't be mad at me."

Hugo took me into his arms impatiently. "Well I can't help feeling sorry for you—you look like death. Come on, let's go outside and wait for Jana."

It seemed like eternity had passed when Jana's Mini Cooper came to a screeching halt in front of us. I did not ask her how many speed limits she had broken. We grabbed the tickets, ran to the check-in, got the boarding passes and kept running to the gate after we had managed to squeeze past the long queue at security. The gate was already empty but a flight attendant was waiting for us at the door leading to the plane.

"Passengers Walther and Krakowski?" she called out when she spotted us. "Hurry up please, the plane is waiting for you! We were about to close the doors."

We ran down the jetty to the airplane and handed our luggage to the purser.

"Row eight, aisle and window," she instructed us. I ignored the furious faces of our fellow passengers staring at me and walked down the aisle, Hugo following me.

When we had found our seats and fastened the seat belts, I finally exhaled. What a nightmare. Now I just had to survive the two flights. I thought of Lars. He probably would have purchased new tickets in this situation, business class of course. I glanced at Hugo. He was wearing his huge headphones and playing with his PSP whilst chewing gum. He misinterpreted my glance.

"Do you want to play?" He shouted and lifted the playstation towards me.

I placed my finger on my lips and shook my head. I turned back to the window, leaned my forehead against the cool pane and finally closed my eyes as the plane took off.

~

I was only really compos mentis when we had arrived at the baggage reclaim on Santorini and somebody called Hugo's name. An attractive woman with blonde hair reaching down to her waist walked towards us. She wore a tight vest, a denim mini skirt, which emphasised her tanned legs, and khaki coloured mules with a wooden heel. My alarm bells rang automatically. I observed her distantly while she greeted Hugo. Before he could respond she turned enthusiastically towards me.

"Hi! I'm Amelie, a very good old friend of Alexia's and over there, that's my husband Tom."

She pointed at a tall blonde man standing at the lost luggage counter wearing jeans and a white shirt. "And you must be Chloé—I've heard so much about you!"

Her charm was disarming. I could not help but smile. "Yes, that's correct—oh, really? Only good things I hope!"

"Of course, only good things!" she laughed. "I am so glad we finally meet! We've been living in Israel for the last two years and only rarely come to Frankfurt so I was hoping to see you here at Alexia's wedding."

Tom walked over and she introduced us. At this vicinity he looked older than I thought. I figured both were in their early forties.

"It seems that our luggage did not make it, darling," he informed her. "It'll probably be here with the next flight."

"Oh dear," I exclaimed. "You poor things!"

Amelie pulled a face. "I suspected that would happen. Our flight from Tel Aviv arrived late in Athens and we nearly missed the onward flight to Santorini. Oh well, never mind, as long as we get our clothes in time for the wedding ceremony tomorrow morning! I've had a new dress made especially for the occasion!"

"And if not, you can wear what you are wearing now!" Hugo remarked.

I shook my head pitifully. "Men! They really haven't got a clue sometimes. Listen, I have two dresses with me—even a new one, unworn—so if you have a problem…" I rummaged in my bag, found my business cards and gave one to her. "Call me."

Amelie took the card, looked at it and raised her head in surprise when she understood. "Wow! That's so amazing!"

I waved my hand. "I just thought, I can imagine you may want to wear something different tomorrow if your luggage does not arrive in time. So the offer stands, anytime."

Amelie gave me a spontaneous hug. “Thank you! We’ll first wait and see whether we’ll get our suitcases later. If not I may take you up on your offer.”

I hugged her back. “Absolutely, please do—it really isn’t a problem! See you later then, and good luck.”

We said good-bye. Hugo and I found a taxi outside the terminal building and asked the driver to drive us to the hotel I had booked. Fortunately Jana had also found and brought the email confirmation for that booking.

~

We drove through the somewhat desolate island scenery. I wound down the window and let the mild evening breeze blow into my face.

“Mucho caldo here, ya?” Hugo asked the driver.

I rolled my eyes. His foreign language skills had not really improved much in the last two years we had been together.

“That wasn’t anything like Greek. Try English,” I suggested.

“Yes, very hot, but in summer very windy,” the driver replied after Hugo’s second attempt. “You come for holiday?”

“Angel, how do you say wedding in Greek?” he turned to me.

“*Gamos*,” I mumbled. It was about the only Greek word I knew apart from *moussaka* and *yamas*. Who had not seen the movie *My Big Fat Greek Wedding*?

“Ah, yes. Yes, we came for a gambas!” he enthusiastically informed the driver.

“Well then *ouopa!*” I murmured.

After about twenty minutes’ drive during which Hugo happily chatted with the driver in Greenglish we arrived at our little hotel. It was situated directly at a steep cliff. The pool had a stunning view of the wide blue sea. Our room did not have any view at all and resembled a cave. I critically inspected the small bed, which seemed to have been carved out of a rock.

Hugo threw himself on the bed, taking up most of its space, yawned loudly and folded hands behind his head. “Finally, a bed!”

“I don’t know. Maybe we should ask for another room—it’s tiny!”

"I think it's fine. Now come here, angel."

I sat down beside him. "Oh well. I'm too tired anyway."

He pulled me towards him. "Not too tired I hope." He grinned mischievously. I withdrew my arm. I could not help but think of Lars and what had happened—what I had done—the night before.

"I still feel awful," I said truthfully. "Perhaps I need some food. The man at reception recommended a restaurant next to the other hotel down the street."

Hugo got up, stretching his body and yawning loudly. "Good idea! I'm bloody starving!"

"What a lovely way to put it. Anyway. Let's just go."

The restaurant was nearly empty. We took a table for four on the terrace by a low wall running along the pavement. I studied the menu the waiter had brought us. Fatty, savoury food was just what my hungover body needed now. And wine of course. We were about to call the waiter to order when I heard somebody call my name.

"Amelie! Tom!" I exclaimed when I recognised them. I waved them over. "What are you doing here?"

"We're staying in the hotel that belongs to the restaurant," Tom explained when they had reached us.

"I don't believe it! What a coincidence! We're staying in the hotel on the other side of the street—up that path over there. Were you going to have dinner? Then why don't you join us?" I pointed at the two spare chairs.

"Great, with pleasure!" Amelie took the chair next to me. She took my left hand into hers and looked at me. "I believe somebody up there has listened to my prayers after all. I was going to call you but didn't really dare to."

I understood immediately and laughed. "The black or the green one?"

"I really don't mind! Seriously, I'm just grateful for anything that doesn't look like I'm coming straight from the beach!" She pulled at her sleeveless T-shirt.

"I think the green one will suit you better with your blonde hair and that gorgeous tan."

"I will never forget this! This is so incredible!"

"What is incredible?" Tom asked.

"Chloé is going to lend me a brand new dress for tomorrow!"

"Oh, did your suitcases not arrive?" Hugo asked.

"I'm afraid not," Tom replied. "We bought some shampoo and toothpaste in the supermarket but I'll have to wear these trousers and this shirt again tomorrow. But I am so pleased that my wife has got something else to wear. That's much more important!" He beamed at me.

"I have a white linen shirt you could wear," Hugo offered. "It's a casual collarless shirt but it could be your size."

I had bought that Zara shirt for him. When he wore it he looked like David Beckham—it was a stark contrast to his fake designer shirts from Thailand.

Tom grabbed Hugo's shoulder. "Man, that's really super cool! Both of you are! This dinner is on us—I insist!" He waved the waiter and we ordered red wine and a large platter with Greek hors d'oevres.

I was relieved. Not only did I get out of being potentially interrogated by Hugo about the night before but I also had the pleasure of sharing dinner with Tom and Amelie and hearing their story. It turned out that she was a trained doctor, had a son from her first marriage whom she raised alone until she met and fell in love with Tom who was also divorced, but childless. Putting her son's well-being first, she only completely let Tom into both their lives when one day her son asked Tom whether he would like to be his dad.

"And what did he say?" I asked Amelie.

"He first said he would have to think about it. Then after a while he said I have thought about it and yes, Nathan, it would be an honour to be your dad. It was months later when he finally asked me to marry him!" She laughed.

"Oh. How wonderful. I can empathise with this a little. I had my first daughter without the birth father being around and when she was about one year old, Jean—my French hopefully soon-to-be ex-husband—appeared in our lives and it was kind of love at first sight between them. In hindsight, I probably only married him because of their special relationship," I concluded.

"It sounds like quite a story," Amelie said.

"Yes, indeed it is. That's why I'm currently not that keen on weddings."

"I understand. But you do seem to have found a very nice man." She pointed her chin at Hugo who was immerged in his conversation with Tom.

"Well, yes. But Hugo will want his own children one day. And I'm not sure I want to go through the whole baby thing again. I think I hoped that my children would be enough for him but I have realised that he does not regard them as his. And how can he—it's a fact, they are not his children." I swallowed hard. Speaking these words out loud felt like I was betraying Noëlle und Marie.

"Sure, they are not, but I do think it is possible for a person to love a child as if it were his own. Tom does. And I would never be able to be with him if he didn't. That may be too much to ask but my child is my biggest treasure and the most important thing in my life." She shot a scrutinising glance at Hugo.

"I know exactly what you mean, I feel the same," I hung my head, watching Hugo from lowered eyes.

Amelie took my hand. "Then maybe he is only your transitional man. But I would still give him a proper chance."

At that moment Hugo looked at me across the table. "Everything alright, angel?" He smiled warmly.

"Uhm, yes, yes. Everythings alright." I forced a cheerful smile but I felt like crying. Deep down I must have known it for a while. I thought of Lars. Of all people he was hardly a better alternative. That would mean that I eventually would have to face another break-up. Not even three years had passed since my separation from Jean. I obviously had no talent when it came to choosing men.

Amelie noticed that I had become very quiet. She squeezed my hand under the table. "I think we need another bottle of wine here," she declared to Tom und Hugo. "We are dying of thirst!"

She turned to me with an encouraging smile. "Everything will be fine. I am sure of it!"

"I guess everything happens for a reason—like us meeting today." I raised my glass, which had been refilled with red wine. "We should drink to that."

Amelie imitated me, Hugo and Tom following her.

"To us!" Hugo exclaimed.

"To Alexia and Alex!" I corrected him. "It's all about them this weekend!"

"To Alexia and Alex!" We all shouted at the same time and clinked our glasses.

~

The next day, the taxi drivers premonition came true: a strong wind blew through the alleys of Fira where the wedding took place. The short ceremony was held in a small church tucked away high above the old town. With Alex being a protestant and Alexia of orthodox faith, they had arranged for a German vicar and a Greek priest to conduct it together, with Alexia's sister acting as an impromptu interpreter. This caused some amusement, in particular with those of the congregation who were bilingual, as it became apparent that each cleric was happily oblivious to what the other was saying in his language. Afterwards we all gathered outside. It was a mixed crowd—rotund Greek aunts with lace shawls, the black-clad colleagues from Alexia's agency, German doctors and their wives. We were all to form a procession and to march along the stairs built into the steep cliff above the sea to the place where the reception would be held. Amelie was holding onto her long hair with both hands so as to keep it from flying loose in the strong wind.

"I feel like I'm going to take off in a minute!" she shouted at me, laughing.

"I'm the same—the wind is really pulling at my hair!" I had to shout, too, because the wind was howling in our ears.

"I don't know about you but I need a drink after any wedding ceremony!"

We decided to walk ahead, right behind the bride and groom. Hugo dropped behind to chat with his doctor colleagues. He always did that at parties—often I would hardly see him all night.

We were the first guests to arrive at the party location. Handsome waiters holding trays with glasses filled with champagne greeted us by the entrance. I accepted the glass offered to me, quickly raised it by way of toast to Amelie and took a large sip.

"Ah! Now I'm much better! Come on, let's speak to Alexia und Alex quickly before everyone else arrives!" We walked the few steps towards her.

"Sweetie! You look absolutely fabulous—congratulations!" I kissed Alexia on both cheeks.

She was wearing a classic white fitted wedding gown. Huge Jackie O. style sunglasses were stuck in her dark hair which had been tamed into a chignon. She looked like a mature Greek version of Grace Kelly.

"Thank you both—I am so happy you could all make it!"

"And this place is so cool!" Amelie said, hugging her carefully.

"It's gorgeous!" I added. We looked around. Bar lounge music emerged from the loudspeakers. The large terrace offered an endless view over the blue sea. Beautiful young and tanned Greek waiters and waitresses dressed in white moved around, balancing silver trays with drinks and finger food. It was perfect.

Alexia seemed to read my mind. "Thank you, dear Chloé! It is only nearly perfect—this wind came up very suddenly as is typical for the *meltemi* winds. They can become very strong and sometimes last for days. Usually though they are expected later in the summer—in July or even August," she explained.

I was always fascinated how Alexia managed to be a walking encyclopaedia and spoke with perfect diction, a hangover from her stint as a TV presenter. But she also had a comic side. "But by tonight, everything will be *ouopa* and we will have one big fat happy Greek wedding party!" She exclaimed with a playful Greek accent.

She was interrupted by Hugo and Tom who had arrived and came over to kiss the bride. I looked at Amelie whose hairdo had surrendered to the wind. She shrugged. "I probably look like Medusa now!" she laughed.

"Fine, I'll let go of my hair as well!" I loosened my grip and my hair started to fly around my head. "Gosh, this is really getting too windy! But look, up there—it looks like that corner is more protected from the wind. Let's get our men, some more drinks and go upstairs." I pointed to a corner on the upper floor, which looked like a lounge area. Several people had already found shelter there.

"Good idea! Come on, guys!"

"You go along," Hugo said. "I'm going to speak to Will and Alex about their new expansion plans. See you later, angel, have fun." He gave me a quick kiss. Amelie, Tom and I walked up the stairs and settled down in the least windy zone for the remainder of the afternoon until it was time to leave to get ready for the evening party.

~

The sun had just set when I stepped out of our hotel room, having swapped my Valentino dress for the evening gown. It was even windier than in the afternoon. Hugo was waiting on a deckchair on the terrace by the illuminated pool, his head turned towards the sea. He looked very handsome in his tuxedo. When I approached him he turned his head. I stopped, stood and waited for him to say something.

"Uhm, I guess the taxi is waiting," he said and got up.

I snorted, shook my head and walked past him. Not even an attempt of a compliment. Of course I didn't dress up only or especially for him but that didn't mean my boyfriend was excused from saying something nice—even if I had been somewhat distant over the last two days. But Hugo only gave after he had received. He would not think in a million years to make an effort for a woman. He was used to women throwing themselves on him. He told me once that he had never made a pass at a woman—allegedly because he was afraid to be rejected. So he would wait for a woman to approach *him*. It had always worked. Two years earlier he had only asked me out when he was sure that I wanted him to and would say yes.

At that time I had indeed made it quite obvious to him that I was interested. I soon realised that the balance of power in a relationship is defined at its very outset. Once we were together I felt I had to continue to take the lead, resulting in: a man who didn't feel the need to conquer me or to grow for and with me—a man who made me feel that I was not worth making an effort for. This was not a desirable outcome.

5

Dazed and Confused

"So, how was that wedding in Greece?" Patricia asked me three days later.

We were having lunch at the sushi bar near the P&W offices. It was a welcome change to the usual tuna salad that I would eat at my desk whilst drafting or reviewing a legal document.

I thought of Hugo and hesitated. Then the memory of Amelie made me smile.

"Well. It was a lovely location and there were some fun people. In particular, I met a good friend of Alexia's—her name is Amelie and she currently lives in Israel with her family. She's really nice and clever. She has this amazing thick, waist-long hair—a natural blonde but the un-blondest woman I have ever met, if you know what I mean!"

"I think I do! She does sound nice. I bet it was a good party, too."

"Yeah, it was. Although—the dinner had been planned to take place on this large terrace overlooking the sea, but then it got so windy in the evening that all the tables had to be moved inside which made it really cramped. Poor Alexia, she was rather distraught, as you can imagine! Everybody tried to cheer her up and distract her—it was nearly comical. The dancing still had to be outside, on the dance floor by the cocktail bar, so with the strong wind blowing, it was quite a challenge to dance—but kind of refreshing too. Here, Alexia sent me a photo this morning."

I opened the attachment to Alexia's email on my blackberry. It was a photo of Hugo and me—it showed me leaning with my back against the bar, arms and legs crossed, apparently watching the people on the dance floor. Hugo is seen standing next to me, putting his head on my shoulder.

Patricia examined the photo. "Very glamorous outfit, Miss Krakowski! And Hugo is really good-looking, isn't he," she stated. She pondered. "There's something odd though—it looks like he is leaning on you, even though he is so tall."

I followed her gaze and had an epiphany. "You're so right. It's quite symbolic—he is the one who always leans on me. And I am so tired of that. I don't know what's going to happen, Patricia, but things aren't right. That's for sure because...well...there's this man I have known for ages...and something kind of happened just before we left for Greece." I recounted the evening with Lars.

Patricia's eyes grew bigger as she listened. When I had finished she laughed. "Chloé, you are hilarious!"

"I think I am just completely messed up! But I can tell you, it's agony—feeling guilty towards Hugo, having these silly fantasies about Lars. I don't really know what to think or what to do."

She turned serious. "No, you're not messed up. You're obviously unhappy and that was some sort of escape, perhaps a wake up call to make you think hard about this relationship."

"Well, it worked. I'm thinking about it. But honestly, I don't think I can handle another failed relationship." I sighed. "And for the girls it would be awful. They are fond of him."

"I'm not saying you should break up with Hugo. All I'm saying is if there is something wrong, perhaps you can do something about it."

I stared at my plate and poked around the ginger with the chopsticks. What was I supposed to do? Force Hugo to love my girls like they were his own? Start to hand him the controls? See whether I could work it out with Lars?

"You know, Chloé, you're lucky. At least you're financially independent. I would never—couldn't ever—leave Michael even if I wanted to. He once said to me that if I ever dare to leave him, I wouldn't get a penny. I just wouldn't be able to face that sort of life."

"That's not true! Of course he would have to provide for you and the boys! Patricia, I know you feel neglected sometimes, and that's terrible. But Michael loves you and he looks after you and the boys. Why don't you talk to him and tell him how you feel? I'm sure he would listen. Instead of letting you buy something expensive, he should spend some quality time with you!"

Patricia smiled sadly. "I kind of try, Chloé, but it's pointless. He doesn't spend any time with me, never goes anywhere with me. I spend nearly every holiday without him, he never comes skiing with us, he doesn't go to parties—he hates them! He says it's all a waste of time. So I do everything on my own. And I get into trouble, too! You know last month when I flew to Dublin for the wedding of my school friend? At dinner I was seated next to this guy, he was really attractive, and single, and of course made a pass at me once he realised I was there on my own. We were dancing all night—it was really fun. And you know what? I enjoyed it! And the only reason why nothing further happened was because I knew I would feel too guilty afterwards."

I took her hand. "You know, if you were to ever leave Michael, you could always count on me—you and the boys could even stay with me. I understand what you are saying and I really believe that you should have a serious talk with Michael, but it also upsets me to see you unhappy—these are the best years of your life! You are young, lovely and a wonderful person and you deserve to be happy!"

Patricia's eyes filled with tears. She pulled her hand away and started rummaging for a handkerchief in her taupe Birkin bag. She found one and blew her nose. It pained me to see this fun-loving woman so resigned to 'this' life. I too loved handbags but I did not want a man who would let me buy a new Hermès bag and a gold Cartier watch but would never make love to me and not even hug me or to show me any tenderness in any other way. At that moment I could have strangled Michael. He was no different to any other partner in a large law firm, with a traditional assignment of roles—the wife at home in the golden cage, him in the office 24/7, even on Sundays, becoming a stranger to his own children and dissociated from his wife, losing respect for her, working more and more, thereby escaping his private life—it was a vicious circle. Until he or she had an affair, then the proverbial xxxx would hit the fan. That was what Patricia was afraid of. In order to be able to get through her day she brushed reality under the carpet and distracted herself with tennis and golf lessons and boozy lunches. But she could not hide from me. It was also my duty as a friend to tell her the truth.

"I have an idea! Why don't you get a job? It would give you a purpose beyond the house and kids, more independence and confidence. And Michael would respect you more," I suggested.

"What? What would I do—who would want me? I haven't worked in ten years!" Patricia was horrified.

"Of course they would! You speak fluent English, German and French, you have organisational skills and you are very good with people. I don't know—I could ask Hugo, he really could do with an office manager. You could work part-time and flexible hours! Yeah, that's brilliant! I'll ask him!" I was suddenly getting excited about the possibility to help Patricia to get out of her frustrated state of mind and her daily grind.

In the meantime, Patricia had turned slightly panicky. "Oh, Chloé, that's really kind of you, but I don't really have the time… and Michael wouldn't want me to do that… it might mess up his financial planning or something."

I sighed. "Well, please think about it. I do believe that something like this would be good for you and your marriage. Maybe the next time you meet some charming guy at a wedding, or on your skiing holidays, you'll be so angry and frustrated with your life that you won't feel guilty enough to show restraint and may do something with him. That's not a solution, believe me. I've never technically slept with somebody else, whilst I was in a relationship, but when I found myself in the situation where I wanted to, I knew something was seriously wrong. Usually that resulted in me ending the relationship."

"That's not always an option? Especially when you're married and have kids," Patricia objected.

"I know! That is why I agreed to marriage counselling with Jean. But it was too late. All that the session's did was to make me realise we were past any counselling. It was awful and heartbreaking—for me and for the girls, and I wouldn't wish it on anybody. So, you're right—if you have doubts about your marriage, you should try to save it first, Patricia. By sitting down with Michael and telling him how you feel," I repeated. Maybe she would be able to gather enough courage.

"I think we both have some thinking to do," Patricia reminded me.

I raised my eyebrows. "You are quite right."

My blackberry rang. I checked the display. "Just a sec, Patricia. It's Isabella." I pressed the button with the green receiver. "Hi sweetie!"

"Hello darling. I did not want to disturb you in the office; I just wanted to say your Edith has arrived and you can pick it up any time."

"You are not disturbing me—I'm having lunch with Patricia. That's great, so I'll pick it up on Saturday."

"Fine! Then have a great day and say hello to Patricia."

"Will do!" I hung up. "That was Isabella—she says hi. The handbag I ordered at Isabella's shop has arrived!"

"Ooh! Which handbag?"

"A whiskey coloured Chloé Edith—it looks like a schoolbag I used to have when I was twelve. It's actually not as expensive as a Paddington, probably because it does not have this massive lock!"

"You and your bags, Chloé!" Patricia laughed.

"You're the one to talk, Miss Hermès! I could get six Chloé or Prada bags for one of your Birkins! Plus, Isabella always gives me a discount at her shop. Most of the time I buy in the sale or online outlets—or both! I buy things that are good quality and timeless. I keep them for a long time, and if I don't want them anymore I sell them at the second-hand shop."

"But I don't think I know anybody who keeps her shoes in the boxes, with a Polaroid stuck on the side!"

I giggled. "Obviously, that's how they don't get dusty or dry out and I don't have to open the box to see what's inside. I actually have also started taking Polaroids of my bags and sticking them on the inside of my cupboard so I have an overview whilst keeping the bags in their dustbags."

I wasn't joking. My view was if you have beautiful things you should look after them properly. The same was true of my home.

When everything was clean and tidy and lovely, I felt some sort of inner peace. Just as the illusory idyllic world of the luxury boutiques made me feel like a million dollars when entering the store, let alone when leaving with a large shopping bag and a happy smile while a doorman—a doorman!—would hold the door open for me (I do sometimes wonder what goes through their minds). I was quite aware that my passion for fashion had, in recent years, led to more and more purchases the pleasure of which faded faster with the more objects I bought. The harder I worked the more I shopped. I was a good girl, so I deserved to be rewarded. That is what I had learned. I was a well-mannered child, obedient and good in school. Whenever I spent time with my father he would buy me beautiful things. Hm. Maybe I should pick up the bag before Saturday.

~

I didn't made it to Isabella's shop before Saturday after all. I had taken Noëlle to a birthday party and only had Marie with me. Isabella had not seen her for a while.

"Oh, she is becoming so pretty!" she gushed when kissing me hello.

"And so content—as long as she can be with her Mummy."

Marie had brought some toys and made herself comfortable on the white leather sofa in the back corner of the shop that was adorned with big cream coloured cushions.

Isabella's boutique was like a second living room for me, it was simultaneously cosy and stylish. It offered chosen young vintage as well as new pieces from the current Chloé, Prada and Miu Miu collections, Diane von Furstenberg wrap dresses and Gucci accessories. On top of that, she exhibited paintings from her favourite artist, Sydney Helfman.

It was a perfect combination. In the past I would have bought so much more but for Isabella's trusted, respected and restraining influence—a cool 'you don't need that' or 'you already have something similar' was all that was needed. Her own style was of simple elegance—she mostly wore black trousers, a cashmere sweater and Chanel ballerinas—and she shared my passion for designer bags.

She provided Marie with chocolate milk and Jelly Babies and chatted to her softly, then joined me at the clothes rack, where I was admiring a black silk A-line Chloé coat with jewelled buttons.

"She is so adorable!" she raved. "I usually don't know what to say to kids but your little angel is just so special!"

I knew what she meant. There are women who take pleasure in every child and others who are not really interested. I had belonged to the latter category until I gave birth myself and had to raise a child, which made me realise how beautiful children were and that every child was loveable. Marie with her soft face, big curls and sweet nature made it natural and easy to love her.

"Yes, I know. Noëlle is also very special—in a different way to Marie but also very adorable. But of course I would say that, I'm hardly impartial!"

"But their behaviour is a result of the way you raise them—just look at Marie being all good on the sofa! I have had children running around in the shop and throwing things off the shelves and their parents saying nothing. Awful!"

I shook my head. "That is terrible. It does take a lot of effort to teach children to be disciplined and have manners. But you don't do them any favours, in the long run, if you tolerate that kind of behaviour!"

For sure I was no expert on child education. But I was convinced that teaching the girls some clear rules gave them a sense of security and self-respect. I was not so certain about my other methods—maybe I spoiled them too much, maybe I was sometimes too strict. I was often unsure whether I fulfilled the role of their mother or their father or both. Perhaps I should spend more time with them, play with them more and listen to them more. Even when she was still alive my mother had not done that. She always seemed to be elsewhere. And when my father left her, for a younger woman, she fell apart and disappeared completely. It was like nobody was home anymore. After her passing I was glad that my father was somebody who was not emotional and just got on with things. So I knew I always had to function for my girls. Provide for them, make all decisions, set the rules and protect them from harm.

Isabella read my mind. "You are doing alright, love. Otherwise they wouldn't have made it so well through the separation from Jean." She pressed my arm. "OK, and now I am going to get your Edith!" she announced and disappeared behind the counter.

"Here she is!" She held up the cream dust bag with the brown logo. I took it from her with awe and opened it. I pulled out the handbag.

"I love it!" I carefully stroked the deliciously soft, light chocolate truffle-coloured leather.

"You can have it for eight hundred."

I stared at her in shock. "No, sweetie! You don't need to do that—you must make your cut out of this!" In fact my heart skipped a beat—in my view the full price of nine hundred was already reasonable, but eight hundred! It didn't even cross my mind how much money that was for most people.

"Don't worry, that's enough," she replied gaily. "It does suit you!" She examined me slowly. "You do look tired though—I noticed that already when you entered the shop today."

I tried to smile. "Well, I am not getting a lot of sleep. My boss is keeping me on my toes. I don't mind the hard work—I've always worked hard. But I have the feeling that she is only satisfied with her team—if at all—if we work day and night."

I suddenly realised I had tried to ignore how unhappy I actually was. I had started my new job with so much energy and good intentions. I had thought Tracey and I would become allies, but it had become very clear that this would be impossible. We were just too different. She was a product of the big law firm system, having learned the rules from scratch and knowing how to get ahead in the firm and take credit for any success—always with a smile and a treacly voice. You never knew what she really thought though.

In contrast, I was undiplomatic and direct. You get what you see. Maybe in the past I had relied too much on my charm as a counterweight. Tracey, however, seemed completely immune to any kind of charm. Only extraordinary efforts counted and only at the moment they were made. Her staff did not receive any recognition from her, let alone any praise. She was like the witch in one of the Brothers' Grimm fairy tales; the one that keeps piling wood upon the boy's back, saying if you can carry that, you can carry more. Was she really so cold and cruel? Surely that was not possible—she, too, was human and had feelings.

"Somehow I cannot imagine you having a female boss. What does she look like?"

Isabella's question propelled me back. I showed her Tracey's photo on the P&W home page using her PC behind the counter and described her dress style as neutrally as possible.

Isabella knitted her brows. "I see. So the devil does not wear Prada in this case. Well, I'm not surprised she's got a problem with you! You are the exact opposite of her—seriously I don't know any other woman who is like you! And to top it all you are supposed to take her job. Now everything is crystal clear."

"Oh, no, you're exaggerating. Anyway, she's got no reason to feel threatened. She is the partner, she has the position and the power. It's not like I'm going to take that away from her—it was always the intention that she would go back to London to fulfil a role that is even more prestigious and I was recruited to become her successor! She's always known that and must have agreed to it."

"Yes, I know, but are you sure that is what she wants? Maybe she just agreed to this because she had to but in fact has quite different plans?"

I thought that over. "That makes no sense. She need not have recruited me."

"Maybe she was full of good intentions initially. Of course I don't know what's going on in your firm but I think I am quite good at putting myself in someone's shoes and if I was her, I would probably do everything in my power to stay in my position. Plus, you don't know what it's like for her at home. She may like working here while her family is in England so she doesn't have to worry about them on a daily basis."

I looked over at Marie who was still sitting on the sofa, playing with the Jelly Babies. "I cannot imagine that she is happy to be separated from her children."

"Then maybe her husband is the problem."

"Whatever—I wish I didn't always have the feeling that I need to check my back in case her knife is stuck in it. That makes me feel insecure and afraid to make a mistake, which I suspect is what she is waiting for." I dug out my credit card and handed it to Isabella.

"You mustn't do her that favour. Trust your instincts," she warned me.

As I signed the credit card slip she took a paper bag and put the handbag inside. Then she pulled a Chloé logo key ring from under the counter and placed it in the paper bag as well.

"And that is a present from me. I can't sell that one anymore anyway—it's from last season. No, I won't hear anything," she said as I started to protest.

I walked around the counter and hugged her. There were few people in this world who understood me as well as Isabella did.

"Thank you," I said solemnly.

The doorbell rang and two women entered the shop.

"Good afternoon," Isabella greeted them cheerfully. "I'll be with you in a moment!" She turned to me. "And now look after your sweet little darling. Don't waste any more thoughts on 'that' woman."

"Easier said than done, but I'll try. I have to pick up Noëlle shortly, then the three of us will have a sushi lunch—they love that."

"Ok darling. Call me."

We kissed each other good-bye, I fetched Marie and we left the shop. My right hand held Marie's little hand, my left one the paper bag containing my new handbag.

"Mummy, did you buy something?" Marie pointed at the paper bag.

"Yes, my love, a handbag for the office," I explained.

"But you already have a handbag," she stated. Hm. I had said the same thing to her when she wanted a new bag for nursery school.

"But none in this colour and every woman needs a brown bag."

There. My five-year-old daughter was hardly going to question the authority of this statement.

"Was it expensive?" she insisted. That was usually my other argument when I refused to buy something for the girls.

"Uhm, actually, kind of—but I had to pay far less than it actually costs." Nonetheless the price was equivalent to the monthly school fee. Something started to tug at my conscience.

"Then you saved money?"

"Exactly, my clever girl!"

I was relieved and pushed that nagging feeling aside. It made no sense to buy a new handbag and then spoil the pleasure of it by allowing feelings of guilt. A new Chloé handbag, and a bargain! I was floating. I felt like a whole new person and was looking forward to taking it into the office on Monday. My grey Escada skirt suit and a white T-shirt would go with it perfectly. And I had shoes in a similar colour. And Tracey would still be in London on Monday, thank god. Thinking about Tracey and my conversation with Isabella dampened my excitement. I had to find a way to improve the situation. I just could not think of any.

~

I tried. It was the sunniest June in years and the most amazing one I had ever experienced in Frankfurt. The city was full of friendly football fans from around the world visiting for the World Cup, and people were celebrating on the streets. Every time there was an evening match Hugo and I would be invited by friends hosting a world cup party. But I would stay in the office instead, leaving Hugo to go out without me and the girls to spend their going to bed hour with Jana, without them even having received a good night kiss from their mother.

I felt utterly miserable.

To make things worse, I tortured myself thinking of Lars. I wanted to see him. I just needed to know whether it had been the heat of the moment or whether it might be more—could he be the One? Oh grow up, Chloé! I was thirty-nine years old and nearly divorced, I had given birth to two children, I had had several suitors and I was still dreaming of *the* knight in shining armour. No man would think along those lines.

--- original message ---
From: Helman, Lars [mailto: Lars.Helman@howardhewitt.com]
To: Krakowski, Chloe
Re: Dinner

Honey,
dinner this evening?

Thinking of you.
L.

--- original message ---
From: Chloe Krakowski [mailto:Chloe.Krakowski@prattwonkey.com]
To: Lars.Helman@howardhewitt.com
Re: RE: Dinner

Doesn't look good. I have a closing tomorrow. It's going to be a late night.

C.

--- original message ---
From: Helman, Lars [mailto: Lars.Helman@howardhewitt.com]
To: Krakowski, Chloe
Re: RE: RE: Dinner

Then come over after you have finished. No matter how late it is.
What are you wearing?

OK, I got it. He just wanted to get me into bed. The worst thing was, I had had similar phantasies of my own. There was no way I would give in to him easily though. Hold on, Mister. Lars knew a lot about fashion. I was sure he had also heard of a certain lingerie brand. I chuckled and typed my reply.

--- original message ---
From: Chloe Krakowski [mailto:Chloe.Krakowski@prattwonkey.com]
To: Lars.Helman@howardhewitt.com
Re: RE: RE: RE: Dinner

A Diane von Furstenberg wrap dress. The rest is my and Victoria's secret.

--- original message ---
From: Helman, Lars [mailto: Lars.Helman@howardhewitt.com]
To: Krakowski, Chloe
Re: RE: RE: RE: RE: Dinner

Wow!! Not sure I can hold out until later, honey.
L.

Bingo. Now I had him on the hook and therefore—at least for now—kept control. Perhaps he would now woo me and spoil me and treat me like a queen. I imagined what it would be like to be with such a successful, powerful and wealthy man. I could talk to him about work and he would be interested and understand. He would take the lead, make decisions, guide me and support me. I imagined a glamorous life with him in technicolour. I indulged in some more fantasies and then turned again to the draft contract on my desk, waiting to be reviewed. I didn't go to see him that night. He sent me several emails but I just couldn't get away.

I concentrated on what I was able to control, and worked like a maniac for the rest of the month. I also wanted to somehow justify my upcoming holidays. After only two months at Pratt & Wonkey I would not normally be entitled to take any time off, but it had been part of the deal from the start. Furthermore, I had been working nearly double time—on average over sixty billable hours each week.

The time keeping system at P&W was the same as at Solomons and Howard Hewitt: from Monday to Friday every lawyer (or so-called time keeper) had to enter at least eight hours into a time keeping system. The smallest time unit was five minutes. The activity code would be the file matter number and one would need to describe, in detail, the type of work undertaken.

The firm's expectation was that each minute of these eight hours would be spent on working for a client, i.e. billable hours. If you had to speak to a colleague, consider issues or read some file, you could bill that time. If you really could not allocate every five-minute unit to a particular matter number, you could use non-billable codes for things like client marketing, know-how development or training. The value of a lawyer to their law-firm is however, primarily, based on the amount of their billable hours. The more of the lawyer's hours the firm can bill to the client, the higher their profitability. So forty to fifty billable hours per week were normal, but the expectation was sixty, seventy or even more. In return, unless a specific bonus system is in place, a lawyer with that sort of performance may receive brief acknowledgement in his or her annual review—the firm considered the monthly pay cheque as sufficient compensation.

So, even with sixty billable hours per week, which meant at least twelve hours every day working for a client, I was about average. Therefore I knew how to interpret Tracey's facial expression when one day before I went on annual leave she wished me 'a *lovely* holiday'.

6

Holiday!

We left at 3 a.m. on the Saturday prior to the World Cup final. We drove through the night and morning to avoid the main traffic and arrived in the South of France around lunchtime.

I had found a two-bedroom villa with a swimming pool and sea view in the hills north of St. Maxime. Hugo and I took turns driving during what was a rather long journey. I was in the driver's seat for the last leg. It felt good leaving my foot on the accelerator and testing the speed of the car. Escaping from all that stress. I realised that the more distance we put between ourselves and home the more the stress and pressure was relieved.

I inhaled deeply. Finally, free. Finally, I would have some quality time with my family. I glanced at Hugo sitting next to me. He had after all been quite patient with me over the last few months. He was faithful and reliable—quite the opposite of me. I was upset with myself about my intermezzo with Lars and, at the same time, relieved that nothing further had happened. I had nearly put everything at stake. Now I was firmly resolved to ensure that we all would have a wonderful holiday.

"I can't wait to see the pool!" I raved. "The house is supposed to have a lovely view of the valley. We should even be able to see the sea!"

"How far is it to the beach, mummy?" Noëlle enquired.

"Well, honey, I guess about forty minutes by car. If you and Marie want we could make a day trip to the beach. But we also have a large pool and terrace—you'll see, you'll like it." I was content. The photos sent by the owner had been promising.

"Then we can teach Marie to swim," Hugo interjected.

"That would be good—I am terrified she might fall into the pool and drown. Maybe you can help her," I suggested.

"Of course—we can manage, can't we, Mariekins?" He turned around and held the palm of his hand towards her. "Gimme five!"

Marie leaned forward, giggling, and just managed to hit his wrist. "That's too high!" she squealed.

Hugo leaned further towards her and she hit his flat hand with hers. "Excellent!" he praised her and turned back in his seat.

"*In three hundred metres turn left.*" The metallic female voice came from the sat-nav.

"The exit for St. Maxime is coming up," I announced. "It's not far from there."

"Yippee! We'll be there soon!" Noëlle shouted, jumping up and down on her child seat as much as the seat belt allowed.

I pressed the indicator. "*C'est—les—vacances,*" I started to sing. Noëlle and Marie continued "*c'est—les—vacances—en—Italie*", as this is how the song went, but I quickly added, singing "*c'est—les vacances—en Pro-vence*". The three of us laughed. Hugo knitted his brow.

"That's a song by a French girl about the summer vacation," I explained hastily.

"I see," he grumbled, looking out of the side window.

I shrugged and winked at the girls in the rear mirror. They both grinned back and continued the song quietly.

A short while later we turned onto the gravel path leading to our holiday home, having passed through a charming little village and a pine forest. I turned off the engine and listened. The only audible noise was the chirring of the crickets.

"How gloriously quiet it is here! Come on, let's go inside!" I took the key from the envelope that the owner had sent to me via DHL.

"You go ahead. I'm going to get the luggage out of the car," Hugo said.

I unlocked the door and entered the house, the girls following right behind me. It was not luxurious but spacious and tastefully furnished. I opened the veranda doors and absorbed the spectacular view of the valley.

"Look, girls, you really can see the sea!"

Like two excited little puppies, Marie and Noëlle ran around exploring the surroundings. "Look mummy, there's the pool!"

"Mummy, there's a bedroom with two beds. Is that ours?"

"Probably, sweetie! I'll be there in a minute!"

Hugo came into the house with the last suitcase. "Where shall I put them?"

"I don't know yet. Just put them down and look around! Isn't it gorgeous?"

"Yeah, yeah. It's all great, angel."

"What's up? You seem annoyed."

"Nah, I'm not. I—uhm—I just think it's a bit quiet and isolated. And this steep pine forest—well, the surroundings are not quite ideal for running. I've got to go for my run every day, otherwise it'll really get too boring for me." He snorted.

That hurt. I averted my eyes. Why could he not share my enthusiasm? I had made such an effort to find something nice. Why then did he leave all the organisation and decision to me? I tried hard to suppress my rising anger.

"Maybe you will give it a try. And also, you can go swimming." I pointed to the pool. The water was glistening in the sun.

"Oh well, the pool is a bit too small for me—three strokes and I'm already on the other side."

I could feel my anger now flaring and decided that it was better to ignore his objection. "I saw a sign for a supermarket down at the big intersection—if you don't mind, I will go and get us what we need for today and tomorrow."

"Uh, yeah, great. With my non-existent French, shopping could become a bit of a problematic experience," he joked.

"You don't really need to speak French in order to go food shopping at the supermarket." I could not help my sarcasm. "Anyway I love going food shopping in France." Just thinking of olives, air-dried salami, unpasteurised cheese, and wine from Provence already made my mouth water.

"Come on, girls, we're going shopping!" I called outside. I took my handbag and calmly looked at Hugo. "I have been really looking forward to our time here and I think we both deserve a rest."

The girls ran into the room. "Mummy, the pool is great!" Marie exclaimed.

"Can we go in later?" Noëlle added.

"Of course, my darlings. We're just quickly going to get some things from the supermarket." I turned to Hugo. "See you later," I said sweetly and kissed him on the cheek. I was determined not to let anybody spoil my good mood. I was on holiday!

"Have fun!" he called after us.

~

We spent the remainder of the day in the villa. The weather was gloriously warm—the girls and I were in our bikinis all afternoon. I read my book in the sun, played board games with the girls, served all meals on the terrace—chicken breast with tomato salad for lunch and grilled fish for dinner.

That evening, having put Marie and Noëlle to bed after their shower, I got myself a glass of rosé and went to join Hugo on the sofa in front of the TV. He was watching the third place play-off Germany vs. Portugal. I sat down next to him and snuggled up to his shoulder. He briefly turned his face towards me and pressed a quick kiss on my forehead. "Shh, Schweinsteiger has the ball."

Hmm, it seemed I had to remind him of the ball we could have together. Within a few hours he had already tanned and looked delicious. I thought of Lars and asked myself which of them I would prefer to be here with me. Either a beautiful and sexy man or a witty and sophisticated one. I guess one could not have both. Neither could I expect Hugo suddenly to be somebody else. He was, for sure, not unintelligent but we always communicated best at a physical level.

I slid upwards and began gently to kiss his ear. He groaned. I fondled his ear lobe and then wandered down his neck. He bent his head back, groaning again. I started slowly to unbutton his shirt. I stopped thinking, leaving free reign to my instincts. He inhaled deeply through his teeth.

"Okay, that's it," he spluttered.

He got up and pulled me from the sofa to sweep me into his arms. From the corner of my eyes I could see the TV screen showing a slow motion repeat of the goal that had just been scored by Bastian Schweinsteiger, the French commentator shouting '*Oui, oui, oui!!*'

Who the hell cares about the match now, I thought as Hugo carried me to our bedroom and closed the door behind us. He placed me gently on the bed.

He tore the shirt over his head, kicked off his shorts and just stood there for a moment. Then he bent over me and pulled off my dress in one short movement. When a groan escaped me, he grinned and held his hand over my mouth. I bit his finger and giggled. Yes, this was indeed the way we communicated best. I didn't need, nor want, to talk anymore. I just repeated, in my head, the last words I had heard coming from the television—oui—oui—OUI!

~

The next day I was lying in the sun on the deckchair watching my belly getting tanned. I tensed my abs and critically pulled at the skin fold that remained. I sighed. I could do as many sit-ups and diets as I wanted—two pregnancies would leave their trace. I knew that considering my age my body was fine, but I wasn't content. I did what my time and budget allowed—expensive anti-wrinkle creams and dermatologist appointments for the face, sports and a healthy diet for the body. I was lucky though—I had little cellulite. On the other hand, I got more and more freckles—really everywhere, except my face. I was used to them. But I so wished for a milky, spotless skin and for physical beauty that wouldn't ever give cause for a man to be critical of me—not in the manner in which my father was to my mother, when her once thick raven hair became thinner and grey, after years of trying so hard to be perfect for him had left wrinkles on her face. I could still hear him telling her: *Look at you. You're getting old. Everything is getting saggy. Look at those wrinkles.*

Well, you cannot have it all, I thought wistfully. But I did want it all—career and children, beauty and brains, and then maybe a fantastic man, who is good-looking, respects my independence and, at the same time, adores and cares for me. Yes, dream on.

Above all a man who loves my children, right? Was that not the most important thing? I sat up and watched them playing in the pool. Hugo helped Marie learn how to swim by establishing the basic swimming motions. Noëlle was also demonstrating how it was done. I smiled happily. Hugo was fond of the girls after all. They were fond of him. I didn't want to be a single mother. My other personal needs would have to take a back seat.

I startled when the aggressive ring tone of my blackberry penetrated my thoughts. It was a P&W landline number. I pressed the green button.

"Hello?"

"Hi, Chloé. It's Tracey. I am so sorry to disturb you on your holiday."

My insides churned and my heart starting beating faster. That was not a good sign. I cleared my throat and concentrated on letting my voice sound friendly. "Oh, hello, Tracey. No problem at all. How are you?"

"I'm fine, thanks. I've had a call from William Hacker at Holman Bank, about a new property deal. It's nearly the same as the one you've just closed, except it's industrial not residential property."

"U-huh. OK?" I tensed up. A new deal on a Sunday? What on earth could she want from me?

"Yes, well, we're a bit stretched here for capacity and I have a meeting in the office all afternoon today, so could I fax you the term sheet for you to have a look at and mark up with your comments? The client wants a call at three."

I knew that her question was a rhetorical one. Of course she expected a positive answer. I had to submit to my fate.

"Yes of course, Tracey. There is no fax here but you can send it by email—I'll read it on the laptop."

"Oh, I see. I always make sure I have at least a fax machine in the vicinity when I go on holiday." That's because you are completely gaga, I thought.

"Yes, that's such a good idea," I said sweetly. "Would it be okay if I send my comments in an email before the call?"

"Alright, then," she agreed reluctantly. "I'll send you William's vcard with his phone number."

"That's very helpful, thanks!"

"Thanks. Bye," she said absently and hung up.

I clicked on my emails. Tracey had already forwarded William Hacker's email and attachment, without any comments. Then a new email appeared into which I was copied.

> Hi William,
>
> as discussed, Chloé will ring you at 3 p.m. your time with her comments on the term sheet. I will send you our fee letter later today. Just to confirm in advance, the cap of €75k is fine, provided we close two weeks from today. All subject to our conflicts check as usual.
>
> Tracey

€75,000 seemed on the low side. But since it would be nearly impossible to close the deal within two weeks we would break the cap and charge more. Tracey was probably counting on that and it would not be the first time she had determined a deal in this manner.

Hugo approached me, dripping with water. "Where is my towel, angel?"

I looked at the deckchair next to mine. It was empty. "It'll be on the laundry rack—there, around the corner."

"Thanks. Oh yes, now I see it. Was that your phone?"

"Yep." I got up to see where the girls were. Marie and Noëlle just climbed up the stairs from the pool.

"So who was it?" Hugo started to rub his hair with the towel.

"Tracey. I have to review a term sheet and then have a conference call with the client."

"You have to review a what?"

"A term sheet. It's a summary, mostly in form of a table, of the most crucial commercial terms of a transaction—for example amount of loan, interest rate, duration, security to be provided, events of default, when the borrower has to repay the loan, and so on."

"Uh-huh." Hugo looked blank.

"It's, so to speak, the start of a transaction," I explained patiently. "The real work then consists of drafting and negotiating all the contracts—loan agreement, pledge agreements, assignment agreements, property mortgages. The term sheet lists all contracts and sometimes provides which law firm represents the lenders and which acts for the borrower. Often it also states the agreed fees for the legal work because the borrower will indemnify the banks for their legal fees. Such an agreed fee is called a fee cap."

"And what sort of fees do you guys get in a transaction like that?" Now I had Hugo's attention.

"Well, that depends—how long it takes, how complex the matter is. Apparently we have agreed a cap of €75,000 for this one."

"Wow—now I'm not surprised that you lawyers earn so much money."

"It's not that much if you think about how many hours' work this will take. A deal with a low cap is only profitable—meaning financially worthwhile—for the firm if a lawyer with a low charge out rate works on it. Tracey, has a partner's hourly billable rate of over six hundred Euros, so will work on it as little as possible."

"That's why she is not doing it herself," Hugo stated.

"Precisely. On top of which, it's urgent, she's got no time, everybody else is busy—whatever, it's the way it is. I don't mind really, the only thing that upsets me is how she doesn't think twice about interrupting her associates' annual leave. Jessica spent most of her last holidays at her laptop and blackberry. When I was at Solomons I sometimes worked during my holidays, too, but I never expected my team to do that." I shook my head. I had to stop dwelling on this otherwise I would get even more upset.

"When is your conferences call?" Hugo said with a furrowed brow, looking at his watch. "Are we going to eat first? I think we're all hungry."

Marie came over to me and hugged my legs. "Mummy I'm hungry," she whined.

"Yes, love, in a minute. First you need to get dry."

I covered her wet hair with a towel and turned back to Hugo. "It's called a conference call. My conference call is at three, London time. I will prepare everything now and while the water for the pasta is cooking I will review the term sheet."

"That's great, angel!" Hugo slumped himself onto the deck chair and grabbed a book with the title *Speed Reading for Beginners.*

"Yes, yes, Chloetta will do everything, at your service," I mumbled. I felt like hitting Hugo with the wet towel on his perfectly built chest. How about offering some assistance for once? I started to feel like I was his maid.

"Maybe you could at least set the table?" My voice sounded artificially friendly. I had a hard time containing myself.

He looked at me in surprise. "Sure. It's just that I have been looking after your children and now need a break."

"My children?" I hissed. OK, now calm down, Chloé, don't flip. I turned to Marie. "Marie, please go and see your sister in your room and put on the dress I have laid out on your bed, alright darling?"

"OK, mumma." She trotted off, trailing her towel behind her.

"Hugo," I started slowly. "Don't you think that it may be hurtful when you say such a thing? We've been together for over two years, the girls see more of you than of Jean and you behave as if you've got nothing to do with them."

Hugo sat up. His face took on a strange expression. "But they are not my children, Chloé. It's not the same. Of course I'm fond of them, but I am not their father. I want my own children and you know that." He looked at me expectantly.

Oh dear. There it was—that dreaded moment—I would be made to make a statement to a topic I had so far avoided carefully. "With me?" I inquired slightly desperately.

He rolled his eyes. "Nah, with Jana. Of course with you. At the beginning of our relationship you told me that you would love to have a son and that you would not exclude having any more children."

"Yes I know I said that—and I did mean it, Hugo, at least at the time. But I'm not even divorced yet, and I'm turning forty this year, and I just started this new job," I responded hastily, my panic rising. Oh the things you say when you have just fallen in love!

"As far as I know your divorce hearing is set for September. The other things are not important. It will be too late at some stage, Chloé." He meant it.

"I'll tell you something," I quickly replied. "I'll decide before my birthday, okay?" That was not for another five months. Many things could happen within five months. As long as this discussion was over for now.

"It's your decision, angel."

He lay back on his deckchair and picked up his book again. I walked slowly into the kitchen, my blackberry still in my right hand. Damn, damn, damn. Now I had given myself an ultimatum, just because I had panicked and was afraid of a confrontation. The clock had started to tick.

Deep down I knew I did not want to be pregnant again and have another baby. I just about managed my life with the two girls. This would change everything. I would lose my independence. Three children from three different men—one of whom would be around constantly and would interfere in the way I raise my children, and, really, honestly—Hugo was the last person I pictured in that role. Good heavens!

So if I didn't grant Hugo's wish, would not the logical consequence be that sooner or later we would break up? Come on, I told myself, as if you hadn't already known that—what about Lars? You would have never allowed yourself to get into that situation if you had been convinced of the viability of your relationship with Hugo. Lars would not want me to have a baby with him, on the contrary. He had children of his own; they could play together, we could be a happy patchwork family…

My thoughts were racing. Currently, I paid rent for the house we lived in together and which Hugo owned, this couldn't go on. I had to acquire my own home. But I couldn't just move out, I would have to have a good reason. Maybe I should buy my own house. With my salary I should be able to get the necessary financing. Hugo could live with us as long as we were still together and, if we did split up, the girls and I would at least keep our home. Unlike when upon discovering my father's infidelity my mother packed two suitcases and took me out of school, in the middle of term, to stay with a distant relative who lived far away. Like a refugee, I had to leave my friends, my home, my beautiful room and my things behind and never saw them again. My father took an apartment and moved in with his new girlfriend and my mother and I had to find a new home.

That would not happen to me again. I would not be driven out of my home again. I would not have my heart broken again. I would not allow it. Ever.

After lunch I tidied up the kitchen and persuaded the girls to have a siesta in their room while listening to a story on the CD player. Hugo had disappeared onto the terrace with his book and his orange noise cancelling headset. I worked my way though the term sheet as quickly as the slow wifi allowed it to load on my laptop, making notes on a pad which I had placed on the kitchen counter. I then summarised the notes in an email to Tracey, which she approved by simply replying *OK*.

At 4 p.m. precisely I called William Hacker and explained my comments on the term sheet.

"It looks like we will have to battle out some major issues in the credit agreement," he concluded when I had finished.

"Well, indeed, to the extent these matters are not dealt with in the term sheet, we will have to make sure that your position is reflected in the drafting."

"And I assume you will do that?"

"I need to discuss that with Tracey, but that should not be a problem."

"Good. Also, there will be meetings on this in London, probably Wednesday the week after next." That would be the second week of our holiday in France.

"Right, excellent. Thanks for the information. As I said I will discuss with Tracey and we will send you the first draft agreement as soon as possible."

"Tomorrow end of play London would be good."

"Of course."

After we hung up I dialled Tracey's mobile number.

"Yes?" she hissed in a whisper. "I'm in a meeting. What is it?"

"Hi Tracey, it's Chloé. I just wanted to let you know I spoke to William. He wants the first draft by c.o.b. tomorrow and there is a meeting on Wednesday the week after next."

"You'll have to do the draft. I told you we're busy here."

I hesitated. "Sure. I'll get Jessica to send me some precedents."

"Send me the draft by lunch tomorrow so I can look it over first."

I replied: "I'll do my best." She had already hung up. I took the earphones out of my ear and placed them slowly on the counter. Hugo would flip if I told him I'd have to work but I had no choice. I walked outside and found him asleep on a deckchair. I sat on the one next to his and contemplated the beautiful view. The sky had become even clearer. The hills beyond the valley opened to offer a view of the waves of the Mediterranean Sea reflecting in the sun. I breathed in deeply and exhaled slowly.

"Hmm angel…your call finished?" Hugo murmured, his eyes still closed behind the sunglasses.

"Yes," I replied gently and took his hand.

"Good."

"The thing is though—I will have to do some work."

"You're kidding." He opened his eyes, withdrew his hand and sat up. "This is really not funny, Chloé. We are on holiday! And it's the final tonight!"

"Yes, I know. What am I supposed to do? I have to produce the first draft of the agreement by tomorrow afternoon."

"And then what? Is it going to be like this every day?"

"No, of course not. I'm just helping out because the others are too busy today. So it should be fine after tomorrow."

"It better be. Neither the girls nor I would appreciate a holiday with you working all the time."

I got up, squatted next to his chair and hugged him awkwardly, leaning my head against his chest.

"Thank you for being so patient with me. I promise I'll make it up to you."

"If you're thinking along the lines of last night, I may be open to suggestions," he grinned and kissed my forehead.

I managed to send the draft agreement to Tracey by the next day. After a brief review she approved it to be forwarded to William, who asked us to send it to the borrower and their legal advisers subject to his comments. That concluded my involvement for the time being. Or so I thought.

For the next three days we enjoyed our holidays. When we returned from a day at the beach, in the late afternoon of the Friday, I checked my emails and saw that the borrower's advisers had just replied with a heavily marked up document. No sooner had I read their message than my mobile rang.

"Hi. You've seen the email I presume," Tracey began. "As you are familiar with the term sheet and have drafted the credit agreement, I have decided it makes sense for you to join the negotiations next week. I have also been able to increase the cap since the parameters have somewhat changed—there is no way this can close by the end of next week."

"Right. Uhm. We are supposed to be still here next week."

"See whether you can get a refund for the second week. We may be able to bill that to the client as a necessary expense."

"I need to speak to Hugo and the girls and will let you know this evening."

"It is not really an option, Chloé. This is now your deal."

"Yes, I understand. I—" There was a click. The line was dead. I placed the mobile on the table next to my deckchair. It was time to wake the girls. They had fallen asleep in the car on the way back to the house and Hugo and I had carried them carefully to their beds to let them sleep for a while. I went through the terrace doors into the living room. He was sitting on the sofa, an open beer bottle at his lips, staring at the TV screen.

"Football? Still?" I commented.

"It's another report on the head-butt. Honestly, the guy was provoked!"

"Maybe, but it was an unfortunate time to let yourself go like that. I still think he's hot though," I sighed as Zidane's face filled the screen.

Hugo clicked his tongue and shook his head. "Will you women ever be able to watch football without commenting on the player's looks?"

"Only if you guys will watch women's sports without doing the same," I retorted.

"Yeah, ok. Point taken."

"I'm going to wake up the girls. But before I do, I need to talk to you."

"What is it?"

"I don't know how else to put it—we will need to cut our holiday short. Tracey wants me back in the office next week to go to a meeting for this deal."

Hugo looked at me stone-faced. "I don't believe it. That bitch!"

"Well, she probably really has nobody else to do this deal."

"Then she should not have accepted it. You are entitled to your holiday."

"Hugo, I am so sorry. Believe me, I wish I could do something about it."

"Easy. Quit this job."

"After just over two months? You know that's not an option. Besides, apart from Tracey's infrequent antics, I actually do like it."

"Is that so? You should think about what it does to your family. I mean your children and me."

"I can't help it right now," I repeated. "I will try to make things better, though, I promise. Please, believe me. It's not fair for you to blame me right now. I am trying my best to make everybody happy."

"Don't cry, angel." Hugo got up from the sofa and came over to take me into his arms. "I don't blame you. I'm just angry with these people. Now, look. We'll make the best of the time that remains. When do you have to be back?"

"Monday," I sniffed.

"Then we will leave Sunday after breakfast, okay? That gives us two more nights and the whole of tomorrow."

"OK. Thank you." I kissed him, pulling out of his arms. "I'm going to wake the girls now."

As I walked away I realised that Hugo probably wasn't too sorry to leave, as he had been complaining about being bored. The girls would be disappointed though—they loved the pool and the beach. And me? I had to admit that it didn't feel bad, being so needed by the firm that I had to make the heroic sacrifice of cutting short my annual family holiday. That would surely go down well with Michael and earn me brownie points with Tracey.

7

London Calling

The forty-eight-storey glass tower of Howard Hewitt was sparkling in the morning sun. We had landed half an hour earlier at London City airport. As so often, due to the side wind, the approach had been rather wobbly and I had asked myself whether there would be enough time and opportunity for me to save my handbag before the little turboprop plane would crash into the Thames. As usual I thought of my girls and of who would look after and take care of them should something happen to me. I detested this airport, almost as much as getting up at 4.30 a.m. to make the 6.40 a.m. flight to London City. Especially when the prospect was, unfortunately, not a shopping spree at Harvey Nichols but negotiation meetings starting at 9 a.m. at the offices of Howard Hewitt, who was opposing counsel and represented the institutional investors in our new real estate finance deal for Holman Bank.

"I have asked Jerome to book you on the early flight to City—I'll meet you at HH's offices in Canary Wharf, an hour before the meeting. I assume that's alright. Can you please prepare a list of all issues together with suggested solutions," Tracey had informed me over the phone while I was still on my holiday in France.

"Sure, Tracey, no problem," I had replied mechanically since it was a rhetorical question not requiring any (or rather, any other) answer.

How I would organise my time, and manage the other tasks that she had given me in addition, would be up to me. A one day business trip would not mean that all other work, that had piled up during my abridged holiday, would just stop. One would simply have to put in extra (even more) time. So that is exactly what I did for those two days before the meeting and, in addition, arranged for Jana to take the girls as they were still off school. On the Wednesday in question, I rose before the birds started their morning song, caught the first flight to City airport and, after a short ride in a black cab, found myself in the monumental entrance hall of the Howard Hewitt building.

"Good morning, my name is Chloé Krakowski from Pratt & Wonkey. I am here for a meeting with Nigel Hancock." My voice sounded surprisingly fresh. That must be the adrenaline. The receptionist looked at me in amused despair.

"Hello, oh right. Uhm could you please repeat your name?"

I sighed patiently. "Of course. Kra-kow-ski. With an 'i' at the end—oh, never mind. From Pratt & Wonkey."

"Thank you, Ms. Crabosky, would you kindly sign in for me please." She pushed a visitors' book towards me. I filled it in quickly and signed my name, whereupon she handed me a visitor's pass. "You will be picked up in a minute—if you could wait over there please."

She pointed at the large dark green leather sofas making up the nearby seating area. I nearly pulled a face. Since Howard Hewitt had paid a PR agency a huge sum of money to procure a friendly, pleasant image to what was one of the world's largest law firms, the new HH green—a dark, fir tree green—was all over the place. All that was missing were some red baubles and the impression of a giant Christmas decoration would be perfect. Yet the partners of HH were no Santas. Thank god I had not accepted their partnership offer—I would have found it hard to identify with this colour. Actually, that could have also been said for the oh-so-happy Pratt & Wonkey yellow and the matching sun logo. Who were they kidding? Since when could one make a connection between a law firm and a laughing sun? Most of their lawyers hardly ever saw the light of day, let alone the sun. The boring brownish taupe of the Solomons logo was more appropriate.

"Good morning. Are you Ms. Krakowski?" A short woman wearing a uniform-like look, widely seen in the City of London (black stretch mini skirt without tights, a white blouse and black low-heeled pumps), pulled me from my thoughts.

"Yes." I stood up, placing my handbag into the crook of my left arm and taking my heavy pilot's case into my right hand.

"Hi! I'm Fenella, Nigel's secretary. Nigel asked me to take you to the meeting room," she began while she led me through the security barrier into a long corridor. "Did you fly in this morning?"

"Yes, I just arrived from Frankfurt," I explained.

"Oh, right—that must have been an early start for you!"

"Quite early, indeed!" I wrinkled my nose slightly.

"That's awful! I hate having to get up so early in the morning!" She continued chatting happily. "Well, you'll find fresh coffee and muffins in the meeting room, so at least you can have some breakfast. Your colleague—Ms. Taylor?—has already arrived and is waiting in the room, as well. Here we are."

I can hardly wait, I thought. Fenella opened the door to the meeting room. I caught sight of Tracey who was standing in the far corner by the window and talking on her blackberry. She glanced at us and summoned me with a wave.

"Let me know if you need anything—my extension is 5691," Fenella took her leave and disappeared, closing the door behind her.

I approached the large conference table, put my bags next to Tracey's and started to unpack the lever arch files from my briefcase.

"Hi, Chloé. Was the flight alright?" Tracey walked towards me. She was wearing a light blue tweed skirt suit and a sweetish smile. So far I had not seen her dressed that formally. It actually looked very smart, although for her young age was too conservative—it would have suited Margaret Thatcher. Also her facial expression didn't seem quite genuine. Suddenly she reminded me of the description of Dolores Umbridge in the fifth Harry Potter book, which I was reading at home. She was a witch in the Ministry of Magic who knew how to get what she wanted from her superiors whilst being relentlessly demanding of those in inferior positions and who spoke with this artificially sweet voice when delivering the cruellest of messages. The vision of meowing cat plates on the wall sent shivers down my spine. I quickly shook off that sensation and forced a smile.

"Yes, everything was fine, thanks." I opened a lever arch file and took out the top sheets. "Here's the issues list. I have printed out a few copies if you want to give them to the client."

"Oh, thanks," Tracey replied with little enthusiasm. She eyed the memo critically. "Well, it's a start anyway. William should be here any minute. I was just on the phone to him. He is on his way. He wants to discuss the RETT issue before the others get here."

Luckily RETT—or real estate transfer tax—was one of the first points on my issues list. You didn't have to be a tax lawyer to know that in all big real estate finance transactions the purchaser wants to avoid, as much as possible, paying a hefty percentage of the purchase price as tax. Such tax is due upon the transfer of the ownership deeds to the real estate. When you have a deal worth several hundred million this may well become a financing issue, and hence, a potential deal breaker.

The door opened. Fenella entered the room, followed by a man with blonde thinning hair in a blue pinstriped suit.

"There they are." Tracey made a beeline for him. "William, how good to see you, how are you? Ah yes, this is my Senior Associate Chloé; Chloé, this is William Hacker. Obviously you already spoke on the phone. William, we have prepared a list of the issues. Would you like to go through it straightaway?"

How I hated to be introduced that way *by her*—it sounded like 'this is Chloé my personal slave'. I extended my right hand with what I considered my most charming smile.

"William—good morning, nice to meet you."

He stared at me with an open mouth and blushed briefly. "Uh, hi. Yeah. Nice to meet you, too. Uh, sorry." He took my hand and quickly pressed it, then turned to Tracey. "Yeah, great. By all means let's have a look at that list, but we need to discuss the RETT issue first."

"Of course, let's discuss that," Tracey gushed. "Although I'm sure they'll find a solution to this. I mean, clearly their tax advisors will have thought of it already." She returned to her chair and took her copy of my list.

William looked at her sharply. "I don't think you understand how important this deal is for us. We need to be seen to be constructive and also come up with solutions, not just sit there and let the borrower deal with it."

Tracey opened her fountain pen. She lifted her eyebrows. "Yes, of course I understand, William."

"I really do hope so, Tracey." William's voice adopted a menacing tone. He leaned over the table and looked at her directly. "I expect you to find a solution and make the structure work. If this deal does not go ahead I will be in big trouble with my board but you will be in even bigger trouble because it will be your fault. Then we'll see whether Pratt & Wonkey will ever work with Holman Bank again." He snorted and sat back.

Tracey examined him coolly. Red spots were starting to show on her neck.

"I see exactly what your concerns are, William, and I am sure we will all work very hard to find a solution. Now, Chloé, would you like to take us through the list?" She turned to me.

Somewhat stunned by that exchange, I quickly had to pull myself together. "Uhm, yes, of course. You will see there are so far thirty-six issues. The main ones are highlighted yellow and appear at the beginning; the remainder follows the clause numbering of the credit agreement."

I passed a copy of the list to William who skimmed through it. His blackberry, which he had placed on the table, started vibrating.

"Excuse me." He pressed it against his ear. "Yah? Oh, right. Just a sec." He pushed his chair back, got up and left the room.

I turned to Tracey whose face had returned to a pinkish colour. I nearly felt sorry for her. William's verbal outbreak had been insulting. "Gosh! That was a bit…tense?"

"Well he is under pressure," she explained with studied casualness. "It was quite unnecessary but I'm used to that, especially from the Holman Bank guys. Like most investment bankers, they make a majority of their money by way of bonus, and this being a one billion Euro deal, he is more than keen to see it through. The bank earns fifty basis points on that amount so he can relax for the rest of the year when the deal is done. Plus, it's a relationship deal—the sponsor is a major client of the bank, and it's his first deal outside Britain. If it goes as well as the numerous domestic real estate financings they have done together, there will be follow-up transactions—for the bank as well as for us. I suspect he is under pressure from his boss, Felipe Nelson, who is under pressure from an executive board member who, in turn, has a close relationship with Patrick Johnson—the investor behind this. I believe they went to Eton together and are in the same golf club." She smiled at me haughtily. "Ultimately, they trust me to get the deal done. That's why they came to P&W and that is why they pay our fees. Sometimes that includes letting them blow off some steam. One's got to be able to take this sort of thing." She turned back to her papers.

If one does not like it, one is welcome to go elsewhere, I added in my thoughts. Thank you for the advice. It was an explanation, but not a justification, for such disrespectful behaviour towards anybody—let alone a female partner of a prestigious law firm. I had done many million dollar deals but most of the time the protagonists were polite and treated each other with respect. Some had flirted with me, some had tried to ignore me but I had never experienced any aggression from the client directed against me. Obviously Tracey was not unused to such bad manners and maybe she did not mind being verbally abused as long as the client was paying her hourly rate of over six hundred Euros. That is how the food chain worked in the City of London. I adopted my poker face and, in true British style, just dropped the subject.

The door opened again and William re-entered, absorbed in conversation with one of the three men who were with him. Judging from the casual but expensive looking clothes, and the confident demeanour of the person talking to William, I concluded that this was Patrick Johnson, the other two being his lawyers—Nigel Hancock, banking partner at Howard Hewitt, and his associate James Elkington. Like many British junior lawyers, who usually obtain their qualification at about twenty-five, he looked very young but tried to come across as confident. I noticed that he was quite cute. At least I could enjoy the view. Though, as my counterpart he had no chance, the poor guy.

After everybody had been introduced and business cards had been exchanged we started the negotiation of the draft credit agreement by reference to the issues list I had prepared. It transpired that the list was in fact complete and the suggested solutions, in principle, useful. William sat to Tracey's left. I was on her right.

"The last issue on the definitions is the valuation," Nigel said and looked at his client invitingly. "I think we take issue with that. Patrick?"

"Yeah, right, Nigel, thanks. William, we're not happy with your suggested property valuer," Patrick said with a cutting voice. "His valuation is completely unacceptable. It's only eight hundred million for the whole portfolio!"

"I appreciate that you'd rather take your valuer, Patrick, but it's the company we always use and they are on the more conservative side. This is quite appropriate considering there are some—to put it politely—rather less attractive properties in the portfolio—such as the supermarket in Erfurt. We can only lend up to eighty per cent. of the value of the properties, and if that's lower than the total purchase price, you'll just have to come up with more equity, or chuck those lower value properties." William leaned back, folding his arms.

Patrick's face turned red. "You know damn well it's the whole portfolio or nothing! The planned twin tower in Berlin alone is worth over half a billion! I don't give a shit about what 'you always do'! We need the full amount. That's what I agreed with Richard! One billion and not a cent less!"

I deducted that Richard was the big boss at Holman Bank—Johnson's friend from school. The so-called old school tie network—men from privileged families who had been pupils at private male-only boarding schools—obviously still worked very well in the City of London. Only that William now had a real problem. Normally the bank was not allowed to lend more than eighty per cent. of the value of the property. If Patrick wanted to borrow the full purchase price of one billion, the valuation had to be increased accordingly.

Apparently either he did not have the required two hundred million of equity or he did not want to use it. Thus the entire risk remained with the bank.

William slid around on his chair and held up his hands. I watched him with interest. A moment before he had been threatening and yelling at Tracey and now he was at the receiving end. Tracey had been right. He was under pressure.

"OK, look. I'll speak to Hugh White who has done your domestic deals and maybe we can use the same valuer. But we need to get it past our credit committee."

"Maybe is not good enough, and for sure we will not pay for the cost of the first valuation," Patrick insisted coldly.

"I'll discuss it internally. We'll find a solution."

"I bloody hope so."

Nigel cleared his throat. "Great, thank you very much, William. I suggest now we skip the representations and warranties, which we can deal with separately, and get to the covenants. What we need to discuss here is the RETT issue. Obviously we cannot covenant that the borrower is the hundred per cent. owner of the property and that Patrick's holding company is the sole owner of the shares in the borrower. The tax advisors have prepared a paper how to get around the issue." He nodded at James. James took a pile of stapled documents and distributed one to each person present.

I read the heading: 'Optimal Ownership Structure from a RETT Perspective'. I swiftly flicked through the document. It provided for two owners—a Dutch company and one in the Cayman Islands. Both were held by a trust in Jersey.

Tracey looked up. "We need to run this past our tax partner Magnus—it seems like a much more complex structure than was originally envisaged." She turned to William. "This would mean we need to revise the loan agreement quite dramatically—we would now have two foreign borrowers who guarantee each other, the Jerseyco as further guarantor—we would require Dutch law advice, Cayman and Jersey lawyers. I'll have to revise our fee letter and get quotes from those jurisdictions."

William stared at the document. "I see," he hissed through clenched teeth. "Let me know by tomorrow. I will also have to discuss this internally."

"I'm not sure I can get our tax people to review all this by tomorrow," Tracey objected.

"They'll just have to. We have our credit committee meeting tomorrow afternoon."

Tracey stiffened imperceptibly, then slowly turned her head to me. "Chloé, send this to Magnus and his team and get quotes from Amsterdam, Cayman and Jersey. ASAP."

And that was how the food chain worked.

The next morning I was back at my desk working on the new mandate letter for Holman Bank. I had started to draft it on the way back from London, having just managed to catch the last flight out of Heathrow.

Suddenly my door was flung open.

"Morning, Chloé!"

I looked up. It was David Byrd and Frank Smith—respectively partner-to-be and new partner. So sorry: Dr. Byrd and Dr. Smith. The obsession of German lawyers to be addressed with their doctorate title (if they had one—if not, they would *per se* be regarded as second class) appeared rather absurd to Anglo-American lawyers. One automatically looked for the physician's bag. Sometimes I asked myself how many German lawyers with a PhD. travelling by airplane would raise their hand when hearing the question 'Is there a doctor on the plane?' I am convinced that here and there a finger would be raised proudly. I prefer the Italian undiscriminating style of addressing every lawyer in a cordial but respectful manner as *dottore*.

"Good morning, my learned colleagues! What can I do for you?"

David carefully felt the top of his hair, which consisted of hard spikes due to the amount of wet gel he seemed to have been using. He unleashed his loud staccato laughter, which I had often heard coming from the corridor. "HA-HA-HAA!"

Uhm, what was so hilarious about my question? Goodness me, he so wanted to be witty. He reminded me of Robin Williams' character's army boss in *Good Morning Vietnam*, who after being unceremoniously sacked as a radio DJ by reason of his very unfunny jokes indignantly snorts: 'Sir, in my heart, I *know* I'm *funny*!' I did love Bruno Kirby's acting though.

Frank grinned, showing a small gap between his incisors. He was not particularly attractive and seemed to be fairly harmless. Apart from a few morning chats in the kitchen and the conference call on my first official day I hadn't really gotten to know him yet.

"We will do something for you, Chloé," he declared generously. "Tracey has a new deal from Paris Bank and thus no more time for your Holman deal—so I will take the lead and David will advise on the German law side."

"Oh I see. That's news to me. Yes, great." I was slightly confused. Tracey had not informed me of this. "How up to speed are you? Shall we go through the structure together?"

"No, no," Frank declined. "We just need the term sheet, the issues list and the latest drafts. We'll get that from the virtual file."

The virtual transaction file contained all documents and correspondence belonging to a transaction and was accessible from the desktop of every lawyer and secretary who had been granted authorised access.

"Good. It's not all in the virtual file yet—I'm just working on the new mandate letter for instance, and the issues list has to be amended following our discussions in yesterday's meeting."

"I would like a copy of your notes from yesterday so that I can consider potential changes to the security documents." David crossed his arms.

I looked at him in surprise. "Sure. Although at this stage we are still far away from thinking about the security documents. It's just that a lot depends on the new ownership structure which is being double-checked by Tax as we speak—there may be more changes."

"Maybe you can speak to Magnus and see where they are on this," Frank suggested to David.

"Good idea, Frank! I'll go and do that now. See you later—and Chloé, don't forget the copies!" He left my office.

Frank grinned again and sat down on the visitor's chair. He crossed his legs. "So, how's it going?"

"Very well, thank you. I think I have acquainted myself with real estate finance and my colleagues are really nice here." I meant it. Tracey was not my colleague—she was my boss, and that was only to be temporary. Frank knew where I had worked before and I assumed he knew that I had been hired eventually to replace Tracey. I therefore behaved towards him as if we were on a level playing field—except for the fact that he was younger than me.

"Well then everything's alright." Pause. "Michael Stone says you're getting a divorce."

"That is correct. The hearing is soon."

"I also separated from my wife at the beginning of this year."

I looked at him. "Oh, I'm sorry. Separations are awful."

He dismissed this with a gesture. "Nah, my marriage was pure stress. My wife always complained about me working too much and when she knew I was going to be made partner all she wanted was more spending money."

I was not surprised. That was the typical scenario. The only untypical aspect was that the separation actually happened.

"Any kids?"

"Yes, two teenage boys and a little girl." For a moment his smile became softer, then disappeared completely. "But I haven't seen them in weeks."

"Why? Don't they live in Frankfurt?"

"Yes they do but my wife has managed to set the boys against me—they don't want to see me. The little one follows whatever her big brothers do."

"That's terrible! But you do have a right to see your children!"

"Right, but I don't want to force them." He shrugged. "Anyway I'm here most of the time and don't really have time for anything else."

I was not going to comment on that. I smiled with empathy, but I didn't really feel sorry for him. A career as a partner did not, by itself, destroy a marriage.

Frank stood up. “Was nice talking to you. Maybe we can have a drink together some time.”

In your dreams. “Yes, sure. There’s the department drinks of course tomorrow—are you coming to that?”

“I’m not sure yet. I’ll have meetings all day so I may not be able to make it, and work comes first, right?” He grinned.

“Of course—always!”

I was relieved when he left my office. He seemed alright enough but I really was not interested in personal conversations. On the other hand, if I wanted to make partner, I had to get on with my partners to ensure I had the support and votes. I just had to ensure that my friendliness could not be misunderstood.

My phone rang. David Byrd.

“Hi. I just wanted to let you know that you need to make some amendments to the credit agreement—I will send you a mark-up, and then you should circulate a summary of the outcome of yesterday’s negotiations. Today.”

I was slightly irritated. Since when did this geek think he could tell me what to do?

“Ah, David. Thank you for your suggestions. That sounds good. Do by all means send me what you have.”

“Have you drafted a documents list and a CP list?”

“My trainee does that.”

“I see, fine. If not, I’ve got Matthew who could do that.”

“Matthew?”

“My junior associate.”

“So, you already have a junior associate?” I quipped.

“Well, I am very busy and require support,” he replied somewhat indignantly.

I see, the young man thinks he’ll be made partner by behaving as if he already was one. Whatever, it wasn’t my problem. I would hardly allow him to tell me what to do. I didn’t like it but I had to put him into his place, as amicably as possible.

“I totally understand that. At Solomons I had five associates and it never seemed enough. But it is very good that you already know how to delegate—not many people do.”

I could feel through the phone how his chest swelled with pride.

"Yes, exactly, I knew you would understand me since you know what it's like. So, I'll tell Matthew to talk to your trainee."

"Super. Thank you."

"With pleasure, any time." We hung up.

There. That was done.

Or so I thought.

~

I realised when the day of my appraisal arrived that I had been so naïve as to underestimate David. It all started rather informally. I got an email from Tracey letting me know briefly that she and Michael would give me an interim appraisal that coming Thursday at 2 p.m. since my calendar showed no entry. Damn. I did have plans, I just hadn't entered anything in my outlook calendar—a long overdue 1 p.m. manicure appointment. If all went well, I would manage to be back just in time. Of course I confirmed the appraisal appointment with Tracey.

I thought about what I would have to expect. I had never had a formal appraisal before—at Howard Hewitt there had only been that one short meeting where I was told I had been selected for the partnership track. The partner reviews at Solomons had been more like a tea party, although there hadn't been anything to be criticised anyway. I had always been a good hard-working girl, but now I could not help but feel that an appraisal given by Tracey would not be a piece of cake.

Tracey, Michael and I met up in one of the smaller conference rooms. Tracey and Michael sat next to each other, facing me. Michael seemed uninterested while Tracey was shuffling with her papers.

"So, Chloé," she started. "We thought that it might be useful to have an interim appraisal at this stage to see where you are and how you are doing." She raised her upper lip and bared her teeth.

I remained silent and waited.

She inhaled. "I must say, when you first started I wasn't sure you really wanted the job."

I was aghast. From where did she get that idea? I got the answer straightaway.

"When I asked you to work at the weekend, you didn't seem committed but instead told me you needed to look after your—children!" Her voice became nasal and more high-pitched at the end of the sentence.

"Well, you asked me on a Friday afternoon and I just was not able to organise childcare for the weekend at such short notice that day." I remained very calm. She could not possibly be serious.

"As I said then, I find I manage to do that in such situations. I just did not feel your commitment."

"I did send you the document on Saturday evening as you requested."

"Did you? I don't remember." She frowned impatiently and rummaged in her notes, then looked up again. "Well, anyway, it does not matter. I've made my point."

"I don't think you can say about Chloé that she does not work enough. Her figures are above the average of those of the entire banking team. She even cut her holiday short," Michael interjected dryly.

"Yes, yes, the figures are quite good," Tracey dismissed him. "Now let's see—what else do I have. Ah yes, your email style—your sentences are too long."

Now I was rather amused. "OK, I will make a note of that." I made a note on my pad: *sentences too long.*

"You seem to get on well with everybody. But David Byrd complained that you do not show enough initiative."

"Is that so? In what way, may I ask?"

"He says he always has to tell you what to do."

I looked at my pad and wrote this down: *more initiative.* I did not know whether to laugh or whether to scream with frustration. Pull yourself together, Chloé. Count to three. I looked up again. "I see. I will have a chat with him."

"I cannot comment on this but clearly team work is very important," Michael said.

I looked at him steadily. "You are absolutely right, Michael."

“So. There does not seem to be much else, is there, Tracey?” Michael asked impatiently.

Tracey’s neck started to get blotchy. She pressed her lips together.

“Then we should talk about what’s next,” he invited her.

“Well, yes, alright.” She looked at me again. “Michael thinks we should get you into the counsel round for next May. I personally don’t think that’s really necessary—people know that you are senior and they are happy to deal with you on the basis that you are an associate. In London, these titles do not matter.”

“We have to arrange the counsel promotion—it’s important for Chloé’s progress and the least we can offer her after one year with the firm.”

I was confused. I did not need a counsel promotion if I was going to be Tracey’s successor. I turned to Michael. “Is that a necessary step towards partnership?”

“Nah, but we cannot offer you partnership for May—we can’t have the two of you as partners. That means until Tracey returns to London you can only become counsel. By the way, Tracey, when are you going back to London?”

“I don’t think that’s a topic for this meeting,” Tracey responded sweetly. “So, as I said, I don’t think it’s necessary, but if Michael insists, of course I will support it.” She looked at me sharply. “There will be no raise, though. Your salary is already way above any standard levels.”

I said nothing. I just continued to look at her calmly while the red blotches on her neck became bigger. Michael shrugged and mumbled something inaudibly. After a short general silence he stood up resolutely. “So, it’s all agreed then—if there is nothing else, I’ve got a conference call to attend.”

“You both go ahead, I have to check this email.” Tracey was busy with her blackberry.

I stood up as well and took my notepad. “Thanks, Tracey. See you later.”

On the way back to my office I reflected on this absurd conversation. I was annoyed with David Byrd. On the other hand, I wasn’t that surprised either. Then it occurred to me that Tracey had not managed to persuade Michael to forget about my counsel promotion. That was a small victory. The question remained what price I would have to pay for it.

8

Freedom

A cutting voice called after me. "Uhm, Chloé? May I ask where you are going? We have a conference call at one."

I turned around. Tracey looked at me through her narrow glasses, raising her eyebrows. "Well?"

I slowly approached her. "I have a court hearing," I said with a low voice.

Her eyebrows now nearly reached her hairline. "I didn't know we do litigation."

"Actually, it's my divorce hearing," I explained reluctantly.

I thought I could see something akin to malicious joy in her eyes. "Oh I see. How dreadful." She attempted a commiserative smile.

"Well, it's not pleasant. Please excuse me. I must go."

"I assume you have prepared everything for the call."

"Of course. Don't worry, I should be back for the call. And I'll make up for the time." I gave her a little smile, turned on my heel and walked toward the exit, her eyes burning in my back.

I took the lift into the underground garage where my car was parked. Inside the car, my heart suddenly started racing and I felt sick. I leaned my head against the stirring wheel. Divorce. Finally. On the other hand, it was the absolute termination of a marriage and the destruction of my hope to have the picture-perfect family. Failure. Feeling guilty towards the girls.

Then I thought of all the horrible things that were contained in the pleadings drafted by Jean's lawyer. I thought of the humiliating fact that Jean sued me for spousal maintenance. A healthy, free man sued his wife, at whose expense he had lived for years, in order to take even more money from her. I started to get angry. It was not a case of personal failure—it was my chance for freedom. I switched on the engine.

It was the summer of 1997. Patricia and I had spontaneously decided to escape the city and, after checking with our respective bosses, had booked a week at the Club Med in Mauritius. Having just returned from a business trip first to Hong Kong and then Chicago, all I wanted to do was to sleep in the sun. On our first evening, I met Jean at the pre-dinner drinks. Tall, French and gorgeous, he was the resident golf instructor and more than happy to give me some private lessons. I wasn't really interested in a holiday fling and initially resisted his flirtation. But the more I learned about him and his life the more we connected and I found myself wanting our time together not to come to an end.

"I think I have fallen in love with you, *madame*," he announced to me on our last evening when we took a moonlit walk on the beach and we had stopped to kiss.

"Oh Jean. This is wonderful and it is awful—I'm leaving tomorrow! And you have to stay here for how long again?"

"Until the end of the season—end of December."

"And then? Will you go back to Paris?"

"They offered me a job in New Caledonia."

"But that's on the other side of the planet! No—you can't go there!"

"I don't know. But it will be hard to give up the beach and the sun. I have to see—maybe I can find something in Paris in the spring."

"Or in Frankfurt?" I asked hopefully. "There are plenty of golf clubs around Frankfurt."

"But I don't speak German. Why don't you get transferred to your Paris office? You could work there, no? They need lawyers everywhere, no?"

I looked at him and knew I could not let this man disappear from my life. So, against all odds, we tried to keep a long distance thing going. But with nearly 6000 kilometres, twelve flight hours and three hours time difference separating us and with each of us working day and night, it was impossible. After three months I was so disillusioned that I broke it off, went on the rebound and found myself pregnant with my first child.

Two years after our first meeting and one year after Noëlle's birth, Jean called me out of the blue. When I heard his voice, my heart raced.

"Jean! Oh my god. It's been so long—where are you, what are you doing?"

"I am back in Paris. I work here now—I try to be an estate agent, ha—can you imagine. How are you? Have you got a boyfriend or did you get married?"

"I'm still at the same law firm. No, I'm not married—I don't have a boyfriend. But—actually, I'm not alone."

"What do you mean?"

"Well, I have a daughter. Her name is Noëlle. She is one year old and she is beautiful."

"Oh, *c'est magnifique*! I want to meet her! I have never stopped thinking about you, Chloé. I was just too scared when we were together. You were so intense, and so—how do you say—*sophistiquée*. Then yesterday I watched this movie—Notting Hill? It reminded me of us and I thought perhaps it could work. If you want to."

I did not hesitate for one moment. "Of course I do. I have never stopped thinking about you either. When can you come to see us?"

"I need to organise a few things but I should be able to come next weekend."

And so he did. When he entered our apartment for the first time Noëlle toddled up to him with a smile, pointed at him and said "Dada!" It was love at first sight for both of them. Two months later he moved in, without money or a job. Patricia warned me to be careful but I was so in love and so happy. We were a little family. We spent our first Christmas with his parents, who adored Noëlle, and were delighted to look after her for a few days. Jean and I decided to revisit the place where we first met, and flew to Mauritius for the new millennium. It was there, a few minutes after midnight on 1 January 2000, that he got down on one knee, presented his grandmother's ring and asked me to marry him.

Of course I said yes. Of course I did not think of money. I was going to be a partner soon and would earn enough for both of us. He promised he would learn German and get a job, if only for his masculine pride. Patricia was happy for me but still worried that I might commit to someone who made himself financially dependent on me. When months later I was about to marry a still unemployed Jean in France, Patricia urged me to at least enter into a standard French law prenuptial agreement. It made perfect sense since I was earning well as a partner at Solomons and Jean had nothing. It did not, however, make sense to my proud French fiancé. Several days before the wedding it came to a head with Jean and his father (‘*zees ees not romontik*!’) but I insisted, threatening to call the wedding off. So one hour prior to the marriage ceremony in the *mairie* in Grasse we sat in front of the notary—who conveniently also happened to be the mayor—and agreed a *séparation des biens*—matrimonial separation of goods. Nonetheless, in the end, it was a beautiful day. This may have been partly to do with the bride and groom relaxing, due to the large glass of champagne served by the notary's secretary after the agreement was signed and sealed.

And now, six years, many broken promises, fights, tears and therapy sessions later, we were in court, waiting for our divorce and for the judgment on Jean's spousal support claim. Life was absurd sometimes, I thought bitterly.

~

Jean appeared, tanned and wearing a cream linen suit. His lawyer was also in a cream tweed suit—was it Chanel? I tried to glance inconspicuously at the buttons—and holding a huge camel Hermès Birkin bag. My lawyer Anthea Voss and I had kept our outfit muted—black skirt suit, understated handbag, flat shoes. OK, *she* wore flat shoes. I had stuck to my principles (no flat shoes with a skirt!) and had for this happy occasion treated myself to elegant dark grey Prada pumps. New shoes make you feel wonderful—and I could use some cheering up. Furthermore, Jean had always liked my legs. There was nothing wrong with a hint of see-what-you're-missing attitude at a divorce hearing.

Really, what had gone wrong here? I had been crazy about this man, had to have him, marry him—even though, deep down, I suspected it might not last forever. I might have had high standards and certain expectations of a man—but what was wrong with that?

I never tried to change him. I thought I gave a man just what I required as well: personal freedom. We all need to be given room for development. If you confine someone—your partner, your child—and dictate how he should lead his life, you don't leave him any choice but to run away from you.

"We have a supplemental motion," Jean's lawyer, Elizabeth van Grossenburg, began and graciously handed copies of a legal document to the judge and Anthea.

Anthea skimmed through the document while I was looking over her shoulder. I could only make out the words 'extension of plaintiff's claim', 'increased demand due to necessary training', and finally 'requiring further monthly spousal support of €5,200'. I felt nauseous. Jean ignored the horrified glance I shot at him. He made the face of a martyr, apparently listening intensely to the whispering of the interpreter sitting next to him.

"I cannot and will not get into this motion since I see it for the first time," Anthea commented, slightly shaking her head.

The judge peered over her glasses. "I am able to relate to that," she replied. "Was this really necessary at this late stage?" she asked Jean's lawyer.

"Your Honour, I'm afraid my client was only able to give us the documents yesterday. In addition they have not been translated yet, but in my view this is a justified motion."

"I tend to disagree. I will tell you now that I think nothing of it."

"Well…" Elizabeth van Grossenburg did not finish the sentence but instead pressed her lips together. She inhaled audibly through her nose, wiggled her head and shrugged indifferently. I suppressed a grin. She deserved it, that cow.

"In any case, should we not first deal with my client's motion—the application for divorce?" Anthea reminded the judge.

"Certainly. I will question the parties themselves on the issue of their separation and the irretrievable breakdown of their marriage.

Mrs. Delorme, when did you separate from your husband?" she asked me.

"At the end of January 2004," I replied calmly.

"Do you consider your marriage as having 'irretrievably broken down'?"

"Yes."

"Do you want to resume matrimonial cohabitation with your husband?"

"No."

"Thank you. Mr. Delorme?"

"*Oui*, eh, yes?"

"When did you and your wife separate? Do you also consider your marriage as having 'irretrievably broken down' or do you want to resume matrimonial cohabitation with your wife?"

Jean looked at the interpreter who repeated the questions in French. He answered her, gesticulating with his hands. She turned back to the judge. "According to my memory it was March 2004. No, I do not want to resume the marriage. I do, however, regret this."

"Thank you. I find that by notarial deed the parties have agreed to matrimonial separation of goods. Regarding the apportionment of pension claims, Mr. Delorme will receive a monthly amount of €298,85 since during the marriage only Mrs. Delorme acquired pension rights whereas Mr. Delorme was not employed."

"At this point we also want to know whether Mrs. Delorme also acquired company pension benefits at her previous firms—Howard Hewitt and Solomons," Elizabeth van Grossenburg interrupted the judge.

"No I did not," I explained quickly. Good god. She really wanted to squeeze the last cent out of me.

"Good. Then that is clear." The judge took her dictaphone and summarised the testimonies. Finally, glancing first at me and then at Jean, she dictated slowly "the parties' marriage is therefore hereby dissolved." She stopped the tape and turned to Elizabeth van Grossenburg. "I assume you will not forgo the right to appeal."

"Considering that we have applied for spousal support for the next two months, absolutely not," she replied.

"That's how they try to get support for a longer period—his claim terminates with the final dissolution of the marriage which only occurs when the written judgment is received plus the two week time limit for filing an objection," Anthea explained to me in a whisper.

"I thought as much," responded the judge. "I have made a note. Good. That was the divorce. Now we turn to Mr. Delorme's motion for spousal support."

Divorced. I was divorced now. I held back the tears I could feel welling up in my eyes. People say this often as an aside—he or she is divorced. It's just a status, but they don't think about the traumatic experience that it represents—that time period preceding the actual end of the marriage and the beginning of the separation. The legal battles. This cold, sober judgment. Naked facts. When people get married the registrar or priest congratulates them. On the other hand, the judge divorcing a couple neither expresses his regret nor his condolences. Maybe this should be changed; maybe the newly divorced couple should also drink to a separate future.

"In my opinion the issue of spousal support is governed by French law since Mr. Delorme is domiciled in France." Mrs. van Grossenburg dramatically put on some rimless spectacles.

"I agree with you. Mrs. Voss?"

"That is indeed correct." Anthea nodded.

"Good. I understand that French law provides for a claim for spousal support up to the effective date of the divorce. However, it is not clear what form this takes—in particular it is questionable whether the support is to be paid monthly or in form of a one off payment—like a lump sum settlement. Do you have an idea, Mrs. van Grossenburg?"

"Indeed we do think that a lump sum payment should be considered because article 303 of the French *code civil* provides for this in the case of spousal support after the divorce; so that would make sense. Since my client was forced to borrow money in order to survive, it would be just what he needs."

Borrowing money to survive?? I was starting to get angry, my short stint of mourning having been blown away completely. Jean nodded vehemently and made a languish face when the interpreter had finished with her translation.

Anthea took the floor. "My learned colleague assumes that there is a basis for a spousal support claims. I have discussed this with my correspondent lawyer in Paris. The law relating to spousal support is much more restrictive in France than it is in Germany. There may be no issue regarding an increased obligation, upon the spouse, to seek employment after the marriage has failed but the responsibility of each spouse to provide for him—or herself is much higher than under German law."

"What needs to be decided, in particular, is whether Mrs. Delorme is obliged to finance his professional training or whether she was only obliged to pay him spousal support until he had sufficient time to gain a foothold."

"Your Honour, may I point out to the court again that my client fulfilled exactly this obligation—if such an obligation exists—since she paid monthly support during the first year of the separation, so that her husband had enough time to seek employment." I quickly whispered something in Anthea's ear whereupon she continued. "And one year was quite enough since, immediately after the separation, he returned to Paris where he has family and friends and where there are no language or other barriers."

Mrs. van Grossenburg jumped up. "He was prevented from working in his profession for many years because he looked after the children!"

I rolled my eyes, simmering with rage. Here we go again—that ridiculous miserable story line. It was such bullshit. Only because once in a while he drove Noëlle to school and threw some eggs into a frying pan for her, he was prevented from working at all. Yes, sure, Jana and I only ever lounged around, twiddling our thumbs. What about his daughter Marie who, in my absence, was predominantly taken care of by Jana? When I would address this issue, he would say: "Oh *mon amour*, you know the babies, it's a bit difficult for the men."

The judge rejected Mrs. Van Grossenburg's objection coolly. "It is irrelevant who looked after the children and when. The court will not require evidence on this point."

I breathed again. Thank God. I think I would have screamed if all this crap from his pleadings had been re-opened.

"Mr. Delorme, I have not understood your Curriculum Vitae properly—you were a golf teacher, and now you require training to become a golf teacher?" The judge looked at Jean severely.

Jean managed to avoid her gaze by turning innocently to his interpreter. I knew very well that he understood more than he pretended. He listened to the French translation and then ranted on in French. The interpreter seemed to have succumbed to his charm in the meantime as she translated in the same vindicatory tone of voice he had adopted.

"Yes, yes of course I am a golf teacher but then they—I think here he means the French Golf Federation—changed the rules and I was required to re-take some of the exams. So when I returned to Paris I undertook training to be a golf coach."

"So you did re-take these exams?" the judge asked.

The interpreter translated the question for Jean, whereupon he whispered his answer to her, which she promptly translated. "No, it was a kind of training to be a coach for managers in connection with playing golf."

I think all of us stared blankly. Mrs. van Grossenburg rummaged in her Birkin and took out some papers. "Ah, yes, here it is—here are copies, unfortunately only in French, of the training programme. It seems to be a kind of behaviour coaching by reference to the game of golf." She handed the copies to the judge and Anthea.

"Hang on, the programme shows that the training comprises a total of fifteen hours over a period of three months—and this is why your client was prevented from working for an entire year?" Anthea quizzed.

"Hm, you are right, Mrs. Voss," the judge agreed meditatively. "What do you say to that, Mrs. van Grossenburg?"

"Uhm, yes. Correct, looks like it indeed—Mr. Delorme, is this correct, there are only fifteen hours per week?" She turned to Jean.

He whispered in her ear. She replied quietly. "Can you get a certificate or something?"

I heard him saying in a low voice "this is no problem, I can get anything", then she turned back to the judge. "My client assured me that the training took up more time. We will submit further certificates."

"We would be very interested in seeing those as well, of course," Anthea interjected ironically, having attentively followed the short conversation between Jean and his lawyer. "We are very curious indeed."

"Good. After having concluded this training as a golf coach in February this year, Mr. Delorme now intends to take up employment this November with a car insurance company?"

"Correct, your Honour—his monthly gross salary will be about three thousand Euros." Mrs. van Grossenburg seemed to be relieved about the change of topic.

"We don't understand this. Where is the connection between the training which was allegedly necessary and this employment?" Anthea demurred.

"My client only accepted this employment because your client stopped making the monthly support payments," Mrs. van Grossenburg retorted pointedly.

"My client financially supported your client during the first year of their separation, to an extraordinary extent, just as she did during their entire marriage. This was an arrangement into which your client practically forced her, due to his idleness. There comes a point at which your client has to support himself. He is a grown-up, living in his hometown, has no children living with him—in contrast to my client who still works full-time and looks after the children. This is really starting to be a joke!" Anthea managed to stay calm but only expressed what I felt. I was grateful to her.

The judge intervened before Mrs. van Grossenburg was able to rebuke. "Well it is quite clear that Mr. Delorme has to provide certificates from the training institution, which prove to what extent he has undergone this training, namely"—she checked her diary—

"by Monday in three weeks' time. Then the deadline for pleadings is 17th October and judgment will be given on 7th November."

She dictated her decision into her dictaphone. Then she looked at both counsel. "Anything else?"

Anthea and Mrs. van Grossenburg both shook their heads.

"Good, then thank you very much."

Everybody got up from their seats and starting packing up. I approached Jean. "I'm sorry, Jean. I hope you will be happy."

He smiled sadly. "*Merci.* I hope the same for you." Oh, that French accent. Still charming.

"I could use a drink now," I joked. "But unfortunately I have to go back to the office. Bye."

"*Au revoir*, Chloé. Give my love to the girls."

And that was that.

~

It was loud, steamy and smelled of Chinese food. But the noodles were delicious and a welcome change from the usual sushi. Patricia was sitting opposite me on a wooden bench and sipped her green tea, lost in thought.

"Gosh. I can't believe you're divorced now. Six years ago I was at your wedding," she declared.

"Yes." I looked around. In this place, like in many other lunchtime hot spots, you had to watch what you were saying. You might sit next to other lawyers and bankers whose ear's would prick up when hearing specific names mentioned. In particular, if you knew a lawyer colleague or banker client not personally but by name only—which is more often the case than not, considering modern forms of communication—there was an even greater danger of sharing your secrets with a stranger who happened to be interested in them. At this moment, there were already four people I knew by sight. I leaned towards Patricia. "Shh. This place has ears."

"Oh, right, sorry. I don't know anybody here."

"But I do. The two guys over there, they are lawyers at Howard Hewitt; that woman with what looks like a blonde wig is or at least was at Solomons, and the Asian girl there is at Deutsche Bank."

"One of the HH guys looks cute," Patricia remarked, unimpressed.

"Patricia! He is a boring German lawyer!"

"So what—I'm married to one. I can't tell you how fed up I am, Chloé. Michael and I were invited to this dinner at the Union Club and, of course, I had to go alone again. With my state of mind, of course I got drunk; I don't even remember how I got home. But when I did, Michael woke up and had a real go at me so I slept on the sofa." She sighed. "That's becoming standard practice now. Oh, that reminds me, I meant to ask you—what's the name of Jean's lawyer?"

"Elizabeth van Grossenburg. Why?"

"Because she sat next to me at that dinner I just mentioned. What an arrogant cow! She was actually talking about how her client is French and suing his wife who was a partner in a big law firm. I interrupted her and told her that I might well know the person she was referring to and that this wife was my friend. She looked me up and down and said in this arrogant bitchy voice *Oooh, well, I seeee*. Then she stopped talking about it—at least while I was there." Patricia imitated the arrogant-despicable facial expression which I had had the pleasure to enjoy just a day earlier.

"Yep. That's her. That's so unprofessional—you don't discuss your client's private matters at a dinner party." I shook my head in disapproval.

"As I said, she is a stupid bitch. Don't worry, she didn't say your name."

I silently dabbled in my bowl of noodles.

"So, tell me, Chloé. How do you feel?"

"Hm. Relieved. Sad. Disappointed and disillusioned. Guilty. Free."

"You know, I never told you this, but at your wedding dinner, Michael and I saw you and Jean arguing and Michael said to me: they will not last five years."

"He was right. Technically of course the marriage lasted six years, but he was right."

"Yeah," Patricia confirmed. "And I'm still married to Michael. I remember I felt awful that day—I had bought this lovely Prada outfit months before and then Michael got me pregnant again and all I could wear from the outfit were the shoes."

"You looked lovely, though, Patricia—your belly was tiny! Yes, Jean and I argued a few times that night. In particular when Noëlle couldn't get to sleep and was crying and asking for me—you know what he said? He said 'zere are enough people to look after her, zeez eez my wedding-eh'. "

Patricia laughed. "Sorry. I know that's not funny."

I smiled sadly. "I was so upset that he was so selfish and did not understand that I needed to look after my little daughter for a while. Especially because he had always been so lovely with Noëlle—I mean, I don't think I would have married him if it hadn't been for the love at first sight between him and her. He is the only father she has known!"

"That's true. He was, and he still is—he makes no difference, emotionally, between Noëlle and Marie, does he? You know, Chloé, you really have to give him credit for that."

"Yes, I know. He still wants more money from me though and he has never paid a cent for the girls, let alone his own daughter."

"That's so dishonourable!"

"Maybe he is now showing his true character. On the other hand, he was very angry and depressed after our separation—he kept blaming me for, as he put it, 'throwing him away'."

"Obviously his ego could not take that."

"Maybe. He quite liked to be the centre of attention. It was like he would compete with me for the sake of it. At his cousin's wedding for example, I wore this gorgeous red Valentino dress in the evening and even I was quite pleased with myself—but I was virtually ignored by everybody because he had this new coat-length dinner jacket and people would compliment him on his outfit."

"He would always tell people how gorgeous you were though."

"Yes, he did—in my presence. But when we were alone, he would tell me that I was such a control freak and so tense about tidiness and money. He would say in the nicest way 'Chloé, you are a wonderful woman but you are not normal, you need a *psychologe*'. It was like brainwashing me. I believed him, until I went to see a psychologist who told me there was nothing 'wrong' with me as such and that I was like any grown-up who has normal neuroses." I sighed. "I think I really did try to make it work, Patricia, but we were just not on the same level of communication. It wasn't a language thing. Perhaps I just didn't bring out the best in him. He didn't bring out the best in me. So, really, it was better to make a painful break than to draw out the agony."

"I think you've done the right thing. How did Hugo react to you being divorced now? I thought he might propose to you on the same day!"

"No! Good god, no!" I exclaimed without thinking.

"That's a fierce reaction! Were you not expecting it—or even hoping for it?"

"Not really—the last thing I want is to get married again! Or have a child. I have fought so long for my liberty. I just want to be free. Have my own house. With my girls."

Were we not already enough as a family? Marie's favourite song currently was *We are Family*. I knew she considered her mother, her sister and herself as being that family.

"Wow, you want to buy a house? That's fantastic!"

"Yes, I am looking around. I don't want to live in Hugo's place, if we were to separate…"

"Who said anything about separating?" Patricia stared at me in surprise.

I backtracked. "No, no. I'm not saying we will separate. But, if I'm honest, things haven't been great, as you know. If I'm going to tell Hugo that I don't want to get married again or have more children, well he should be free to find a woman who does."

"That sounds very cold and rational. If he really loves you, that won't matter."

I rolled my eyes. "Come on, Patricia, be realistic. Anyway, there's no use talking about it. Let's eat up—I want to have a quick look at some winter coats before I go back to the fun factory!"

Patricia giggled. "The fun factory—I am soo glad I don't have to go and work at Howard Hewitt anymore! Urgh, can you imagine?"

I contemplated Patricia in her Hermès-laden outfit. "No way."

"Exactly. Oh, and can we go to Cartier, too? Michael said he might allow me to buy a *ballon bleu* watch as my Christmas present from him."

"Really? Wow, that's generous of him! Of course we can!" I waved at the waitress to get the bill.

~

Cartier was just around the corner. While Patricia was shown different versions of the *ballon bleu* I browsed the rings on display. I couldn't really wear the Trinity ring, that had the names of Jean, Noëlle and Marie engraved on it, any longer. That is when I saw it. Brushed white gold, about one centimetre in width, with the Cartier double C in the middle which was encrusted with diamonds. Ohhhh. I was in love. With a ring. But I could hardly buy that for myself. Theoretically I had the means to buy it, but such a special ring should be given to a woman by a man—for a special occasion or simply because he adores her (and can afford to buy it). A sales assistant appeared by my side. She must have sensed my interest.

"May I show you any particular piece?" she asked gently. She had obviously noticed my steel Roadster watch on my left wrist and accepted me as a Cartier client.

I looked at her regretfully. "No, thank you very much. I was just admiring this lovely ring while waiting for my friend." I pointed at the ring and then at Patricia.

The sales assistant leaned over the showcase. "Do you mean the one in the middle? That is the last one in the old design—next year there will be a newly designed C-motive ring." She unlocked the case and took it out, placing it carefully on a red velvet tray.

"Oh really? That is a pity—it is a gorgeous ring. May I ask its price?"

"In this size about two thousand—I would have to check for the exact price."

Two thousand? I would have thought it more expensive. "That's fine—don't trouble yourself," I declined politely.

"What's going on?" Patricia appeared. She looked at the ring. "Oooh, very nice."

I sighed. "Yes, it is beautiful." I smiled again at the assistant with regret. "Thank you."

"You are very welcome."

"Did you find your watch?" I asked Patricia.

"I am not sure which one I want—the yellow or white gold one. I'll come back, with Michael perhaps—if he ever has time."

"Right, let's go then—I have to go back to the office."

As we left the shop I thought of what the hotel manager insinuatingly says to Richard Gere's character in *Pretty Woman*, when the latter returns the diamond necklace worn by Julia Roberts' character to the opera: 'It must be difficult to let go of something so beautiful'. It was indeed difficult. But maybe this ring—and what it represented for me—would one day come to me after all.

I walked back to the P&W building, crossed the entrance lobby and just managed to squeeze into a lift as the doors were closing.

"Hold it!" a male voice shouted as the doors were nearly closed. I quickly pressed the hold button.

"Thank you—oh, my learned colleague!" Michael Stone entered.

"Hello! What a coincidence—I just had lunch with your wife!"

Michael made a sarcastic expression. "Well, that must have been a very important meeting."

I raised my right eyebrow. "It was, actually."

"Oh yes, of course—did you not have your divorce hearing?" he asked.

"Yes, I did."

"Well then—congratulations." His voice was now dripping with sarcasm.

"Hm." What was I to say to that.

He noticed my displeasure. "Now, it's not really great, is it Chloé? A single mother with a full-time job in our world—I don't know how you think you'll manage in the long run."

"Excuse me? A divorce does not make any difference!" I did not know whether to take him seriously.

Ping. The lift stopped. We had arrived on our floor. Michael charged ahead and held the door, leading to our offices, open for me. "Well then, have fun. Bye."

He paced into the direction of his office while I slowly, and in a bit of a dither, turned the other way towards mine. Did he really mean that? Back in my office I sat down on my chair without taking off my coat, staring at the black computer screen. I activated it and clicked on my time entries. I already had over two hundred billable hours for this month, and it had yet to end. What did he mean I would not manage? Had I not sufficiently proved it? Just you wait. If I achieved two hundred and fifty hours this month he would no longer doubt me. Obviously only the financial figures mattered to the Partners. I knew this only too well. Only the figures counted; everything else was negligible. After all I was in one of the most conservative professions. Lawyers don't like not being able to pigeonhole a colleague. To them, the best lifestyle would still be that in which they preferred to see themselves as having: an (outwardly) stable family life where the husband works hard, pays the bills and drives a big car whilst the neat, but not too attractive, good wife looks after their home, their two to three children and their dog. Naturally the 'good wife' doesn't work at all or at most has an non-strenuous part-time job. All lawyers living outside that box—unmarried women of child-bearing age, single mothers, homosexuals, foreigners and handicapped—would be regarded with distrust and have to work even harder in order to prove themselves.

I shook my head imperceptibly. No, I would not accept this. There was still a lot of work to be done, in every sense.

9

It's My Party and I Cry If I Want To

Panic. That was my exact feeling when I thought of my approaching fortieth birthday.

Panic—for many reasons. Forty was—if the universe treats me well—the middle point in my life. My wish was, on the one hand, to look back with content at the things I had achieved in the first half of my life whilst, on the other hand, looking forward with confidence to my prospects in the second half. How do I compare, to my own high standards? Let's see.

I had given birth to two wonderful children whom I had partly raised by myself, sometimes against all odds. I loved them above everything and everyone and was looking forward to watching them grow. So far, so good.

In my career I had achieved everything that one can achieve—to be equity partner in a large international law firm. Although that lay in the past I still had a reasonably good reputation in the legal market, a job with prospects at a prestigious law firm and earned good money. Not too bad either.

In the last twenty years I had been looking after my body, most of the time, and still looked good, even without resorting to the occasional botox treatment. I also liked the fact that whilst taking away my youth, the passing of time had added an attractive mature quality. Therefore I did not mourn the loss of youth or youthful appearance as such. I was quite proud of my physical condition and the work that I had put into it. I really did not want to be twenty anymore.

But now here goes.

When I thought of my relationships, I felt ill. I had always been a romantic and a firm believer in deep, real love and in the one person who really sees me. Who would look into my soul and read it and hold it in his hands like a precious liquid. Who would listen with me to Ella Fitzgerald's *April in Paris* or Debussy's *Clair de Lune* and understand the tears of melancholy in my eyes.

Silly, little, Chloé.

Of course, I had been convinced a couple of times that it happened—that I had met The One. Regrettably, and slowly, I had started to doubt whether it was possible at all. Men seemed to like my strong mind and physical attractiveness. Nobody ever bothered to look behind that. Really—nobody. Maybe once. One single time. The French student in my first year in London. Patrice. I was twenty-one, he was a year younger. We had spent hours discussing love and the universe, had written love poetry to each other, had (only) kissed. It had been incredibly romantic. I opened my soul to him. And then? At the end of the summer he came back from Paris and announced to me: *I don't love you anymore.* Just like that. I didn't understand, but I pretended to, then retreated and broke down inside. I suffered for weeks. I felt so alone, so unworthy of love. Out of deep despair, I even took a knife and pressed it into my wrist. Then I thought of my mother, and of her mother, and decided to break the chain. One day I knew I was over the worst. Then, slowly and carefully, I firmly shut that door to my soul, through which he had been allowed like nobody before.

Of course, I was still able to fall in love again. But nobody after that was allowed through that door again. Not Jean, nor Hugo.

The panic rose again when I reminded myself of my boyfriend. Hugo! Something inside of me was entirely resistant to the idea of a firm commitment with Hugo. I realised I had already made my decision. No further wedding, no more children! I didn't mind at all that both fathers of my children lived far away and were not able to interfere with my precious time with the girls or the way I raised them. I had to get back into the state in which I felt most secure: independence. That was, potentially, the prospect for the second half of my life. Only I had not yet reconciled myself to this, at that point.

A quiet knock on the door pulled me away from my thoughts. I was still in the office—it was late. The lamp on my desk gave off a warm light while the rest of my office was left in a gloomy semi-darkness. It was November and the deals that had to be closed by year-end were thriving. I had prepared the girls, as well as Hugo and Jana, for the reality that I would have to work rather late for those last two months.

Frank entered my room and sat on one of the visitor's chairs. "Hey, how're you doing? Have you also been kept in detention?" It sounded like a question but in fact was a statement.

"Hm," I agreed smiling and blinked a few times. In view of my stream of thought just now, I was not really in the mood for a chat. On the other hand my melancholic mood had lowered my usual defences. He seemed to sense this, as he grabbed the opportunity.

"Yes, uhm. I wanted to ask you something," he began.

I looked at him with suspense and encouragement. What now? Did he want to ask me for personal advice? I knew he was getting a divorce and nearly was through with it—only the spousal support claim was yet to be decided upon. I was happily prepared to listen to him and maybe make him feel a little better.

"Yes, uhm…I don't really get out much and want to meet more people …and I thought about joining a salsa dance class." He grinned, slightly embarrassed.

"Well, that's a nice idea. Good for you!"

"Do you think so? Me too! The only thing is, uhm, I am looking for a dance partner because it's kind of silly to go there by yourself." He waited expectantly.

I deliberated—whom could he ask? I couldn't think at that moment of any suitable single women. I leaned back and let my mind wander while staring at the dark ceiling. "Hmmm, let me think if I know somebody."

"No, no—you don't need to—I was going to ask you whether you would like to come with me—I mean to the dance class."

My gaze bounced back to him. "Me?" *Huh?*

He held up his hands with a short embarrassed laugh. "Yeah, not like a date or something—I just thought you might want to come along."

Now I was confused. "Yes, uhm, of course, why not—when is this supposed to be?"

He took a piece of paper from his pocket, unfolded it and examined what I could just make out as a timetable. "This says every Wednesday from eight to ten. Or Saturdays, same time."

"I can't do Saturdays, because of my children, but… Wednesdays… yes, sure—if we get out of here in time."

I smiled without enthusiasm. If I went out with a partner, to socialise, one could hardly use that against me. Could I record this time somehow as non-billable hours like for internal meetings or know-how development? Probably not.

Frank stood up. "So, great, I'll send you a mail with all details and we can start next week."

"Super…" I tried to sound more enthusiastic now.

Oh dear. I needed this like a hole in the head. I already had such little spare time. On the other hand, maybe it would do me good to do something apart from my job, children and household. I suppressed the feeling of guilt rising inside me by telling myself I would also be doing Frank a favour. Things were not easy for the poor guy either. Maybe he could even meet a hot salsa dancer.

~

We were both a little nervous. Outside of the safe sphere of the office we did not quite know how to behave towards each other. It was not a date but we weren't friends either. When the minuscule Cuban teacher, called Paolo, whose lisped accent was barely comprehensible ("and-eehhh now-eeh togedaahhrrr, venga, venga!") asked everybody to take the dance position, I had to force myself to put my right arm around Frank's waist and my left hand into his. It was no more pleasant to allow him to hold me.

Dancing—in particular Latin American dancing—is very sensual and with the right partner even erotic. My memories of Lambada classes as a student in London mainly consisted of dancing all night with my tall and hot Brazilian dance partner. Whenever Felipe would gently sing *Desafinado* in Portuguese, I would feel like Jamie Lee Curtis' character in *A Fish Called Wanda*, who was close to orgasm when John Cleese's character would start speaking in Russian. Now, comparing Felipe's sensuously swaying hips to the stiff movements of the pale, teutonic, Frank I sighed regretfully. At least he was tall and, albeit not athletic, he was quite burly. And he made an effort. He kept watching his feet intensely and counted with the teacher. "*Uno, dos, tres*! *Uno, dos, tres*!"

That distracted me such that I stepped on his feet. "Oh sorry!" I laughed.

He looked at me with relief and blew in his face. "Whew, this is so complicated!"

"In particular if you can't make out the instructions!" I giggled, pointing to the teacher who, counting loudly and clapping his hand with the rhythm, walked from couple to couple in order to correct their position.

"Watch it, here he comes!" Frank hissed.

Indeed it was our turn. We looked down at Paolo. As I was over six foot tall in my heels he just about reached my chest.

"And-eeeh, herrre, nonono, closerrr togedarr, *venga*!" He pressed our upper bodies closer together with surprising force. "And-eeh now-eeh, *uno*, *dos*, *tres*!" He watched us with a wrinkled brow dancing a few steps, clicked his tongue disapprovingly and went back into the middle of the dance floor. He pointed at me. "No wiggelingeh weez dee heeps! Is-eeh no Lambada!" He exclaimed.

Now Frank and I both laughed. The ice was broken. We relaxed.

"OK, let's try again, now weezout zee heeps!" I said.

"And don't lead again!" Frank retorted.

This time we found it easier to follow Paolo's steps, although it was still difficult for me to let Frank lead. It was like he was trying to pull and push me around the room. As mentioned, no comparison to Felipe. It required physical confidence to dance well, not confidence as a lawyer. But maybe he would improve. I was an optimist after all.

When the class was over Frank invited me to have a Corona beer at the small bar in the room adjacent to the studio.

"Cheers, we earned this!" He clinked his bottle with mine. "I think we did quite well together!" He declared enthusiastically.

"I agree," I replied honestly. "When the women had to swap partners and I had to dance with each of the other men in turn, I realised that all of them had very little rhythm! Except Paolo of course, but that was an altogether different experience"—it's deceptive how much strength and energy this tiny man had! "Nonetheless, a dancing couple should match physically—with my height I just cannot dance well with a man who is so much shorter than me!"

"I absolutely agree, that really is much better," Frank said and stretched himself to his full height.

"My boyfriend is about the same height as you," I said. He should not get any ideas.

"Uh-huh." Frank appeared mildly interested. "What does he do again—dentist or something?"

"No, otolaryngologist."

"Yuk—that must be disgusting to examine people's mucus all day." Frank pulled a face.

"That's not how he sees it. I think it's all quite abstract to him. Just as we don't see the jobs or human problems, which may be affected by our projects, but only the legal issues."

"Hm. Maybe. Do you want another beer?"

"Oh no, thanks, I've got to get home." I took my bag and jacket from the adjacent stool. "Thanks again for the beer. See you in the office tomorrow."

"See you tomorrow. You go ahead, I'll stay for another drink." He glanced at Paolo who was talking in loud Spanish with two dark-skinned women skimpily dressed in colourful clothes.

I followed his gaze, took in the women and understood. He was wasting his time with me, so he needed to look elsewhere. I winked at him. "Well then, have fun. And good luck!"

~

As my birthday rapidly approached, my workload distracted me from having any more panic attacks, as well as further dance lessons. Frank did not seem to mind at all as he told me, grinning contentedly, that he had found another dance partner, a Cuban girl. Judging by his grin, they did not leave it at dancing.

At the beginning of December—it was the Friday before my birthday—Tracey called me into her office.

"I had a telephone message from a client from Francobank—it seems like they have a new deal. I thought it might make sense for you to be there when I call him back," she explained quickly while dialling a London number on her spider.

After two rings a male voice answered. "Deepak."

"Oh, hello, Deepak, it's Tracey, from Pratt & Wonkey," Tracey chimed into the phone.

"Hi Tracey," replied a grumpy voice.

"Hi there!" Tracey was unperturbed. "I'm here with my senior associate Chloé who is working with me on some deals."

I leaned towards the loud speaker. "Good afternoon."

"Hi," the voice replied curtly.

Tracey continued. "I understand you may have a new transaction you might like us to help you with?"

"Yeah. It's a huge property deal for the real estate investment arm of Holman Bank, HOLREF. Two point five billion. Euros. We don't have much time though. They absolutely need to close at the end of the week after next."

I mouthed a 'no way' to Tracey. That wasn't even a full two weeks—impossible.

She briefly met my eye. "Do we know how many properties there are?"

"About one hundred and eighty. All in Germany."

"Right, and the number and jurisdiction of borrowers?"

"Don't know exactly. About fifty. German limited companies—GmbHs I think. You can ask Nigel from Howard Hewitt. I think you know him. He's already drafted the loan agreement."

Now it was Tracey's turn to mouth 'no way' to me. I wrinkled my brow. I knew why she was irritated. Traditionally, the credit agreement is drafted by the lender's lawyers, because otherwise it would be too borrower-friendly and negotiations would be extended.

"Yes, I do know Nigel, Deepak. But—on the assumption that we have no conflict of interest and can assist you on this—you should insist that your lawyers draft the credit agreement as is customary."

"Look, Tracey, I don't really care. I'll tell HOLREF but it's their call; they have the timing issue and they will pay your bill in the end." Deepak sounded even more impatient than initially.

"I'm sorry to insist, Deepak, but I really cannot advise you to accept that because it is not in your best interest. We have our P&W/Francobank precedents we could use and that would also save us a lot of time—which I understand is of the essence."

"Hmm. I guess you're right. OK, I'll speak to Steve Fry from HOLREF. He is in charge of this project."

"Lovely. And we will do our conflict check and prepare a fee estimate." Tracey pressed on the red button, smiling contentedly, and the loud speaker fell silent.

"I know Steve Fry," I explained. "He used to be a lawyer at Howard Hewitt. Not a very friendly chap. As far as I know he was up for partnership, didn't make it and then his boss arranged for him to get the job at HOLREF."

"He obviously left on good terms if he now instructs his old firm."

"I know—that happens a lot, doesn't it. Didn't some of the Francobank guys work at P&W?"

"Yes, nearly half of their real estate finance team. Francobank is a major client of the firm and looks to us to fill their internal legal requirements. So the London office regularly sends associates for secondment. The ones that we don't need to come back are kept on and become permanent employees of Francobank. It's a win-win for all."

"Very clever. Now, let's see—I can prepare the fee quote if you want, and of course I'm happy to do the deal—it's a very tight deadline though. I'll need my trainee and Jessica or Indira to assist me. I assume Frank Smith and his team would do the German corporate and property law aspects?"

"Yes, why don't you ask him. And you can take Indira. I need Jessica myself."

Indira was our new colleague who had applied directly from India. She was shy and, having only started that month, still needed to be shown the ropes. That would be making things more difficult considering the tight time frame.

I just rose from my chair when Tracey's telephone rung. She picked it up by pressing the loudspeaker button. "Tracey Taylor?"

"Tracey. It's Steve Fry. I just spoke to Deepak." The voice sounded unfriendly.

Tracey motioned me to stay. "Oh, hello Steve. Is Nigel on the line too?"

"No."

"In that case, I hope he does not mind me talking to you directly. We do take the rules of professional ethics seriously."

"Whatever. Deepak told me you object to our lawyers drafting the credit agreement."

"Well, Steve. I am sure you know that this is highly unusual and that as bank's counsel we would usually draft the credit agreement."

"I DON'T GIVE A DAMN WHAT'S USUAL! THIS IS OUR DEAL, WE PAY ALL THE LEGAL FEES AND WE CHOOSE WHO DRAFTS THE CREDIT AGREEMENT!" Fry started to scream.

Tracey went bright red in the face. She breathed in, obviously trying to keep her poise. "It is my duty to advise the bank that this is not in their interest. I just don't think it's done."

"THE DRAFT IS READY, AND I AM NOT GOING TO LET MYSELF BE TOLD WHAT IS DONE AND WHAT NOT! YOU ARE JEOPARDISING THE DEAL! THIS IS A MEGA TWO POINT FIVE BILLION DEAL AND IT HAS TO BE DONE NOW!!" Fry's voice almost cracked.

"There is no need to scream at me, Steve. I still owe a duty to my client," Tracey said coolly.

Steve's voice went quiet but with a twang. "Nigel will send you the draft agreement. Either you accept that or you're off the deal." He hung up.

The red blotches on Tracey's neck disappeared slowly. She looked out of the window. I didn't dare to move. I still had a vivid memory of that banker William's behaviour in London. This one here wasn't even our client.

She turned back to the telephone and dialled an internal number.

"Yes, what is it?" Frank Smith's baritone answered.

"Hello, this is Tracey," she said, sounding like a little girl.

"Yes, I see that—what can I do for you, Tracey?" he replied benevolently.

"I just had a call from Francobank and then from HOLREF." She quickly summarised the calls.

"Hm. I do sympathise, Tracey, but considering that our likely fees on this will probably be three to four hundred thousand Euros I guess we can make an exception?"

"I just don't want to create a precedent," she replied defiantly.

"I'm sure we won't," he appeased her.

"What about the timing? Can you do it?"

"Yes, sure. There are twenty four hours to a day and seven days in a week."

She sighed. "OK. We'll do the conflict check, draft a fee letter and copy you into all correspondence. Thanks." She hung up.

I rose from my chair again. There was nothing to be added. Every minute counted now. I thought of my birthday at the weekend. I might as well forget about that.

I was about to leave her room when she called me back. "Oh, Chloé? Uhm… can I just say something?"

"Yes?" I waited. She looked at me sharply.

"Casual Friday means no jeans. I know the other partners do not care about this but I want the rule to be upheld in my team."

I looked down at myself. I was wearing tailored Seven for All Mankind jeans in a dark wash and with ironed creases down the front and back, a tan Hermès belt, a white shirt, a bouclé Chloé blazer and light brown high-heeled Tod's loafers. With a blank look I perused her outfit, which consisted of beige baggy corduroy pants, a white blouse and a long thickly knitted patchwork cardigan decorated with tassels, all in a beige-ochre-orange-brown mix. These trousers of Tracy's were hardly any better than their white summer counterpart, with an elasticated waistband, which Jessica called pyjama pants behind Tracey's back. *No comment.*

"Uh-huh. OK. I actually didn't know." I said slowly, which was true. Many colleagues and even partners wore denim on Fridays, and I mean the faded blue ones, drainpipe style with a pleated front. Hello from the Eighties.

She blushed, visibly crossed. "Well you always look very smart and glamorous of course, but that's the rule—no denim."

Was there a hidden compliment? I didn't think so—it was more of a statement.

"No problem, Tracey. Thanks for letting me know."

Thus having clarified this important matter, I walked passed Jessica's office to get to Indira whose office was next door. Jessica saw me and wildly waved at me, motioning to me to come in. "Come in, quick, and close the door," she whispered with excitement.

"What's going on?"

"Haven't you heard? It seems like Tracey has to go back to London by May next year! David told me that his boss told him that the Frankfurt partners do not intend to extend her secondment contract! That means you're going to be my boss soon, yay!" She bounced on her chair several times.

"Really? No, I didn't know about this. That would explain her particular nasty mood today." I related to Jessica how Tracey had criticised my outfit.

Her eyes nearly fell out of their sockets. "What! She dares to criticise you, whilst wearing pyjama pants and some old carpet? I mean, really!"

I could not help but laugh. "That cardigan really is something else."

Her eyes twinkled with malicious joy. "And it's her fluffy favourite—goes sooo well with her frizzball hair!"

Jessica's telephone rang. She checked the display. "Ooops, here we go—talk about the She-Devil!" She winked at me as she picked up the receiver and cheerfully said something to Tracey.

Outside her door I reflected upon what Jessica had told me. This was just the sort of news that I needed. Another five months and we would all be free. And I would no longer have to play the uneasy role of her *senior* associate.

The next morning I woke up when a door was slammed shut. I grunted, turned onto my other side and felt around for Hugo. I was alone. Please let me fall asleep again. I don't have to go to the office today. Slowly I drifted back to sleep.

Suddenly I was widely awake. Hang on. It was my birthday. Forty! It had arrived. Having dreaded it, it now felt like any other day. I checked the alarm on my nightstand. Twenty to eight. I listened. I could make out my children's voices downstairs. I threw the duvet off me, got up and went to the bathroom, grabbing my blackberry out of my black Marc Jacobs bag on my way. The red light was flashing. While I brushed my teeth I quickly went through my emails. HOLREF's lawyers had been industrious and had sent the draft credit agreement over night. Judging by the data size of the attachment it should consist of at least one hundred and fifty pages. I would have to print them out and review them later.

I walked down the stairs and opened the door to the girls' rooms.

"Good morning my darlings!"

Marie and Noëlle sat on the floor, playing with their 'Baby born' dolls. Marie was dressed up as a pirate, eye patch inclusive, Noëlle as Barbie's Rapunzel.

"Hello Mummy! We are playing pirate and princess" both crowed cheerfully. Noëlle struck what she considered a regal pose. Marie waved a plastic sword at her with an attempt of a menacing growl.

"I can see that—you look very pretty, honey, and you, Marie look very scary—I hardly recognised you! Darlings have you seen Hugo?"

"Yes, he said he had to go to work," Noëlle replied.

"I see. Oh well. Have you two had anything to eat yet?"

"No."

"I'm hungry, Mummy!" Marie moaned.

"Then I'll go downstairs and prepare some breakfast. You two follow me shortly, ok?"

"Okay! Mummy can we have pancakes?" Noëlle asked.

"Of course, we'll have a special breakfast!"

"Oh, yes—Marie," Noëlle nudged her sister. "Get that drawing for Mumma!"

I waited, smiling at Marie waggling to her desk and returning—her one visible eye beaming with pride—with a large piece of paper. "For you, Mumma!"

I took it from her and examined it. It was a scrawled drawing of a pirate and a neatly drawn princess. Underneath they had handwritten, in slightly faulty French, '*Bon aniversair MAMAN*', and signed it *Noëlle* and *MaRIe.*

"That is so beautiful, thank you so much my angels—it's the best present ever! Come to me for a hug and a big kiss! Mwa! Mwa!"

"Did you get a big present from Hugo?" Noëlle asked.

"No, not yet. He left before I woke up."

She looked disappointed. "But it's your Birthday, Mummy! You have to get a cake and a party and lots of big presents!"

"But I'm all grown up, darling. It's not so important."

"I'm gonna draw you another picture!" Marie announced and hugged me.

"That's so sweet my darling, thank you! Mwa!" I kissed her again. "Now! As to those pancakes. I'll make myself some coffee and then we can prepare the pancakes together, ok?"

"OK, Mummy."

"I have to go pee-pee!" Marie ran out to the bathroom, pulling at her pirate trousers.

I went downstairs to the kitchen to make myself a big cup of coffee with frothy milk. I fixed their drawing, with magnets, to the door of the fridge. I leaned against the counter, holding my steamy mug and looking outside into the garden. Tiny snowflakes had started to fall on the lawn. I felt all warm inside. I loved it when it snowed on my birthday.

That was when I spotted the present next to the toaster. It was wrapped in Christmas paper and had an envelope on top. I looked at it more closely—my name was written on it. I opened it curiously and pulled out a card with a photo of a vintage car. I turned the card to read it.

> *My angel, I wish you all the best for your big birthday! May you always be of good health and may your dream of your own house come true! My present for you is a contribution for your new kitchen and one for your new bathroom! With love, Hugo.*

I peered inside the envelope. There were four green one hundred Euro bills. Then I carefully unwrapped the present. It was an ultrasonic toothbrush. I stared at it, waiting for my reaction. It did not come. Somehow I felt nothing.

~

I checked again the changes I had made, at the client's instructions, to the CP letter as well as addressees on the distribution list. Then I pressed *send*. I inhaled deeply and exhaled with relief. It was closing day of the HOLREF transaction. We were nearly there. I did not want to think about having to spend another all-nighter in the office, and it being nearly noon already. At that moment my telephone rang. I recognised Deepak's number and picked it up.

"Hi, Deepak."

"WHAT THE FUCK HAVE YOU DONE!! I *TOLD* YOU TO SEND THE LETTER TO *ME* FIRST!!"

My heart fell somewhere between my knees; my empty stomach churned. What?? I had followed his instructions religiously. He had said: once you make the change, send it out.

"Deepak, I am so sorry, I must have misunderstood you—you saw the draft, there was only that small change, which we have discussed and then you said make the change and send it out." I was stunned and absolutely sure that I had not made a mistake.

"YOU FUCKED IT UP! YOU REALLY HAVE FUCKED IT UP!"

"Again, I am so sorry! I was sure you told me to send it—I can send an email to all saying that it was sent by mistake if you want."

"IT'S TOO FUCKING LATE, YOU HAVE FUCKED IT UP AND THAT'S ALL! NOW I HAVE TO SEE WHAT I CAN DO TO GET US OUT OF THIS SHIT!" He hung up with a bang.

My body was shaking. I felt sick—I was in shock. In my entire career nobody had ever spoken to me like that. Apart from the fact that no damage had been done—the letter had not been signed by the bank and I knew it did not contain anything to the bank's disadvantage. Maybe there was something I didn't know. Of course we were all overtired and Deepak, particularly, was under enormous pressure to get the deal done. Above all it was about huge sums of money. Just think of the fees that the bank would receive, not to mention there was the important business relationship between HOLREF and Francobank. Still. Nearly all conditions precedent—CPs—for the drawdown had been fulfilled. The conditions which the borrower was allowed to fulfil later were set out in that CP letter. The bank was not yet obliged to pay out the two and a half billion Euros. The letter set out all the points that Deepak had instructed me on.

My telephone rang again. Deepak. I tried to calm down and stop my hands from shaking.

"I spoke to HOLREF and told them the letter was fine as it is but they really need to make sure to fulfil the outstanding CPs next week."

What???? So where had the problem been? "Right, Deepak, understood. Thanks for letting me know."

"Yeah. So we are going to transfer the money now. Thanks." He hung up again.

I left my office to go to the ladies' to wash my hands. I looked in the mirror and saw my pale face with the deep dark circles around my eyes. Now I definitely looked older than forty. Was this job really worth it all? Was all the money really worth being screamed at and working yourself half to death whilst neglecting your children?

I had no answer.

10

Wherever I Lay My Hat

Finally the wandering years were to come to an end. I had stopped counting how many times I moved house in my life. It is one of the most stressful things to do yet, to look for a new home is so exciting. It was new for me to look at the "For Sale" listings and to calculate what I could afford. Even though our real estate finance transactions were usually commercial investment properties, I had an idea what to expect from the bank in terms of mortgage and equity requirements. I also realised that I was about to make an enormous commitment. First, this was to be the permanent home for my family, and that included Hugo. As the ultimatum was still not yet overdue I assumed we would continue as we were. He would hardly leave me just because I might not be ready to have another child. However, if for any reason things didn't work out, in the long run, I would be independent and the girls would not have to move house. Secondly, I would always have to have a job that was so well paid that I could afford the mortgage payments. That part was scarier. The cost of maintaining a house would be so much higher than just renting a place. I would have to stop going shopping. As that made me depressed, I decided that I should give myself a monthly allowance.

I checked the estate agents' website daily and viewed all properties that were remotely appropriate, but one, or more, things were wrong with each property. I looked at a house where the only bathroom and toilet was en suite to the master bedroom; a house where each room was as small as a rabbit hole; a house where the garden was the size of a doormat; a house that reeked of the twelve cats and seven dogs that inhabited it. Then, one sunny Saturday afternoon in late autumn, the girls and I went to see a house that was in the right area, large enough and affordable. I had not received any photographs in advance and when we pulled up in front of it I knew why: from the outside it rather resembled a barrack. I was about to restart the engine and just drive away when the estate agent spotted us and waved us in.

The house was a relic from the 1960s which was when it had been built: it had avocado green bathrooms, partly ancient felt carpet or lino floors, internal flower beds integrated in the floors—I had never seen anything like it—and glass brick components around the main entrance door. But when I stood in the enormous living room, looking through the terrace doors onto the unmown lawn, strewn with dry leaves, and listening to Noëlle and Marie running through the spacious rooms, my instant thought was: Christmas. This house deserves to be filled with warm light and children's laughter.

So I did it—just before Christmas I actually closed on the acquisition of this huge vacant house, which was in dire need of complete refurbishment. It had been the ultimate shopping experience. A new handbag at Louis Vuitton, shoes at Prada or a cashmere coat at Chloé—that was exhilarating but there was no comparison to buying a house. A detached, real house. With a large garden and old trees. I would not be able to wear it but maybe that was exactly why the feeling of happiness lasted longer than a week. It would be our home. No annoying and loud neighbours anymore, just peace, light, harmony, permanence, stability. For the girls and me—as well as Hugo, of course.

So I rolled up my sleeves, hired a builder friend of Hugo's, gave him a carefully calculated budget and nine weeks, starting in January, and we got to work on my project. Tiles, bathtubs, wash basins, taps, flooring, windows, radiators—every Saturday I would spend hours on the building site and in the home improvement store. Over two hundred and fifty square metres had to be completely refurbished, three bathrooms had to be re-built and re-designed—in spite of a three-star budget, I wanted them to look like those in five-star hotels: brick and tile washing stand, mirror embedded into the tiling, brick and tile walk-in shower. My biggest challenge was to compose a kitchen at Ikea (after all for which I already had 400 Euros thanks to Hugo's romantic birthday present…!). How am

I supposed to know how many cupboards and drawers I needed? In the last twenty years I had always somehow managed with every kitchen I moved into. However, I knew I definitely wanted a freestanding oven integrated into a counter in the middle where one could sit on bar stools. There was just enough space for that purpose. Everything else would sort itself out somehow.

When all that was left of the house was a shell, all the flooring and bathrooms having been ripped out, the walls and ceilings stripped, all wiring and pipes laid bare and fifteen windows removed, I experienced a flash of panic. How on earth would we be able to live here in a few weeks' time?

But we managed it. The paint on the wall was just about dry when the removal van arrived. Nearly one hundred packing boxes were unloaded, the furniture roughly placed in the rooms into which it belonged. Hugo got to feel and hear a lot of my tension, because, in my view, he had avoided all the hassles and trouble.

It so happened that we did, after all, address the topic I was dreading. One night, not long after my birthday, I announced to him that there was no way I would have any more children or get married again. I don't know what kind of reaction I expected—maybe something like 'it does not matter, my angel. I love you more than anything else and the most important thing is that we are together. Besides, you already have the cutest children in the world'.

But, no. He tensed his shoulders and answered very soberly. "In that case it would be better if I don't move into your new house properly. I will keep the basement flat here and just have a cupboard at your place."

I felt stunned and deeply disappointed. Three years into the relationship the moment of truth had arrived. I actually never thought that he had seriously imagined taking the conventional path with me—a middle-aged divorcée with two children, having a full-time and demanding job. I just thought that he really loved me and that we'd just continue as we were.

"I guess," I replied. I was hardly going to beg. What did I expect after all? I was not able to give Hugo what he wanted. However, a potential separation in instalments did not promise to be less painful. Somehow I could not imagine our life without him.

I didn't have much time, however, to dwell upon it. After the pre-Christmas all-nighters the New Year 2007 didn't get off to a slow start either. Since the closing of the Holman deal had been done so quickly, and with so many items left open, it meant that the credit agreement, despite running for over two hundred pages, was incomplete. It would now need to be amended (Tracey had been right of course—we should have drafted the agreement from the start). In addition, numerous conditions precedent had not been fulfilled but turned into conditions subsequent. Even for the seven lawyers involved on our side this financing of more than one hundred properties for thirty borrowers had been too much to get done properly in such a short timeframe.

It was precisely at that hectic time that I received an invitation by email.

> Dear Oxonian, you are herewith cordially invited to the first dinner of the Oxford Society in Frankfurt. Our guest speaker will be Professor...

The invitation was for the coming Tuesday at 7.30 p.m. I was at first tempted to ignore the email. I had not been back in Oxford since our very pompous graduation ceremony in the Sheldonian Theatre. Having spent only one academic year in Oxford, most of which I had spent practically chained to my desk in the Law Bod, trying to prove that even as a non-native speaker and without a first class undergraduate law degree I deserved my place on this prestigious course, I had managed to convince everyone that I was bright enough. I felt immensely privileged but I never felt that I really belonged there. It was the hardest time, but it had also been the most wonderful and special time. So why not revive some of that? It might lift my mood. I would manage somehow to get out of the office in time. I knew a few lawyers at Howard Hewitt in Frankfurt who had also studied at Oxford University. If they also attended it might be fun and if not, I could always leave early. The guest speaker was not uninteresting either. Apart from that, I had no expectations.

~

Our eyes entangled at first sight.

He was tall, with short blondish hair, alert blue eyes and a face somewhere between innocent and dangerous. He approached me and introduced himself in the finest Oxford English.

"Good evening. I am Thomas Adorno." He tilted his head slightly, indicating a bow.

"Adorno? Like the philosopher?" I raised one eyebrow.

"Yes, but no relation."

"I see." I shook his hand. "My name is Chloé. Chloé Krakowski."

He shot me an amused look. "Krakowski? Like Krakow, the city?"

"Indeed, but no relation," I grinned.

He laughed, showing a row of perfect white teeth. "Touché! So, you studied in Oxford?"

"Yes. Postgraduate law."

"B.C.L. or D.Phil.?"

"I see you do know your degrees. B.C.L. One year."

"Wow. I am impressed. It usually takes two years, doesn't it?"

"Uh-huh. And you? No, let me guess."

He had a very self-confident demeanour. That could only mean two things: (i) he had attended one of the rich, large colleges and (ii) he had read PPE—Politics, Philosophy and Economy—a degree for which Oxford is particularly renown.

"PPE. And you were at St. John's."

"Not bad! PPE yes, but at Wadham. And you?"

"Exeter."

"Lovely chapel and gardens. Awful food."

"I know. But I lived outside—just up the Iffley Road."

"And what do you these days, Chloé?"

"I'm a lawyer. At Pratt & Wonkey."

"Hm. Good firm. I myself had a brief career at Howard Hewitt but left to set up my own management consultancy with my old college friend Sebastian over there." He pointed to a man with dark hair and glasses standing nearby.

"Really? Interesting. Talking about food—I think we have to join the others for the dinner. Shall we go inside?"

"Of course. Please—may I?" He led me to the room next door where people had sat down at a large dining table. He found the nearest unoccupied chairs, pulled one out for me and then sat down himself. While I was studying the menu, he leaned to me and whispered.

"You know, I nearly did not turn up tonight. But now I am very glad I did." He looked into my eyes with a slight smile.

Whoops. My heart sank somewhere into my stomach. It was really amazing how one single sentence could create an erotically tense atmosphere. After a while the man on my right started trying to engage me into a debate about Einstein—which was the topic of the after dinner speech. I could hardly concentrate, as I could sense Thomas was watching me throughout the entire meal, even whilst he was engaged in conversation with the person on his left. When the guest speaker stood up after desert, Thomas leaned towards me.

"Did you know that Einstein's theory of relativity is all about energy? If you think about it, any communication between two people is just a form of exchange of energy."

I glanced at his mouth. I imagine the energy with which I would kiss those lips of yours, I thought. He had followed my glance, guessed my thoughts and now curled his lips. I sat up straight and cleared my throat a little too loudly, turning the irritated speaker's eye on me. I gave Thomas a meaningful look and put my index finger to my lips. "Shush."

Thomas winked with amusement and, demonstratively, turned his attention to the speaker.

I didn't listen to the speech. Instead, I honestly wondered what I was about to get myself into. Again. When the speaker had finished I immediately rose from my chair.

"I've got to go."

Thomas seemed surprised. "How unfortunate. I was hoping we could continue our discussion at the bar."

"I promised my babysitter not to be too late."

"You have children?"

"Two girls."

"How lovely, and you work full-time. Amazing."

He didn't ask whether I was married but, after all, I did no wear a wedding ring. Neither did he, by the way. "In that case, please let me make sure you get to your cab safely."

"That's very kind. I am fine though. My car is just outside."

"I insist."

He accompanied me to my car and waited until I had unlocked it. I turned around to find him standing very close.

"Good night." I elongated a little so as to give him a kiss on the cheek. He pressed me softly against the driver's door, took my face between his hands and kissed me passionately. I went all weak at the knees and for a moment my mind was blank, save for my mouth melting into his. It took me enormous discipline to disengage myself from him.

"Stop—somebody could see us!" I panted. It just occurred to me that Patricia and Michael lived around the corner.

"I've got to see you again. Soon. Here's my card. Call me." He kissed me again. Oh God.

"I really have to go." I pulled away and got into the car. "You can find me at Pratt & Wonkey. You know where that is."

"I do know where that is. I will find you. Drive safely."

He was still standing where I had left him as I drove away. I chuckled, shaking my head. What on earth was that about? I really had a talent for getting myself onto this kind of situation—like that evening with Lars. Why was I not adored and courted like a coy princess? How come every man I found attractive (and there weren't that many!) immediately wanted to strip off my clothes? Did I give off any obvious signals? For sure this was not to be mixed up with romance. Even if a man was as charming and eloquent as Thomas. As well as being such a fantastic kisser! I knew I wanted to see him again, but there was no way I would initiate it.

I did not have to. Nine days, four emails and two telephone calls later I saw him again.

We had arranged to meet at Bar 22—almost equidistant from both our offices. I only had to ensure not to wear the same black Max Mara skirt suit, that I had worn at the Oxford dinner. Since, in the meantime, it had become nearly as warm as in spring, I wore a Chloé light linen skirt suit with a white T-shirt and brown Jimmy Choos, plus my most recent purchase: a chalk white to light grey ombré beautifully soft deer skin Prada handbag. Which had come with the matching wallet. I had not been able to resist buying the bag, but I would and had to be able to resist letting things go any further with Thomas. After all, there was Hugo. Still. One—albeit very passionate—kiss was not sufficient to throw all that aside.

He sat at the bar, a glass with what looked like whiskey on the rocks in front of him. He rose from the bar stool when he saw me. "Hello, gorgeous you."

Gorgeous? I thought: *you are divine*! I had not remembered him being that handsome, still I was firmly resolved not to flirt with him, let alone do anything else. I ordered a Vodka Martini.

He looked at me in amused surprise. "That's quite a strong drink, young lady!"

"I know, but it's so delicious and I need to unwind. I just had a discussion with my builders and have been told that we won't have a front door for another week."

I told him about my house, mentioning in passing that I had a boyfriend who was 'sort of' living with us. I told him about Tracey, my career plan and my past career. Maybe the vodka loosened my tongue. On the other hand he really seemed to listen and to know what I was talking about. He finished my sentences and uttered my thoughts. It was almost creepy. It turned out that he was half German and half English and, like me, had spent half of his life living in various countries. English came as naturally to him as speaking German.

"As you know, I did the whole lawyer thing, too. I worked for the same partner at Howard Hewitt that you had worked for—it was after you had left to go to Solomons. They were still talking about you—you left quite an impression there."

"What a coincidence! But I really don't see you slaving away at the sweatshop—you seem so unspoilt! Not at all like the typical big city lawyer!"

"I take that as a compliment. You're absolutely right—I hated the job and, thankfully, got out of it after a few years. Now I'm quite happy doing what I do. I'm even trying to persuade my girlfriend not to qualify as a lawyer and find another path."

Right. There we were. Of course he had a girlfriend. I made a neutral-interested face. "She is a law student?" Why did men have to go for women so much younger than themselves? He had earlier mentioned that he was thirty-four.

"Yes. Our parents have known each other for ages. She's moving to Frankfurt next month and is going to live with me. She is a sweet girl—very young and I kind of feel responsible for her." He looked at me apologetically.

"I see. Well, that's nice."

I breathed a secret sigh of relief. There was something about this man that I could not grasp. He knew how to build a connection with me in a way that confused and scared me. If you want love, you may have to take some risk. Up to now I had always kept control over my emotions and never let anybody come really close. I sensed that this man might be dangerous for me in that way. So it was good if he also was already taken.

Several Vodka Martinis and Whiskeys later we left the bar.

"Do you mind if we just drop by my office? I want to get out of this suit and put on my jeans for my bike ride home."

"No, of course not. I'm taking a cab in that direction anyway."

We went to a building nearby and took the lift up to the seventh floor. He unlocked and opened the door to a suite of offices. It was dark and abandoned but he did not switch on the lights. Some light from the street lamps was seeping through the shutters. He took my hand and led me down the corridor. My heart was nearly bursting in my ribcage. Then he stopped. He turned around and came so close that I had to lean against the wall. He took both my hands into his left and gently pinned them over my head. He looked into my eyes and let his fingertips slowly run down my temple towards my lips.

"I just can't help it." He kissed me until I could not breathe anymore. He kissed my face, my neck. I stopped thinking. We slid down the wall on to the carpet. He moaned. "You are amazing." His hand started to wander under my skirt. "I want to feel you."

At that moment I knew that I didn't want this to go any further. I pulled his hand away and put it around my hips. We kissed again. Then I forced myself to disengage from him, got up and smoothed my clothes. "I must go. This is not a good idea."

"I know. I'm sorry."

"I'll go now." I started to walk towards the door.

"I…I will call you."

We both knew very well that we could not see each other again. No good would come of it.

~

The coming days shed a surreal light on that evening. Yes, sure, we had had cocktails but we had not been completely drunk. I had to come to terms with what I had felt and then get closure on the whole thing. At first I did not even want to speak about it with Isabella when Noëlle, Marie and I visited her in her store one Saturday.

"Oh I love it!" Isabella raved when she spotted my Prada bag. "And so soft! Just adorable!"

"Yeah, at least the bag is adorable—unlike me!" I burst out.

She looked at me with bewilderment. "What's going on, my love?"

I thought of Hugo and of the conclusions I had drawn from the encounter with Thomas. "I don't know, sweetie. I think I have to break up with Hugo."

Isabella shot a glance at the girls. They were sitting on the white sofa, arranging according to length and colour various belts Isabella had handed to them. She pulled me into the kitchenette. "Come on, we'll make some coffee."

I followed slowly. Whilst she was preparing coffee, she began her cross-examination.

"What happened?"

"Nothing. Not really. Well, I met someone—but that's not the point; I won't see him again anyway."

"Then what about Hugo?"

"Isabella, what can I say? The man wants to get married and have children! I can't do that!"

"Of course you can. Do you want to?"

"Goodness, no!" I panicked.

"Don't you love him?"

"No!" Oops. There it was.

Without thinking about it, the word had escaped my mouth. I couldn't take it back anymore. I didn't love Hugo, at least not enough to give him what he wanted.

Isabella froze for a moment. "Then there is no point, if he wants something different from what you want," she replied calmly. She continued placing the mugs on the tray.

I hung my head. "I know. He is hardly ever there anymore and I have started to bitch at him, both of which are bad signs. We have been invited to another wedding, which means he'll have moist eyes throughout the ceremony and I'll have a crisis."

"I have to say I am quite shocked about your reaction—I really thought you still loved Hugo. But if you don't, then you must take the consequences. Think about it," she sighed.

"I know you're right. As usual."

"Mummy, your phone is ringing!" Noëlle came into the kitchen, holding my blackberry.

"Oh, thank you darling." I took it from her and checked the display. "Urgh. It's Tracey." I said to Isabella.

"On a Saturday?"

I signalled Isabella to be quiet and pressed the green button. "Hi Tracey."

"Hi. I am so sorry to disturb you. We have an emergency here. Jessica has been taken to hospital—she was in the office to finish a draft credit agreement and apparently broke down—David was there at the same time and called the ambulance."

"Oh my god! What's wrong with her?"

"I don't know—she had complained about stomach pains apparently. Anyway. We need to get this loan agreement out. Can you come to the office and finish it for her please. I realise you will need a bit of time to get into the matter but I'll grant you admission to the virtual file and send you the term sheet together with a summary of where we are."

I hesitated. Tracey knew full well that I had to look after my children, but I would manage somehow. I wanted to help out for Jessica and I needed to for my impending counsel promotion.

"Of course, Tracey," I replied calmly. "I'm on my way."

I hung up and looked at Isabella. She understood and pulled a face. "That old witch!"

"My colleague has been taken to hospital. Honestly, I'm not surprised. In the last few months she has spent day and night and every weekend in the office—that verges on the illegal."

"You don't work that much less yourself."

"At least I sleep every night and rarely work on weekends."

"What's going on Mummy?" Noëlle re-appeared in the kitchen, Marie trotting behind her.

"My sweethearts, Mummy has to go to the office for a while and you can come along and help, okay?"

"You can leave them here," Isabella offered.

"But I want to go with Mummy," Marie whined.

"Then I will come too," Noëlle decided.

"It's fine, Isabella. I'll just print out what I need and then work at home, but thank you anyway." I hugged her.

The girls and I hurried to the office where I logged into my computer, found Tracey's email and started printing out documents. Marie would bring me each document from the printer just outside my office and then Noëlle would hole-punch it—sometimes on the wrong side of the sheet and not quite straight, but I was very touched and proud of my little girls. I felt terrible to have to neglect them again, later whilst working at home, even if they were very excited by the treat I promised them as a reward—to watch a Disney DVD at home and order a pizza from the delivery service.

On our way back to the lift I took the route past Jessica's office. The screensaver was flickering on the monitor. The desk lamp was switched on, her desk strewn with piles of documents. Her little water bottle was open, a straw sticking out. I noticed a ballpoint pen lying on the floor and picked it up. I hesitated before switching off the lamp. Hopefully it was nothing serious, I thought worriedly, and felt tears of rage welling up. Tracey had made her work until she required hospitalisation.

"Mummy, come on, the lift's here!"

OK, Chloé, you will handle this and Jessica will be fine. I pulled myself together and followed the girls.

~

I had not thought it humanly possible to work even more than I had already been doing but Jessica left a huge hole which needed to be filled urgently, of course. She spent three weeks in hospital and I never found out for sure what had been wrong with her. When I went to see her, to give her a present from me as well as the flowers so generously donated by the banking partners ("Do go ahead and buy a big bouquet, Mrs. Krakowski, with our best wishes!" Francis Mayer, the head of department, had instructed me), she looked so young, pale and thin. When I dared to ask her, she mumbled something about kidney stones and was grateful when I changed the topic, albeit to something equally unpleasant.

"Hey, guess what! Tracey is going to let Indira go before the end of her probation period. I mean, I know she didn't fit in so well but she did come over here specifically to work with us, and all! She'll have to leave Germany now!"

"Poor thing. I found it impossible to work with her, though," Jessica replied. "She drove me crazy. I would show her how to do something, then explain it to her again in an email, and then she would drop into my office two hours later and ask me if what I wanted or meant was this, that or the other."

"I know what you mean. I suppose, from Tracey's point of view, it is probably the right decision—but still, it means her visa will be terminated and then who knows what will happen to her?"

"Of course it doesn't improve the staffing situation either. David told me you've taken over most of my deals," she remarked sheepishly.

I didn't have to fake my cheerful tone. "Oh, you know, it's fine—the others are too junior to do them and two of the deals are closing next week, as you know; it should be quieter after that." I didn't mention having to do double shifts. "Really, don't worry about that—the most important thing is that you get well, as soon as possible! You must make it back in time for the big office family party."

"Oh. Right. I forgot about that. Saturday at three, right? Are you going?"

"Sure. I'll take Hugo and the girls. We have been to that beach club and the girls really liked it."

"I'll definitely try to be well enough by then. I feel so bad already, for missing so many working days, and it doesn't reflect well on David."

I pressed her hand and realised that she was unlikely to make a big fuss out of this incident, in order not to jeopardise her fiancé's career prospects. There was no comparison between her emotional pressure and my current 16-hour working days. In contrast to hers, my boyfriend would probably spend more time by my bedside than in the office. I felt grateful that Hugo had stuck by me in spite of all the problems we were currently having (and despite my escapades, which were unknown to him, of course, but still…!), and that he had not complained for one second when I had explained to him that I would have to take over Jessica's work for a while. Maybe I didn't love him enough to compromise, and fulfil his dream of marriage and babies, but he was always there for me and that was worth a hell of a lot.

Jessica did make it to the party. The weather gods were merciful and had done everything to complete the illusion of a day at the beach. The dress code was casual so I had chosen long flowing linen dresses for the girls and I and had even braided some flowers into their hair.

"Oh my, what a picture perfect family!" Beatrice exclaimed when we arrived at the beach club and had made it past the bouncers. She was standing with Jessica and had spotted us.

"Hugo, this is my colleague Beatrice, and this is Jessica," I introduced them.

"Nice to meet you." He shook hands with both women.

"Very nice to meet you! Chloé is a lucky lady. I wish I could introduce my husband to you but he is away, on business. Again!" Beatrice rolled her eyes.

"At least that is what he said." I could hear Jacob's unmistakably sarcastic voice behind me.

"Oh shut up, Jacob," Beatrice retorted. "Don't be such a pain in the neck. At least not until I've had a few more drinks. Claudia, can't you teach him any manners?"

A dark haired woman had appeared next to Jacob and behind her a boy of about Noëlle's age.

"Hi, Beatrice," she said. "I've tried for two years and failed—so probably not," she laughed.

"I know what you mean," I said. "Hi Claudia, I'm Chloé. This is Hugo and these are my daughters Noëlle and Marie."

"Ah, you are Chloé! Nice to meet you—I have heard a lot about you."

"Have you? That surprises me."

"Uhm I might have mentioned you once or twice," Jacob interjected quickly and offered to shake Hugo's hand. "Hi, I'm Jacob. And this is my son Antonio. Where are your brats, Beatrice?"

"My baby is at home and Georgie is at the chocolate fountain like all the other kids." Upon hearing those magic words Marie and Noëlle started tugging my dress whilst Antonio nudged his father.

"Ah—a chocolate fountain. Yes, I can see it over there. That looks amazing. Hang on, girls. How old is Antonio?" I asked Jacob.

"Ten. Yours?"

"Six and nine." I turned to the boy and looked into a pair of big brown eyes. "Hey, Antonio, since you are clearly the oldest child here, what do you think about going ahead with the two girls here to see the chocolate fountain?"

"Sure, ok. Papa?"

"Yeah, good idea. Go ahead." We watched them walk to the nearby stand that boasted a huge white porcelain fountain with chocolate sauce pouring down its sides.

"There's a big open air cocktail bar next to the dance floor," Jessica suggested. "Shall we go?"

"Sounds good to me," Hugo responded.

Claudia agreed. "Perfect! Something for the grown-ups!"

"Now that I'm no longer breast-feeding, I am ready to get hammered!" Beatrice announced.

"I'm going to see how the girls are doing first, you go ahead," I said to Hugo. "I'll come and join you in a minute."

"I'll come with you if you don't mind," Jacob said to me. "My son and chocolate—that usually ends up messy. Yes, go ahead," He confirmed to Claudia.

With Jessica leading the way Hugo offered an arm to each of Beatrice and Claudia who accepted and giggled. Jacob and I slowly walked towards the chocolate fountain where a queue of children had begun to form.

"Good looking boyfriend you have," he remarked.

"Hm, yes."

"He doesn't have kids?"

"No. He's never been married either. He's genuinely lovely with my girls."

"I see. Doesn't he want children?"

"Yes he does, but I don't—anymore. He gave me an ultimatum but I missed it. I'm forty, I'm divorced, I have a demanding job with an upcoming promotion. What can I say."

"Oh dear. Has he been complaining? Tell me about it. Claudia is all about wanting to get married, have more kids, have me working less."

I spotted the girls and Antonio feeding each other chocolate covered fruit sticks and laughing. "Look at them! They seem to have fun. Your son seems lovely."

"And your daughters are super cute." He stopped and smiled at me. "You know, you and I should be together. We have so much in common—we are perfect for each other!"

"Haha. Very funny. Now let's make sure they don't make a complete mess and then we can go and join my boyfriend and your girlfriend for a drink."

I ignored the strange expression on his face and walked on. We found the children and took them to a kind of guarded playground that was attended by child minders and was just across the beach from the open air cocktail bar. I spotted Hugo in the middle of a crowd of women talking to Tracey. When I came closer I could hear her giggling.

"Hello Tracey," I said. "I see you have met Hugo."

She blushed. "Ah, yes. Hello Chloé. I was just saying how helpful you have been recently."

"I just asked your boss for how much longer you would have to work double shifts and when she thought the girls and I would see more of you again," Hugo explained. Here we go again, I thought.

"Hugo, you are so lucky, to have this wonderful profession where you can have regular hours. I mean a doctor! It's so admirable," she gushed. Was she batting her eyelids? "But we poor lawyers are at our client's service, day and night—it's not just our job, it's our calling!"

"Yeah, I've been hearing this crap for years." A short, burly man who had been standing behind Tracey and talking to David Byrd turned around, a beer bottle in his left hand.

"Oh." Tracey turned a shade of crimson. "Chloé, Hugo, this is my husband Kevin."

"A man to my liking, I see," Hugo said and shook Kevin's hand.

"Another poor bastard married to a lawyer, I see," Kevin grinned. Tracey's face got darker.

"We're not married," I said quickly regretting it immediately. Hugo shot me a strange glance.

"Oh come on, guys, be nice to your beautiful and hard-working women!" Jacob came up from behind and put his left arm around my shoulder and his right arm around Tracey's shoulder. For once I was grateful for his blunt manner. "Ladies, you seem to be in need of a drink! What can I get you?"

"Uhm, thanks, Jacob. I'll have a Vodkatini," Tracey said, the colour fading again from her face.

"I don't know yet," I said. "I need to look at the drinks menu—I'll come with you." I needed to escape Hugo who had shot me another stone-cold stare, as Kevin began to involve him in a discussion about the Premier League.

"Thanks for that, Jacob," I said when we were standing at the counter, waiting to order our drinks.

"Any time," he said kindly. "It must be hard for you to be with someone who does not understand you life."

I looked at him and said nothing.

When we returned to the group, Hugo seemed to have calmed down and soon asked me to dance which I readily agreed to—better than having to talk and venture into any dangerous topics like work, children, and marriage. Neither he nor Claudia seemed to notice Jacob staring at me frequently, which I could only escape by making us leave the party as early as possible, using work commitments as an excuse.

It wasn't really so much as an excuse but the truth, as I was still on double shifts.

Just before Jessica had fully convalesced, the worst was over for me. The two biggest deals had closed, after many late nights in the office and at home, but without any all-nighters. It was the first evening in weeks that I could make it home in time for the good night story.

I was just tidying up my inbox on outlook when a new email from Tracey popped up. I reluctantly clicked on 'open'. Please, I want to go home so badly.

I think we are done.
Thank you for your amazing effort over the last weeks.

Your Counsel promotion has been approved.
Congratulations.

T.

There. So it had been worth it, working myself half to death without complaint.

My promised promotion to Counsel.

Oh, and what a miracle. After one year's hard work and several eighty-hour weeks.

I finally got praise from Tracey.

11

Don't Leave Me This Way

Seven minutes.

And not many more words.

"I don't love you. I want to get married, I want children. You've already had everything. Amongst all women, you are like a Ferrari, but I don't want a Ferrari. It's too much. I just want a Volkswagen bus."

"Hugo, please stay, you cannot leave now, let us talk about it!" I sobbed.

"I can't. I have to go." His face was hard but his voice sounded chocked.

He turns around, walks to the front door. Opens it.

Closes it from the outside.

He is gone.

Oh god, it cannot be. Please, no. That had gone completely wrong. Our agreed time out of two weeks was over this evening; I had been looking forward to seeing him, I wanted to dispose of all problems once and for all, make up for everything.

I could feel the rug being pulled out from under me. I slumped down.

I somehow managed to grab my mobile and press Isabella's name on the favourites list.

"Love? What's going on? Didn't Hugo want to come by this evening for your big talk?"

"Yes—he was—here—he doesn't—love—me—anymore," I babbled breathlessly. "I—can't—breathe."

"I'll be with you in ten minutes! Lie down and try to breathe very slowly—inhale, exhale! Are the kids asleep?"

"Yes—"

"Good. If necessary, wake them up and send them to your neighbour to get help. I'll be there soon, love, I will hurry! Hang on in there!"

"OK." I hung up and stared at the phone.

She must have knocked on the door and I must have opened it for her. At some point I was no longer alone on the sofa. I leaned my head on Isabella's shoulder, my arms wrapped around my legs. I couldn't cry. My entire body was trembling. The pain was physically perceptible—somewhere in my chest, taking my breath away. It hurt so much I was not able to think of anything else. I just couldn't comprehend. Not Hugo. Hugo could not leave me. Hugo, who had told me one week after we got together that he loved me (and I had thought he was crazy). Hugo, whom I had taken for granted. Whose needs I had not taken seriously.

"Love, you're in a state of shock. Please tell me at once if you are starting to feel any worse and I will call a doctor immediately." Isabella was very gentle but I could sense her determination.

"There was one here just now."

"My god, of course. I did not think of that. That's even more irresponsible! He has an ethical responsibility as a doctor, doesn't he? How can he, just like that, end your relationship, your life together with one sentence and then just disappear immediately? I can't believe it!"

"He was here for exactly seven minutes."

"My love, I am so sorry. You have my deepest sympathies. I appreciate that you've been carrying around this fear since your childhood trauma with your father, the feeling of being abandoned and now it's like a nightmare come true. I'll promise you something, you will not end up like your mother. Yes, you will suffer like a dog for three months. You will wake up every morning and think you cannot take it anymore. Then, one day, after three months, you know this page will have turned. It is no longer your first and final thought, it hurts less and less and it starts to heal. Please don't forget how much your girls need you."

"I know," I whispered, "they love Hugo as well. Especially Marie. She has spent more time with him than with Jean, and now—" I couldn't finish the sentence. I could feel myself welling up. I had made a complete mess of it. My children had had a chance to have a normal family life and I had messed it up. "We were going to go on holiday to Croatia in two weeks' time. The girls were so looking forward to it!" The thought of having to disappoint them and to look into their sad faces was too much.

"Here, take two of these." Isabella handed me a small white plastic pill container. The label read *Happy Camper* and showed a simple colourful drawing of a boy happily stretching out on a cloud.

I instinctively wrinkled my nose. "What is that?"

"It's Kava Kava, don't worry it's all herbal. It's mood-improving, just like hypericum and valerian. You can only buy it in the U.S.," Isabella explained.

I took my glass of red wine and flushed down two capsules with a large sip. "I'll write him a letter now. I have to do something. I can't believe it has come this far."

"You do that honey," Isabella encouraged me. "I will stay here."

I went to my desk, took out a writing pad and started to write. I appealed to him to consider that our love was something special which should not be thrown away; I understood that my selfishness had driven him away but I could also be a Volkswagen bus if that is what he wanted, I could defer my needs to his needs, have another child… I wrote a plea that was built on logical arguments and designed to invalidate Hugo's statements. I could do no more than that. Satisfied with my powers of conviction, I placed the letter in an envelope and sealed it. I reminded myself, with some unease, of my conversation with Isabella where I had told her that I didn't love Hugo. Clearly I had said that in some mood. Of course I loved him and I had to get him back. He wouldn't be able to refute my arguments.

Isabella looked up from the newest edition of InStyle magazine when I returned to the living room. "Look, here is a photo of Kate wearing that Chloé top which you bought the other day," she remarked and held up the magazine.

"Yes I saw that—of course it looks better on her," I sighed and plunged on the sofa. "Oh, honey, how could it come to this? Since my counsel promotion Tracey has pushed even more transactions on to my desk, in which I'm to take the lead—although she does not fail to remind me of the oh so important hierarchy: '*but of course, do copy me into all correspondence, as I am still your supervising partner*,'" I imitated Tracey's nasal tone.

Isabella sniggered at my attempt at parody.

"In addition it's expected of me to do lots of marketing, which I like—at last that means I can reactivate all my contacts. However, it means, in addition to the normal work load, that I have to do lunches and dinners and travel more. All of which means I'll have even less time for Hugo, let alone the girls." I sighed again.

Michael Stone had been right. How on earth could I imagine I was able to reconcile all these factors? I always had wanted everything—a career, children and a man—but somehow it didn't seem to work. On the other hand, there were so many fabulous women—beautiful, successful, independent and intelligent—who seemed to have it all. Although, personally, I didn't know of one who had actually found, in her relationship, the fulfilment that she longed for. Admittedly, my relationship with Hugo did not fulfil me either; hence my conviction at some stage that I didn't love him. That wasn't the point though—Hugo had to learn to create the space that he needed and I had to learn to give him that space.

"Hmm. When is that woman finally going to return to London? Shouldn't that have already happened?" Isabella interrupted my stream of thought.

"Tracey has not mentioned her return to London for a while—indeed, when I think about it, she never mentions it and only smiles in a strange way when Michael Stone, Richard Keel or another banking partner raises it. I am starting to believe that she doesn't intend to return to London, in the near future, at all."

Isabella looked at me with astonishment. "No! You really think so?"

"The more I think about it the more I'm convinced that that is the case. She insists that she is the only English banking partner in the office, you know! Her peculiar way to insist on that reminds me of this Welsh character from *Little Britain*—'*I'm* the *only* gay in the village!'" I made a bad attempt at imitating a Welsh accent. It came out sounding more Caribbean.

"That makes sense—why should she give up her position here when she would probably just be one of many in London? Now I understand everything," Isabella mused. "That means of course that you are in her way!"

"Come off it—I'm no danger to her—she's the partner, not me!"

"Why not? You are in every respect a danger to her. You have personality, style, a career, adorable children, a gorgeous man, a great figure plus you are a kind person—that's too much for her, she cannot possibly bear to face this every day. One has to be very self-confident in order to do that. I can only do it because I love you so much!"

"Oh dear," I protested. "Darling you are very sweet but you know very well what it is really like behind the façade—and which gorgeous man? He's gone, remember?" I was tearing up again but the thought of Tracey prevented me from bursting into tears. I paused to collect myself. "Tracey has to go back to London eventually—her husband and children have already moved into their new house in Blackheath. Tracey flies to London every weekend."

Since she often arranged for important client meetings on Fridays or Monday she was able to bill the flight costs to the firm's marketing budget, which was quite common practice. Although she wouldn't be able to do that too often. Also, even considering her work mania, I could not imagine that any mother would be able to bear being separated from her children on weekdays over a protracted period. I dismissed the thought.

"I'm just saying, watch your back. If she stays, you will have to push past her."

"That's not my style. I would have to make an even greater effort to be made partner, even though that has basically been promised to me. Anyway, at the moment I don't care, I just want to have Hugo back!"

"Then go to his house and put the letter into his letter box. I'll come with you."

I sniffed. "OK. Actually Jana is staying here tonight anyway as I thought Hugo and I may go out. I'll just leave her a note in case she wakes up."

I went into the kitchen and scribbled a message for Jana.

We drove the short distance to Hugo's apartment and posted the envelope in his letterbox. Ten minutes later Isabella dropped me back home.

"Are you sure you don't want me to come back in?" she asked anxiously, through the open car window. I was already by the front door, searching in my bag for the keys.

"No, don't worry, love. I'll try to get some sleep—with the help of a bottle of red wine and some valerian capsules." I felt drained. All I wanted to do was to crawl under my blanket.

"OK, but you know you can call me any time, day or night. I will leave my phone switched on." Isabella blew me a kiss and drove off.

I waved her good-bye and then dropped my hand. I looked at both my hands. Hugo had given me those rings. They were not Cartier but they had come from his heart. Big teardrops were now falling onto them. I unlocked the door and went inside.

~

Two days and three sleepless nights had gone by and I had not heard from Hugo. It was Monday. I had somehow dragged myself into the office and was now staring out of the window, incapable of thinking about anything else. I gathered all my courage, took the telephone and dialled Hugo's office number.

"Dr. Walther's office, how can I help you?" The receptionist answered.

"Hello, Mrs. Johnson. It's Chloé Krakowski—can I speak to him please?"

"Hello! Yes of course—I think he is free right now. Just a moment please."

While I waited I could feel my heart beating fast.

"Uhm, Chloé?" Hugo answered hesitantly. He hardly sounded pleased.

"Hello, Hugo." I swallowed. "Have you read my letter?"

"Uhhh—ahem—no. Which letter?"

That was strange. Hugo checked his letter box every morning, even on Sundays when there was no postal delivery. "The one I dropped at your house Friday night. Did you not check your letter box?"

"Uhm. No."

The blinkers fell from my eyes. "Oh my god. You have not been home since Friday night."

He hesitated. "No," he admitted.

"Oh god. Hugo. Who is she?"

"Her name is Alina. She is twenty-six. She wants children, she—"

"Hugo, please. I don't believe it! OK, I understand you. I'm not angry with you but please read my letter before you throw away everything that we have!"

"Chloé—I can't."

"Do you love her?"

"No! I don't know. I—"

"Please Hugo! Think about us!" I was desperate. Was it too late?

"I still mean what I told you, Chloé—I don't love you."

It somehow sounded rehearsed but there it was. The deal-breaker. I could not argue with that and he knew it.

"OK," I whispered. "I understand. Take care." I carefully replaced the receiver as if it was fragile. At that moment my landline rang, nearly giving me a heart attack. Tracey. Great timing.

"Hi Tracey," I managed with enormous effort.

"I have a small deal here; we won't get a lot of money for it as it's a favour for Holman Bank, but I thought you could do it."

She made it sound like good news. In fact, however, this would be bad news for my performance statistic since I would not be able to make any profit. Tracey was aware that good figures were essential for a partnership business case, but I had no choice and she knew it.

"Yes. Sure," I replied. "I'll come over."

I hung up again, dried the swelling tears and walked to her office with my head down, hoping that nobody would talk to me on my way there.

She looked up from her draft. "So, the client needs the first draft by tomorrow—is everything okay? You look ill." She studied my face.

I could not contain myself any longer. "Hugo left me!" I burst into tears.

"Oh dear!" Tracey exclaimed. She got up from her chair, walked around her desk and hugged me. "You poor thing!"

"He—he—was my rock!" I sobbed.

"Oh I know! I can't imagine what I'd do if Kevin left me—well, he'd probably end up getting all the money and custody of the children, considering I'm never home—oh this is terrible! You have to work this out, Chloé. Don't you think you'll work it out?"

"No—he already has a new girlfriend—she is twenty-six!" I pulled away and blew my nose. "Sorry about this, Tracey. I didn't intend to cry."

"Oh no—don't worry. Really? A younger woman? Seriously, that's ridiculous—I mean, you look twenty-six!"

I managed a crooked smile. "That's not the point. She is willing and young enough to give birth to his children."

"Still—he'll come around, I'm sure! I know Kevin would not really want to give up the lifestyle. They all moan and bicker about us working hard but in the end they realise they can't do much better, especially if we slacken the reins and turn a blind eye. Maybe it's just a phase and he needs attention from a bimbo in order to feel less emasculated. Still, it must be so hard for you! In the circumstances I would understand if you don't want to do the Holman deal. Look, Chloé, you tell me how much work do you want—do you want lots to take your mind off things or do you want me to leave you alone?"

"To be honest, I find it hard to concentrate on anything," I replied with relief. "I'm not sure how I can—" I broke off. The tears were choking me up.

"Then why don't you go home—or go and see a doctor?"

"Yes, I think you are right. My doctor is nearby; she may be able to see me at short notice." I looked at her gratefully. "Thank you so much, Tracey."

"That's OK, Chloé. Just get better soon. No man is worth it." She lead me out of her office and closed the door behind me.

Wow. I had completely misjudged Tracey. Deep down she was a warm-hearted, empathetic woman. First she wanted to impose a loss-making deal on me then she hugged me and sent me home. Wow. I went back to my office, grabbed my bag, briefly told Jerome where I'd be and left the building. On my way to the doctor I called Alexia to put her in the loop. As soon as I mentioned Hugo's name she began cursing Hugo in what must have been very rude Greek. When I told her about Tracey's reaction she was not surprised.

"Chloé, I always say that, in situations like this, women stick together. They have to! It's the unwritten sister code. Nonetheless I think that's really great of your boss."

"Yes I know! Oh Alexia, what am I going to do? I could just cry the whole time."

"I understand, believe me. But there is no point. Like most men, Hugo seems to be able, just like that, to press a switch and immediately start a new life with a different woman. Every time this happens I am amazed how men can do that. They don't reflect on things, let alone on themselves."

"What do you mean start a new life with her? Have you seen her?"

"No, I refuse to. But apparently he took her to Will's last night. Alex was there. As you know, my husband does not talk much but my impression was Hugo is committed to her and is prepared to introduce her to everybody."

"What? Already? But they can't have known each other for more than a couple of days!"

"Actually, Alex said that Hugo mentioned that they met at that wine festival."

"Oh my god. That was the day after we had agreed to go on a two week break."

"See? I told you. They can switch just like that. By the way, Sabrina was there as well. Maybe she can tell you more."

Will was Alex's work partner and Sabrina his fiancée. The invitation to their upcoming wedding, addressed to Hugo and me together, was at home. Marie and Noëlle were to be flower girls at the wedding and I had secretly planned with Will's brother Robert to sing Will and Sabrina a song at the reception with Robert accompanying me on the piano.

"Good idea. I'm meeting up with Sabrina anyway this week, when she has her last fitting, to pick up the girls' dresses."

"Just do me a favour please. Focus on yourself from now on. We are going out Saturday night! There—don't argue! Until then cry all your tears, get drunk, whatever, but let it all out!"

I laughed reluctantly. "Yes, Ma'am!"

~

I followed Alexia's advice. I was actually able, after a few days of suffering, to pull myself together and follow my usual zest for action. I was even able to enter a bridal shop without having a nervous breakdown. Of course it didn't hurt that the shop owner had offered Sabrina and me a glass of champagne.

"Oh Sabrina, you look divine!" I exclaimed when she stepped out of the changing room.

She beamed. "Do you really think so?"

"Of course! You look like a princess—not tacky at all! All those little sparkling rhinestones make you look like you're out of a fairy tale!"

"These are all tiny Swarovski stones!" Sabrina explained. She turned with her back to the mirror and looked over her shoulder. "It's so gorgeous, from behind too—I love this train," she added.

"When I look at you like this, it puts me in the mood to get married again!" Hello? Did I just say that?

"You know, sweetie—I'm sure things are going to work out with Hugo," Sabrina encouraged me. "That girl is not for him—she's got nothing on you!"

At that moment I had had an epiphany. Or was it that I had made a decision?

"Sabrina, I'm going to get married next year. If it's not to Hugo, then it'll be to somebody else. I can't tell you why but I just know it," I declared. Lars still hadn't stopped calling and was begging to see me again.

"Then that's the way it will be! I'm so excited!" Sabrina clapped enthusiastically.

I raised my glass at her and took a large sip. "Indeed so be it! First—it's your turn! Oh, it will be such a lovely wedding!"

She chuckled. "I can't wait! Do you already know what you're going to wear on our day?"

"I ordered a plum-coloured Vera Wang bustier dress at Net-A-Porter and had it delivered to the office. I immediately tried it on in the ladies', totally gaga!" I laughed. Then a thought crossed my mind. "Tell me—did Hugo RSVP?"

She looked at me anxiously. "Yes, he is coming, Chloé, but we told him he can't bring *her*. Is that OK? We could hardly disinvite him."

I swallowed. "It's your wedding, of course he must come. It would be considerate if he came without her, also because Noëlle and Marie will be there, and they would be shocked and disturbed—but that's his decision."

"Do you want to bring anybody? We are quite full already but if you want to, and if it makes you feel better about seeing Hugo—"

"No, no. Thank you so much for the offer, but no. That would be so obvious and pathetic—and beneath me. No, it'll be just me and the girls."

"Those two will look so cute in their long white flower girl dresses! By the way, where are they? How are they keeping up?"

"At home with Jana. School is out for the summer. Noëlle is quite ok I think—or at least she doesn't show if she's upset. However, Marie has these moments when she cries for no reason and she's having trouble sleeping. She feels that I am not well and it unsettles her. I try not to let it show too much in front of the girls but it's an undeniable fact. Hugo is gone and we miss him."

I looked through the shop window to the street outside and, for a moment, I wished Hugo would come into the shop, get down on one knee, ask me first for forgiveness and then for my hand in marriage—just like in some Hollywood extravaganza. Instead, my blackberry drew my attention by vividly blinking its red light.

"I think I have to get back to the office. Tracey is still going easy on me with new things but my ongoing deals have not yet closed."

Sabrina contemplated herself in the mirror. "Urgh, always that stupid office. Once we're married I will stop working. Will and I want to concentrate fully on having children," she declared.

"Really? Don't you want to keep some independence? Do you always want to have to ask him, when you want to buy something nice for yourself? I admit, the job is sometimes annoying but it's also fulfilling to enjoy the success."

She pouted. "Nah. He can work and earn money for both of us. I'll do everything else for him. One miscarriage was enough. I don't want to risk that again."

I hugged her carefully so as not to put creases in the dress. "I'm sorry, sweetie. I didn't mean it in that way. I'm sure you will both be even happier when you have a child together. I just know that you will be a wonderful mother."

She still had plenty of time—she was only thirty, ten years younger than me. I thought of Hugo's new girlfriend. Twenty-six! And he was already almost thirty-seven, so ten years older than her. Such a large age gap was of course no problem from a man's perspective. If I showed up with a new boyfriend who was only thirty, everybody would bitch about me behind my back. Alexia was also ten years older than Alex, and even though she looked much younger than her age—sometimes even younger than him—it did seem to make a difference in the way they are viewed by others.

"In principle it makes no difference at all," Isabella objected when I talked to her about it later on. "I'm six years older than my husband. So what? Now stop reducing yourself to the role of the old abandoned woman. In particular, stop behaving like a victim. You're not a victim. You're no longer the little girl who was abandoned by her father. You decide who is allowed to stay in your life and who isn't."

"Yes. I know. I'm just afraid of running into Hugo and her at the wedding—or anywhere else for that matter."

"Forget about him! He doesn't get you at all. He never did. As for her—she is probably afraid of you. You grasp things so quickly that others find it hard to follow—which applies also, and in particular, to Hugo. You're not just quick—you are supersonic! You are Mrs. Supersonic! Now call him and tell him you are absolutely fine with him coming to that wedding, with or without that bimbo. Turn the tables on him."

No sooner said than done. Thankfully, I only reached his mailbox. I left the message I had prepared, my voice trembling only slightly. It was like a weight had been lifted from my shoulders. Hugo had indeed never understood who I was. I had to guide him through his life while dealing with my issues by myself. I could rarely lean on his shoulder or even be weak—he wouldn't be able to cope. The more I tried to fulfil his expectations of physical perfection, the less depth our relationship had and the more distant I grew. That was another reason for my escapades. When you're not happy and loved, you cheat. You look for something that your partner cannot give you. It becomes a vicious circle. Both of you change and then, one day, one of you will get out. The other one is left out in the cold but still has the possibility to rise like a phoenix from the ashes. Which was my plan exactly.

~

Contrary to all forecasts, the sun shone brightly on Sabrina and Will's wedding day. Nonetheless I was shivering out of nervousness. I was waiting with the children in front of the church for Sabrina to arrive.

"Don't forget, girls—walk slowly in front of Sabrina and stay next to each other, OK?" I reminded them with chattering teeth and fumbled with Marie's floral headdress.

She disengaged from my grip. "Stop, Mummy, it's ok—Hugo!" she suddenly exclaimed and, laughing, ran towards Hugo who was approaching us, holding his arms wide open. He caught Marie in his arms, then Noëlle who had followed her. I stood still. My heart was beating fast. Calm down, Chloé. Keep cool, I told myself. I forced a nonchalant smile. "Hi."

He laughed sheepishly. "All three of you look so beautiful!" he declared and twirled Marie around.

She firmly put her little arms around him. "Hugo, we missed you so much!" she exclaimed.

"I missed you too!" He still didn't look at me but, instead, planted a big kiss on her cheek, letting her down carefully.

Noëlle took his hand. "Are you going to come home now?"

Hugo bent his knees until his head was at the same level as hers and took her other hand. "Not now, sweetheart. I have to live in my house for now. But I will come and see you soon, OK?"

"OK." Noëlle replied slowly, visibly disappointed.

Suddenly Hugo's mobile rang. He got up from his knees and reached for his pocket.

"Angel!" he shouted enthusiastically into the phone. Then he saw my face. That had always been his pet name for me. Now he had given her the same name. I snorted, slightly shaking my head. He blushed and walked away towards the church entrance, still talking on his mobile.

"Come on, girls." I took Marie and Noëlle by the hand and led them to the curb. "I think Sabrina's car is arriving." Indeed, a dark limousine stopped in front of us. She let the rear window down and waved to us.

"Chloé! I'm so nervous—I feel sick," she moaned.

"In that case I have the perfect remedy for you," I replied and took a small hip flask from my Prada clutch. I unscrewed it and offered it to her. "Here, take a sip of vodka—I brought this just for you, in case your nerves were going to falter."

She looked at me with horror. "Oh, no, no! I promised Will not to drink anything before the ceremony!"

"Rubbish! He won't be able to smell the Vodka on your breath! It's better than vomiting, out of nerves, in the middle of the church!"

"Oh, alright." She took a sip. "Hmm, you are right. That's good!" She grinned. "I think I'm ready now." She turned to her father who had followed our short conversation with amusement. "Let's go, Dad! Are you ready, girls?" she asked Marie and Noëlle who nodded enthusiastically.

"Fine. Then I will go ahead and let Will know that the bridal party is ready," I said.

I looked at the open church doors. We could hear that the organ music had started. Hugo must have gone inside. Good. I had no appetite for another confrontation. I tightened my shoulders, pulled my shawl around them and walked towards the entrance all alone.

Next year, I thought. Next year.

~

I took the microphone and cleared my throat. "Good evening. May I have your attention, please?"

Everybody fell silent. The last course of the wedding dinner had just finished; the speeches had been given. Will and Sabrina watched me curiously. At the adjacent table, Hugo seemed to stare at me with his mouth open. I tried to tune him out and addressed the bridal couple.

"Dear Sabrina, dear Will. Robert and I want to give you a special present today—a song that reminds us of your love. This is your song. Please bear with us as we did not have much time to rehearse."

I walked onto the stage, where the band had set up, and joined Robert who was already seated at the grand piano. I turned around and nodded at him. He started playing the introductory chords. I inhaled deeply and began to sing the beautiful words from Alicia Keys' *If I Ain't Got You.*

My song was for Sabrina and Will but I also sang to Hugo. It was my goodbye song for him. While I sang I felt that it wasn't so difficult to say goodbye. I thought of his silly speech about Ferraris and Volkswagen buses. I realised, if you want to drive an exclusive and fast car then you must be able to afford it, look after it and drive it properly. Sadly, Dr. Hugo Walther was just not up to it. But I knew who was.

As soon as I had finished the song, and had hugged a very moved Sabrina and Will, I checked on the girls and went outside. I waived to Alexia and Alex smoking on the terrace and found a quiet corner. My clutch was big enough so that I had brought both phones. I took my blackberry that held Lars' contact details and dialled his mobile.

He picked it up straightaway. "Is that who I think it is?"

"Hi. How are you? Are you busy?"

"Actually, I just came back from dinner with my kids. I took them back to my ex-wife in my ex-house and now I'm alone and about to open a bottle of very expensive wine. Why? Are you lonely and finally willing to see me?"

"Hm, maybe. I'm at this wedding."

"Sounds dreadful. I don't know why women are so crazy about weddings. Weddings are so boring—bad speeches, bad food, bad wine and bad company. At my house, there's good wine and even better company."

"Well—I'm not crazy about weddings either. Your idea is tempting, but I've got the girls with me and no babysitter."

"Then I'll come to your house. In one hour?"

The hell why not? I had had enough of feeling miserable. Lars was sexy, successful and a real man. "Make it an hour and a half. I'll text you the address. When you're there, don't ring the doorbell—text me instead."

"As your highness wishes. See you later, gorgeous." We hung up.

I walked back inside and made my way to the children's table, where the girls were still playing Nintendo with Alexia's son. "Darlings, it's getting late. Come with me to say goodbye to Will and Sabrina. Simon, your parents are on the terrace."

"OK, Mumma," Noëlle said. She shot a stern glance at her sister. "I think Marie is tired anyway."

Marie stifled a yawn. "I'm not tired!"

"I think maybe you're both tired."

"Mummy, your song was so beautiful!" Marie said. She got off her chair and reached for my hand. "Will you sing it to me again when I'm in bed?"

"Of course, my love. I'd be happy to."

We made our excuses to Will and Sabrina and took a taxi home. After I had gotten Marie ready for bed and tucked both of them in with a kiss, I duly gave a subdued rendition of my earlier performance while stroking Marie's curls.

"Thank you, Mummy. Good night," she murmured, nearly asleep. I tiptoed out of their bedroom and left the door ajar. I checked my watch. I had perhaps ten minutes if Lars was on time. Suddenly I felt unsure whether I still wanted him there. What if this was just a booty call? I shook off that thought. He wasn't really that kind of guy and I wasn't really that kind of woman. This was more. This had real potential. I went to check my blackberry. He had just sent a text. *Am outside*. My heart beat faster. Then I heard a very quiet knock on the front door. I went to open it. He was leaning against the doorframe, a bottle of champagne dangling from his left hand.

"Wow. What a dress." He looked me up and down.

"Oh this old thing," I giggled. "Come in."

"Don't mind if I do." He grabbed me by the waist with his right hand, pulled me towards him and kissed me.

"I've waited for this for a long time," he said later when I was lying in his arms.

"And was it worth the wait?"

"Every minute, honey."

"I think so, too," I said softly. "It makes me wonder what I have been doing all this time." I looked at him and gently touched his cheeks.

He cleared his throat. "Uhm, right. So—some more champagne?" He freed himself of my embrace and poured our glasses. "There you go, love." He checked his blackberry. "Hm, I better go home soon and get some sleep."

"What, now?"

"I do have to catch a flight to Warsaw in the morning."

"Uh—Warsaw? You are going to see Magda? I thought you had broken up?"

"It's complicated. What does it matter? You and I always had the hots for each other and now we've finally done it."

What does it matter? Oh my god. I felt so foolish. My little romantic head movie just burst into flames. I quickly grabbed my dressing gown and wrapped it tightly around me.

"Nothing. Just wondering. I need to get some sleep too."

"Hey, honey—are you alright? Are we cool?"

"Of course we are, Lars. It's all cool."

What was I thinking? That a rich rainmaker partner with plenty of ex- and current lovers would make a better boyfriend and stepdad material than Hugo? That I would be more than another of his conquests with which to satisfy his ego?

I really had some serious thinking to do.

12

Supersonic

"Could you please tell me why they plan the department outing to take place on a weekend? I hardly see my family as it is and now I am also supposed to sacrifice my precious spare time, only to be able to pretend to have fun with those idiots? You can't be serious!"

A few weeks after Sabrina and Will's wedding I was sitting in Beatrice's office to discuss a new deal when an email from Tracey, addressed to the whole practice group, announcing the department getaway arrived in her inbox.

"That's obvious—that way we don't waste chargeable hours, and there's nothing more precious than chargeable hours," I replied.

"No! I am not going to play along with this! They are out of their minds! First they tell me, only after I reduced to sixty per cent., that, as a part-time associate, I can never become counsel because I don't work enough, then I work like a maniac, neglect my new-born second child and now—tell me, whose glorious idea was this?" she interrupted herself.

"Tracey's. That's why I already knew about it. She told us that she has come up with lots of team building activities which will be such jolly good fun!"

"No shit. Yeah, of course I'm really looking forward to jumping on the bouncy castle with David Byrd!" She shook her head.

I laughed. "Or leapfrogging with Keel," I suggested, "imagine—him and Mayer doing the hula-hoop or an egg race!"

"Hahaha, stop it! I can't bear it!" she laughed.

"What's going on here? Can anyone join in?" Jacob stood in the doorway.

"We're just imagining how much fun we'll have on our departmental trip," explained Beatrice. "In particular with the team-building activities." Her voice was dripping with sarcasm.

"I'm sure there will be some sort of party in the evening. Although, I think I can only bear the sight, of so many uncoordinated lawyers on the dance floor, with lots of alcohol," I added.

"Hmm. Interesting," Jacob replied. He gave me a provocative look. "Maybe I can drink champagne from your boots." He chuckled mischievously.

"Huh? I'm not wearing any boots!"

"What on earth is going on in here? Are you having a tea party? Haven't you got sufficient work to do?" Michael Stone had suddenly appeared behind Jacob. His eyes twinkled in playful severity through the big round glasses sitting on his long nose. For a moment he resembled an old owl.

"We just learned of the plans for the outing for the banking group," Jacob explained.

"Surely you are going to come along?" I asked innocently even though I knew from our mutual past at Howard Hewitt that he despised that sort of event.

Stone snorted. "No effing way! Do have fun without me though. I don't have time for games. The other banking partners, above all our dear Mrs. Taylor, are welcome to make fools out of themselves. The English just love that sort of thing," he concluded and turned to leave.

Jacob and Beatrice giggled.

"See you later," I threw at them and quickly followed Stone.

"Michael, do you have a moment?"

"Hm. If necessary," he growled and held the door to his office open. He took a seat behind his desk. It was covered with paperwork piled several feet high.

"What is it, Ms. Krakowski? Is Tracey bugging you?"

I shook my head. "Wow, I wonder how you still manage to keep an overview," I remarked and pointed at the piles of documents. "Anyway, what I wanted to say or rather wanted to ask—do you now have a specific date for Tracey's departure to London? Shouldn't this be happening soon?"

He slowly took off his glasses and leaned back in his char. "Well, here's the thing. She doesn't want to go back to London, and we can't really force her to go. After all she currently has the highest billings here."

My stomach churned. "But—you said she would leave this year for sure and then I was to succeed her? The counsel promotion was only an intermediate solution," I insisted.

I would not let this go so easily. We had a deal. They had promised me.

"She'll leave sooner or later—maybe at the beginning of next year. There is no space here for two English banking partners at the same time. In any case you have to build your business case and you'll need her for that, as your sponsoring partner."

"She will never support me if she wants to stay here."

Michael shrugged. "That's the way it is, Chloé. You can't get around her. She is the one who can really judge and support you, and it does not seem to be going too well at the moment. I saw your figures—she complained to me that you don't work enough and that under those circumstances she is not willing to support your promotion. What's going on there?" He took off his glasses and studied me sternly.

I was appalled. "Excuse me? Tracey told me herself that she would give me less work, when Hugo left us. She was so understanding!"

"That may have been so, but not for an extended period of time—certainly not for two months. I have told you before, you have to watch out with her. Apart from that, this is objectively bullshit and won't be tolerated." He narrowed his lips.

I felt myself blushing. He was right. In my self-pity I had allowed my work to be neglected. On the other hand, why had Tracey not spoken to me first before complaining to Michael?

His telephone rang. He took the receiver and looked at me expectantly. I understood. The discussion was over.

I walked back to my office, thinking hard. I knew exactly what Michael had meant. The partnership process was very similar in most big law firms—you needed a business case and a personal case that had to be approved by at least a majority of the existing partners. To start with, in order to be even considered for the process, you clearly had to exceed your chargeable hours target over a period of several years. Then you had to demonstrate, in written detail, that you didn't only do a good job on your transactions but also acquired follow-up deals, that you would in the future acquire new transactions and fulfil the high demands on turnover and profitability. Lars, my learned partner at Solomons, had summarised it very accurately: we are neither a charity nor the civil service.

Alternatively you worked for a partner who was generating so much business that it could sustain two partners. In both cases, however, you would need at least one sponsoring partner—namely the one you were working for primarily. The overall goal was to generate more income for all partners and to ensure the continued growth of the firm.

Last, but not least, you had to be 'partner material': self-confident, assertive, hungry, with the necessary scruples and ready to give one thousand per cent., day and night. Many large firms would test their candidates in assessment centres; where they would be made to play through all sorts of catastrophic scenarios which may or may not happen in the legal business world, watched closely by those partners constituting the new partners committee. I had survived and passed the three-day assessment centre at Howard Hewitt. Maybe it had not been like fighting in a war but it had felt close to it. If you showed any sign of weakness, you would be shot down.

Take my colleague Harold who worked for Dr. Keel. Richard Keel was very influential and prepared to use his influence in order to push his prodigy into the partnership selection process, after having let him work towards this goal over many years. Harold's financial performance was good and Keel had sufficient business. Then the kind, quiet Harold was sent to the assessment centre and failed miserably. Keel dropped him immediately and chose his next prodigy who, applying the right mixture of ambition, ruthlessness and brown-nosing, went straight to Mount Olympus with flying colours. Meanwhile, Harold sat in his office, contemplating the photos of his family and asking himself why on earth he had sacrificed spending valuable time with his wife and children, one of which had been diagnosed with a serious illness.

Did I really want that? Becoming a partner at P&W had been my, eventual, promised outcome. Somehow I could no longer be bothered to take notice of the proverbial carrot dangling. I no longer believed I'd be allowed to grab it. Tracey had pleasantly surprised me when she appeared to show sympathy and a human touch; but when I took her word for it and let down my guard for a while she stuck a knife into my back.

Wasn't my family and my relationship more important? I would see even less of Marie and Noëlle. I had already lost Hugo but I would not allow something like that to happen again. Life had to continue without him. If he did not want to be my partner in life, then someone else would.

~

A few days later on a Saturday morning at the end of August, I was sitting in a rail compartment with Jessica, Jacob and Mike and had just seen Beatrice walk past us.

"I say, I thought Beatrice wanted to boycott the outing?"

"She is always like that," Jacob replied. "First bitch then yield." He handed Jessica a bottle of beer. "Here—for you to relax, babe." He chuckled.

Jessica refused. "I don't think that's a good idea—if the partners see us!"

"Crap. They are drinking more than everyone else!" Jacob shook his head. "Besides—which of the partners have turned up at all? Up to now I have only seen Tracey and Frank Smith, and they have gone to the bar with your fiancé and are downing one beer after the other!"

"I saw your boss, Gunther White, and Francis Mayer. I don't think any other partners will be joining us," Mike interjected. "They consider themselves far too important, especially Stone and Keel. As far as I know they have never been to such an event. They probably don't think that it's a good idea to socialise with associates."

"My partners at Solomons had the same attitude," I confirmed. "Most of the time they would cancel at the last minute under the pretext of a life-and-death transaction which they would have to save personally. In fact, however, they'd know from the start that they just couldn't be bothered. It's simple really; showing social skills and seeking personal contact with the associates neither increases their profit nor improves their ranking in the league tables."

"Well, at least four of them made an effort. Chloé, did you see Dolores wearing her pyjama pants again? She has pleated her hair in braids?" Jessica giggled. "I mean, look at you! You are so stylish! I have these ugly walking shoes and rain jacket and you arrive with designer wellies and a Burberry coat!"

I laughed and lifted my colourful Pucci print wellies. "Of course, my dear! You can never be too glamorous, even at an office outing!"

"Who's Dolores?" Jacob and Mike were bewildered.

"That's our code for Tracey. It's a character from Harry Potter—Dolores Umbridge, a particularly nasty and mean witch," I explained.

"Talking of which—I better go and check on David. He may be wondering where I am." Jessica rose and left the compartment.

Mike watched her walking away. "Haven't they been engaged for more than a year now?"

"Hm. About two years, as far as I know," I confirmed. "I don't think they have set the date yet."

"Maybe it's better to leave it that way. In my experience, relationships between two lawyers don't last," Jacob declared laconically. "My ex-wife, Jasmin, is a lawyer. Claudia is a lawyer."

I quickly turned my face towards the window in order to control my tears. "It doesn't need two of them," I whispered without looking at anybody.

Jacob had heard me. "Chloé, I'm also already divorced. It's not because she was a lawyer. It just wasn't right, and because it wasn't right I didn't make her my priority." Jacob's voice sounded sympathetic. "As far as Claudia is concerned, I should have broken up with her ages ago."

I looked at him with surprise. "Why? I had the impression your relationship is quite stable."

"Well, she wants children, get married—but I don't. At all."

"Do you love her?"

Jacob weighed the question. "She is really a sweet girl, but, to be honest, now that you ask me—no." There was that expectant look again he had given me at the office family party.

Then aren't you just wasting her time! That's very selfish of you!"

Mike nodded in assent. "Natasha—my girlfriend—also wants to get married and have babies. I can imagine having all that with her, but not just yet."

Jacob frowned. "I was hoping all summer that she would find somebody else. By the way, she really liked your ex-boyfriend, this Hugo guy. I must say he is attractive—but of course I am much better looking, hahaha!" he declared with a husky Marlon Brando playing Don Corleone voice.

I rolled my eyes. "Why do you guys all think this Godfather imitation is cool? It just sounds daft!"

Jacob protruded his low jaw, lifted his cheeks and wrinkled one brow, and with a rough voice spoke under his breath "You know why? Because we can!", which threw Mike into fits of laughter.

"You're so silly! For once we're having a serious conversation and you just have to turn all juvenile again," I snorted.

"I'm sorry—you're right," Jacob appeased me. "I do have to split up with her, if she doesn't split up with me. Up to now I just didn't have any reason to do so."

Something in his voice made me sit up and take notice. I watched him rummaging for something in his travel bag. I noticed his tanned upper arms. I had never seen him in a T-shirt, only a suit and long-sleeved shirt. He had seemed to me to be rather too slim for my taste. Actually, he wasn't. Hm. Those biceps looked strong. I meditatively took a sip from my beer bottle and picked up my magazine. Then I lowered it again.

I said, "You know, it strikes me that men just do that. They stay in a relationship just because it is comfortable. Even if they aren't particularly happy, they won't make a change unless or until they are somehow forced to."

"Well, why not?" Jacob asked.

"Because the woman thinks it's all fine, she is investing her time and love and making plans and then bam! From one moment to the next they just leave and move on. They decide it's over and that's all it takes. Like flicking a switch."

"It's not like that. It's just—guys hate break ups. We are terrified of it. Hence the break-up by text or email," he explained. "Once we've decided it, we just want to get it over and done with as quickly as possible."

"The fact that you're breaking someone's heart is of no concern to you?"

"We just don't want to deal with it," he admitted.

"Then you've never had your heart broken."

He took a deep breath and nodded slowly. "In order for a heart to be broken, it must have loved. So maybe I have never really loved someone before." Again he gave me that meaningful look.

I was lost for words. Was Jacob trying to tell me something?

For the remainder of the journey I found it impossible to get his words (and his upper arms) out of my mind. Nor did he leave my side. Each time we had to change trains he stayed with me, naturally, as if we somehow belonged together and he had to protect me. When we arrived at the hotel and stepped out of the bus, Tracey was standing in front of the entrance, holding a clipboard and grinning like a school teacher, both of which was in stark contrast to her Pippi Longstocking hair style.

"Now, please, would everybody come to me, one at a time, so I can let you know which room number you have and which group you have been assigned to!" she shouted at us.

"Group? Are we going to do group sessions now?" Mike asked with a tortured face.

"Maybe group sex with Tracey! Don't worry, you'll get your turn," Jacob teased him.

"You really don't seem to have any other topic!" I rolled my eyes. "Urgh! I don't even want to think about it!"

Jacob was highly amused about our reaction to his flippant remark.

"So, Jacob, you are with Beatrice, Mike and—let's see," Tracey smiled. "Oh yes, me." I thought I detected something like a flirtatious undertone.

"Oh, super, Tracey," Jacob replied, adopting her tone of voice, "and what exactly will we be doing together?" He grinned at her provocatively.

She blushed. "Uhm, actually it's a surprise—but I'll let you know anyway, hehe, just don't tell the others—we will be going white water rafting and the groups are made up by those who will share a raft."

"Wow, that sounds cool," I commented.

Tracey shot me an irritated glance. "Uhm, yes, as I said, don't tell anybody." She consulted her list. "Chloé, you are with David, Jessica and Francis Mayer; although I think he may not be able to make it—he has an important conference call."

Anything else would have surprised me. These kinds of conference calls are welcome excuses on such occasions. I made a sympathetic face. "Oh, that's a shame." But Tracey had already turned to the other people who had been waiting behind us.

Jacob grabbed my trolley case. "Come on, I'll help you with that. Wow, that's heavy—have you packed bricks in there?"

I shook my head. "Very funny. No—files, of course. Tracey provided Jessica and myself with homework. After all we must not waste any valuable working hours!"

"Hm. I guess then it's up to me to ensure that you have at least some fun here!" Jacob's eyes twinkled. You are such a flirt, I thought. Even Tracey was not able to resist his provocative charm.

"Hey, Chloé!" Jessica followed us into the lift. "You're in a raft with me and David!"

"Yes, I know. I'm not sure that's good for you though—I've never been rafting!"

"Oh you'll pick it up—it's such fun! Apparently the bus leaves in half an hour."

"That leaves just enough time to check my emails."

Jessica pulled a face. "I'll have to pop into the business centre and log in properly. Tracey wants me to send the revised fee letter to Francobank."

"Well then girls, off you go and do some work!" Jacob parked my trolley in front of my room and walked down the landing, looking for his room number.

I unlocked the door to my room, rolled my suitcase in and looked around. It was a little on the rustic side, but clean and spacious. After having unpacked my few things and placed the files on the small desk, I pulled my blackberry out of my bag. Of course its little red light was blinking. I scrolled through my emails which also contained some instructions from Tracey addressed to Jessica and I. In fact they were instructions to Jessica, I was only to check her work. Sometimes I suspected that Tracey was particularly tough on Jessica precisely because she was the fiancée of a partnership candidate, so as to make sure she would get no ideas about expecting any privileged treatment. Jessica allowed it to happen—as if she wanted to prove that she would always hang on in there. Even following her breakdown and hospitalisation she hadn't really made any adjustments to her working manner.

I replied to several mails and then locked my valuables in the small safe. Looking at my watch, I realised it was time to go. I grabbed my waterproof anorak which I had specifically purchased for this occasion, stuffed my bikini into one of the side pockets and my blackberry, lipstick and handkerchief into my Louis Vuitton pochette (which in my view didn't contravene Tracey's instructions of 'no handbags to the rafting!') and ran down stairs to the bus where Tracey was waiting, again with the clipboard, but this time with a sour face.

"It's about time, Chloé!"

"Sorry! I was only answering your emails, Tracey!" I triumphantly held up my blackberry and climbed on to the bus. She mumbled something and followed me.

"There's a seat next to me. You can sit there," she reluctantly instructed me and pointed at the row behind the driver.

"Thanks."

I plunged into the empty window seat. I turned around and saw Jessica sitting behind me. "Good, you made it! I saw you sent the fee letter; well done, sweetie."

She gave me a grateful smile. She pointed with her chin towards Tracey's back, rolled her eyes and winked at me. Tracey was already emerged in her emails. I leaned back and concentrated on watching the road ahead of us in order to fight my usual travel sickness.

When we arrived at the white water rafting station we were handed wet suits and helmets. All women had to change together behind a curtain. I found a corner and managed to put on my bikini discreetly. I couldn't help but get a glance of Tracey's pale English body and to feel a sense of pity. She suddenly appeared very vulnerable and was just a woman trying not to show her hang-ups. Jessica eyed my stomach.

"My goodness, Chloé, it's unbelievable that you have given birth to two children!"

I shook my head, hoping that Tracey hadn't heard that. Anyway I felt like I was cheating due to my botoxed forehead and that I didn't deserve any compliments. I probably had as many hang-ups as Tracey, if not more. As far as I knew she neither went on a diet nor to the gym nor had any beauty treatments. Maybe she had the fortune to be convinced that she deserved to be loved the way nature had intended.

I squeezed into my wet suit with great effort and joked about it in order to override Jessica's remark. "Now I look like a real sausage!"

We went outside for the group photo. With our safety helmets we all looked like right idiots. I noticed Jacob in the back row winking at me. I quickly protruded my chin so that my lips looked fuller and zipped up my life jacket a little which, rather painfully, but effectively, squeezed my breasts together; at the same time I gave him my best rehearsed smile, tilting my head slightly to the back. Indeed he understood, looked at my cleavage and grinned at me. Mike caught him looking at me and nudged him in the ribs. "Jacob, let's see whether we can make Chloé fall off the raft into the cold water," he said loudly so that I could hear him.

"Ah-ha-ha! You're so funny." I shouted. He better not mean that. I had a flashback to a school outing, when I was in fifth grade. In my minds eye I saw a little ten year old me (in a yellow anorak, yuk, but at least with colourful wellies which *I* thought were really cool but all the children made fun of them) sliding into a muddy stream in the forest. The memory of my muddy wet trousers and the roaring laughter of my classmates made me panic.

"Don't worry, David and I have done this quite a few times," Jessica encouraged me. "It's just a question of technique."

Oh no.

I rowed for my life. The raft of Mike's team (including Tracey) came dangerously close a few times but we were able to avoid it.

"Look, we are nearly there." David pointed at the shore on the right where one of the organisers was standing and waving at us. On a meadow behind him they had set up marquees with long tables and benches. Smoke smelling of barbecued meat was rising from a large barbecue grill.

"Yay! We made it!" Jessica cried happily.

"No! Don't stop rowing!" I screamed in panic because suddenly the raft of Jacob's boss, Gunther White, appeared on our left.

David and Jessica just turned around, dumbfounded. It was too late. The raft rammed into us with full force. David and Jessica managed to hold on but, since I was at the front, I fell into the water sideways. The last thing I saw was White's amused face. I emerged from the ice-cold water with my mascara smeared and my hair soaking wet, making my colleagues roar with laughter. The water wasn't deep but I wished I could have submerged in it for good.

"Fuck it's cold!" I stammered, while David gave me his hand with a suppressed grin in order to pull me onto the raft.

I scrambled back to my seat. Despite the wet suit I was shivering from being cold. When, after a few more strokes, we reached the shore we left the raft to the organisers who showed us the changing tent where they had deposited our things. Once I had changed back into dry clothes and wrapped a towel around my head (having been told, by the mirror, that not only had part of my dignity but all of my make-up been washed down the stream) I strolled to the drinks buffet.

"Where is the alcohol?" I asked the lady from the catering team when I only spotted soft drinks and water bottles on the table. She raised her eyebrows, frowned and pointed at the refrigerator behind her. "We've only got Beck's beer."

I asked her to open a bottle of Beck's for me and took a large sip. It was too bitter for my taste but the alcohol helped to return some of my coolness.

"So, Mrs. Krakowski, everything alright again?" White appeared by my side. He was back in his corduroys and checked shirt.

"Of course, the dip in the stream was nicely refreshing after the vigorous rowing exercise!" I emphasised casually.

He nodded with satisfaction. "I knew you would be a good sport about it."

"At P&W you have to be prepared to jump into the cold water; harhar!" Francis Mayer added, joining us.

"Ah-ha-ha. Unfortunately you missed the race, Mr. Mayer—as far as I know you were supposed to be on our boat," I reminded him. I really felt like giving him a kick—no, actually both of them.

"Ah, yes, unfortunate indeed. Important telecon. The client insisted on having me there."

Somebody put his hand on my shoulder. I turned around and looked into Jacob's concerned face. "Is everything OK, Chloé?"

I turned away from White and Mayer who were already being schmoozed by David. "Yeah. I'm alright, but that really wasn't funny." I looked at the ground and kicked some bits of grass away. Don't cry, Chloé, just because somebody shows you a little sympathy.

He touched my upper arm. "Come. I have saved a seat for you at our table. I can also get you something to eat."

"That's really kind of you. Thank you, Jacob."

He returned my smile …nearly tenderly. Uh-oh. I knew that kind of smile. He was not flirting anymore. He really *liked* me.

I followed him to a table at which Beatrice, Jessica and Mike were already sitting. As we were walking I noticed his broad shoulders and that the hair at the nape of his neck were slightly too long. I resisted the urge to lift my hand and touch the short soft curls. We sat down next to each other, not much space between us due to

Mike taking up a large part of the bench. Neither Jacob nor I told Mike to make more room. It felt good to be close to him.

"Oh, sorry," Jacob said when our legs touched inadvertently. This time it was my turn just to smile at him.

He did not leave my side again throughout the picnic.

After the outing we all returned to the hotel by bus. Back in my room I unlocked the safe, took out my wildly blinking blackberry and scrolled through my mails. I saw that Francobank had negotiated, with Tracey, another fifteen per cent. discount off of our fees. Great. That wasn't good news for my business case. The last email was about two minutes old and from Jacob. He asked me to join him and the others in the spa. I deliberated briefly. It would probably be wonderfully relaxing to warm up in the sauna. I replied "OK" and put my still damp bikini back on, covering myself with a big fluffy towelling robe that I found in the bathroom.

The heated swimming pool outside was steaming invitingly, a contrast to the already snow-covered mountains in the distance.

"We're here, Chloé!"

Jacob was standing in front of a small wooden hut at the other end of the pool with only a towel wrapped around his hips. I deduced that the hut was a sauna when the door opened and Mike stepped out looking very red in the face. "Phew! It's fucking hot in there!" he laughed.

"Please, tell me, who's in there?" I asked Jacob when I reached the hut.

"David, Mike, Tom, Roger and the new trainee—I don't remember her name."

"Me neither. Ahem. Oh well, fine." I took off the robe and hung it on a hook. I grabbed a towel form the shelves.

"What, you are wearing a bikini to the sauna?" Mike held the door open for me.

"You must be joking. I am certainly not getting naked in front of you!" He had some nerve!

I stepped into the sauna room. It was dimly lit. Once I recovered some sight, in the semi-darkness, I nearly had a heart attack. Everybody was sitting *naked* on their towels—the trainee even with her legs drawn under her, offering a full view of her private parts. Oh. My. God. I quickly turned my eyes to the ground and sat down at the lower bench just by the door.

All I could make out, from the corner of my eyes, was naked flesh and skin and… urghhh! Roger got up, poured water on the hot stones and started to swing his towel in the air in order to spread the hot steam. I covered my eyes with my hands.

"Sit down, Roger! I don't want to see you naked! Actually, I don't want to see any of you naked!" I felt my panic rising.

Everybody laughed. Then even Tom got up and started wiggling his bottom. "So, Chloé, you really don't want to see us naked?"

That was enough. I grabbed my towel and fled from the sauna. I quickly put my robe back on, relieved that I did not have to stay any longer.

"Too hot, wasn't it?" Jacob had followed me. He suppressed a grin.

"That was disgusting! Eeek! Did you see the trainee?" I started laughing now, too.

"Not her, only her beaver!" he cracked up.

We were still laughing when the lift stopped at our floor. I held up my key. "Now I am going to have a nice long shower—dinner's in an hour's time. See you then?"

"Shall we dine together—uhm, I mean share a table?"

"Sure! See you later."

I unlocked my door. He walked on towards his room, turned around again and gave me a little wave with his hand. I felt all warm and fuzzy. Somehow I had the feeling I was no longer alone here anymore.

My suspicions were confirmed as the evening progressed. Even Jessica noticed how much attention Jacob paid to me ("I think he likes you, Chloé, I have never seen him make such an effort for a woman!"). After dinner we all went to the hotel bar for cocktails. I found myself at the bar, surrounded by male colleagues and the female trainee (I could not get *that* picture out of my head anymore). Somebody ordered a round of Mojitos. Jacob took two, handing me one of them.

"Let's go over there—it'll be quieter." He slightly hustled me to the nearest pillar.

"Cheers." He clinked his glass with mine. "That was quite a nice day."

"Yes, surprisingly so. Except for my involuntary bath in the stream and the even more involuntary sightings in the sauna!" I shivered with disgust.

"They did that partly on purpose, particularly Roger."

"Phhh. It's like being in kindergarten." I took a large sip from my Mojito. "Hm, yummy." I eyed him up surreptitiously. Why hadn't I previously noticed just how cute Jacob was?

"How long have we known each other?" I asked.

"Let's see—that Australian deal was about five years ago. After that we exchanged a few calls and emails. For the last year and four months you have been my office neighbour. By the way, when we did that deal five years ago? I thought at the time that it was really totally sweet of you when you called me and offered your help."

"Really? I did that? I can hardly remember that telephone call."

"It was just before Christmas. We had to draft all these contracts at short notice and were under immense time pressure. I don't know why but I told you then how crappy I thought that was and that I wanted to go and see my little son for Christmas. I remember very well, you said that you sympathised fully because you also had young children. You were so nice, I was really surprised, and somehow, it made me feel less depressed. I have never forgotten that."

"Oh yes. Now I remember. I thought it was very endearing that you told me about your son. It was a human moment in all that chaos."

His eyes beamed so warmly it touched my heart. On impulse I leaned forward. "I think I have to kiss you tonight," I whispered in his ear.

He grinned at me in happy surprise. "Really?" He put his left arm around me and stared at me intently. "Then go ahead," he challenged me.

"Not here, in front of all these people!" I replied indignantly, "but I was going to go back to my room soon anyway," I said casually.

"Chloé, all the guys think you're hot. I'm no exception."

"Rubbish! That's nonsense," I protested in horror and glanced at our colleagues standing in the vicinity. "After what they did today?" I had a brief vision of Gunther White's gloating face when I fell into the water.

"No, it's true. Believe me. Whatever—I would be proud if you chose me. Though I hope you know what you are doing." His face took on a serious expression.

I slightly leaned my head onto his hand, which was still around my shoulder. At that moment I felt very drawn to him. Then I slowly disengaged from his arm.

"No idea," I replied. "Let's find out. Room 103."

I left the bar, without turning around, and went to my room.

A few moments later there was a quiet knock on the door. When I opened it, Jacob was leaning against the frame. I grabbed him by his shirt and slowly pulled him in. We stood in front of each other and just looked at one another. He pulled a face. His lips trembled when he bent forward and found mine. He was no longer the cool wise arse but a vulnerable and sensitive person. We kissed tenderly for a while. Then he gently nudged me towards the bed, causing us to fall on it together. When he started stroking my breasts I stopped his hand.

"I'm not going to sleep with you," I said.

"I know," he replied.

I paused. "What do you mean you know?"

"Because this is not about sex—well not only," he grinned.

I grinned back. "Fine. In that case you may kiss me."

And so he did.

13

That's Amore

I have never been to Rome. I had saved this city for a very special trip—a *romantic* trip.

On the Monday morning, following our office outing, I sat at my desk at eight thirty, as usual, but this time with my heart beating fast. Jacob rarely appeared before nine thirty. So I had one hour to plan how I should behave when having to face him. I couldn't help smiling when I thought back to the previous Saturday.

We had spent the night talking, kissing and embracing each other. On Sunday morning we had taken our breakfast together, which nobody considered unusual. He also took the early train back home, whilst others planned to stay for the afternoon. On the train ride, Tracey occupied the row in front of us and he sat next to me. We kept holding hands, secretly, and exchanging tender glances. When we arrived at the train station, he declared he had to pop into the office in order to get his briefcase. Both Tracey and I had our cars parked there.

"So whereabouts do you live?" I asked him as the three of us were travelling up in the lift.

"Westend. Not far."

"That's on my way. I can give you a ride if you want." I was demonstratively casual. It was just a favour among colleagues. Tracey appeared to ignore us but one never knew with her.

His eyes twinkled with conspiracy. "Oh—that's kind of you. Thanks!"

"Good. I just need to get a file from my office."

The doors opened. Tracey turned right. "Bye, you two. Have a nice weekend."

Or whatever was left of it, I thought. “Bye Tracey. Thanks, you too.”

Jacob and I turned left.

“Are you really going to take me home?” Jacob whispered.

“Of course! I have been waiting the entire journey for an opportunity to kiss you.”

“I came along to the office on a pretext. I actually don’t need anything from here.” We grinned at each other. “Me neither. Let’s go then.”

We turned around and got into the lift. When the doors closed behind us Jacob took me into his arms straightaway and kissed me. I nestled up against his neck. Oh that was so nice.

Ping. The doors opened. We had arrived in the underground car park.

“Careful, there are CCTV cameras everywhere,” I warned him as we walked to my car.

As soon as we had gotten into the car he put his hand on my leg. “There are no cameras here.”

I pressed his hand happily and selected the reverse gear. We left the garage and I took the turning towards the Westend, which was the opposite direction to where I lived.

“Having a parking space here really can be useful. I don’t live far but if I have to take lots of files—well, I guess I will get one as well soon,” Jacob announced.

“How come? Aren’t they only for counsel and partners?”

“Yes, exactly. I’ve got my counsel interview this week.”

“Really? I did not know that! Good for you! Isn’t it too late for this financial year?”

“Yes and no. White missed the May deadline but it’s still possible for the second half year starting 1st November. I told him if he doesn’t manage to push it through now I’m going to leave.”

“Jacob, that’s great! I’m really happy for you—after all, you’ve been there for over six years.”

He attempted to make a nonchalant face but was not entirely able to conceal his pride. “It’s not done yet, but thanks.”

"But it will be done! If you want I can give you a hand with the presentation—as you know I had to do it six months ago."

"That's so sweet of you. Yes, perhaps. We'll see. Here we are—if possible, please stop on the right here."

I steered the car to the right hand curb. "Are you able to reach your bag?"

"Yes I am. Chloé—" He hesitated.

"Hm?"

I waited for him to come out with it. What was it going to be? A rebuff? It was great but let's stay friends? Actually, what did I want to hear?

"Oh, nothing. Have a lovely Sunday with your girls." He took my face between his hands and kissed me.

Suddenly it occurred to me that Claudia might be waiting for him. I felt a pang of guilt. "Oh dear—I'd forgotten about your girlfriend, Jacob. I—I honestly don't usually do this sort of thing. This is really bad."

"Don't worry. We discussed this quite a while ago. Take care—see you tomorrow."

He got out of the car, closed the passenger door and walked towards his front door. I switched the engine on and engaged a gear. If he turns around now, then he does really like me. Please turn around. Please.

At that moment Jacob stopped at the front door, keys in his hand. I held my breath.

He turned around and smiled at me.

~

The memory of that moment made me smile again. My heart beat faster, not simply because of the memory but also because I could hear noises from the neighbouring office. I froze. What was it again that I had decided to say and how to behave—cool, wasn't it? At that precise moment he appeared in the doorway.

"Hi."

It was the same smile from the day before. Thank God. I exhaled and relaxed a little.

"Hi," I replied equally gently.

"May I?" He pulled my door shut and sat down on the chair across the table. I said nothing. What was going on now?

"I split up with my girlfriend," he announced calmly.

My heart skipped a beat but I tried not to sound too happy. "What? Yesterday?"

"Last night," he confirmed.

"Oh, Jacob, are you sure? I'm so sorry. For her, I mean."

"Of course I'm sure. I should have done this months ago. She immediately asked me whether there was somebody else."

"Oh, and what did you say?" My heart was skipping again. Several beats.

"Well—I didn't lie. I told her there was a colleague I liked, and then she said I bet it's Chloé!"

I stared at him aghast and open mouthed. "Really? Why would she say that?"

"Well, maybe in the last few months I have been talking about you more often than I had realised. When you joined us last year, of course, I spoke about you and also after the office family party, where she met you and your ex. I also told her that you two had split up."

These revelations had shut me up. It had to all sink in first.

"If I'm honest," he continued, "I liked you from the very first day. I just would have never thought that you might be interested in me." He waited. I couldn't help but be honest.

"Me neither, Jacob. Colleagues are taboo. Normally. But this is somehow different. We have a lot in common. As you said a while ago, it could really work. I really like you too."

He beamed. "Then can I ask you on an official date? On Saturday I will cook dinner for a few friends at my brother's house. Would you like to come?"

"Yes. I would like that." I had to laugh. "That's new for me—having the first date after we spent the night together."

His answer was interrupted by the telephone. He got up. "I'll leave you to it," he whispered as I was lifting the receiver, I winked at him.

"Krakowski?"

"Can I speak to Chloé Krakowski please?" a male voice answered.

"Speaking."

That happened a lot. Non-Germans become irritated by the German habit of answering the telephone stating one's last name. It does have something of a military tone about it and might sound, to the other people, like an order. The Anglo-Saxons usually state their full name or just say "hello" or—more common with stressed stockbrokers or lawyers—"yep". Italians stick to the universal *pronto*, the French limit it to *oui allo* or just *oui* (which may well remain the only affirmative statement in that telephone call).

"Oh. Hi Chloé. This is Luke Miller from Francobank." There it was, the slight irritation as if I had feigned something.

"Hello Luke. How are you?"

"Fine. I'm calling about that new deal, where your colleague sent the fee quote."

"Sure, what can I do for you?"

"We need to send a draft of the financial covenants section of the credit agreement ASAP."

"Oh right? We have only just about started the draft credit agreement."

I was astonished. The provisions in the credit agreement dealing with the financial covenants were deadly complicated and had to be negotiated individually—either in the term sheet (which had not happened in this case) or in the context of the otherwise ready draft agreement.

"That can wait. We need the provisions by 3 p.m. today. Your time. I'll send you some bullet points."

"Uhm. OK. Fine, sure."

We hung up. I got a bad feeling in my stomach. I wasn't sure at all. OK, calm down and wait for his email. I would manage somehow. *Ping*. The email arrived. Hm. Oh God. I understood nothing. It made little sense to me—it looked nothing like anything I had seen before. I took a know-how file from my shelf and researched some examples. Nothing. I logged on to the internal know how system and started a search. 289 hits. That could take a while. I hesitated. Considering my charge-out rate I should not spend too much time with research—that was too expensive. On the other hand we had agreed a low cap with Francobank anyway. I clicked on 'show all results' and called our local know-how lawyer. Damn. I got her voicemail: "*I'm not in the office today. I will be back next week on…*" I hung up before the message had finished. Next week would not be good enough. I had to at least manage a first draft. I checked my watch. If I skipped lunch I would be able to send something by 3 p.m. Unfortunately he said our time, not London time. Whatever, I would have to do my best.

The next five hours flew past while I was hammering out ten pages of complex provisions for an agreement that only existed in rudimentary form. Ten minutes after I had sent the email to Luke, Tracey appeared in my office. Whilst the air temperature seemed to have gone down by a few degrees I felt hot in my stomach and my ears when I saw her angry face.

"Luke just called me. He complained about your draft."

I threw my hands up in the air. "I did all I could with the little information provided and in such a short timeframe. It was just a first draft," I defended myself.

"He also complained about your correspondence style. Apparently you sent him a rude email."

"What? Me? Rude? I have no idea what he is talking about!"

"Well he must have a good reason. Think!"

"Wait—the only thing—no, that cannot possibly be it."

"What? What is it?" Her voice acquired a menacing tone.

"I mistakenly sent him a draft of the email before I finished the first sentence, so it finished after the words 'please find attached'. But I noticed my mistake and sent the proper email afterwards."

"No, that can't be it. It must be something else."

"I really don't understand! Especially when his email style is like he is shooting short orders, no hello or goodbye, no please or thank you."

"That's very London investment banker style. Anyway! He is the client. He can do what he wants. I've gotten you another chance with him but beware, they expect you to do this properly." She left my office without any further word.

I felt like a chastised schoolgirl. Tracey, Michael Stone, Richard Keel, Francis Mayer; even Frank Smith (whom I had turned down elegantly) and David Byrd—they all had this ostentatiously patronising style, which I had never encountered in so many people in one place before. Amongst lawyers in big law firms there were (male) prima ballerinas, divas, megalomaniacs, workaholics, schemers or simply the emotionally juvenile, reckless and greedy people without scruples. My friends, who worked in investment banks or in advertising, told me it was the same in their world. Maybe that was due to the money, the power and the prestige you can gain in these worlds. I had always been, more or less, aware of that but played the game anyway, as long as, overall, I had a positive experience and met a sufficient number of people who were not that way—which had been my experience so far. Although here, in the banking department of P&W, the abovementioned characteristics were to be found in an astonishing concentration. I realised that this extended, also, to the clients. In my previous firms I had always encountered nice clients. No client ever verbally abused me. My colleagues and partners never made me feel like a complete loser. Until now! Here you got criticised all the time. No matter how much you worked or how good your work was, it was never enough or good enough. Jacob had told me at the weekend that this was the way it was. One got used to not taking it to heart. He should know—he had already spent over six years in this firm. Perhaps men were more thick-skinned than women. For sure, Jessica and the other female lawyers (of which there were but a few) didn't seem to be immune to it. However, they seemed to be resigned to putting up with it. Would I be able to do that? If so, for how long?

"Chloé, this is my brother Luke and these are Lisa, Wayne, Annabel, Christian and Sabine."

We were standing in Lucas' kitchen that was big enough to have room for a table for eight at which five people were already sitting. I shook Lucas' hand. He looked like a blonde version of Jacob.

"I can see that you two are brothers," I declared.

"We are only a year apart, but I am, of course, the much better looking brother!" Lucas replied in that smug Don Corleone tone of voice that I already knew from Jacob.

"Ey bro', don't you dare hit on my chick!" Jacob laughed.

I went to join him at the stove. "You really are cooking? I'm impressed. Cooking isn't one of my strengths."

He waved nonchalantly with a wooden spoon. "Of course! I told you I'm going to cook. I'm a fantastic cook."

"For a change, this is not an exaggeration," Lisa confirmed and waved for me to sit next to her. "Come, Chloé, why don't you sit here. Jacob mentioned you have two daughters? Where are they now?"

"That's right—they are at home. I have a nanny," I explained.

Lisa had managed to break the ice immediately. I sat on the chair she had shown me and gratefully accepted the glass of red wine that Jacob handed me with an encouraging smile.

"That's handy! Tell me—is it still so awful at P&W? I worked for Francis Mayer for four years and it was a complete nightmare. By the way, Christian and Wayne also used to be at P&W."

"Oh! So there is a life afterwards!"

"A much better one," Wayne confirmed. "It is amazing how the partners, who have treated you like an idiot, all of a sudden start courting you when you go and work for a client."

"I'm not surprised. Have you already mandated P&W?"

Wayne chuckled. "Hell, no! But every time I have a deal I let them pitch for it and then reject them!"

Christian shook his head. "They are so stupid. If they treated their associates a little better they would get work from them once those associates—like Wayne, Lisa and I—are, one day, post-P&W, in a position to give mandates."

"That's a bit like in Pretty Woman, when Julia Roberts goes with all her shopping bags into the boutique she went to on the first day and says: *you wouldn't serve me yesterday—that was a mistake. A BIG mistake*," I quoted one of my favourite movie scenes.

Lisa, Anabel and Sabine understood and laughed. Wayne looked blank. Christian rolled his eyes. "Girls!" But Jacob threw a glance at me over his shoulder and smiled proudly.

Three courses, many bottles of red wine—with which we celebrated Jacob's counsel promotion—and two bottles of vodka later we were all more than tipsy. Suddenly Jacob got up from his chair, pulled my arm and declared: "Let's dance the tango, Chloé!"

I let him drag me off my chair, protesting weakly "but I don't know how to dance the tango and there's not enough space in here!" I laughed when he started twirling me, and bending my upper body backwards in a dramatic movement.

After the second twirl I lost balance and fell, Jacob on top of me, against the radiator under the window. It broke off the wall with a loud bang. The tray with the glasses that had been sitting on the wide windowsill fell on to the marble floor, causing the glasses to break into a thousand pieces. For a moment the others stared at us in shock, then they started roaring with laughter. Lucas helped us to get up from the floor. I rubbed my painful backside that had hit the radiator.

"Careful! Don't cut yourself on the pieces, are you hurt?" Jacob asked worriedly.

"I didn't know that my bum is a match for a radiator!" I beheld the chaos with horror.

"That was already wobbly and anyway it doesn't work," Lucas explained calmly. He had already grabbed a broom and dustpan and started to sweep up the pieces of broken glass. "I think Jacob needs to go home."

Jacob sat on a chair and held his head in his hands. "I actually don't feel so great. Chloé, could you take me home?"

I had sobered up, a little, due to the fall but I certainly had had too much to drink beforehand. "Sure. We should call a cab though."

"At this hour? Forget it. I need to go home now. Please. It's not far."

I hesitated. He was as white as a sheet. "OK, come on. Let's go." I offered him my arm.

"You gorgeous, wonderful woman. Thank you." He took my arm and got up from his chair. "Lucas, I'll come over tomorrow to help you tidy up," he told his brother.

"Don't worry about it, bro'. You just go and get some sleep. Chloé, nice to have met you."

I quickly said goodbye to the others. Lisa hugged me. "I don't understand why Jacob always has to drink so much! You'll have to watch him in the future," she whispered to me.

We left Lucas' house. I led Jacob to my car.

"I feel sick," he moaned.

Oh shit. I wasn't sure I was ready to see vomit on the first date. "We will be at your place shortly. I'll hurry."

It was Saturday night, we were in the centre of town and I was drunk. Not a good idea at all, but taxis were indeed rare at this time. One look at him and I pulled myself together. It really was not far to his apartment. We got into the car and I pulled out of the driveway and onto the street. Luckily it was empty. After several minutes' drive Jacob opened the window, leaned out and threw up. I just continued to drive, stroked his left leg to comfort him and concentrated on the road with all my might. We arrived safely at his house. After I had parked the car, more or less in an orderly fashion, we stumbled to the front door.

"Uhh—I am quite embarrassed," he mumbled sheepishly. "I think I have to lie down and go to sleep straightaway. Will you come in anyway?"

"Of course." I pressed his hand. "Give me the keys." I unlocked the door. We took the lift to the second floor where he showed me his apartment door and waited until I had unlocked that too. We went in. One bedroom, a living room—a little bare but furnished with taste.

"Where is your kitchen? I'll get you some water."

"Thanks. It's through the living room. I'll disappear to the bathroom."

I went to the kitchen to find glasses and mineral water. A short while later he joined me, wearing brown tortoiseshell glasses, a white t-shirt and striped pyjama bottoms. He looked like a little schoolboy.

"I had to get rid of the contacts, I brushed my teeth and took mouth rinse," he explained.

"Aw, that looks cute. I like attractive men who wear glasses. It makes them look so intellectual and so vulnerable at the same time."

"I'm glad you like it." He took my hand and led me back through the living room into his bedroom. "Will you stay here? I don't want you to leave." He nuzzled his face like a puppy into the nook of my neck.

"That tickles!" I laughed. "Alright, alright. My babysitter is staying over at our house anyway, but I must be home before the girls wake up."

"Good. Then get undressed," he grinned.

"Hey!" I protested, laughing. "No funny business! You must sleep it off, mister!"

"I'm not that drunk anymore." He pulled me towards him and kissed me.

When you have just fallen head over heels in love then even drunken lovemaking is wonderful. Already high on adrenaline with intense feelings of tenderness and intimacy you hardly realise the added intoxication by alcohol. Or do you maybe mix up one with the other? In the early hours of the morning I got up and got dressed quietly so as not to wake him. He was curled up under the duvet and looked so peaceful. I planted a light kiss on his cheek and tiptoed out of the apartment, closing the door with as little noise as possible.

~

Back at home, everybody was also still asleep. I decided to take advantage of the peace and quiet and went back to bed, too. I woke up several hours later to a strange sensation in my face. I opened my eyes and looked into Marie's smiling face on the pillow next to mine. She giggled. "Hello, Mumma."

"Hm, good morning my angel. Did you just blow in my face?" I tapped lightly on her nose.

"He-he. Only a little. Noëlle told me to wake you up."

"Okay, it worked," I laughed. "I'm awake. Come here for a cuddle." I opened my arms.

She obliged willingly. I inhaled the baby shampoo scent of her long curly hair and covered her head with kisses. Noëlle came in to the bedroom, balancing a tray. "Good morning, Mummy!"

"Good morning my darling! Oh, is that coffee?" I sat up, Marie still clinging on to me.

"Yes, with hot milk, just as you like it, and I made toast with Nutella for all of us so we can have breakfast in your bed," she replied, beaming with pride.

"I am so impressed! You are such a brilliant girl!"

"Jana helped me—but just a little bit."

"How nice of her. Is she still here?"

"No, she went home."

"Well, then, take off your slippers and come in! Let's have a picnic in my bed!"

"Yay!" Marie cried. Noëlle handed me the tray and climbed on to the bed. She sat cross-legged at the foot of the bed so that I could place the tray on the duvet in the middle.

"Yummy! What a good idea, my love. Toast with Nutella—this is exactly what I fancied right now!" Noëlle took one slice in her hand and bit off a small piece.

"Did you have a nice party last night?" she asked after she had stopped chewing.

I nodded. "Very nice. Do you remember the beach party?"

"Yeah, that was so cool with the chocolate fountain!"

"And there was this boy we played with," Marie added. "He dug himself in the sand, remember Noëlle?"

"Yeah, he was funny," she agreed.

"Right, that boy—Antonio? He was there with his daddy—you met him, too."

"Ah yes. He brought us ice cream cones when we were playing in the sand," Noëlle said.

"Did he? You hadn't told me about that. Well, that was nice of him. Anyway, he was at that party last night, too. Hey—I just had this idea—why don't we invite Antonio and his dad to our house?"

Noëlle weighed the question. "Okay. I don't mind. We could show him our new Wii."

Marie, having watched her sister for a cue, quickly added "yes, me too!"

"Great! I'll call him." I picked up my mobile and dialled Jacob's number. He picked up after three ringtones.

"Hi! Good morning," he said softly.

"Hi! Did I wake you?"

"Actually, my alarm just went off. I have to get up soon, to go and pick up my son from his mother's house. I didn't hear you leave. It must have been very early this morning."

"It was." I glanced at the girls who were listening attentively. I cleared my throat. "Anyway. I'm here with my daughters having breakfast, and we were wondering whether you and Antonio would like to come over this afternoon. We've got a new Wii and lots of games."

"That's a good idea." He paused. "I'll check with him but I'm sure he would like to. I'll find a way. I also definitely want to see you."

"Hm. Yes. I agree," I replied casually. "Fine then. Shall we say around three?"

"Perfect. Text me the address."

"Will do. We'll see you later then!" I put the phone back on my nightstand and turned back to the girls. "So they're coming around later. That'll be fun! Shall we bake a cake together?"

"Can I lick the bowl?" Marie asked. "No, I want to!" Noëlle protested and nudged her. "You always eat all the batter!"

"Mumma!" Marie whined.

"Girls! Calm down, you two. Honestly! When we finish the mix I will scrape the bowl with two big spoons and you can each have one. Alright?"

"OK". Marie exchanged glances with her sister.

"Good. Let's finish this wonderful breakfast that Noëlle prepared, then I'll take a shower and we can get started on that cake."

No sooner said than done. Just before three o'clock, Jacob texted me: *we're on our way*. I positioned myself at the kitchen window from where I had a good view of the street. When I spotted Jacob's black Beetle convertible I opened the window and waived at them. "Hello! We're here! You can park behind my car!"

Antonio waived back enthusiastically. Jacob turned onto our driveway and stopped the car. Antonio jumped out and ran up the stairs to our front door where I was waiting.

"Wow, your house is huge!" he exclaimed.

I laughed. "Hi Antonio. Come in. Yes, it is quite spacious. Ah, here are the girls. Marie, Noëlle, come and say hi."

"Do you know Wii?" Marie asked him.

"Sure," he answered casually. "We've got one at my mum's house."

"We've got Cars, Wii Play and Wii Sports," Noëlle said.

Jacob appeared at the door. "Hi! Hi, Chloé." He quickly winked at me. "Hi girls. Nice to see you again. Thanks for having us over. We brought you something." He held up a colourful paper bag. "I wasn't sure whether you'd prefer chocolate or gummi bears so we got both. Of course ask your mum first whether you may eat them."

"We like both." Noëlle said, took the bag and peered inside. "Yummy, *kinder* chocolate! Thank you!"

"Of course you can have them," I confirmed. "Thank you both."

"We baked a cake!" Marie announced.

"That sounds wonderful!" Jacob said and squatted down to her. "Now why don't you and your sister show Antonio around and I can help your mum in the kitchen?" Marie studied his eyes and nodded. "Okay."

As the three trotted off, Jacob whispered in my ear. "Look at them. Marie is so tall—from behind the three of them look like they are the same age. We could be like Brad and Angelina with all those kids."

"They do look cute together," I admitted.

"Like a real little family," he added and squeezed my hand.

Maybe it was this remark that made me sit down at my computer, after they had left in the evening. I wanted to search the Internet for weekend trips. The autumn school break was only a few weeks away and Marie and Noëlle were going to go to Paris to see Jean. So Paris was out of the question. Suddenly I knew where I wanted to go with Jacob. I had never been to Rome; he had been there a few times. He was the right man to show me Rome.

I decided to surprise him. I knew I'd be taking the risk that he might have to cancel because of work commitments. On the other hand his boss Gunther White seemed fairly laid back and didn't expect him to work at weekends. As far as I was concerned, I would manage my work if necessary by putting in overtime beforehand.

The next day, after having lodged my day off request and asked Mike for hotel recommendations, I booked the flights and a small hotel near the Spanish steps. Mike had just been to Rome and lent me two guidebooks, marked with his recommendations for eating out.

I printed out the etickets, cut out the itinerary and glued it onto a postcard showing a painting by Monet of Venice in the sunset. It was not Rome but at least conveyed the right atmosphere. I wrote on the picture (thinking of the Norah Jones song) '*Come away with me…*' and above the itinerary on the other side '*…to Rome*'. Underneath I stuck a picture of the hotel I had printed out from the Internet.

That evening—the girls were already in bed and asleep—Jacob sat on my sofa with a glass of red wine.

"Here." I handed him the card.

He looked at the postcard, frowning. "Come away with me?" He was puzzled. "What does this mean?"

"Turn it around!"

He did as he was told and continued reading. His facial expression changed from confused to incredulous and then to joyous.

"You want to go to Rome with me?"

"Yes! I've never been. I always saved Rome for a very special trip."

I was relieved. He seemed to like his surprise. He pressed me against him. "That is so sweet, baby. You are really perfect. I am starting to believe I should marry you."

What? My heart seemed to stop. I giggled nervously. He could hardly have meant that. Or could he? My heart started beating again, but now faster. He noticed my hesitation. He took my face into his hands and looked at me.

"Would you say yes if I asked you?"

"There is only one way to find out," I evaded the answer.

He grinned. "That's true."

He studied the card again. "This is really such a wonderful idea. Hang on. Oh bugger. Chloé, that Monday is Antonio's birthday and the return flight would get us here after five p.m. It's not going to work."

I crashed straight from my romantic high into the cold reality. Well, it would have been too good to be true, wouldn't it? I tried to hide my disappointment. "Oh. OK. We could take an earlier flight back."

"No, no. I was going to spend the afternoon with him, in particular because I'm not going to have him that weekend."

"I see. What about the weekend before that? Maybe I can change the booking."

"Let me check." He consulted his blackberry. "Yes, that should be fine. Look, I'm really sorry but surely you can change the booking."

"Yeah. Sure. I understand. It's Antonio's birthday. I'll change it tomorrow."

For him, that seemed to be the end of it.

I was able to change the booking but ended up paying nearly double the price. I told myself I would have expected him to do the same thing for me. Jacob was a doting parent who would plan everything around being able to spend time with his son. Unlike some of our other male colleagues who had children, Jacob really seemed to put his child first. He was a responsible father, a good lawyer and a romantic lover.

Things between us developed very nicely. In the office we kept our relationship a secret, which made it all the more exciting. We had much fun taking the same lift by feigned coincidence, stealing kisses when we were unobserved and shooting each other secretive glances when hanging out for a coffee with our colleagues. Sometimes we would even meet at his apartment for a tête-à-tête in our lunch hour. At home, he would join me and the girls for dinner whenever he could and bring Antonio with him at the weekends.

~

When, a few weeks later, we arrived in Rome and drove in a taxi from Fiumicino to the Via Flavia, I happily breathed the still warm air through the open window and pointed at the palm trees by the roadside.

"Oh look how lovely! Palm trees!"

"Just wait until you see Rome. It is the most beautiful city in the world. I have already planned some lovely walks. We'll start at the Spanish Steps, then pass the Fontana di Trevi and end up at the Pantheon. Close to the Pantheon there are some traditional restaurants where we can overindulge on pasta and Chianti."

"That sounds wonderful. I would also really like to see the Vatican and the Colosseum and Forum Romanum, tomorrow or the day after. Also if possible—but only if you don't mind—walk down the Via Condotti. I don't necessarily have to shop!"

He laughed.

"Of course. You can do whatever you like and, by the way, I also like to go shopping in Rome," he winked at me.

I was happy. It had been the right decision to visit Rome with Jacob. Just like me he seemed to appreciate the right combination of sightseeing, culinary delights and shopping. I rejoiced inside. Prada, Gucci, Dolce & Gabbana! I'm coming!

Rome exceeded all my expectations. It was overwhelming to finally view the historical sites and feel the pulse of the city for real, after having only seen or read about it in movies, pictures and books. With every minute I felt closer to Jacob. He was a resourceful guide and kept stopping here and there to show me something special or just to kiss me. By the Fontana di Trevi he took a selfie with his mobile of us kissing. That turned out so nice that afterwards we continued to apply that technique and made numerous selfies of us kissing in front of Rome's famous monuments. Actually you saw very little of the relevant landmark in the background.

Saturday was another perfect day. On the way back from the Pantheon I stopped in front of a huge MaxMara boutique. "Oh! I love MaxMara!"

"Why don't you go ahead inside? I saw some shoes in that shop over there. I'll come and find you."

I wasn't listening anymore, as I had already entered the boutique and, mesmerised like a child in a sweet shop, gone straight for the cashmere coats. Then I spotted a gorgeous little black dress, and another one! With matching sandals! Oh and these adorable bolero cardigans!

"So did you find anything at all?" he grinned when he found me an hour later.

I looked at my four shopping bags, a little embarrassed.

"Uhm, yes. A few things. But there is no MaxMara boutique at home and here in Italy it's so much cheaper!" I justified myself.

He laughed. "If you bought something dressy, wear it tonight. I have planned a surprise. I don't know whether it's going to work out but I hope so."

I was thrilled. I couldn't have planned it any better!

We returned to our hotel. Post-shopping lovemaking felt like having your cake and eating it. Later we called our respective children and got ready for the evening. When I finally emerged from the bathroom, all made up and wearing my new MaxMara dress, he nodded with appreciation.

"That really is a beautiful dress. In fact I'd like to rip it right off you again but we've got to go. The concierge called—our taxi is here."

I picked up my Damier Ebène Speedy that did not go with the dress but had enough space for the guidebook. I had only taken one handbag on the trip and chosen Louis Vuitton as I figured the pickpockets might not be interested in it as it could be one of the many copies one could buy illegally on the streets of Rome.

"OK. I'm ready."

We took the lift downstairs. This time he did not kiss me. He looked at his watch several times and checked the knot of his tie.

When we stepped out of the hotel the doorman opened the taxi door for me. "*Buona serata, signora.*"

"*Grazie.*" I got in. Jacob followed on the other side.

"All Saints Church, Via del Babuino," he instructed the driver.

"*Va bene, signore.*"

"A church? At this hour?"

He grinned nervously. "Just wait. I hope it will be a good surprise."

A short ride later the taxi stopped at a neo-Gothic church made out of brick. The way to the portal was lit. Jacob took me by the hand. Next to the portal an old lady was sitting behind a foldable table on which some brochures were fanned out.

"Two tickets please," he asked.

I curiously studied the brochure entitled *Accademia d'Opera Italiana*. Then the coin dropped.

"They are performing an opera? Here in the church?"

"Not just any opera, Chloé. *La Traviata.*"

He led me inside. Dimmed light shed from the candelabras and the reading lights of the members of the small orchestra in the wing. In front of the altar, which had been covered by a velvet cloth, there was a chaise longue, a table, two chairs—it was the stage set. We found a space on a marble bench. At that moment every little corner of the church began to fill itself with the mesmerising music of the prelude. My scalp started to tingle. Goose bumps spread from the back of my neck to the base of my spine.

"Good surprise?"

I nodded and looked at him silently, too moved to talk. I swallowed. "That's the opera from *Pretty Woman.*"

He smiled tenderly. "Yes. Exactly. I know you like that movie." He took off his coat and put it around my shoulders. "Here. I don't want you to be cold."

I was bowled over—no, more in a state of shock. He had just found a way to the hidden place in my heart. I was no longer able to say anything. At that moment I knew with utter conviction. He loved me.

The next morning I woke up in his arms when the bells of all of Rome's churches were calling for Sunday mass. I carefully tried to get out of his embrace in order to go and brush my teeth, but he pulled me closer to him with his right hand that was around my shoulder and buried his face on my hair.

"I love you," he murmured.

I lifted my face in surprise. "What?"

"I love you," he repeated firmly and kissed my forehead.

I pressed against him and held on tight. "I love you too, Jacob."

This time I meant it.

14

Tango Nuptial

Part I

There is only one thing more wonderful than the Christmas season: to be in love, happy in a new relationship and to look forward to the first Christmas together. Even the less wonderful side of the season, namely the crazy year-end transactions dictating our work life, couldn't spoil this. In spite of my workload preventing me from being able to enjoy my Christmas shopping in peace and quiet, I was in a festive mood for the season of love and giving. Therefore vulnerable!

Tracey noticed the change in me. She must have observed me during a conference call, that we had with Luke Miller and his team of Francobank. Jacob had walked past the glass door of her office and grinned at me. I had grinned back. After the call was over she looked at me knowingly with her cold blue eyes.

"I must say, Chloé, you seem so much better than the summer, when your boyfriend broke up with you." She gave her voice a tone that I readily interpreted as kind interest.

"Uhm. Actually, yes. I am," I replied hesitantly. Then I could not help breaking out in a smile. I was, after all, happily in love.

"That might not, by any chance, have something to do with a certain colleague?"

There it was. What was I supposed to do? Lie to her? The official firm policy allowed relationships between colleagues of the same level of seniority—see David and Jessica—which did make sense. If you spend so much time in the office it automatically becomes a type of hunting ground. As long as the relationship worked, it could even be good for the firm when the couple worked in the same office so that both would have an additional reason to spend more time in the office and less distractions outside of it. The practical consequences could be very different. I wasn't sure how Tracey would react. On the other hand even though things between Jacob and me were fairly fresh, they had become serious. In addition, we had known each other for years.

Tracey didn't wait for my reply. "I had noticed that Jacob and you were very close at the office outing," she pressed on. She leaned forward. She had this conspiratorial *come on you can tell me* look.

I felt unable to lie. "Well, actually, we have been together since then. We're getting on very well, and so do our children." I don't know why but somehow I hoped that a relationship with a good and loyal P&W man would finally make Tracey welcome me as one of them. Or to congratulate me that P&W was now effectively present in every minute of my private life.

Instead a triumphant smile escaped her. "I knew it."

Then she changed the subject and gave me a long list of to do's regarding the Francobank transaction, which I was to complete by the end of the day.

"Don't forget, we have to be tough on these points we just discussed with Luke," she reminded me.

I left her office a little confused but relieved.

On the way to my room I stopped at Jacob's door and cleared my throat demonstratively. He looked up with a furrowed brow, then smiled when he saw who it was.

"Just quickly," I whispered. "Tracey knows about us."

He immediately made a worried face. "You told her? Chloé, that wasn't really a good idea. You don't know what she will make of it. You do have to watch out with her."

"She asked me a direct question! I could hardly lie to her face," I defended myself. "Anyway—she doesn't seem to mind, and why should she."

He didn't seem convinced. "Well, now it's too late anyway." He shook his head.

I was annoyed. Did he not want things to be made official? I murmured "whatever!" and left before he could notice my annoyance.

I didn't get to think about it any further for the remainder of the day since I was drowning in work. When I had circulated, by email, the newly revised draft agreement which contained all of the points we had discussed earlier with Luke, my counterpart at Lakes Solicitors, an English lawyer I hadn't come across before, wrote an almost instant reply.

From: Paul.Johnson@lakes.com
To: Chloe.Krakowski@prattwonkey.com
Cc: Tracey.Taylor@prattwonkey.com; Luke.Miller@francobank.com; Peter.Jonas@worldpropertiesfund.com
Re: WPF

Chloé,
We have received the revised draft. The undertakings are unacceptable. Furthermore, WPF will not bear any tax risk or risk of increased costs.

Paul

What? I was flabbergasted. The borrower's undertakings in the agreement were to some extent negotiable. They could be drafted in a way that would make it easier for the borrower to be able to fulfil its obligations. No lender would ever take any risk of taxes resulting from a deal, or of costs imposed by banking regulators who decided that this sort of transaction would require an increase in the bank's capital or payment by the bank of any special fees. For the borrower to take the risk of taxes or so-called increased costs was absolute market standard and had already been agreed upon by WPF in the signed term sheet. Disputing this meant going back to square one. I decided to call this Paul to find out where this all came from. When his assistant informed me that he was not available, I left a message asking to be called back. Instead of returning my call he sent a further email.

From: Paul.Johnson@lakes.com
To: Chloe.Krakowski@prattwonkey.com
Cc: Tracey.Taylor@prattwonkey.com; Luke.Miller@francobank.com; Peter.Jonas@worldpropertiesfund.com
Re: Re: WPF

Chloé,
Just to make sure you understand - Francobank's cost of doing business, and any risks associated with the transaction, should have been priced in. This has nothing to do with WPF.

Paul

This was ludicrous, in particular considering that the fees Francobank was going to make on this deal were considerably low. Remindful of Tracey's instructions I decided against my instincts and usually diplomatic style to write a tough reply.

From: Chloe.Krakowski@prattwonkey.com
To: Paul.Johnson@lakes.com
Cc: Tracey.Taylor@prattwonkey.com; Luke.Miller@francobank.com; Peter.Jonas@worldpropertiesfund.com
Re: Re: Re: WPF

Paul,
Surely this cannot be right. I tried to call you to discuss but was told you are not available. I suggest we talk this through before exchanging further emails.

Chloé

I pressed 'send', feeling slightly uneasy. However, this was the sort of email I had seen from others, including the P&W partners.

Two minutes later my phone rang. Tracey. "I don't believe you just wrote that. What on earth were you thinking?" she hissed without further ado.

I could feel my head getting all hot and my stomach churning. "His arguments were ludicrous and you told me to be tough on these points," I replied feebly.

"I don't know how you could get that idea! Luke just called me and went ballistic. This is a really important deal for him! He does not want you to work on this anymore. I will take over. Send me all drafts and make sure the virtual file is up to date." She hung up.

I stared at the receiver. This had never happened to me before. *Fuckfuckfuck.*

Tears started to run down my cheeks. I quickly tried to dry them. Damage control, Chloé. Maybe Tracey would realise that I had not done anything terrible. I checked the virtual file. It was up to date. I quickly printed out the last draft agreement, filed it in my working folder and called Jerome to print out all drafts for Tracey. Checking my watch, I realised it was 7 p.m. already. I could hear Jacob on the phone next door. He was angry with me too, so no sympathy was to be expected from him. I switched off my computer, grabbed my bag and coat and left the office, taking the direction that did not lead past Jacob's door.

On my way home I called the only person who always understood me.

Isabella answered immediately. "Unbelievable—I was just about to dial your number!"

"Oh—everything alright? I just had a shitty day. But you go first."

"No, sweetie, you sound very down. What happened?"

I quickly filled Isabella in.

"Oh dear, that was bound to happen sooner or later. She has been trying to get at you, hasn't she?"

"I guess so. I am so angry with myself! I went against my instincts and stepped right into her trap!"

"Maybe it wasn't a trap. But who knows."

"I'm so tired, Isabella! So tired of being scared of her, of constantly having to watch my back, of all this hostility and duplicity."

"Can't you get a job elsewhere?"

"Not that easy at such a senior level and, somehow, I feel I shouldn't allow her to push me out."

"Hm. Perhaps it's better than being unhappy."

"Yes I know. Anyway. Why were you going to call me?"

"I don't think now is the right time to tell you."

"To tell me what? You know you can't just say that and then tell me nothing."

"OK, then. We are moving to Berlin."

"What? Why? What about the shop? What about us? When?"

"Darling, don't be upset. Please. As you know Joe has been going to Berlin a lot for business and now he's got a project for which he needs to be there full time. As far as the shop is concerned, my assistant Sylvie will look after that. If it goes well maybe she'll take it over. In Berlin I can do what I've always wanted to, Chloé—design jewellery. You know I've had individual pieces made after my design and now I have found a goldsmith in Berlin to assist me. Joe has rented a small apartment near the park. We are moving after Christmas."

"So soon? I mean, sorry, it all sounds exciting and I am happy for you if you are. It's just that it's far away and, oh what am I going to do without you?"

"You'll visit. You'll see, Berlin is the place to be now—it's exciting, new, free—I love it!"

"Of course I will come to see you. Still, I'll miss you so much."

"I'll miss you too, sweetheart. You've got Jacob, and his boy, now, as well as the girls of course. I also think you'll be very busy soon, planning your wedding." She chuckled.

"What? You think so? I mean—Jacob mentioned it already and he had sounded quite serious. Oh my god! Maybe he'll propose this Christmas! Or New Year's Eve! It's a bit soon, but why not?"

"Darling, I've told you before, you are supersonic, so why not indeed!"

Somehow things didn't look so grim anymore.

~

The positive aspect of having been taken off the Francobank deal was that I had time, in the last days before Christmas, to buy presents in actual shops and not all online, to decorate the house and the Christmas tree and to bake cakes and cookies with the girls. On the eve of my birthday, Jacob, Antonio, the girls and I had watched *Mamma Mia* on DVD, singing and dancing on and around the sofa. After having taken our respective children to bed—I had turned the spare room into a guestroom for Antonio—Jacob and I reconvened in the living room.

"Phew! I am exhausted from all that dancing!" I complained. "I must be getting old!"

Jacob checked his watch. "Not old, but a year older soon! It's almost midnight." He smiled nervously. I waited.

"Uhm. Would you mind if I gave you your present tonight? I don't think I can wait any longer—I want to see whether you'll like it."

I tensed slightly. That sounded mysterious. *Omigod.* Maybe he was going to ask me? What will I say? I smiled encouragingly.

"Of course! If you want to—that's very sweet of you."

He checked his watch again.

"It's midnight. Happy Birthday, darling."

He bent towards me and kissed me tenderly, trembling slightly. My heart started beating fast. Was this the moment? He let go of me, reached behind the sofa and pulled out a large square package. I breathed a secret sigh of relief. That was too large to be a ring. I opened the blue bow and then the wrapping paper. It was a fifty-by-fifty centimetre, framed black-and-white print on canvas of the selfie we had taken in Rome in front of the Trevi fountain.

"Oh wow! What a fantastic idea! And so romantic!" I exclaimed.

Jacob beamed at me proudly. "You like it?"

"Of course I do! That is the sweetest, most original birthday present ever! Thank you so much!" I kissed him tenderly. I really did like it. I was relieved because I would have been a bit disappointed to get a proposal on my sofa. I pictured something more romantic, a special occasion. Anyway, there would be still plenty of opportunities.

Christmas came and went, Jacob having gone a step further and given me something perfect wrapped in blue: a platinum necklace with a diamond cross from Tiffany's, nearly identical to the one I had lost a few months earlier. "I was so touched I wept a little," I told Patricia when she came to see me at home, on the Saturday afternoon just after New Year, to pick up Lucas from his play date with Marie.

She examined the little cross. "How sweet of him to remember! I am impressed—this must have cost him well over a thousand Euros. He certainly seems very generous."

"He is! It's a nice change to be with a man who is willing and able to buy nice presents."

"Hugo was generous! He just didn't have the same means as Jacob has," Patricia reminded me. "I miss Hugo. He was fun," she added solemnly.

I shrugged. "I know you two got on well. You still see him, right?"

"Once in a while at parties. So where is this boyfriend of yours?"

"He's on his way over. Ah—talk of the devil!" I heard the key in the door.

"He's got a key already?" Patricia hissed.

"Hi darling, we are in the kitchen!" I shouted out to Jacob and frowned at Patricia. He entered the kitchen, holding two plastic bags from the supermarket. "Jacob, this is Patricia—Michael Stone's wife," I introduced her.

"Hello," Patricia smiled coyly. Jacob put the bags on the floor and shook her hand.

"Patricia! Very nice to meet you! Chloé has told me all about you."

"Has she now?" Patricia raised her eyebrows at me. I squinted and shook my head slightly as if to say *don't worry.*

Jacob put his arms around me. "Sure. Chloé has no secrets from me." He placed a kiss on my forehead.

"Uhm, 'course not," I replied vaguely, still signalling Patricia with my eyes. "So uhm, darling, have you been shopping?"

"Yes. I stopped at the supermarket on the way here. I got a fresh duck, dumpling mix, vegetables and chocolate gateau. I'm going to do a roast duck for lunch now."

"You are going to make lunch, now? It's three o'clock! We have had lunch already and I had planned for the girls to make their own pizza this evening," I objected.

"So? I'm hungry now," he stated and started to unpack the bags.

"A man who can cook and buys lovely gifts! Very impressive," Patricia said.

"You have seen the necklace? Ah, that's just a small gift. Chloé is such a good little woman. There is plenty more where that came from."

"Hm! That's nice. Anyway. I've got to get back home to my lord and master." Patricia shot me a glance. "Lovely to meet you, Jacob."

He smiled at her. "Come over any time."

"I'll see you out," I said to Patricia.

"Thanks. Lucas!" She shouted into the hallway. "We're going!" Lucas shuffled out of Marie's room, dragging his jacket behind him. As he put on his shoes, Patricia hugged me. "See you soon, perhaps for lunch?"

"That would be great. Tracey took me off this deal so I'm not too busy at the moment."

"Fine. I'll call you on Monday."

"Are you alright, Patricia? You seemed a bit off just now."

"Sure, sweetie. As long as you're alright."

"Jacob can give a bit of a false impression but he is a really nice guy."

"I'm sure he is, Chloé." She kissed me good-bye and left with Lucas. I went back into the kitchen where Jacob was already busy with several pots and pans. I watched him for a moment until he noticed me.

"Darling, you haven't yet said hello to me properly—come here, beautiful." He pulled me into his arms, grabbed the back of my neck and kissed me passionately. Oh he was a good kisser. I soon forgot about Patricia's visit.

~

Back in the office, after the Christmas break, Gunther White suggested that Jacob and I should attend an aircraft industry finance conference in Geneva. Luckily I had become quite busy with aircraft finance deals, that he required help with, otherwise it would have been more painful to realise that Tracey continued to ignore me and to load all the work onto Jessica. I was glad with not having to work with Tracey whilst I enjoyed spending time with Jacob and looked forward to our trip to Geneva.

Several weeks later we arrived in the Hotel des Bergues in Geneva. Jacob and I checked into our separate rooms, having ensured that they were adjoining. As I was unpacking, I heard a light knock on my door and went to open it.

"I just checked the conference schedule. We don't really have to be there before 6 p.m. for the cocktail reception. What do you say I take you for lunch?" Jacob suggested.

"Good idea! Just give me a few minutes. I know a lovely little restaurant near the Rue du Rhône. We can walk—the weather is glorious and it's actually not that cold."

"Isn't that where the designer shops are?"

"Yes, why?"

"Well, because I was thinking I may have a look at watches. They may be cheaper in Switzerland, and they are tax free."

"Right. Maybe. I don't really know anything about watches."

"You know, for example Omega—the James Bond watch." He did that Godfather voice again.

I laughed. "Of course—what else! Sure, if you want. Maybe after lunch if we have time."

We walked across the Pont des Bergues, across the Place du Rhône and found the little bistro on the Place de la Fusterie. Once we were shown to a table by the window, where we could have a view of the square, Jacob ordered two glasses of champagne.

"Champagne?" I enquired.

"Why not? I feel like celebrating," he declared.

"Celebrating what?"

"You and me, and everything."

I smiled. "That's sweet. Actually, I don't ever need a reason to drink champagne."

Lunch was rather uneventful because we were both busy on our blackberrys and just interrupted typing or reading once in a while to take a bite of the delicious food or a sip of the champagne.

After lunch we left the square and turned right into the Rue du Rhône. I spotted the Omega shop on the left, as well as Louis Vuitton next to it. I said nothing at all as we stepped inside Omega and were greeted enthusiastically by an attractive female sales assistant. Jacob asked to see a selection of the *Seamaster* range. When she returned with a tray on which three watches were displayed, he tried each of them on whilst negotiating a discount. Then he turned to me.

"What do you think? I mean—it's a lot of money. I have never spent that much on a watch, but it's tax free—and she is giving me some extras."

"You deserve it, darling. You make good money but you don't really spend any—I think you should buy it."

"You are probably right." He inhaled deeply. He signalled to the sales assistant, who had stepped away discreetly, and nodded his agreement.

When we left the shop, Jacob proudly holding a little Omega bag containing his old watch, the new one gleaming on his wrist, he hesitated. "And now?"

I automatically turned my head to the left towards the Louis Vuitton store. He followed my movement, misread it and grinned. "Now what a coincidence—there is Cartier! Well, let's go."

I held my breath in surprise. "Really?"

"Yes." He took my arm and led me to the boutique. I hardly noticed the window display at Louis Vuitton when we passed by. The doorman at Cartier greeted us cheerfully when he opened the door.

"*Bonjour madame, monsieur. Est-ce que je peux vous aider*?" An elegant lady approached us inside.

"Hello. Yes. We would like to look at engagement rings." Jacob stated resolutely.

My jaw dropped. I turned to stare at him. He smiled nonchalantly and ignored me.

"Of course, with pleasure! May I say congratulations?" The lady beamed at us enthusiastically.

"Not quite yet," Jacob replied smugly.

She led us to a small desk and asked us to take a seat while she left to get a selection of diamond rings. I was too stunned to say anything. Jacob just sat there and grinned.

She returned with a small black velvet tray containing three solitaire rings and held it out to me.

"Oooh. They are gorgeous." I carefully touched the biggest one in awe.

"Why don't you try these on for size? Then I can bring you more," the sales assistant suggested.

I slowly put one of the rings on my right ring finger. Jacob picked up the ring with the largest stone and looked at the small price tag. He gave a slight cough. "Forty thousand—that is a little outside my price range," he explained to her with a charming smile.

"*Pas de problème*!" She replied with enthusiasm as if he had just said the opposite. "How is the size?" she asked me.

"This one is good. But can I ask—do you have the ring with the double C?" I remembered the beautiful (and not so expensive) ring I had seen with Patricia in the Frankfurt Cartier boutique.

"Ah, *oui*! I will get it for you." She got up, walked to a cabinet, took out a ring with her gloved hand and came back, placing the ring on the tray sitting on the table.

It was not the one I had seen before. This one was larger, rounder, in shiny white gold, had more diamonds and was just perfect—not a ring I would buy for myself but also not a typical boring solitaire engagement ring. I put it on my finger and stretched out my hand. It fitted perfectly. I looked at Jacob and smiled at him. He smiled back at me.

"How much is it?" he asked her.

"In Euro—I think about five thousand seven hundred but I can check," she replied.

"We'll take it."

"*Fantastique*! I will prepare everything and my colleague will bring you some champagne in the meantime!" She took the ring from me, discreetly accepted the credit card Jacob handed to her and walked away to the back room.

"Jacob, are you sure? I mean—I didn't think you would actually buy something. I thought we were just looking!" I exclaimed truthfully.

He laughed and slightly shook his wrist with the new Omega watch. "I am obviously having an uncharacteristic fit of generosity, but yes. I am sure. Actually, I have never been more sure about something."

Tears of joy welled up in my eyes. I swallowed hard and gratefully accepted the glass of champagne the sales assistant offered us. For once I was speechless.

That evening and the entire next day at the conference was a blur. I took part in meetings, sat in conference rooms listening to other people and even gave a talk myself. Jacob was in the first row of the audience, beaming with pride and all I could think of was: he bought a ring. An engagement ring! For me!!! I felt so elated, I wasn't even pondering on when he would give it to me, and what that would entail—a marriage proposal. If I was a man, I'd be terrified to do that. Not so much because of what it means, more because you only have one moment to get it right, to say the right words, not to sound corny, to do it in a dignified, romantic but not cringe-worthy way.

On our last morning in Geneva we decided to skip the final sessions of the conference and instead have breakfast in bed in my hotel room.

"This is such luxury—croissants in bed with you, no kids, no office!" I stretched my arms joyfully.

"Actually, we've made a bit of a mess—and you've got some crumbs in the corner of your mouth—wait." Jacob leaned over and tenderly kissed the crumbs off my lips. "There you go, now that's better." He contemplated me for a moment. "Uhm. I think I'm going to go to my room to take a shower—do you mind? I'll be back soon."

I suspected he wanted to go to the toilet discreetly. "Of course not, I'll get up soon as well." When he had closed the door behind him I snuggled into the duvet and decided to have another little snooze before getting up to prepare for our departure. I must have dozed off because the next thing I heard was Jacob's voice.

"Chloé, darling, are you asleep?"

"Mhmm. Five minutes more please," I mumbled, leaving my eyes closed.

He stroked my hair. "Darling, do you want to be my wife?"

"Of course—what?" I tore my eyes open.

He was lying next to me in his bathrobe, his hair still wet from the shower, and holding the red Cartier box in his hand. The lid was open, the ring sparkling inside. I jumped up.

"Oh my god! Yes! Yes, of course!" I hugged him, laughing happily.

He chuckled. "Well then let me put the ring on your finger." He took it out of the box and carefully slid it over my right ring finger. I stretched out my hand and admired it.

"It's so beautiful, Jacob! It's the most beautiful and valuable thing anyone has ever given to me."

"And it is so you. I'm very happy."

"And I'm going to make you even happier!" I exclaimed and threw myself at him so that he lost balance. We kissed and I fumbled with the belt of his robe, desperate to make love to my future husband. I finally felt I could let down all my defences, allow myself to be protected and guided by him, the man to whom I belonged. Within minutes I felt like a train was slowly approaching inside my body, starting at my feet and then driving with an explosion through my brain.

~

At Geneva airport we had some time to spend before we could board the plane. Jacob took out his blackberry and scrolled through it.

"Darling, can you not put that thing away for once?" I asked.

"Honey, I am looking at dates."

"At dates? For what?"

"Uhm—for our wedding? Remember? This morning?" He held up my right hand with the sparkling diamond ring.

"Uh, yeah, but already? I'm just trying to get over the fact that I am actually engaged!"

"Haha, very funny. Now look—I thought that last weekend in June would be perfect because that's when the school holidays start and then we can go on a family honeymoon with the kids."

I took out my diary and checked the dates.

"A filofax? I thought nobody uses these anymore," Jacob remarked with amusement.

"It's not a filofax! It's a Louis Vuitton *agenda* with a filofax calendar inside!" I corrected him. "Anyway! That weekend is less than four months' away!"

"Chloé. You and I have done zillions of transaction closings before—this will be like another one, getting all the required documents and papers and things organised!"

I laughed. "OK, persuaded. Sounds feasible but you'll have to take the lead on the paperwork so I can concentrate on the fun stuff like dresses and make-up."

"Done!" He grinned with satisfaction. "I can't wait for you to be my wife. We'll be *the* power couple."

"Ahem, yes. Now I better tell my bridesmaids—Isabella and Patricia."

"We'll tell the kids together when we pick them up at Jasmin's." Jasmin was Jacob's ex-wife and Antonio's mother. Their marriage had only lasted a couple of years. Shortly after their separation she met Martin whom she married, immediately after the divorce from Jacob had been finalised. Jasmin and Jacob were on good terms. Jacob was often at their house, not just to see Antonio but also to coo over the little daughter Jasmin and Martin had together. He had taken the girls and me there on several afternoons.

"Perhaps I should tell the girls separately when we are back in our own home?"

He frowned. "We're all effectively a family already anyway, so what's the problem?"

"I don't want to put them on the spot. They might feel pressured or confused."

"You should give Jasmin some credit. After all she has had a couple of days to bond with them."

"I guess." Jasmin adored my girls. In the absence of any alternative childcare, I had accepted her offer to look after them whilst Jacob and I were in Geneva. I was curious to see how she would react to the news. She was cool and I liked her but you never really knew.

I picked up my mobile and texted Isabella and Patricia.

> Big news from Geneva - Jacob proposed! Planning a summer wedding on June 21! Save the date! C. xx

Isabella's reply was instant.

> Congratulations! So excited! Promise you go wedding dress shopping with me!!! xxx

Patricia followed.

> Wow - That's quick! Don't think I can be there - I'm invited to go to the South of France with a friend, leaving that day. P xxx

I couldn't believe she really meant that.

> Can you not leave one day later? It's my wedding and I need you to be there 😊

Apparently she did.

> Then I may not be able to go at all. Sorry!!

I knew Patricia had liked Hugo a lot and had not yet met Jacob properly but I had counted on her support. Well, I wasn't going to let my big day be spoiled by anybody. I sent a message to Alexia who texted me back straightaway.

> I am so happy for you Chloé! Of course we will be there!!

I was touched. I reminded myself that the two people who had been there for me most when Hugo left were Isabella and Alexia. So I replied.

> Thank you! Will you be my bridesmaid??

Her reply was instant.

> Yes! And I will organise a hen night for you that you will not forget! 😉

I closed my phone with a satisfied smile.

~

"Hello you two! Welcome back!" Jasmin greeted us, holding the door open.

"Mummy, Mummy!" Marie and Noëlle jumped up from the sofa and ran towards me when I entered the open living area. A board game was spread out on the coffee table, which Antonio and Martin were bent over and now looked up from. Some cartoon was showing on TV in the background. Antonio's little sister was standing up in her playpen and rattling at the bar so that her mother would pick her up again.

"Mhmm, I've missed you!" I kneeled down, hugging them both at the same time and burying my face in their hair.

"So, how was the conference? How was Geneva? You're probably exhausted. Do you want coffee?" Martin got up and made space for Jacob to sit next to his son.

"Come here, my little Antonino!" Jacob gave Antonio a cuddle.

"Get off, Daddy!" Antonio giggled, pretending not to like it—that was their ritual.

"Actually, we had a great time," Jacob answered Martin's question. "Girls, Antonio, we have something we want to tell you."

I took the girls by the hand and led them to the sofa. Jacob winked at me encouragingly. He took Marie on his lap, one arm still around Antonio. I sat on the edge of the coffee table, hugging Noëlle from behind. We waited and I looked at Jacob, who drew a deep breath.

"So—I have asked your mum to marry me. Is that OK with you, girls?"

"And is that ok with you?" I held my hand out to Antonio.

Antonio took it and beamed. "Yeah! That's really cool!"

The girls nodded. "Okay," little Marie said.

"We'll be a real family?" Noëlle asked hopefully.

"Yes, a real family," Jacob replied.

"Oh my god! That's wonderful! Congratulations!" Jasmin had been watching us discreetly from the back of the room. She came over and hugged me, and then Jacob. She seemed genuinely pleased.

"Excellent! Congratulations! No coffee then, I gather—I'll get some champagne!" Martin declared and disappeared into the kitchen, returning shortly thereafter holding a tray with four glasses and a bottle of champagne. He placed the tray on the dining table and opened the cork with a loud pop.

"Just as well we haven't opened that yet—It's as if we had known we would need it for a special occasion!" Jasmin joked. "Now, Chloé. Did Jacob you get a ring?"

"Yes—here it is! It's from Cartier." I proudly held out my right hand.

She took me aside and examined the ring. "That's gorgeous!"

"You know, I never got such a nice engagement ring from Jacob. He was, of course, a poor student then!" She winked at me with a smile. "However, I would have bet on him still being too stingy to spend that much money on a ring! Chloé, I really think you have cracked Jacob. I have never seen him so happy and relaxed and nice!"

"But he is nice!"

"Yes, of course he's a nice guy! But, as long as I have known him, he has always found it hard to show his true feelings. You seem to have brought out his soft side."

"I hope so. I know what you mean, and that's certainly the Jacob as I knew him, before we got together—cracking sarcastic jokes, holding people at a distance, but he is lovely with me. He seems to love me just the way I am. I hope you don't mind me saying that."

"Oh no, no! Please don't misunderstand me! I'm glad we're not together anymore! It was a disaster, for both of us! I am very happy with Martin of course." She squeezed my arm in a reassuring manner.

I was relieved. I looked over at my fiancé, huddled with all three children and talking and laughing with them. I knew it was the right thing to do.

~

When I entered the office, the next Monday, I felt as if my right hand had doubled in size and the ring was screaming *look at me*! I was able to contain myself for a few hours then went to see Jessica in her office. She looked up from her papers with panic in her face when I opened the door.

"Oh thank god it's only you, Chloé." She breathed a sigh of relief. "I thought it would be Dolores—she's on my back to get this out at lunchtime." She pointed at the pages strewn over her desk.

I giggled as she was referring to the nickname she had given Tracey. "In that case I'll come back later."

"No, no—it's fine. I'm nearly done. So how was Geneva?"

I grinned and approached her desk, holding out my right hand. She understood immediately.

"Ooooh wow, Chloé! Jacob proposed?" she exclaimed enthusiastically.

I nodded. "Yes. We got this at Cartier in Geneva. It was quite spontaneous."

"That's so lovely! I am so happy for you!" She jumped up from her chair and hugged me.

"What's going on?" Tracey stood in the door, frowning.

"Chloé and Jacob got engaged, isn't that great?" Jessica announced gaily.

Tracey looked at my hand. Her face took on a crimson colour. "Really? Are you quite sure?"

"Uhm—yes?" I was confused.

"I see. Well, if you are sure. Congratulations."

"Thank you, Tracey," I replied nicely. Not even Tracey could spoil my happy mood. Then I noticed her shoes. They were light green pumps with green piping and a little green bow. They looked quirky but quite cool. "These are very nice shoes!"

She looked down at her feet. "Ah, yes." She raised her eyebrows with a slight smile. "I thought you might like them." She turned to Jessica. "Jessica, I need this CP confirmation letter now. Send it to me. Thanks." She turned and left the room.

Jessica rolled her eyes. She motioned me to stay. "Wait, I need to tell you something," she hissed. "I just want to send this letter to her."

I sat down on her visitor's chair and watched her. She typed on her keyboard, clicked the mouse a few times and then turned to me. "This is confidential info—I've got it from David who's got it from Francis Mayer. Apparently Tracey has extended her secondment contract!"

"What? For how long?"

"I don't know but secondments are normally for a period of two years."

"Oh no! That's not good. Unless she'd promote me nonetheless however, I'm afraid, as long as she is here, my career prospects are zilch." I put my head in my hands.

"Maybe you'll have to suck up to her more," Jessica suggested. "Like that compliment you just made her—that was a good start."

"I actually meant what I said to her—those shoes are nice. I cannot pretend. That's just not me."

"Recently she has become a bit friendlier. She has been wearing some nicer clothes. I always felt she was jealous of you, your figure and your style. Maybe you have inspired her and she is making an effort now. Give her a chance."

"You're right. I don't really have a choice anyway. I know what I'll do—I'll invite her to our wedding. You and David will come of course, won't you?"

Jessica smiled. "Certainly! I cannot wait to see your dress! What are you going to wear?"

"Ah, now you're talking! I have a few ideas, but I've not decided yet. It'll be a surprise!"

"In that case, will you help me to go shopping for my wedding guest outfit?"

"Absolutely!"

Jessica's phone interrupted us.

"Oops! There's the she-devil again!" Jessica laughed and picked up the receiver.

I got up from the chair and waved goodbye, then left her office, closing the door behind me.

I envied Jessica for being so thick skinned and for her apparent ability to take Tracey with a big pinch of salt and a lot of North American humour. I would have to make an enormous effort to be that way. On the other hand, it was a different situation. Tracey didn't feel threatened by Jessica, who was so much more her junior, eager to please and ambitious to start climbing the career ladder.

I would not only have to make an enormous effort, I would have to change.

Part II

I was in the land of my dreams. Every bride knows how stressful it can be to organise a wedding, and even more so with only four months to go to the big day, but, in my case, I had received excellent training—if I could organise a closing, within several weeks, for a real estate finance transaction involving one hundred properties and multiple borrowers, I should be able to do this with my eyes closed.

Jacob and I very quickly settled on the location, a big country hotel outside the city with lovely gardens. The guest list comprised no more than eighty people—a mixture of nationalities and professions (not all lawyers!). Jacob chose the menu and the wines whilst I had decided on blue hydrangeas as a flower decoration. We planned a civil ceremony in one of the festive rooms in the morning, followed by a reception with piano music, champagne and a small lunch buffet in the adjoining hall of mirrors, which boasted a huge balcony. The evening festivities would start with a drinks reception at 7 p.m. before the black tie dinner, followed by a dance with a D.J. and drinks from a cocktail bar. The children and their little guests would be looked after by two nannies in the adjoining room and would have a special kids' buffet and plenty of games and other entertainment.

But the biggest pleasure was choosing my outfits. Yes! I planned on more than one. One for the bachelorette night, one for the wedding ceremony and reception, one for the evening black tie dinner and one for the dancing after dinner. Not to forget one for the wedding night and one for brunch on the morning after.

Isabella, who was the only person privy to my plan, came over from Berlin to open her shop exclusively for me one Sunday. The girls would be at home with Jacob and Antonio. I would have several hours to myself. Or so I had planned.

As I was about to leave, Jacob and I were standing by the front door when the doorbell rang. An elderly couple stood outside.

"*Mama, tata*!" Jacob exclaimed. "*Co niespodzianka*!"

"*Mój chłopcze*! My boy!" Jacob's mother shouted and spread her arms wide, smacking kisses on his cheeks.

"We are sorry to barge in on you like this. We have just been to see your brother and decided to surprise you. Lucas also gave us Chloé's address," Jacob's father explained.

"That would be me," I said. "So nice to meet you both, Mrs. and Mr. Wronski! Please come in."

"Oh please call me Józef and this is Martha."

"Hello Chloé!" Martha hugged me warmly. "Lucas was right—you are very beautiful!"

"Why, thank you! I am so glad you came over. I know we have spoken on the phone before but meeting you in person has been long overdue."

"Well, as Jacob may have told you, we enjoy our retirement. So we are always on the road to see old friends. Today we spontaneously decided to come and see our sons; I hope you don't mind," Józef said.

"Of course not, on the contrary! You can meet my girls as well—and of course your grandson is here, too. Ah, there they are."

Antonio came running down the hallway, the girls following behind him. "Grandma! Grandpa!"

"Oh, come here my darling!" Martha showered him with kisses. "And who are these lovely young ladies?"

"This is Noëlle—she is nearly ten, and this is Marie who will be seven next month."

"What beautiful names! Aren't you two precious!"

"Ma, Pa—what can we offer you? Shall I make some coffee? We could get some cake from the bakery," Jacob said.

"Uhm, Jacob. You know I need to go," I reminded him. "I'm so sorry, Martha and Józef. I was actually about to leave the house, I have a special appointment to look at wedding dresses with my friend who owns this boutique. I would reschedule but she's only here today."

"Oh, don't worry, I understand," Martha said.

"Hang on—I have an idea. Why don't you take my mother with you?" Jacob suggested.

"What on earth for?" Martha asked.

"To get you a nice dress for the wedding!"

"Your mother doesn't need a dress," Józef objected.

"I really don't, darling," she confirmed. "I have this blue one I wore at your grandma's eightieth."

"Ma. You're not going to wear some old dress at my wedding. It's my treat," he added quickly.

"Ah, in that case, Martha, you should go," Józef said jovially.

I had followed this entire exchange. "Of course, Martha. Please, do come along!"

"I guess—if it is ok with you and your friend—I don't want to intrude."

"It's not a problem at all! I'll just quickly call her and let her know." I went into my bedroom to call Isabella.

"Darling, what's the matter? Everything alright? I'm waiting for you." Isabella said when she had picked up the phone. I quickly described the circumstances.

"Sure! She can come, too. I think it's nice, Chloé! This is an opportunity to bond with your future mother-in-law, I already have some ideas for her outfit. Very classy and elegant."

"You're a star. I must tell you though she is a little round," I said without thinking.

"So? Not every woman can be like a size zero! I actually don't know many women who have your figure and who aren't actresses or models. I'm also of average womanly shape and height and I still find nice clothes."

"I didn't mean it that way, and I'm not a size zero either and I would not want to be! Anyway. I'm sorry, I just wanted to prepare you."

"OK, fine. I'll see you soon, sweetie."

Phew. That was close. Isabella was my best friend. The last thing I wanted was to upset her.

"Did you speak to Isabella?" Jacob had come into the room.

"Yes. She'd be delighted to meet your Mum. I think it's really sweet that you want to buy her a dress, Jacob."

"The wedding will be glamorous, the guests will be well-dressed. I want my mother to feel comfortable and to look the part."

"I'll help her find something. What sort of budget do we have, Jacob? You know designer clothes come at a price. She will need an outfit for the day and an evening gown, perhaps some accessories. I'd say around two thousand?"

He ran his fingers through his hair. "Two thousand Euros? Wow. That's a lot of money. But—it's my mother. She deserves the best. OK. Fine."

"Good. We'll be off then—we'll probably be back in about two hours."

"Take your time."

A short drive later Martha and I arrived at Isabella's store. As it was a Sunday we were able to park right in front of it.

"Ooh! That looks very elegant," Martha remarked when she got out of the car and saw the window display. "And expensive."

"Don't worry. Your son has given me a generous budget for you," I appeased her and led her to the door. Isabella had spotted us, came to unlock the door and invited us in.

"Hello! You must be Jacob's mother! Lovely to meet you. I'm Isabella Moyer. I have already laid out some outfits for you."

Martha blushed. "You two are so kind. I never go clothes shopping, let alone in such an exclusive boutique!"

"In that case, I'll make sure you'll have a memorable afternoon," Isabella replied. "The champagne is cold, I've got some nibbles and you can try anything you want!"

She led us to the seating area and poured some champagne. "Please. Enjoy," she handed each of us a glass. "Now then, Mrs. Wronski, if you would like to start with trying on the dresses hanging next to the changing room—I believe I may have gotten the size right but let me know if I haven't."

Martha took another sip from her glass and walked over to the clothes rack Isabella had pointed at. She carefully took the silky material of one of the dresses between her fingers, sighed and then looked at the price tag. "Oh! This is eight hundred Euros! No, no! That is too much money! I have never spent more than eighty Euros on a dress!"

"Martha, please. Just try them on. Jacob insisted," I urged her.

"Of course you will get a discount here," Isabella said.

"Oh. I see. I guess I can try them." She placed the glass on the table, took the dress off the rack and held it up. "I will start with this one, then."

"Great!" Isabella said to her. When Martha had disappeared behind the door of the changing room, she turned to me. "How sweet is she? Now. As for you, I have also had a few ideas."

"Actually here are a few outfits I printed out from Net-a-porter," I began as Isabella started looking through her order book. I showed her a white A-line Chloé dress with trumpet sleeves. "That would go with tan Louboutin sandals or peep toes and this huge tan straw hat, see?"

"I like it," Isabella declared, "it's quite low key."

"Indeed! I'm an over forty year old bride, so it's got to be quite low key—yet elegant and fresh. Otherwise I'll look ridiculous."

"You would never look ridiculous!" Isabella laughed. "OK, what else?"

"This is also Chloé, black silk chiffon, not too mini, A-line again, perfect for the dancing. With silver mid-heeled sandals—here like these Jimmy Choo ones."

"Ooh. I love that. Yes! I can order this for you."

"Great. Then I will order some sexy bridal lingerie from Victoria's Secret and I have this white linen Chloé day dress for the breakfast the next day—I got it in the summer sale last year and haven't even worn it yet. Add some flat sandals—that's it!"

"Hm. Yes, I love it all—but as I said I had some ideas too." Isabella disappeared into the back room and returned, grinning mischievously and holding up two suit covers. One was black and had the letters *GV* printed on it and the other was white and read *Alexander McQueen*.

She hung the white cover on a rack and carefully opened the black cover by slowly pulling the zipper downwards. She flapped the cover back, displaying the most gorgeous dress I had ever seen. It was a white, about knee-length, fitted silk bustier dress with a few large black flower heads printed on it.

"Isabella, it is so precious! This looks like haute couture!"

"It's Giambattista Valli prêt-a-porter but yes it's almost like haute couture—nearly two thousand though," she added in a whisper.

"Yeah, please, don't talk about prices in front of my future mother-in-law—you saw how shocked she was! This dress is a dream! Can I try it?"

"Of course—that's what it's here for. I saw it in a magazine on Victoria Beckham—I think she was wearing it going out for dinner with her husband—and I thought: this is you. Glamorous, sexy, not bridal but can be depending on the accessories. Absolutely stunning and unique."

Martha emerged from the changing room. She wore a light blue silk pantsuit that flattered her figure. She stopped in front of the mirror and contemplated herself.

"Martha, you look so elegant—and at least ten years younger!" I said.

"I tried the two day dresses but they were both too small around the bosom and I don't want to show so much of my legs. I do, however, like this," she agreed.

"You could wear a silk scarf with it, like that one here," Isabella said and draped a chiffon scarf around Martha's shoulders. "Also—if you wanted—a hat. Plus medium high heeled pumps and a clutch like this one here." She handed Martha a Lanvin clutch. "It looks younger than a handbag."

"That's beautiful," I agreed.

"Oh, I don't need a handbag. I have another one—it is similar to this, but smaller and beige." She pointed to the black bag she had placed on the floor next to the sofa.

Before I could open my mouth, Isabella shot me a warning glance and said gently: "Beige should be nice. Do you have shoes that would go with this?"

"Yes, I think so. I have a black and a beige pair." Martha turned sideways and looked over her shoulder to get a different view of herself. She nodded with content. "Okay. I'll try on the two evening dresses now."

"Fantastic, and you, Chloé, put this one on," Isabella said.

I accepted the Giambattista Valli dress from Isabella and went to the second changing room to try it on. The many hooks of the boned bodice were not easy to deal with but, eventually, I managed to close a few of them and zipped it up. I stepped out from behind the door to look in the mirror. The person staring back at me seemed only vaguely familiar. I looked like some (minor) Hollywood star.

"Oh my god. It is amazing what clothes can do to you. I feel like a million dollars!"

Isabella grinned and said nothing. I turned around, looking at myself from behind. It was really perfect—simple but elegantly cut, the beautiful fabric letting the dress do the talking. I was not wearing the dress, it wore me—yet it upgraded my entire look.

"There's no doubt about it. The poor white A-line Chloé just got bumped to the hen night. I can't stop looking at myself! This is it!"

Isabella just continued to grin smugly. "I knew it BUT I can top that."

She reached for the white suit cover, held it up and unzipped it slowly. She let the cover fall to the ground and held the hanger a little higher. It was again a bustier dress, but long, with several layers of cream chiffon silk, ruched at the bust and the side, and cascading softly to the ground.

"That's your real wedding dress, Chloé. Actually it's an evening gown, but the colour and style is quite bridal."

"Oh! That is divine! But you know how I feel about being a forty plus bride. I don't want to look ridiculous."

"Try it." She opened the back zipper of the Giambattista Valli dress slightly and handed me the Alexander McQueen gown.

"Oh, Chloé! What a beautiful dress!" Martha emerged from her dressing room just as I was about to disappear back into mine. She was wearing a navy silk flowing evening gown with chiffon sleeves. I hardly recognised her.

"And you, Martha, look like Barbra Streisand!" I said with astonishment.

"She does, doesn't she?" Isabella agreed.

"Now you are exaggerating," Martha replied, blushing but visibly pleased. "It actually fits perfectly, even the top half."

"Jacob will be so thrilled! Now I'm going to put this one on and then we're nearly there, I'd say."

I managed to get out of the Valli dress and put it back on its hanger. Then I carefully slid into the McQueen gown. It was so delicate and ethereal—I wasn't sure whether it was right for me. I stood on my tiptoes as it was very long and opened the door. Martha clasped her hands before her mouth. "*Oj!*"

As I slowly strode towards the mirror, I could feel I was welling up. I turned to Isabella. She nodded smilingly, one tear running down her cheek.

Yes, I was going to be a bride.

~

If there was somebody even more organised than me it was Alexia, who was in charge of my bachelorette night. Two weeks before the wedding I was picked up by a white stretch limo and six ladies: Alexia, her best friend Elena, Isabella, Amelie, Patricia and Sabrina—all gorgeous, dressed up and—except Sabrina—in their fabulous forties. As I got in, they were loudly singing to Beyoncé's *Single Ladies* and pointing at their ring fingers.

"I think you've all had a few already!" I shouted, as somebody handed me a glass of champagne.

"Here this is for you—you've got to wear this!" Elena gave me a white square box decorated with a pink ribbon.

"Oh no—I don't have to do anything silly, do I?"

"Open it!" Amelie nudged me. The others cheered. I undid the ribbon and lifted the lid of the box. There were two things inside: a blue lace garter and a white satin Alice band with rhinestones.

"Aha! I see! OK, there you go. Ta-dada-dadada, ta-dada-dadada, ta-dada-dadada, ta-da-dadah!" Imitating the introductory music of Joe Cocker's *You Can Leave Your Hat on*, I pulled the garter over my right foot and slowly up my leg until I reached my upper thigh. Then I stretched out that leg and rotated my foot, causing the others to wolf-whistle.

Next I placed the Alice band over my long curls and checked my reflection in the small mirror above the bar area of the car.

"Alright, I can agree to wear that! So what's next?"

"It's a surprise! You'll see. You are at our mercy tonight!" Alexia declared mischievously.

It was not long before the limousine stopped and the driver opened the door for us to get out. We went inside Harrys New York Bar where Alexia had organised a table and cocktails. Once we had made ourselves comfortable at the table the first round of Cosmopolitans appeared. "Of course—what else would we order?" was Alexia's self-satisfied comment.

"So, Chloé, what's your wedding dress like?" Sabrina asked. "Is it one of those you saw with me at the shop last year?"

"Ah—no, it's a secret!" Isabella responded in my stead. "All I can tell you is that she has several outfits!"

"Actually, Isabella, I have some accessories planned that not even you know about," I teased her. "Now that I have something blue"—I held up the seam of my dress and pointed to the garter—"all I'm missing is something borrowed."

"Oh, then you'll have to give that back to me afterwards," Alexia said. "I wore it at my wedding, so it's old, too."

"Excellent, agreed! Let's all drink to *something old and something new, something borrowed and something blue*!"

Just as I was ready to order a second round, the pianist spoke into his microphone—"and now I would like to ask Chloé and her friends to come up here."

"What?" I turned around in surprise while the others got up from their chairs as if on cue.

"Come on, Chloé. Don't worry, you know this—*That's what friends are for*!" Alexia appeased me.

We all huddled next to the piano when the music began. I did know this. I smiled at Alexia who started singing the first verse and then we all joined in the refrain. It sort of got a little muddled at the end but nobody seemed to care and the audience whistled and clapped when the song was over.

An attractive young man was waiting by our table when we got back, holding a red rose and looking at me. "Hello Chloé," he greeted me, making a sad face.

"Uhm, do I know you?"

"I wanted to ask you: please don't get married—please go out with me." He handed me the rose with a serious air.

I laughed. "Very funny. I'm afraid it's too late."

"That is such a shame. Okay. Good luck then. Bye." He gave me a kiss on the cheek, turned around and left. I looked at the others who made an effort to keep a straight face.

"Aw, that was so sweet and he was gorgeous!" Elena exclaimed.

I laughed and shook my head. I was about to sit down again, only to be interrupted by another even better looking young man who was holding a red rose.

"Oh Chloé! Please don't get married!" He handed me the rose, grinning.

"Ah yes. OK, I'll think about it," I joked and stuck the rose in the small vase the waitress had brought us in the meantime. He bent towards me and kissed me on the cheek.

"That's wonderful. I hope to see you soon. Bye!"

"Hey! Leave her alone!" A third man appeared, holding a red rose. He was gorgeous—short dark blonde hair, slightly tanned, his muscles bulging under his tight white shirt.

"Oh and who would you be now?" I asked provocatively.

"My name is Justin and you, actually, are really hot. Please don't get married!" He handed me my third red rose and showed his white teeth in a brilliant smile.

"Hm. Now this is getting difficult," I replied with a smirk, "but I will stay firm."

"Can we at least have a drink together? Maybe I can still persuade you." He lowered his voice, trying to sound seductive.

"No, thank you—girls' night only!"

"Shame. Good luck, gorgeous." He kissed me goodbye.

As he left, I sighed and turned to the others. “So? Whose idea was this?”

Alexia giggled. “My sister’s—she knows these guys and organised for them to turn up here and beg you not to get married.”

“How original! I must say the last one was just my type and would’ve been at least good for a flirt.”

“We admire your restraint, Chloé!” Amelie cried.

“Quite! I would have already gone for the first one!” Patricia commented.

“Hm, I thought the second one was really yummy!” Sabrina added.

“Huh! Now all of you! Really, I’m shocked! You’re all married!”

“We can still window shop,” Isabella grinned. “Are you sure you don’t want a last *shopping trip* before you get married?” She winked at me.

“No, thank you. That is absolutely out of the question!” I declared indignantly. “I may have been a bit wild in the past”—this caused roaring laughter—“but I am a faithful fiancée and will be a faithful wife!” I held out my right hand with the Cartier ring, as if to emphasise my words.

“We’ll drink to that!” Alexia held up her glass. “Here’s to Chloé—the faithful wife!”

The others followed suit and we clinked our glasses together. “To Chloé, the faithful wife!”

~

Two weeks later, I woke up in the morning and was disoriented. Sunlight was seeping through plush curtains. I listened. It was quiet. Where was I? The room looked unfamiliar. Then it dawned on me. I was in the hotel, on my own. This was my wedding day! I jumped up and opened the curtains, taking in the stunning view of the park below my window and the skyline in the distance. I walked to the bathroom, passing the wardrobe where my dresses were hanging. I stroked each of them carefully—the Giambattista Valli, the Alexander McQueen, the black Chloé party dress. Then I bent down and looked at the shoes that I had displayed underneath the dresses—dove grey Lanvin satin pumps with sparkling heels for the morning, silver Jimmy Choo sandals for the evening. Now I only had to make myself look worthy of these beautiful clothes. I showered and washed my hair, leaving it to air dry. I called room service and asked for coffee and some croissants in case I was able to eat something. Then I called Jacob at home.

"Hello?"

"Darling, it's me. How are you? How are the girls and Antonio?"

"All is well. Jana is helping them to get dressed."

"Oh, good, and you?"

"I'm a bit tense, to be honest."

"That's normal, isn't it? I'm nervous—and excited! The lady doing my hair and make-up will be here soon."

"I'm sure you will look beautiful. I'll pick you up from the room five minutes before the ceremony, so just before eleven."

"Fine. See you later! I love you!"

"I love you too." He hung up.

I smiled to myself. He did sound tense. I hoped the girls would feel at ease. Their dresses were lovely—two-tone sleeveless linen dresses with bows in the back, which I had ordered online at Bonpoint, a light rose and grey for Noëlle and a baby blue and grey for Marie. Antonio was to wear a navy suit, a blue shirt and a navy striped tie. I had also helped Jacob to choose his navy tailored suit and Hermès tie.

An hour later there was a knock on the door. The stylist had just left, having helped me to close the numerous hooks of the internal bodice of the Valli dress, so I thought she had forgotten something. When I opened the door, Alexia, Elena and Isabella stood outside.

"SURPRISE!"

"Fantastic!" I laughed. "Come in! Actually this is perfect timing—I'm getting quite jittery!"

"Darling, you look gorgeous!" Elena exclaimed.

"Where are the glasses? We brought some champagne!" Alexia held up a bottle of *Moët et Chandon*.

"Ooh, great idea! There, by the mini bar."

"I love the fascinator with the feathers—so flamboyant," Isabella commented on my headdress. "Oh and I adore the shoes—let me look at that heel. So those are your secret accessories!"

Alexia handed out the filled glasses when we discerned another knock on the door.

"I'll go," she announced, walked towards the door and opened it just wide enough to see who was outside.

"Hi Alexia. Is Chloé there?" I heard Jacob's voice. I rushed to the door but hid behind it.

"Jacob! What are you doing here? You are not supposed to see me yet!"

"Sweetheart, I just came to say the ceremony will start about twenty minutes late. A lot of guests aren't here yet because, apparently, there is some traffic jam on the motorway."

"What? But—what about the registrar? Is she here?" I started to feel panic rising.

"Yes, she is and she is happy to wait for a while."

"I don't want to miss our appointment! Are you sure she will wait?"

"Yes, calm down—drink something. I'll pick you up in about half an hour."

After Alexia had closed the door, I took a big gulp from my glass. "I don't like this. I need everything to go according to plan! If we are late for the ceremony, we will be late for the reception and lunch and—oh it's a mess!" I declared desperately.

"Sabrina just texted me." Alexia looked up from her new Iphone. "She says the room is filling and everybody is very relaxed. So sit down and have another drink."

She poured me another glass and it helped. I slowly started to relax and was even able to giggle at Elena's comical rendition of *That's What Friends Are For*. When there was another knock on the door, it seemed to be just five minutes since the first interruption. Now, however, I was in the best of moods and opened the door to Jacob with a brilliant smile.

"Oh my," he smiled back. "You look amazing and hot. If your friends weren't here and people weren't waiting downstairs—" He left the sentence unfinished and offered me his arm. "Shall we go?"

"Yes!" I glanced back to Alexia, Elena and Isabella.

"We'd better go ahead quickly," Alexia said and the three of them walked towards the lift. I turned to Jacob. He looked very handsome in his suit. I gently ran my fingertips over his cheek, touched the knot of his tie and placed my hand on his heart.

"OK. Let's go." I took his arm as we slowly walked down two flights of the wide staircase. Neither of us spoke.

As we approached the ceremony room, we could discern people murmuring loudly inside. My heart started to beat faster. I squeezed Jacob's arm. On entering the room, I spotted Marie and Noëlle sitting with Martha and Józef and next to Antonio all in the front row. Alexia and Isabella were standing next to the registrar, by the large desk in front of the windows, facing the room. Suddenly everybody started clapping and cheering and I realised that was meant for us. Jacob and I laughed and waved as we walked to the front. I stopped to kiss my daughters and Antonio, then turned to greet the registrar.

"Ms. Krakowski, Mr. Wronski! Good morning. I hope the delay has not inconvenienced you. During this adjournment I have prepared all papers and checked the passports of your witnesses—Mrs. Moyer and Mrs. Baker on your side, Ms. Krakowski, and your brother Lucas on your side, Mr. Wronski. I understand you also wish your children to sign the register, in a symbolic gesture, so I have explained to them when and where they may do that. So we are all ready to go. The question therefore is: are *you* ready to get married?"

Jacob and I looked at each other.

"Are you ready, my love?" he asked me gently.

I nodded. Yes, I was.

15

Lady Macbeth

A lawyer is not profitable, according to the firm's calculations and budget, if he does not achieve at least his targeted billable hours. If lawyers aren't profitable then they are effectively worthless. "We are not a charity," Lars had once said to me when he was managing partner at Solomons. Of course, law firms are profit-oriented, just like any other business, but everything is relative. The continuously increasing performance criteria of billable hours, hourly rates and invoice collections appear to become less and less achievable.

~

On our post-honeymoon, with the children, on the French Atlantic coast, neither Jacob nor I were thinking about billable hours or other work matters. We were coming to terms with the requirements that our newly defined relationship was imposing upon us. From being lovers with independent lives we had turned into a married couple. To me that meant I had him to protect me and my girls, while I made us our home, looked after our children and did my part to contribute financially. So when we arrived at our rented summerhouse near Lacanau, the first thing I did whilst everyone else jumped into the pool was to unpack, put sheets on all the beds, get towels for everyone, go food shopping and stock up the kitchen.

"Come on, wifey," Jacob shouted from outside, "come swimming!"

I poured two glasses of the red wine that I had just acquired at the local wine shop and took them outside to the terrace. Jacob and Antonio were swimming lengths while Noëlle and Marie were looking at something in the lavender bed, that framed the pool terrace on the south side.

"The water is too cold for me," I replied. "I got you some wine, though." I held up the wine glasses.

"*Moja dobra żona*! You're such a good little wife!" Jacob crawled to the stairs, climbed out of the pool and took the glass from me. "Cheers, darling!" He downed the glass in one and planted a kiss on my lips. "Mwa!"

"Careful!" I laughed. "You're getting me all wet!" I looked down at my sundress, which was showing a big water stain. "I better get this off." I went through the French doors into our bedroom. He followed me, a towel wrapped around his hips.

"Oh, darling! Have you followed me to be naughty?" I turned to hug him and started kissing his neck. "I mean, the children are outside but perhaps we can go to the bathroom—after all, this is our honeymoon."

He took me by the shoulders and slightly pushed me away. "Uh, no. I just wanted to get a polo shirt, and I'm tired."

"Oh." I let go of him. "Here, in the closet."

He opened the doors of the cupboard. "What the—? Chloé, how much stuff did you bring? We're only here for two weeks. I mean, there are at least six pairs of shoes and four handbags." He turned around, shaking his head in disapproval.

"Darling, we are on our honeymoon! I want to look pretty for you."

"You look pretty enough without all this stuff. My mother never travelled with more than a couple of things." He took out a polo shirt and banged the doors shut. "I'm going to lie down on the sofa," he announced. "Please tell the children to be quiet and wake me up at seven, OK? I'll then get the barbecue going. Did you get any charcoal?"

"Oh damn. No, I forgot. I'll go back to the shops."

"You forgot? But you spent like two hundred Euros—what on earth did you buy?"

"All sorts of things. The wine I got wasn't cheap. Don't worry, I paid with my money."

"What do you mean? This is now our money. Seriously, darling. You still have so much to learn." He planted another kiss on my forehead, took the wine glass out of my hand and emptied it in one go. "You won't be needing that when you go shopping." He grinned and gave me a light slap on my bottom. "Off you go then."

When I got back from the shops Jacob was curled up on the sofa, sound asleep. I went outside to place the bag with the charcoal next to the barbecue. The three children were at the table by the pool playing what looked like Monopoly.

"Are you OK, kids?" I asked them.

"Yeah, sure," Antonio answered without looking up, apparently contemplating his next move.

"Shh, not so loud. Your Dad told us to be quiet," Noëlle reminded him.

He dismissed her with a short laugh. "He won't hear anything anyway. He's had lots of wine."

"Mummy, can we have some sweets?" Marie asked.

"It's a bit late, darling," I replied. "But I could bring you a bowl of grapes for you all to share."

"Yeah, thank you Mummy!" Marie replied and Noëlle nodded. Antonio shrugged and counted the steps of the little racing car he had chosen as his game piece.

I went back inside. As I passed the sofa, I noticed the empty wine bottle and nearly empty glass on the coffee table. I decided to pick it up slowly so as not to disturb Jacob. As I did so, he suddenly woke up with a jolt.

"Antonio! I told you not to wake me up!" He started ranting. The he noticed me. "Oh. It's you. Man! The kids have been so loud! I haven't been able to sleep properly!" He ran his fingers through his tousled hair.

"They are outside, playing quietly. Did you finish the bottle by yourself?"

"Hm. I must have." He let out a short growl. "I guess I might as well get up." He started lifting himself up from the sofa but fell back again, knocking over the wine glass in the process. The glass fell on the terracotta tiles and shattered into pieces, its contents being sprayed onto the side of the sofa.

"Oh no!" I exclaimed. "I think that glass was crystal!"

"So what—we are paying enough money for this place."

"We have to take a note of everything that we break. I better get a dustpan. I'm not sure how I'll be able to remove the wine stains though."

He clicked his tongue impatiently. "Just leave it for the fucking cleaner tomorrow!"

"But Jacob, the splinters are dangerous and the stains may not be removable tomorrow," I objected.

"Gawd! I did this so I decide how to deal with it and I say leave it!" He got up, brushed some of the larger pieces aside with his deck shoe and shuffled to the master bedroom.

"Mummy, what happened? Did something break?" Marie came in from outside.

"Stop! Careful, honey, don't come closer—you're not wearing shoes. Yes, a glass fell on the floor."

"Ouch!" She stopped and lifted her foot. I quickly went to examine it.

"Yes, you have a small cut. Here, the splinter is gone. But please, no more walking around. Come, I'll carry you to the bathroom so we can put a plaster on it." I carried her back to the terrace door, opened it and shouted: "Noëlle, Antonio, please don't come inside—there are some pieces of glass we need to clear up first." I then went to the master bedroom in order to get to our bathroom, where I kept the first aid kit. Jacob was lying on our bed, asleep again.

"Mummy, why is he sleeping so much?" Marie whispered in my ear.

"He has been working a lot, so he's just tired," I whispered back. In the bathroom, I placed her on the edge of the bathtub and went to get my sponge, which was back with the medical supplies. Next to it was Jacob's toiletries bag. It was open. I noticed a pillbox with the lid not fastened properly. I picked it up to screw it back on and read the label—*Imipramine*.

"It stopped bleeding, Mummy."

I quickly placed the bottle back in the bag and turned around. "Good. We'll put a plaster on it anyway, OK? Then you can go outside through the terrace doors. I will hoover the floor and let you know when it's OK to come back inside."

"OK, Mummy."

We tiptoed through the bedroom again, Marie left through the French doors and I went to clean the floor. When I finished and saw that Jacob was still asleep, I decided to let him sleep and prepare dinner myself. Antonio woke him up when everything was ready and we had set the table outside. Jacob appeared from the bedroom to join us.

"Hm, sorry guys. I'm just so tired." He yawned. "My wifey, you've been so good, letting me sleep and preparing everything."

"That's OK. The children were a great help. Are you feeling better now?"

"Yeah, thanks." He gave me a kiss on the head and sat down. "Again, thanks. I'll prepare the barbecue tomorrow, OK? How about we make a trip to the beach tomorrow?"

That got the children all excited. All three started talking at the same time about what they needed to take and what they wanted to do in the sea. The shattered glass incident was not mentioned again.

A few days later we decided to make a day trip to Bordeaux. As we emerged from the parking garage near the Cours de l'Intendance, I spotted a Louis Vuitton boutique.

"Oh! They may have the new leo print scarf, it's sold out everywhere else! Jacob, do you mind if I have a quick look?"

Jacob did not look pleased "Hm. OK. We'll wait outside—Antonio and Noëlle can try out their new Heelys. Be quick though, and don't spend any money."

"I'm going with Mumma!" Marie announced and took my hand. As we entered the shop I saw the leo scarf in one of the displays. I humoured the shop assistant, who made a fuss about it being sold out everywhere, and completed the transaction much quicker than I normally would've and without looking twice at the beautiful temptations that winked at me from the shelves. Marie had stood next to me when the price was announced so as we were leaving, I turned to her. "Don't say anything about how much this was, OK darling? In case Jacob asks."

"Why Mummy? Can you not buy what you want? It's your money, isn't it?"

"Well, it's complicated, honey. Let's just not talk about it."

We found Jacob outside, watching Antonio and Noelle rolling up and down the street.

"So you obviously found what you were looking for," he stated with a glance at the brown paper bag.

"Yes—such pot luck! This scarf costs more on eBay than in the shop itself! They even had this handbag, that I thought was not for sale any more—it's the handbag that Carrie gives to her assistant Louise in *Sex and the City: the Movie*."

He frowned. "You didn't buy that as well though, did you?"

"Well no, but really, I should—it would be a good investment." I looked back at the window displays.

"Chloé. If you buy another handbag I will get a divorce."

"Very funny," I laughed.

"I mean it. If you buy another handbag I'll get a divorce," he repeated sternly.

At that moment, it dawned upon me that he was serious. Being married to Jacob meant that he really expected us to share our salaries, and that in future I had to account for my purchases. I looked at the beautifully wrapped box inside the paper bag and no longer felt any enjoyment. For an instant I had the urge to go back and return it but then I felt an even stronger urge to go back and buy that handbag.

However, he was my husband and I wanted this marriage to work. Upon further reflection, therefore, I decided to be a good 'Polish wife' like his adored mother. So on our return to the holiday home I took my notebook—a navy linen-bound book with blue ruled paper and a Prada logo that Isabella had once given to me—and started to write down all my daily expenses. I continued to do so after our holidays. Jacob was content. Our marriage was on track.

~

Job matters soon become predominant again. It was the beginning of September 2008. That morning, having switched on my PC, I had noticed that Jerome had put an appointment in my outlook diary for 10 a.m.: *review with Tracey*. Yay. That was never a pleasant exercise and I didn't expect anything different this time. Still, she had been quite friendly to me after we had come back from our post-wedding vacation—congratulating me and politely admiring my rings—and she certainly seemed to place more attention on Jacob, being nearly flirtatious with him at times. I took that as a sign that she was relaxed both with me and with my personal circumstances. Maybe I could relax now as well.

When I entered her office she barely looked up from her papers.

"Come in, Chloé, and close the door, please. I am just looking at the print-out of your financial performance. As far as I can work out you have only got about one hundred and thirty chargeable hours a month on average over the last three months." She looked up at me and raised her eyebrows. "How can that be?"

"Uhm—we did not get the last two deals from Holmans and the other two pitches I sent out are still pending?"

"This is not acceptable. These figures are far too low. I have also had to write off too much of your time on the deals that we have billed in the second quarter."

"Well, the fee caps we offered were quite low and the structure of the Amsterdam bank deal changed completely so I had to put in double the amount of work. Also, there was a bit of duplication of work by Jessica when she filled in for me when I was on holiday."

"Her hourly rate is lower than yours and she deserves to be able to have her time invoiced when she works so hard. If I did not know you better I would nearly have the impression that you have become less willing to work and instead are enjoying an extended honeymoon."

I could feel my face getting flushed. "No. I haven't. I'm not."

"Be that as it may, all I can say is these figures must improve drastically within the next three months. Otherwise we may need to reassess your counsel status."

At this point my scalp and the top of my ears were burning, which only happens when I feel the adrenaline of danger shooting through my veins. Notwithstanding my racing heart I managed to respond calmly. "I understand. I will do my best. Is that all?"

"Yes, that's all."

Back in my room, I closed the door and sat turned towards the window. This wasn't good. Not good at all. Granted, the expected monthly chargeable hours target was one hundred and sixty and at one hundred and thirty I was below that. However, I simply hadn't been that busy and, I admitted to myself, I had enjoyed not being frantically busy all the time. However, Tracey's threat had contained a dangerous undertone, which, since she was a woman, was relevant and not to be ignored. She had meant much more than she had actually said. A man would have clearly said 'if you do not perform, you will have to go'. I found the business card of my preferred head-hunter, Steven Quinn, in my purse and dialled his number on my private mobile.

"Steven Quinn?"

"Steven, hi! It's Chloé—Chloé Krakowski from Pratt & Wonkey."

"Chloé! Good to hear from you. How are you—how are things at P&W?"

"That's why I'm actually calling. I'm considering a change and was wondering whether you have any searches going on."

"In fact, we do. Two firms are looking actively at the moment. They aren't top ten though—they are small and don't have any banking law capacity. Other than that, it's fairly quiet in that area—thc financial crisis is taking its toll."

"Yes. I know. Would you enquire anyways, with these two firms, on a no names basis?"

Sure! I'll do that and get back to you."

"Thanks." We hung up. I was unsure what might come of it but it was important to set up a plan B if matters deteriorated here.

~

Two weeks later, on a Monday morning, when stepping off the lift at 8.30 a.m., I was surprised to see that many associates and partners were already or—judging by their state—still in the office. I spotted Jessica who was about to rush past me with a little stressed wave of her hand. I stopped her.

"Hey, what's going on? Why is everybody here already?"

"Haven't you heard? It's Lehmans! They have filed for insolvency! AB bank made a money transfer to their German subsidiary on Friday afternoon for the GREF deal which is to close today. We have to try and get the money back before it lodges its insolvency application with the German bankruptcy court! Sorry, I've got to see Tracey *now*!" She ran off.

At P&W we had known of, and been affected by, the subprime crisis over the preceding year because many of our real estate finance transactions were put on hold, or stopped altogether, due to the rise in the interbank interest rate. Banks were simply no longer able to lend money at the low rates clients were willing to pay and able to afford. This, however, was unbelievable. One of the largest US investment banks was insolvent?

Once I had reached my office, and was online, I scrolled through the websites of the various financial newspapers, which all had the same topic. Even the tabloids were dominated by screaming headlines about the fall of Lehman Brothers. I was shell-shocked. What would this mean for the world economy? I still remembered the stock market crash on Black Monday in 1987 but at that time I was a student and only theoretically interested in the financial markets. Things were of course different now. P&W's main clients were banks. They—and we—would be clearly, and dramatically, affected by this.

Sure enough, a while later, an email from Tracey, to her entire team, informed us of the immediate consequences.

From: Taylor, Tracey (BK)
To: Krakowski, Chloe (BK); Allen, Jessica (BK); Jones, Mike (BK); Holmes, Joanna (BK)
Cc: Panzer, Jerome (BK)

Dear all,
I have spoken to AB Bank, Holmans/HOLREF, Holland Bank and Francobank. ***All*** transactions are on hold. DO NOT write down any time on any of their deals until further notice. If you have any questions let me know.

Tracey

My heart sank. I was involved in two of those transactions and needed the billable hours. I certainly had not forgotten Tracey's words: '*these figures must improve drastically, within the next three months, otherwise we may need to reassess your counsel status*'. The aircraft finance restructuring for Bavaria Bank that I had been working on was not affected by the crisis, as this was not a new money loan. The airline had received their loan years before but now had problems repaying it so the bank agreed to lower the repayment instalments and extend the term in which they were payable, in return for receiving additional security and guarantees. However, even taken together with some other small matters I was busy with, it would not be sufficient to increase my hours drastically. Which reminded me of plan B. I closed the door again and dialled Steven Quinn's mobile. When he did not answer I left a brief message, asking to be called back.

A short while later he returned my call.

"I was going to call you in the next few days anyway," he began. He was the only legal head-hunter I knew of who did not need to be chased for information.

"The two firms I mentioned to you—they were interested, initially, but now everything's on hold. They are not sure they want banking law capacity in this current market. Do you do restructuring?"

"Not really," I replied. "Only in respect of deals I have previously done but I'm not a restructuring or insolvency specialist."

"Shame. That's what everyone will want. All I can say is you better hang on to your job."

"Sure. I was just checking the market," I lied. "I have no reason to leave."

I did leave though—the office, early, at 6 p.m. It was glorious to have non-hurried evening time with the girls, eating pizza with toppings we made ourselves, playing with foam and huge bubbles in the bath, cuddling in Noëlle's bed with her reading a story to me and Marie.

When Jacob came home I was just washing up the oven trays.

"You left early," he stated with raised eyebrows as he placed his briefcase on the kitchen counter.

"Hm. I was looking for you but heard you were in that crisis meeting all day."

"Yeah. The whole Lehman thing is a nightmare. I need a drink." He opened the cupboard and took out a whiskey glass.

"Yes. I know. Nearly all my deals are on hold. So I left early to have dinner with the girls and give them a bath. I have even done the washing and tidied up."

"How exciting."

"It's not about being exciting or not. I'm really trying to be a good wife, Jacob. I have the same job as you, yet I do all our housework and look after the girls and Antonio as much as I can."

He shrugged his shoulders. "If it's too much for you, just don't do it."

"It's not too much. It's a pleasure. I love looking after my family but I feel like you're taking everything for granted. I need your appreciation once in awhile. Like, you no longer tell me that I'm pretty or that you love me. I miss that." I firmly held eye contact. It was not easy for me to do so but I thought if he wanted to make me happy then I had to verbalise my needs. There was no point waiting—any longer—for him to realise this by himself.

"I'm a good husband. I work all day. I don't beat you. I don't cheat on you."

He was actually serious, which only got me more upset. When he noticed that, he smirked and took me in his arms. "Darling, darling! You are so pretty, I love you so and we have such a nice home," he said in a baby-like voice.

I pulled out of his arms. "You don't have to make fun of me!"

He laughed. "Oh come on." He grabbed my breasts from behind, made a grunting noise and rubbed himself against my bottom. "Let's have sex, oomph-oomph."

I pushed his hands away with my wrists and took off my dripping rubber gloves. "Let it go. That's really not a turn on. I don't know why you always do that when I am washing up and can't defend myself."

"That's exactly why it's fun!" He shook his head and let go of me.

In an attempt to placate him I hugged him and kissed him softly. "Can we not be more tender? Let me show you what I mean."

He pulled back impatiently. "No. I don't have time for that now. I've got work to do."

I turned away, pretending to check the dishwasher program, so that he could not see my tears. "Alright. I'll wait for you in bed." When I looked up again with a forced smile he had left the kitchen.

~

From: Hart, Christopher (CEO)
To: All Fee Earners (Global); All Support Staff (Global)
Cc: James, Bryan (SP)
Re: Global restructuring programme

Dear All
In order to anticipate the effects the financial crisis may have on the firm it has been decided that a restructuring of all Pratt & Wonkey staff will be required globally. The aim is to reduce the head count overall by 9 per cent. within the next two months. This will affect all offices and all departments, and fee earners and support staff alike. If you have any questions please consult your local HR department.

Best regards
Christopher Hart, Chief Executive Officer
Bryan James, Senior Partner

"Do you think the banking department will be affected? I mean—with all the restructurings we are still the most profitable department overall," I said to Jessica when she called me as soon as the email had arrived.

"That's true, but David told me that although there is a worldwide increase in turnover, the profit per equity partner is expected to fall because of staff costs and underperforming departments, like real estate for example. He also told me—well, but you must please keep it quiet." David had, in the meantime, been made partner so this was first hand gossip.

"Of course, what is it?"

"Apparently Michael Stone and Krystle Cann from HR have drawn up a list of staff to be made redundant. And Mike is on it."

"What, but he is fairly busy and he's only on a junior lawyer's salary! His girlfriend is pregnant—he just told me yesterday."

"I know! Maybe they will change their minds. I heard that the list is to be finalised by this afternoon."

After we had hung up I pressed the short dial for Mike. I felt somehow responsible for him as I had taken part in persuading him to work in our team and, apart from being a fine person, he had been an invaluable help on my aircraft transactions.

"Hey, Chloé! What can I do for you?" He was as obliging as ever.

"Just quickly—have you told Tracey yet that Natasha is pregnant?"

"No, not yet—I mean why should I, it doesn't affect my work."

"You should tell her ASAP. Don't ask why. Just do it. Please. Now."

"Uhm. OK, sure."

Good, maybe it would get him off that list. The whole thing was absurd. Even following the stock market crash, in October, we had been busy with restructuring various deals we had completed in the last two or three years. There wasn't a great outlook for new transactions in the near future but as soon as the banks would be back in business, so would we. No firm would take such a short-term view.

I was wrong.

"So, Chloé. I trust you have read the CEO's email this morning. As it said, every office and department is affected, also this one. A list has been drawn up of members of staff who are affected by the restructuring. Actually, Mike's name was on the list but I took him off it as he will have to provide for his girlfriend and a baby. I had to give another name instead. So, now your name is on it."

I was standing in front of Tracey's desk. She had called me and asked me to come and see her. I only managed to stare at her incredulously.

"You will be offered the same as everyone else. The firm will pay you three months' salary in return for signing a termination agreement and you can leave now." She spoke in a business-like manner, as if she was talking about a new transaction.

"And what if I don't accept?"

"Then we will lawfully terminate your employment contract by giving you the required notice period."

"I will have to take legal advice."

"Of course." She smiled sweetly. I left her office without a further word and without closing the door.

"I don't believe this! They are firing my wife? What assholes!" Jacob freaked out when I told him, having straightaway walked to his office. "You must contact an employment specialist! Here, wait—there was an article I saw a while ago about this lawyer who successfully represented some high-profile CEO." He rummaged through a pile of business magazines on his shelf. "There it is. Ah, page 23—there—his name is Peter Weaver. Just Google him, and call straightaway. Three months' salary as a severance payment is ridiculous. You should get one to two years' worth."

"But I don't want to have to leave! I want—I need—this job!"

"You'll get another one and until then we have a shit load of cash." He grinned with glee.

I couldn't feel any glee at all. Peter Weaver did confirm Jacob's view about what was an adequate severance package in my case and responded to management, accordingly, on my behalf. P&W, however, didn't move at all on their offer 'accept three monthly wages severance or get fired'.

Thus, after several weeks of being isolated and ignored in the office, whilst keeping strict working hours at the advice of my lawyer, I received Tracey's version of Lady Macbeth's letter. I now found myself—a hard-working, highly experienced, former equity partner, Oxford-educated barrister and solicitor and mother of two—out of work.

~

"I doubt that they will let this go to trial. I expect them to make a decent offer now."

I found myself in court with Peter Weaver, waiting for the lawyer representing P&W and the judge to arrive. Immediately after having received my termination notice and being escorted out of the building within an hour thereof, I had called Peter Weaver who lodged our case one day later. It took another month for the judge to summon the parties to court for a negotiation meeting.

"Well, I need it. I am struggling financially, to be honest. I get less than ten per cent. of my monthly net salary as unemployment benefit. This just about covers my daughters' school fees. My husband is lending me money to cover my part of the mortgage payments and all other costs."

"He is *lending* you money? Doesn't he earn about the same as you did?"

"Yes." I looked at the ground. That had been another unpleasant conversation with Jacob. I couldn't blame him. Yes, if I had spent less money on clothes, shoes, handbags and holidays, I would have more reserves. But did I ever—*ever*—contemplate being without income? No. Maybe that was naïve. I regarded it as an inherent lack of existential fear. Deep down I felt I would always be alright. Yes, if necessary, I would do any work to support us. It would just not be logistically possible to change my lifestyle completely from one day to the next. If they were to make me a decent offer now, I would accept it and discuss with Jacob how to downsize our life. We could sell the house, sell the car, rent a small apartment. Whatever happened, never, ever, did I want to have to work within this type of culture or for those people again.

We were interrupted by the arrival of Krystle Cann, P&W's HR manager, and Angela Lang, employment law partner at P&W. So the management had chosen to be represented by one of their partners, who thus would have a vested interest in this case. The door behind the bench opened and a young-looking woman with an Ellen de Generes-style blonde pixie haircut and blue-rimmed glasses, wearing a judge's gown, entered the court, causing all to rise.

"Good morning," she began. "In the matter of Chloé Krakowski versus Pratt & Wonkey LLP.—are all parties and their legal counsel present? Ah, good. I would like the parties to consider negotiating a settlement."

"My client is not interested to settle, Your Honour. We consider this dismissal as having been made on lawful grounds," Angela Lang replied.

"I see. Are you absolutely certain? Very well, then I will order pleadings be exchanged as follows," the judge ruled. Checking through her calendar, she set the dates for four sets of pleadings. "That will take us to a trial date in September," she concluded.

So now we were in full legal action mode and it was going to take months. The nightmare was not yet over.

~

Somehow the time went by more quickly than expected. The summer came and went while I played the good housewife and mother (who was amassing debt, with her husband, in order to be able to pay her half share of the outgoings) and tried to deal with the mounting tension in our relationship—with little success.

"So the trial is on Monday?" Jacob had come into our dressing room while I was switching handbags.

"Yes. Weaver said since we have exchanged pleadings twice and submitted all evidence in writing we might even get a judgment on Monday."

"I doubt P&W will let it get to that. They will make you an offer and then you should take it whatever it is. I mean—you are suing my employer! How do you think that affects my position? If this gets any worse, I can forget *my* career!"

"Jacob. They haven't made any offer at all. I had no choice but to sue. Anyway, I'm going into town now with the girls." This discussion was pointless, especially when he was getting angry.

"What? You're unemployed and are going shopping to spend our money?"

"Jacob, I did not say I was going shopping and I still have some of my own money."

"It's not your money, it's our money! What is this—a new handbag? Don't you have enough of those stupid fucking handbags? My mother has only ever had one handbag and it certainly did not cost more than a hundred Euros! This really makes me sick!" He kicked the Prada bag I had emptied. I picked it up carefully and moved away from him towards the corner opposite the door where he was standing.

"Please don't do this. I understand you're upset, Jacob, but it is me who is being kicked and treated like shit by *your* employer. I don't ever want to work in that kind of place ever again!"

"How dare you talk like that! Sometimes I think they were right to fire you! You are brainsick! You better get a fucking job when this is over and if you have to work as a fucking waitress I don't fucking care! I can't believe I had the fucking idea to have this fucking wedding and move into the house of princesses! It's all your fucking fault!" He banged his fist against the cupboard door, threw me a hateful look and left the room. Several moments later I heard the front door bang shut.

After I had dried my tears, and poured myself a glass of wine, I went to see the girls downstairs. They were playing with our cat Peppermint, laughing as it tried to catch the red light being projected by the little torch Marie was holding in her hand.

"Mummy, can we go to the sushi place where the plates go around on a belt?" Noëlle asked.

"Sure, sweetie. Then we'll go to the Japanese supermarket and buy some mochi as well."

"OK! Will they make me fat?"

"Of course not! What on earth makes you say that?"

"That's what Jacob said to me. He said I was getting fat because I was eating toast with Nutella."

I quickly went to hug her. "No, no! Not at all! I'm sure he didn't say that!"

"He did, then Marie said Noëlle is not fat! And then he said to Marie, you don't understand anything you're a dumb-ass."

What?! I pulled Marie into my arms as well. "Come here, darling. I'm sure that was a joke, you know like you say silly-billy."

"OK." Marie did not seem upset. Good. I was livid though. It was one thing to scream at me, quite another to abuse my sweet little girls verbally.

In my arms, Noëlle seemed to feel protected enough to speak further. "But Antonio said nasty words to us the other day and told us he will beat us up if we tell you."

"What? Why? What did he say?"

"I can't tell you, Mummy. It was horrible."

I pressed them both at me. "I'm so sorry, my loves. Boys can be quite mean sometimes. I'm sure he didn't realise what he said. Please tell me, immediately, next time this happens. I'll speak to Jacob about it anyway."

"I don't like Antonio anymore," Noëlle said.

"I don't like Jacob anymore," Marie added. "They are both mean."

I just hugged them tighter. I didn't know what to say.

~

The evening before the trial, I sat down to write a letter to Jacob. When I had called Alexia to ask her for advice and tell her of my fight with Jacob she had recommended I should do just that.

"Write a letter—do what it takes. I'm sorry, Chloé, but you got *married*. For the second time! You've got to pull yourself together and make this marriage work at all cost," Alexia had said.

"But the girls are unhappy, too."

"Not if you make things work. It's up to you, Chloé."

"Maybe, but there is something I haven't told you. Jacob takes anti-depressants."

"Oh! Do you know which ones?"

"Imipramine. I have Googled it. It would explain his low sex-drive and his mood swings."

"Have you talked to him about it?"

"Not really. One time I asked him what that was, when he had popped a tablet, and he says it's to help him be less nervous when he has a presentation."

"Well, I mean the current situation can't be that easy for him either. I guess in his mind he married you *with* your job—it was like the basis of your relationship contract. Now the essential terms of that contract are being changed, which he doesn't understand, doesn't support and doesn't want to live with."

"Maybe you're right. The last months have been hard on both of us."

With that conversation in mind, I started to write the letter to Jacob. I was not sure I could reverse anything that had happened but I was going to try to rescue what was left.

Dear Jacob,

I need to tell you how I feel before things get out of control. Please take this seriously.

I don't want to be patronised.

I don't want to be shouted at.

I do not want to be cursed at. That is verbal violence. It hurts deep inside, destroys my feelings and scares me.

I should be allowed to be angry, especially when it is justified.

I want rules of manners to be accepted and supported.

I want appreciation for my thoughtfulness, not criticism or indifference or derisive lack of respect.

I want my needs to be taken seriously.

I want my husband to understand me and to love me and my children, and not for us to be subjected to your authority and constant criticism.

I never wanted the man whom I love and married to expect me to change and to adapt to his image of a wife.

I want a man who, in the case of existential or money issues, does not look for fault in me. I may be neurotic and sometimes superficial but that cannot be the justification for any disdainful behaviour towards me.

I want a man who does not leave me in times of trouble and who is also interested in my feelings.

I want my man to be happy for me if I spend my time doing something that makes me happy and fulfils me. I would like him to encourage me and support me in doing so.

I don't want to be despised and criticised when I 'm tidy and look after our home and our things (like fluffing up sofa cushions and using coasters).

I want my man to love and admire me for grooming and looking after myself.

I want a man who loves looking after, and looking out, for me.

I don't want to be despised for spending my money. It ignores who I am and what I have achieved in my life and what I achieve now.

I don't want to be punished with disdain and withdrawal of affection if my man does not like the way I am or behave.

I want to be spoiled once in a while by my man. I work hard and I deserve it.

It's not all my fault and I don't want to hear that anymore.

I also want to be treated with respect and tenderness physically. Crudely grabbing my breasts and other body parts particularly in inappropriate circumstances repels me.

I want my man to trust my decisions and to take them seriously.

I want to exercise my personal rights freely.

I want my children and their education to be respected.

I want criticism to be given kindly and constructively and not to be seen as an opportunity to impose an opinion on me or to give me a telling off.

I want to be loved and understood just the way I am.

I want our marriage to work and I want to be happy. Is that too much to ask?

I love you

Chloé

~

The next day I was waiting outside the courtroom, waiting for Peter Weaver. My stomach was in knots. I hoped that nobody I knew would see me. As if I had just wished for the opposite, I spotted a partner from Solomons in his robe walking up the corridor towards where I was sitting. He was engaged in conversation with what I assumed to be a client. When he looked up and saw me he appeared surprised.

"Oh, hello Chloé!" He hesitated as if to say something else and, when I only nodded at him, turned back to his client and walked on, not without glancing at the board next to the door to the courtroom which showed that my case was up next—*Chloé Krakowski v. Pratt & Wonkey LLP.* Oh shit. Lawyers cannot resist such sensational gossip. By tomorrow everybody in the legal community would know that I dared to take the big almighty firm to court.

Several minutes later, Peter Weaver arrived as well as Krystle Cann and Angela Lang. I wondered briefly whether the rumours Jacob had told me were true—namely that Angela was also a victim of the cleansing programme at P&W and was to be demoted to non-equity partner.

We all rose when the judge came in, this time with two lay judges. She still had this cute hair cut but this time was wearing red-rimmed glasses.

"Good morning." She sat down and ruffled through her papers. "Right. I have received and read all pleadings and have come to a conclusion. Before I pronounce my decision, however, I would like to ask the parties whether there have been any further negotiations for an out of court settlement."

I turned to Peter Weaver in surprise. He replied immediately. "Your Honour, we have never received an offer after the initial one several months ago before my client was dismissed."

"I am astonished to hear that. I must say, I am indeed astonished, that Pratt & Wonkey have let this case go to trial at all."

"We have offered an amount equal to one year's salary," Angela Lang quickly declared as if that was no news.

"This is the first time we've heard about that," Peter replied.

"Well, that is a good start," the judge commented, "but in the circumstances, and looking at similar cases, I was thinking more of eighteen months. I expect Mrs. Krakowski will have considerable difficulties to find a new job any earlier than that. She is a very senior lawyer in a highly specialised area of the law, over forty years old and a mother of two young children." The judge looked expectantly at our counterparties. Krystle Cann whispered something in Angela Lang's ear.

"I have no authority to offer one cent more than that," Angela replied stiffly, "and in my opinion, that offer is absolutely adequate."

"Hm. Mr. Weaver, do you want to consider this offer? You know that if we rule in favour of your client she will have to go back to her job where, I daresay, she will not be welcome."

Krystle Cann nodded in assent and shot a cold glance at me.

"May I have five minutes outside with my client?" Peter Weaver replied.

"Of course." The judge rose, causing all attendees to follow her example. "I see you all back here in five minutes." She left the room through the door behind the bench. Peter Weaver and I went outside and found a quiet corner.

"What do you think?" he asked me.

"I can't believe she acted as if that offer had always been on the table! Why have they not come up with this earlier?"

"Clearly, in order to increase the pressure on you until the very last moment."

"No. We have come so far. The last six months have been a nightmare. They shouldn't get away with this so easily."

"I agree but it's up to you. I wouldn't take it either. There is a risk you will lose altogether but I'm quite confident we will get a judgment in our favour. You know what that means."

"Yes." I swallowed hard. "I'll have to go back into *that* arena."

He pressed my arm in encouragement. "Fine. Let's go and inform the judge."

Back inside the courtroom, I tried to ignore the poisonous looks from the Pratt & Wonkey ladies. The judge entered the room and sat down. She looked questioningly at Peter. "Mr. Weaver, has your client made a decision?"

"Yes, your honour. We will not accept the offer." That prompted excited murmur from the other side.

"Very well." She switched on her dictaphone and took the microphone.

"In the matter of Krakowski—spelt K-R-A-K-O-W-S-K-I—versus Pratt and Wonkey—spelt W-O-N-K-E-Y—is that correct Mrs. Lang? Thank you. All claims—there are two claims, Mr. Weaver, aren't there? That the dismissal was void and unlawful and that the plaintiff has to be re-employed? Yes, thank you—that all claims of the plaintiff are herewith granted. I hereby pronounce judgment in favour of the plaintiff. Mrs. Lang, Mr. Weaver, a fully reasoned judgment will be available by tomorrow afternoon. Thank you all."

And thus came the evil spirits *I* had summoned.

16

I Will Survive

It was Thursday, 1 October 2009. I was back in the lion's den. I stood in the lift and pressed the button for the reception floor. My hands were trembling. I didn't know what to expect. For sure the P&W partners were livid with me after the negative press coverage. My name had not been mentioned anywhere—that was not allowed—but as soon as the judgment had been made public the legal press, as well as the Financial Times, had a field day. None of the lawyers who had been made redundant, during the banking crisis, had dared to sue their firm and see it all the way through. All other cases had been settled prior to judgment. This was new and, most importantly, it was a sensational slap in the face of one of the most powerful law firms in the world.

My knees were still trembling when I was shown into a meeting room—the same I had been hired and fired in—and I looked into the stone cold faces of Michael Stone, Krystle Cann and Henry Struther. I had met Henry the previous year at a European associates' meeting where he had declared to me that P&W better make him a partner soon or they would lose a major client. That obviously worked because here he was, as Tracey's successor and my new boss.

"Good morning, Mrs. Krakowski," Michael said stiffly. "Take a seat."

I managed a small smile. "Good morning."

"We want to establish some rules," Michael began.

I waited. My heart was pounding.

"We want to monitor you, so that we can see what you do and for you to know what you are allowed to do," he continued. "One. Any work you accept from within the office needs to be cleared with

Henry. All partners will be notified of that." He paused as I took out a notebook and pen and started making notes.

"Two. Any delegation of work is to be cleared with Henry. Three. To the extent you do German law work you need to clear with Henry and a German partner who the supervising partner will be. Four. There will be a monthly review and analysis of your activities. We may decide at any time that a more frequent review meeting may be necessary. Five. Any marketing activity or participation in training has to be cleared in advance with Henry. Six. We will monitor your busyness. You will fill in and submit your time sheets daily. You will submit a weekly summary report about your activities to Henry. Seven. If you're allowed to undertake a specific marketing activity, provide a short summary afterwards to Henry. Eight. There has to be a new agreement on objectives."

"I do not have any agreement on objectives. I never had one, because my salary does not include a variable bonus element," I interjected slowly.

"Prepare a first draft before the end of the week—before Thursday if possible. Nine. We will treat you in compliance with our legal obligations. We will perform our side of the contract. If you feel treated unfairly, tell Henry or myself. Any questions?"

"No. I only want to make one thing very clear. I never contacted the press."

"Noted. You can go to your office now. Reception will give you a key card."

I got up and left the room without any further word. Enough had been said. I collected my key card from the receptionist, travelled up two floors and walked past some secretaries who stared at me with round eyes.

"Chloé!" A friendly and familiar voice made me turn around. Jerome was quickly walking towards me, his smile in stark contrast to the cold faces I had been stoically looking at earlier. I gratefully accepted his hug.

"It's so good to have you back! I saw you had a meeting with Henry, Dr. Stone and Krystle Cann. Are you OK?"

"Sure, Jerome. Good to see you, too. I assume nothing has changed around here?" I walked into my office and noticed a small bouquet of flowers in a vase on my desk. "Flowers?"

"These are from me actually. A little welcome present," he replied with a bashful smile. "Yes, it's all the same. Except of course that Tracey is back in London and Henry is in charge here now."

"Thank you so much, Jerome. And? How is he to work for?"

He turned to see if anybody was listening. "Actually, so far so good. He is very organised, polite and keeps reasonable hours."

I raised my eyebrows and nodded. "Right. Well—I better get started. As far as I'm concerned nothing is the same. I'm back now but I have a new boss and I intend to make the best out of it."

"I'll leave you to it then. Let me know if there is anything I can do for you."

"Thanks, Jerome. I really appreciate it."

Once I had settled in and started my computer, I opened my inbox and waited, for the over 1,100 unread emails which were shown, to load fully.

My thoughts went back to the previous Friday—my last weekend of freedom—which I had spent with Isabella in Berlin. Noëlle and Marie had still been with Jean and his parents in France, for their half term autumn break. Jacob had stayed at home. Isabella had booked us an early dinner at the Grill Royal, our favourite restaurant in Berlin.

We'd just finished our main course, the waiter having cleared our plates. The table next to ours was being set for the next guests. As I poured Isabella some water I looked up and saw two men walking towards us, being led by the headwaiter. I recognised one of them.

"Shall we ask for the bill then, sweetie?" Isabella asked me.

"Uhm—not yet. I know this guy." I widened my eyes and rolled them to indicate there was something behind her. By then the waiter and the two men had arrived at the table next to us.

"Here you go. Enjoy your dinner," the waiter said to them and handed each of them a menu.

"Oh my god, it's Chloé!" The man exclaimed when he saw me. I got up to shake his hand. He blew me two kisses left and right.

"Giles! What a surprise! I haven't seen you for ages! Isabella, this is Giles Rocher. He is a partner at Olsens—so, a colleague, and his father is French in case you are wondering about the accent. Giles, this is my best friend Isabella Moyer. She is a jewellery designer."

"How fabulous! Enchanté! Ladies, this is my husband Marcel. Marcel is a fashion designer," Giles said with his slight French accent.

"So, how do you two know each other?" Marcel asked.

"Darling, you remember the film financings where I represented the Hollywood studios? Chloé was nearly always the bank's lawyer," Giles explained.

"Oh, how I miss those first class trips to L.A.!" I sighed.

"Well, yes—no more of that in this horrible economy!" Giles said. "So, how are you these days?"

"Oh—I'm fine. I've been at Pratt & Wonkey for a few years now. And I got remarried last year."

"Congratulations! That calls for some champagne!" Giles signalled the waiter. "However, that's not good news for me."

"Why? You can hardly mean that you want to switch allegiance!" I winked and pointed at him and Marcel.

"Of course not! Chloé, you are the most glamorous lawyer I know, but no," he laughed. "I was hoping you'd tell me you're unhappy so I can finally lure you to come and work with us in Berlin."

Isabella exchanged a quick glance with me. "I think that sounds really interesting. Who knows? Perhaps Chloé will think about it," she said.

"I like this woman!" Giles exclaimed and clinked glasses with Isabella. "Yes, do think about it, Chloé. The offer stands. I will send you a signed contract with all details and whenever you are ready you just sign it and send it back to me."

Eventually, we agreed to get the bill and leave Giles and Marcel to enjoy their dinner for two. As we stood outside, waiting for a taxi, I sighed. "Thanks for not saying anything, Isabella. I mean, Giles is a sweetie and such a rare gem in our world, but I wasn't ready to tell him about my failed job and my failing marriage." I held up my right hand with the beautiful Cartier engagement and wedding rings.

Isabella squeezed my arm. "I know! However, this was such a chance encounter—who knows what it's good for? At least you know there is a plan B if everything fails."

"Yes, you're right. For now, though, I have to go home and face my husband on Sunday and then the lion's den on Monday."

A knock interrupted my thoughts. Jessica was standing in the doorway, holding two lever arch files. Over the last six months I had not had any contact with her or anybody else from P&W, even including Patricia Stone. "Hi Chloé," Jessica said stiffly. "How are you?"

"Hi Jessica. I'm fine, thanks. And you?"

"Fine, thanks. Henry asked me to bring you these files. We have a big refinancing transaction for the Plastic Group with subsidiaries in fourteen jurisdictions providing security. It's Tracey's deal but Henry is running it day to day. Joanna, my trainee, needs help with coordinating CPs and security documents." She placed the files on my desk.

"So I am assisting Joanna?" I asked calmly.

She seemed embarrassed. "Henry told me to ask you," she repeated. "Look, Chloé, I am sorry. I am not supposed to talk to you about anything other than active work matters."

"Sure. That's fine. No problem. I will look at this straightaway."

"Thanks. If you have any questions, you can ask Joanna—or me, of course. Oh, and we are supposed to record our time *generously*. Apparently we made a loss of about thirty per cent. on the initial financing but we don't have a fee cap now so now Tracey wants to make up for it. Sorry, I can hear my 'phone—I'll see you later." She left.

I frowned. Recording time generously? I knew what that meant. Whilst under pressure to meet, or even to exceed, their billable hours target some lawyers have developed the habit of recording their time on client matters for every minute they were in the office, whether they actually worked on such matters or not. However, a direction from the file partner to record more hours than the actual time spent was not something I had heard of since that scandal in the late nineties when a Wall Street firm was exposed for "padding" bills. That was very odd. Tracey knew that this was in effect fraudulent. Maybe it was a trap. I certainly would not fall for it.

Ping. I looked at my screen and my stomach churned. A new email had arrived. Sender: Tracey Taylor. I opened it.

From: Taylor, Tracey
To: Krakowski, Chloe
Cc: Struther, Henry
Re: Review of security document

Chloé,
Please review the attached security document and send me your comments on any deficiencies (and your suggested corrections) by 2 pm CET today. If you require any other documentation please let me know.

Kind regards
Tracey

I opened the attachment and scrolled through the document. The recital explained that a company was to provide security, on the same terms as certain chargors under an existing security agreement, by acceding to that security agreement, although there was no accession mechanism in the original security document. The definitions section and other provisions cross-referred to other documents. I clicked on reply all.

From: Krakowski, Chloe
To: Taylor, Tracey
Cc: Struther, Henry
Re: Re: Review of security document

Dear Tracey,

Thank you for your email.

Of course I am happy to review the attached document. I assume this takes priority over the work I have been asked to do for Henry on the Plastic Group transaction. I would be grateful if you could arrange for the following documentation to be sent to me: Senior Credit Agreement, Restructuring Deed, Security Deed, Intercreditor Agreement, Accession Documents. Alternatively, perhaps it would be easier to grant me access to the virtual file (is it the number on the front page?) so I do not have to bother you with further requests.

Kind regards
Chloé

From: Taylor, Tracey
To: Krakowski, Chloe
Cc: Struther, Henry
Re: Re: Re: Review of security document

Chloé,
I attach the Security Deed, which is the only other document I currently have access to. Given the timing, please note in your mark up which precise terms require review of other documents.

Kind regards
Tracey

Fine. That would have to do. Peter Weaver had warned me that P&W would probably try to provoke what they would regard as misbehaviour in order to collect reasons to fire me properly this time. He had briefed me that I should stick to doing the work I was asked to do, undertaking reasonable efforts—judged by the standard of someone of my level—and within reasonable business hours. They wouldn't be able to fire me if I didn't adhere to (unreasonable) deadlines or even if I made a mistake. Nonetheless, I was going to be careful stepping around this minefield. I was going to do my best and adhere to prescribed timeframes, even if the task was clearly designed for this purpose only or even completely fake and came from a partner who was not only no longer my immediate supervisor but not even in the Frankfurt office.

While I was working on the security document, Tracey sent me another email requesting a report on the satisfaction of conditions precedent for a real estate finance transaction that we had closed two years ago, giving me a deadline of close of business the next day. I automatically panicked at first, thinking maybe I did something wrong then; they have found something against me and now they are trapping me. I tried to remain calm, which was not easy. I inhaled and exhaled slowly. It was only half way through the day and I was already a nervous wreck. I briefly replied to Tracey that I was of course happy to start with this after 2 p.m. CET and continued on the first assignment.

I sent Tracey my mark-up two minutes before 2 p.m. The document had contained obvious mistakes and was badly drafted, even using different defined terms to describe the same thing.

I recorded the time I spent on it to the exact minute on the number I had found on the cover sheet of the document. Tracey had not said anything to the contrary.

I then started on the next assignment. My door was firmly closed. I didn't want to speak to anybody, let alone Jacob who, in my absence, had conveniently moved to an office down the corridor and further away from mine. By 7 p.m. I had made good progress and decided there was no reason to stay late for any of this. Just then I received another email from Tracey.

From: Taylor, Tracey
To: Krakowski, Chloe
Cc: Struther, Henry
Re: Client bulletin

Chloé,
We require a client bulletin on common structuring issues in acquisition finance in Germany and an update on market developments, covering recent legislative changes

and court decisions as well as any other topic you identify in this area. Please research those issues and draft a memo of not more than six pages. This is not chargeable so please manage this around your client chargeable commitments. If you think you need to obtain input from colleagues please let me know and I will ask the German banking partners whom you may contact. In the meantime please base the memo on your own research. The deadline is close of business this Thursday.

Kind regards
Tracey

I shook my head slightly. This wasn't the sort of thing I should be asked to do, or indeed, the most appropriate person to be asked. The entire tone of the email was very artificial. What was going to be next?

I realised the battle had just begun.

Over the next few days I was kept busy by my newly dedicated supervisor, Jessica's trainee solicitor Joanna. I'm not sure she enjoyed her task, which was to ask me to assist her. I didn't really care, at least it was not fake work and it didn't come from Tracey. My suspicions, in respect of fake assignments, was confirmed when I received an email from a London associate querying why I had recorded time on a matter number which I recognised to be the one I used for the review of the security document Tracey had sent me on my first day back in the office. I responded to her.

From: Krakowski, Chloe
To: Granger, Georgina
Re: Re: Project ABF

Dear Georgina,

Thank you for your email.

I recorded time on this matter because I was asked by Tracey Taylor on that day to review, comment and mark up a security deed. I assumed you or the matter partner knew about this and I was asked to assist because of lack of capacity. Was that not the case?

Kind regards
Chloé

From: Granger, Georgina
To: Taylor, Tracey
Cc: Krakowski, Chloe
Re: FW: Project ABF

Hi Tracey,
My name is Georgina Granger and I am in charge of sending out weekly invoices for Project ABF. We have 3.2 hours of Chloé's time recorded on this matter. I think this must have been mistakenly charged to Project ABF. The file partner, Dave Miller, asked me to confirm this with you.

Many thanks
Georgina

From: Taylor, Tracey
To: Granger, Georgina
Cc: Krakowski, Chloe
Re: Re: FW: Project ABF

Thanks Georgina, I will speak to Dave.

Tracey

Gotcha, I thought. She hadn't thought this through, even when I had asked about the matter number. My little victorious moment was short-lived. I should've known—we weren't in court anymore, where justice and the law protected me. I was back in her territory where she had all the power. Tracey's revenge came two hours later.

From: Taylor, Tracey
To: Krakowski, Chloe
Cc: Struther, Henry
Re: Major client standard documentation

Chloé,
Please can you prepare a standard form real estate finance credit agreement for use with UK or non-UK borrowers and/or guarantors, UK or non-UK real estate, with options for fixed or floating interest rate and including all recent developments under English law and recent changes to the LMA standard documentation and addressing the issues that have resulted from the banking crisis. The deadline for the first draft is opening of business on Monday. If you require any further information or you think that you require additional time to complete the task, please let me know today. Please use the client marketing file number and let me know how many hours you spent in total when you send me the draft.

Kind regards
Tracey

That would be a mammoth task! I knew I would have to collect, and review, material on all legal and Loan Market Association developments that had happened while I was away from the office—and the market—over the last six months. I should be able to do this research but there were over thirty emails containing know-how from that period alone. I replied to Tracey, saying that considering the volume of know-how to be reviewed and taking into account the chargeable work I had been given to do, I estimated that I would need five to seven business days to complete a meaningful first draft. She replied in turn, granting me three more days.

Meanwhile, I submitted the acquisition finance memo a few minutes before 6 p.m. The entire afternoon she kept sending me emails with further nagging, cross-examination like, questions on the CP report I had sent at the beginning of the week. It was quite obvious what she was doing. I sent her my polite and concise answers, careful not to step into any trap, always asking innocently which assignment was taking precedence and, of course, always copying in Henry. With each email from her I was getting more wary. I knew these were her tactics—if they couldn't fire me they would wear me down until I would be ready to leave voluntarily.

By the end of the working day on Friday, I felt physically and mentally exhausted. I had been going into work every day like I was going into psychological warfare. Dealing with those emails from Tracey, working as the trainee's assistant, encountering administrative hurdles, facing the cold atmosphere in the office—all of that showed me clearly that I was regarded as the enemy number one. In their eyes I should've accepted the dismissal and taken any settlement they had offered. They didn't care what consequences that would have had for me and for my family. Now I still wanted to keep my job but I was not going to swallow it all. In compliance with 'The Rules' I prepared an email to Michael and Henry.

From: Krakowski, Chloe
To: Stone, Michael; Struther, Henry
Re: Weekly summary

Dear Michael and Henry,

Please see below for a summary of my activities this week so far.

1. Conditions precedent/Plastic Group transaction for HS -- 31.4 hours

2. Project ABF security agreement for TT -- 3.2 hours

3. 2009 transaction closing report for TT (non-chargeable) -- 4.3 hours

4. Acquisition Finance client bulletin for TT (non-chargeable) -- 7.7 hours

5. Standard form real estate finance agreement for TT (non-chargeable) -- 2.2 hours

6. Administration (Monday: going through 1100 plus emails) -- 2.1 hours

7. Preparing draft agreement on objectives -- 2.6 hours

Please find attached the draft agreement on objectives as requested.

For the avoidance of any doubt, I take the liberty to summarise the rules you informed me of in our meeting on Monday morning.

1. Any work I accept needs to be cleared with Henry. All partners will be notified.

2. Any delegation of work is to be cleared with Henry.

3. To the extent I do any German law work I need to clear, in advance, with Henry and a German Partner who the supervising partner will be.

4. There will be a monthly review and analysis of what I have done. If necessary, the review will happen more often.

5. Any marketing activity or participation in training has to be cleared with Henry beforehand and Henry will decide upon it.

6. You need to monitor my busyness. I am to fill out and submit my time sheets daily. I am to submit weekly summary report to Henry about my activities.

7. If I am allowed to undertake a marketing activity, I am to provide a short summary afterwards to Henry.

8. If I feel I am treated unfairly, I may report it to Henry or Michael.

Please kindly let me know who in Henry's absence is to take his role in this respect. Unless you inform me otherwise, I shall report to Michael during that period.

In the meantime and as for rule number 8: I am still waiting for the allocation of the parking space and on the crediting of my 19 days' holiday entitlement for this year. Furthermore, my profile has not been re-entered on the P&W homepage. I attach the relevant correspondence below for your convenience. Please would you kindly arrange for this situation to be remedied and for those conditions of my employment to be reinstated.

Many thanks and kind regards
Chloé

I pressed the send button just before I left the office. Once outside the building, I enjoyed the ten-minute walk to the car park where, at short notice, I had been able to rent a space once I discovered that P&W was not going to re-allocate me a parking space in the underground garage of the office building.

After I had given the girls a bath, I went to the kitchen and poured myself a glass of red wine. I heard the key in the door.

"Hi." Jacob walked in slowly, blackberry in his hand, briefcase in the other. He placed the briefcase on the kitchen counter, threw his coat on a chair and took a glass out of the cupboard. I watched him silently.

"This is shit, Chloé. You should have taken what they offered you. This is really shit. Three partners were in my office today asking me why I have no control over my wife. They told me that all of this might affect my position soon as well." He ran his hand through his hair and looked at me for the first time. "This is getting too much."

"I'm sorry. That is awful. Believe me, what they are doing to me all day is worse. It's psychological warfare. Not just work but things like cancelling my holiday entitlement and not giving me my parking space back."

"They have the right to do that. You've been away for several months—they can deduct that from your holiday entitlement for this year. As for the parking, it's not in your contract."

"Whose side are you on? I know about the holiday but Peter Weaver thinks the parking has become part of the contract and that we should sue."

"Are you crazy? Do you want to get me fired as well? It's unbelievable. I'm start to think they are right about you. Anyway, I've got work to do." He shook his head and left the kitchen. That night he slept in the guest room and the night after—and after that, he moved his personal belongings in there.

~

A few weeks later I woke up in the morning with my head on fire. I stumbled into the bathroom, took a thermometer and two aspirin out of the medical cabinet and continued to the kitchen, the thermometer stuck under my left armpit while I made coffee. When it beeped I checked it—39.5 degrees. Not good. I swallowed the aspirin, went back to the bathroom and took a shower. There was no way I would call in sick. They wouldn't believe me anyway. I got myself ready, woke up the girls and helped them get dressed. When we left for school, Jacob was still asleep in the guest room.

By the time I got to the office I knew this was not just a fever. I felt dizzy, I was sweating, coughing badly—actually the same symptoms Antonio had shown the previous weekend when Jacob had brought him over from Jasmin's house. I called Jacob on his mobile.

"Have you heard any news about Antonio?"

"Ah, yes, actually. Jasmin called. The doctor suspects it may be swine flu."

"What? I told you it was irresponsible bringing him into our house and in the vicinity of the girls! Now I'm really sick—he might have passed it on to me!"

"Well, that is the risk we took," he replied coolly.

"We? You mean you! Without asking me! Thanks a lot!" I put the phone down with a bang, then rang Jerome's number.

"Jerome, I have got to go to the doctor. I'm very sick and I may be contagious with swine flu—probably got it this weekend from Jacob's son."

"Oh dear! OK, I understand. I will divert your phone to mine—what shall I say if somebody asks?"

"I am sick but I am working from home."

"Understood. Get well soon—I hope it's not the swine flu!"

"Thanks." I hung up, packed some files in a briefcase and left.

~

The doctor was worried and prescribed strict quarantine at home until he had the results back from the lab. So I settled on my sofa, laptop on the coffee table, blackberry beside it, files all over the floor, tissue boxes and tea mugs around them. I felt the energy draining out of me with every passing hour. It was hard to keep the girls at a distance—Marie even saying "I don't care if I get sick, I want a good night kiss from Mummy!" Jana stayed late every evening to give the girls their bath and put them to bed.

"So? Where is your husband?" she asked on the third night.

"Good question. He hasn't called, he comes in late, he leaves without a word. It's as if he doesn't exist."

"Oh, Chloé, I didn't want to say anything then, but I need to tell you now. I have heard him a few times screaming at the girls. Even on your wedding day." She looked at me with sadness.

I nodded. "I'm not surprised about that now. He has said pretty nasty things to them in my presence since." I felt the tears in my eyes again. I was so tired of fighting. "I will not allow it anymore."

The next morning before Jacob left the house he came and stood in the doorway to the sitting room where I was lying on my sofa. "Antonio doesn't have the swine flu after all."

"Great."

"How are you?"

"Since when do you care? Jacob, I can't go on anymore. I feel drained. I feel I have nothing left. I have been so sick and you haven't even called me. I feel you may have even been with someone else. I am so unhappy, so deeply, deeply unhappy." I started crying.

He didn't move.

I wiped my tears away. "I really think I'd be rather reasonably happy on my own, than so desperately unhappy like this."

He waited.

"Jacob, I can't go on anymore. I think—I think it's better we separate."

He shifted his position. "I think that's a good decision," he replied calmly, attempted a smile and turned to leave. Twenty seconds later I heard the front door close.

"Isabella, it's over." I had called Isabella as soon as I had stopped sobbing.

"Oh no, Chloé. I know things with Jacob have been going from bad to worse, since you had to go back to work. It's all her fault, that stupid bitch!"

"Of course it's not her fault. Yes, I'm going through absolute hell but this is between Jacob and me. I feel embarrassed because we only got married last year! I wanted it to work. I thought he loved me the way I was and I tried so hard to become the wife he wanted me to be. I have failed."

"I am so sorry, darling. I really don't understand how he can let you go just like that. He is crazy! *You are his wife*!"

"It's become all too much for him. This is not what he bargained for. I just feel so sad and hopeless. I don't know what's wrong with me. I just don't know anything anymore."

"How are the girls taking the situation at home?"

"That's the other thing. I don't know. They actually seem fine. I'll tell them he is staying with his brother—which I assume is true, but who knows. At least they won't notice at Christmas, as they'll be with Jean in Paris."

"What—you are going to be alone this Christmas?"

"Yes, and I actually want to be. If the girls can't be with me, I don't want to see anybody. We'll have a little celebration before they leave and then they will be back for New Year's Eve. I promised them a girly party with their friends Paulina and Louisa."

"That's sweet. I do have some good news for you though if you are interested."

"What is it?"

"I went back to the Grill Royal the other day and bumped into your friend Giles again. He reminded me of his offer. I told him I'd let you know."

"Oh—thanks. It's good to know. Work is hell and now I'm separated. So maybe it is time to start considering this." I sniffed and suppressed a tear. I had cried enough. I needed to be stronger than ever now, in order to find the best way out of my misery.

~

The months went on. Christmas had come and gone. Jacob had moved out and tried his best to ignore me in the office. It turned out that he did have a new girlfriend, as I had suspected, but I locked my pain away and concentrated on having a positive attitude to work. Shortly into the New Year of 2010, Henry became so busy with several large transactions and he realised that I could be of actual use to him and actually take work off of him, instead of being downgraded to assisting the trainee. I diligently took on every assignment and put in late hours and weekends again, running up nearly 300 billable hours every month. Winter was over, spring came and I started to believe that maybe, just maybe, this could work out, in the long run. Tracey left me alone and the monthly review meetings were short. By June I felt I had proven myself to be trustworthy again. Henry and I worked well as a team and there were moments when he seemed to forget that I was supposedly the enemy. So I thought—until the next monthly review meeting came along.

I knew something was different because Krystle Cann attended the meeting in addition to Michael and Henry. I was on high alert when I sat down opposite them.

"So, Chloé. How have things developed since the last meeting you had with Henry?" Krystle Cann began probingly.

"Fine. We have been very busy. We had a successful closing last week."

"Right. We will get to that. I want to focus on three topics. Let's deal with your marketing activity and your progress in fulfilling your business plan. We need to see more activity. Henry expects to be approached regularly with requests for specific client marketing initiatives. I note from the target list you have sent us that no significant progress has been made."

"Well, I've been caught up in billable work but I have contacted most of them, for the purpose of setting up meetings at next week's aircraft finance conference, where they will all be."

"Yes. I see that here, as well as in paragraphs 2 and 3 of the business plan or your agreement on objectives as you call it. However, meetings should be set up anyway. Waiting for the conference is not necessary to re-establish contact."

"Okay." The less said the better. The HR lady didn't know my business.

"So we will make a note of this. Next topic. Taking responsibility within the team."

"Yes?"

"Apparently you left in the middle of a closing," Michael said sternly.

I stared at him incredulously. "What? When?"

"It was the Dutchbank closing," Henry clarified. "You and Joanna were collecting CPs in the evening. I had to go to a meeting and when I came back you had your coat on."

"Uh, not quite—you, Joanna and I went through the CP list together; all that was missing was for us to send out our legal opinion which Joanna was about to do; I asked you if that was fine because my nanny had to leave. You said yes, I left and was online again twenty minutes later when I logged on at home."

"There was still work to be done and the matter was not yet closed," Henry insisted.

I exhaled and shook my head slightly. This was all wrong.

"In your position of seniority you must see what work there is to be done and not leave a trainee in charge. You are expected to assume responsibility within the team, act proactively," Michael said.

"You are expected to perform at the level you are employed. Your own perception of what you should be doing is in no way adequate. The guidelines we provided you with nine months ago do not prevent you from taking responsibility and working proactively within the team," Krystle Cann added.

I silently looked at all of them in turn.

"This leads to the third point," Michael continued. "You recently seem to be keeping quite standard office hours—nine to six. Why is that?"

"I am usually in at eight thirty after I have dropped my children at school. I have childcare until seven so I try to be home by then. Once my children are in bed I log on at home, if necessary—as in the Dutchbank closing or other recent deals."

"Standard office hours are in no way acceptable for a senior lawyer. This seems to be indicative of a general attitude issue," he replied coldly.

"Logging on, if necessary, is not sufficient," Krystle Cann agreed. "Your accessibility is necessary whether or not you anticipate receiving anything. We have a note of one recent evening when you did not respond to a query from the office."

"I only saw that email after eleven o'clock as I was looking after my youngest daughter who was sick. I responded first thing in the morning."

"Blackberrys are issued to lawyers so they are accessible at all times as necessary, especially after hours," Krystle Cann reiterated. "We will make a note of that, too. I suggest we meet more frequently now. The next meeting should be in two weeks' time and then we will review the matters discussed again."

I had nothing to add.

I left the meeting room, firmly closing the door behind me. I was so livid, I thought my head would explode. I decided to walk straight to Gunther White's office. He was the only one I could speak to openly. He was one of the most decent people at P&W and I knew that he had always liked and respected me. He looked up from his papers, when I knocked on the open door while entering his office.

"Chloé. What can I do for you?" He smiled kindly.

I took a deep breath. "Have you got a minute? I would like to speak with you."

"Yes, of course." He put his pen to the side and took off his glasses. I closed the door and walked towards his desk.

"Gunther, I have had enough. I have been mobbed and mentally tortured for the last nine months and yet I have worked my arse off. I have just had it. This review meeting was the final straw. If you want me to leave then make me a decent offer. Tell your partners that I know of at least one case where Tracey Taylor instructed the team to record more time against a deal than they actually spent on it! I recorded my time properly but when I saw the invoice to the client the number of my billed hours was much higher. I am quite sure the entire invoice was padded. You know this is fraud. If this has happened once, in this firm, then it has happened before."

Gunther looked worried and alarmed. "OK, OK. I will speak to management. There is a big meeting going on anyway, here on the conference floor. Yes, they never intended to give you a chance, Chloé. Look, I'm sorry about how you have been treated. Please just don't do anything rash."

I stared at him. So it really was true. I guess I'd been naïve to believe anything else. I swallowed before my tears of relief could show. "Thank you, Gunther. Thank you for your honesty."

He lowered his head and sighed. "You've been so brave. I really am sorry."

I left his office and went back to mine. My whole body was shaking. I closed the door and sat in my chair, staring at the view outside.

Then I picked up my private mobile telephone, scrolled through my contacts and pressed the dial button, once I'd found the number I was looking for.

"Chloé! What a lovely surprise—I've nearly given up hope!" Giles sounded truly pleased.

"Giles, I'm ready. I'll send you the countersigned contract."

"*Superbe*! You won't regret it."

"I've got to go. I just wanted to let you know."

I put the mobile back into my bag and tried to concentrate on the twenty plus unread emails that had arrived since I had left my office for the review meeting.

Ten minutes later Gunther knocked on the glass door. I waved him in.

"I have been sent to let you know, formally, that the partners have agreed to offer you a settlement worth three annual salaries including a ten per cent. bonus. The managing partner is on the phone to your lawyer now. Until the formal agreement is signed, you can take paid leave as of now."

I nodded slowly, letting the information sink in. On a quick calculation that was nearly one million Euros! I tried to maintain a poker face.

"Oh, and something else." He seemed to suppress a smirk. "I shouldn't tell you this but I think you deserve to know—there will be an internal investigation into Tracey's invoicing files. She has been suspended with immediate effect."

"I see. Thank you, Gunther."

He nodded with a smile. "It's the least I could do." He softly closed the door behind him.

When he left I bit on my lips, suppressing a grin. It was nearly too good to be true. I would finally get justice, to the tune of almost a million Euros! With a new job already lined up!

I looked around my office. Would I miss it? I had spent four years of my life in this firm and, somehow, had felt I belonged here. I took the silver photo frame, containing a picture of Noëlle and Marie—the only personal item I had brought, when I had returned nine months before—and placed it carefully in my bag. I checked my emails. There was none that was only addressed to me. That was the advantage of working in a team. If one team member drops out, the others can continue. I turned on an out of office reply and typed.

> Dear sender,
> I am currently out of the office. Please contact Jerome Panzer on extension 5703 or **Jerome.panzer@ prattwonkey.com** for further assistance.
>
> Best regards, Chloé Krakowski

Suddenly the door was pulled open with force. I swivelled around and stared at her in shock.

"Hello, Chloé." Tracey stood in my office. Her hair was frizzier than ever, she was pale and had her hands clenched in fists.

"Tracey! What are you doing here?"

"That's hardly relevant. How *dare* you blackmail the firm! How dare you elevate yourself above the *partners* when you should just shut up and do as you are told! I will see to it that you will *never* practise law again!" she hissed loudly. Her neck showed dark red blotches.

Suddenly I felt very calm. "It's hardly blackmail if I tell your partners what you are up to. As for not practising law again, I wouldn't worry about *me*."

"Ha! We will see about that!" she snorted and turned to leave. Then she stopped in her tracks. "I know you despise me, Chloé. You think you are so superior with your morals and your principles but you have absolutely *no idea* who I am and what I have had to sacrifice to get to this position. You would have *never* made it here as a partner. You never *fitted in*." She smiled haughtily. "I must admit—I have nearly envied you at times for being different, for wearing what you want and for insisting on spending time with your children. You cannot have it all. There is a high price to be paid for the privilege of making it in this firm and you were never willing to pay it."

I smiled. "One million Euros plus your suspension feels like the right price to me."

Her jaw dropped. She drew her breath as if to start another tirade. The she pressed her lips together, shot a deadly glare at me, turned on her heel and stormed away.

Turning back to the screen, I saved the out of office message, closed all windows and logged off. I switched off my blinking blackberry and placed it on the desk.

I took my bag and walked to the door. I slowly took in the room, the filing cabinets, the desk and the chair. Then I turned out the lights and left without looking back.

Epilogue

My name is Chloé. Chloé Krakowski.

Today is my first day as a partner at Olsens. Nobody had any problems with my surname. The spelling of my name on the office door is correct, as are the smart black business cards.

A vase with a large bouquet of lilac tulips is standing on my clean white desk. Next to it is a card showing the first Concorde operated by British Airways. I turn it around and read it again. The words are handwritten in blue ink.

A warm welcome, dear Chloé.
We are happy that you have joined us and we are looking forward to exciting times.
Giles and your Olsens team in Berlin

I put the card back, lean back in my chair and smile.

Nine hours later. My first day in the office had not been a long one. At 6 p.m. sharp Giles had urged me with a wink to go home.

Berlin, Kollwitzstrasse. I'm lucky, in finding a parking space right in front of the house. I get out of the car, take my nearly new LV Neverfull Damier Azur shopper and shut the door. I inhale deeply. It's still warm. Summer, in July, had arrived. In the café next to our house the tables outside are all occupied. I recognise the couple sitting next to the entrance and briefly wave at them. They are our neighbours from the first floor, Paula and Louis. I look up to the third floor and see the windows of our dining room, where, I believe, the girls are preparing an early dinner with Isabella. I walk towards the front door and unlock it. In the hallway, Jonah's little cuddly toy bunny lies forgotten in his buggy. I pick it up carefully and walk up the stairs to the third floor.

On the second floor I stop briefly, put the bunny on the foot mat and ring the doorbell. As I continue to walk up the stairs, I turn my head to hear the door open and Angela's voice.

"Look, Jonah! There's your bunny! I told you, he probably went for a quick walk!" She winks at me and blows me a kiss.

I finally arrived at our doorstep. I paused for a moment, lightly touching the oval brass plate next to the bell.

C. Krakowski
N. & M. Delorme

I fiddle with my keys at the lock. Suddenly the door is being pulled wide open, the girls burst out and envelope me into a hug. "Mummy, Mummy!"

I stand there in their embrace and look at Isabella, who is watching us with a smile. She nods and I nod back.

I'm finally home.

THE END.

Acknowledgements

I would like to thank my first editor, Liz Garner, for not only understanding Chloé's character and her story but for bringing out the best in me. Her review of the manuscript's second version has inspired me to turn *SUPERSONIC* into a book I felt ready to be published. It took another review by Anna Prokopidu-Schulz, my daughter Anastasia Dubourg and Kieran Marchant to fine tune certain aspects, so my heart-felt thanks to all of them.

I am also indebted to my friend Victoria Smith, a brave single mother, and former lawyer herself, for editing the early versions of the first three chapters so that I could submit them to literary agents—alas, with no success—and for encouraging and motivating me over so many years to find a way to publish this novel.

Thank you also to Jan ter Haar, an old friend and colleague who reviewed the first version of the manuscript as a beta reader and gave me valuable feedback from a male perspective.

I owe more than gratitude to Anna and Achim Schulz who were there for me when the going got tough and who showed me *That's What Friends Are For*.

Finally, words cannot express my gratitude to Karmen Hoyer who has read everything, who knows everything and who has never stopped believing in me. I will love you forever.

Inspiration: Music and Movies

There are many moments in my life when I've felt inspired by a song that I have heard or a movie that I have seen. Here is a selection of those appearing in *SUPERSONIC.*

New Kid in Town (The Eagles)

Indecent Proposal

Every Time We Say Goodbye (Ella Fitzgerald)

She Works Hard For the Money (Donna Summer)

Witness For the Prosecution

My Big Fat Greek Wedding

Dazed and Confused

Holiday (Madonna)

C'est les Vacances (Ilona Mitrecey)

London Calling (The Clash)

Good Morning Vietnam

Freedom (Wham!)

We Are Family (Sister Sledge)

Pretty Woman

It's my Party And I'll Cry If I Want To (Lesley Gore)

April in Paris (Ella Fitzgerald & Louis Armstrong)

Clair de Lune (Claude Debussy)

Desafinado (Stan Getz & João Gilberto)

A Fish Called Wanda

Wherever I Lay My Hat (Paul Young)

Don't Leave Me This Way (Thelma Houston)

If I Ain't Got You (Alicia Keys)

Little Britain

Supersonic (Oasis)

Harry Potter and the Order of the Phoenix

The Godfather

Come Away With Me (Norah Jones)

That's Amore (Dean Martin)

La Traviata: prelude (Giuseppe Verdi)

Single Ladies (Put a Ring on It) (Beyoncé)

You Can Leave Your Hat On (Joe Cocker)

That's What Friends Are For (Dionne Warwick)

Mamma Mia

Sex and the City: the Movie

Macbeth

I will Survive (Gloria Gaynor)

Lightning Source UK Ltd.
Milton Keynes UK
UKHW04f0723210918
329294UK00001B/1/P

9 781785 388675